ESCAPING CYPRUS

D1715882

Gus Constantine

ISBN: 150754720X
ISBN 13: 9781507547205

DEDICATION

First and foremost: I'm dedicating this book to all the Haji's and Rebecca's who escaped Cyprus; and those who were not able to escape.

To my bride Georgia of thirty-six years. Your faith in me is second to none. You never lost confidence in me. Not only in my writing, but in everything I have ever done. *You are the glue that not only held me together, but the glue that continues to hold our entire family together.*

To my three children; Cristina, Jackie, and Charlie. Always asking: Hey Dad, how's the book coming? I can't wait to read it.

To my niece Eleni Lacas who has helped me with the technology of Microsoft Word.

Last and certainly not least:

Gus Leodas: Author of eight bestsellers; including two book of the year awards.

Gus; I never could have done it without you. Your countless hours of encouragement, your brilliance in editing, and your phone calls while you were away on vacation encouraging me to write. I thank you with all my heart.

ESCAPING CYPRUS

This novel is based on true accounts. I have conducted many interviews here in America and have even traveled to Cyprus for additional research. The atrocities described in the novel are factual.

"When Turkish soldiers invade his Cypriot village in 1974, twelve-year old Haji witnesses brutal atrocities, including the torturous murders of his father and sister while his pregnant mother was being raped.

With the help of his beautiful teacher, Rebecca, (dishonored many times by the soldiers) they flee their village only to face constant life-threatening danger wherever they went as the barbaric Turkish soldiers continue to pursue them.

Their struggle to survive the Turks and then erase the horrors that haunt them lead to the dramatic ending."

CHAPTER

1

Cyprus, 1974. The Turkish Invasion.

He was awakened in the middle of the night by the sound of screaming, Help! Help! Help! He thought he was dreaming. Suddenly he realized it wasn't a dream. The screams were coming from the kitchen, opposite his bedroom door. It was his mother, father, and little sister Mary. He was too scared to move.

Finally, with fear and a racing heart he left his bed and tiptoed to the door. When he opened the door he couldn't believe his eyes.

He saw his sister Mary with a rope around her neck hanging from the rafters. Her hands were tied behind her back as she stood on his father's shoulders. If his father moved away, her neck would snap, and she would swing from the rafters. His pregnant mother was totally naked, tied to the kitchen table spread eagle screaming. There were many Turkish soldiers taking their turn with her. His father dare not move. He just screamed to Mary to keep her eyes closed and to keep her feet on his shoulders as he held on to her ankles.

As a soldier pulled out his knife and started to walk toward his opened door, he saw his father run towards him. Then he heard the snapping sound of his sister's neck as she swung from the rafters. The soldier then pulled out his side arm, and shot his father dead.

The soldier then grabbed him by his hair and forcefully threw him across the room where he fell.

What was he to do?

He was only twelve-years old.

As morning approached, many soldiers came and left his mother in agony. As his mother laid there begging for mercy, one very young soldier that just finished dishonoring her took out his knife and asked all who were around what they thought his mother was carrying, a boy or a girl? Then he cut her belly open and produced an unborn baby boy.

His father laid there dead.

His sister was swinging by her neck in the middle of the kitchen.

His unborn brother laid there in a pool of blood on top of his dead mother.

By morning he was sitting in the corner of his kitchen in shock. He cried without any tears. There were no more tears left. But there was still plenty of laughter left within the Turkish soldiers.

Suddenly the front door flew open. In came his school teacher Rebecca Economou being dragged by her hair by another

Turkish soldier. Then the young soldier who cut open his mother asked: "Hey kid, have you ever gotten laid?" as he groped Rebecca.

Rebecca was in her late twenties, beautiful in every aspect of a woman. She was always well-dressed and well-groomed. Her clothes always emphasized her beautiful figure. She was never without a smile.

Whenever her students had any problems with their school work she always made herself available for extra help.

Now, to see his beautiful teacher who has done nothing in her life but inspire her students, being treated and tormented like this, added to his helplessness.

"Hey kid, I asked you a question."

He dare not pick up his head.

"Hey kid, I'm talking to you. Pick up your head now if you know what's good for you."

He slowly raised his head and saw the young soldier grab Rebecca by the hair and fling her to the opposite corner of the kitchen, but not before stripping her of all her clothing.

What seemed to be an eternity, they discussed what violating acts they were going to do to her as she cried helplessly. As he threw her across the kitchen she landed head first on the hard wood floor, she cried out for help.

But who could help her?

Nobody could help her.

They had heard the day before that the Turkish Army landed in northern Cyprus and was approaching their village. What did they want in their little village of Vavla?

Rebecca got her bearings and looked around at what was going on. She saw her student's dead family. Then she noticed him. He couldn't look her in the eye.

The young soldier said, "Hey kid, I asked you a question. Don't make me ask you again. Have you ever gotten laid?"

He looked the young soldier in the eye with complete embarrassment and answered.

"No."

"Well, you're going to get some now."

With total fear, he looked over to Rebecca as she sat naked in the corner of his kitchen with her knees up against her breasts crying.

"Kid, what's your name."

With his head down he answered, "John Haji Ioannou."

Suddenly, another soldier came barging into the house.

"Let's go everyone, now. The Cypriot soldiers are coming just on the other side of the hill."

With that announcement the Turkish soldiers gathered their stuff, and left them like they didn't matter. But not before the young soldier groped Rebecca again, and told her that he would see her again sometime soon. Then the Turkish Soldiers left without any regard as to how drastically they changed their lives.

Rebecca slowly stood with pain and embarrassment, put on her torn dress, went over to Haji, and held him tight. Haji laid there crying in his teacher's arms.

"What's happening?" he asked.

"I don't know."

But they knew.

Archbishop Makarios, the President of Cyprus, had been worried about this for some time now. Archbishop Makarios had been refusing to allow Henry Kissinger and President Richard Nixon additional military bases in Cyprus. In 1973, America needed additional military bases in Cyprus to prepare in case the United States needed to retaliate against any attacks from Russia. All Cypriots knew Archbishop Makarios was against any additional American military bases in Cyprus.

Archbishop Makarios was a peaceful man who did not want Cyprus overrun by military bases.

Then negotiations broke off that same year. Most Cypriots thought the negotiations would continue at a later date. Well, that later date came. July 20, 1974. It came in a way that Cyprus would never suspect. Basically it was like this. Turkey said to Kissinger.

"We'll do it. We'll help you. You can add as many military bases in Turkey as you want. Need anything else? How about our communication towers? How about our airfields? It's all yours Mr. Kissinger."

Now Turkey had a new best friend.

The United States of America.

CHAPTER

2

Rebecca went into Haji's parents' bedroom to get blankets to cover the bodies. She also came out wearing one of Haji's mother's dresses. It was weird for Haji to see someone as beautiful as Rebecca wearing his mother's clothes. Haji cried as he watched Rebecca carefully cover his mother's body with his dead unborn brother on top of her. Then she covered his father's body. At the same time she looked up at his six-year old sister hanging from the rafters. Then they looked at each other. Rebecca told Haji that she cannot get his sister down.

They would have to leave her hanging by her neck.

"No Miss Economou, we can't leave Mary here like this. We must get her down," Haji cried.

"Listen Haji, and listen to me good. Mary is in heaven with your mother and father now. There's nothing we can do for her, or your parents. There's nothing anyone can do. Get hold of yourself Haji.

We must leave this house and find a place to hide. The Turkish soldiers will be back. I'm sure they're regrouping. We must go hide in the hills. You saw what those barbarians are capable of doing. They don't care. Your family is with God now. We must save ourselves."

They hurried to the window and looked outside at what looked like a war zone. There were bodies in the street. Mothers were carrying their breathless newborns, and children hovered over their mothers' naked bodies.

Outside they felt the death around them.

They smelled the death.

They heard the cries of death.

"Uncle Socrates, Uncle Socrates," Haji cried when he saw him lying on the ground and ran to him calling out; "What happened to you?"

When Haji reached him, he realized Uncle Socrates was dead.

Haji's Uncle Socrates was born with many health issues. He never married. He was never able to hold down a job or support himself in any way. He was the old man in the village that everyone knew. Most of the villagers always did whatever they could do to help him. At 75-years old, Uncle Socrates was living in Haji's great grandmother's house that she left to him. If not for Haji's great grandmother, Uncle Socrates would not have a home of his own.

When Uncle Socrates was 18-years old he got hurt. He caught a very high fever from a cut on his leg from a rusty nail. Haji remembered his mother telling him the story of Uncle Socrates, (her uncle). She told Haji that his wound became infected just below his knee. After weeks of several doctors coming to their house and his fever setting at 103-degrees for three weeks, one of the doctors decided that if Uncle Socrates was to live he would have to amputate his right leg. So, at 18-years old Uncle Socrates had a wooden leg.

Now as Haji looked at his Uncle Socrates lying in the road he noticed smoke coming from his charcoaled wooden leg. The

Turkish soldiers humiliated him by burning his wooden leg and just left him there. Then he couldn't believe what he saw. Uncle Socrates laid there dead with his other leg cut off.

"Let's go Haji," Rebecca cried out. "Let's get out of here before they come back."

Before they knew it, there were other survivors.

People were crying in the street while embracing one another and asking; "what's happening, what's going on, who were those people?" Everyone was looking for answers.

Finally, they saw comfort in the face of Father Demitri, the village's spiritual leader. He had been the village priest at St. George for fifty some odd years. He married and baptized everyone in the village.

Who else can they turn to?

Their very own Fr. Demitri was the only one who could give them comfort.

"Everyone, please, come into the church," Fr. Demitri announced. "Right now the only one who can help us is God."

They all walked the quarter-mile to the church. As they passed the schoolhouse they noticed all the broken windows and doors.

Haji saw the way Rebecca was looking at her one room schoolhouse. You could tell by the way she had her eyes glued to her school that she wanted to look inside but would not dare leave the group to walk off alone.

The villagers always found comfort in Fr. Demitri and St. George Greek Orthodox Church. As they approached St. George, they noticed that the door was wide open. Fr. Demitri would *never* leave the church door wide open. Vavla had lots of stray animals; cats especially. Everywhere you looked there was a stray cat. Stray animals always found their way into the church. One thing about Fr. Demitri, he didn't allow animals in his church.

Fr. Demitri hesitated as he walked up the steps to St. George to enter the church. Already, everyone sensed what had happened.

Halfway up to the altar Fr. Demitri fell to his knees and broke down and cried.

The church was ransacked.

Many pews were tipped over.

"The Holy Altar! Oh my God! The Holy Altar!" Fr. Demitri cried out, as he noticed the bullet holes in the icons. "They destroyed God's church!"

"Why would they destroy a church, a house of God?" asked Rebecca.

Fr. Demitri controlled his emotion. He knew as the villagers' Spiritual Father, everyone not only looked up to him but looked to him for strength and leadership. He knew he had to keep control.

The entire village, what was left of it, would look for him to lead.

Fr. Demitri slowly stood and approached The Holy Altar. He and all of the villagers stood there in shock.

"How dare they? How dare they?" Fr. Demitri cried.

Someone defecated on The Holy Altar, and next to the defecation they put a toilet; the ultimate insult to the church. Fr. Demitri turned to all those in the church and said, "Everyone, please come closer. Come inside."

Using his handkerchief, he picked up the defecation and placed it in the toilet. With tears in his eyes, he carried the toilet out the backdoor.

When he returned, he reassured everyone that this was *still* God's house. As everyone entered the church and looked around, the sobs grew louder and plentiful. Most of them stood. The elderly sat on the few remaining pews that were not tipped over. The injured sat on the floor. Some tried to lift the heavy pews. But for many, they were much too heavy. After a moment of silence, Fr. Demitri started like he always started every Sunday.

"Let us pray to the Lord. Let us bow our heads to the Lord. Lord have mercy. Oh Heavenly Father, please protect us from any further pain. And Heavenly Father, please find it in your heart to forgive those who have trespassed against us."

Imagine that, after all this, Fr. Demitri was asking God to forgive those savages.

After Fr. Demitri led them in prayer, they waited for his instructions.

"Listen up everyone," said Fr. Demitri. "We are not safe here in Vavla. The Turkish soldiers know we are here. I'm sure they're regrouping. They know we're defenseless. We must go into the hills. We will go to The Holy Cross Monastery."

Fr. Demitri looked around at his flock. He was their shepherd, they were his sheep, and they would go wherever he would lead. There were thirty-five of them.

"Follow me." That was all Fr. Demitri had to say.

He walked down the three steps of The Holy Altar holding close to his heart what was left of the torn Gospel (Bible). As he passed his flock, they followed behind. He stopped at the front door, took a deep breath, and stepped outside.

If there was a knife, he'd take the blade.

If there was a gun, he'd take the bullet.

That's how much Fr. Demitri loved his parishioners.

They followed Fr. Demitri down the steps into the street. Two by two they started walking east towards the hills. They knew the four-mile walk would take them three hours. Despite the comfort they felt with Fr. Demitri leading them, they were all still terrified as they heard the gunshots in the distance.

How many more people were being killed?

How many more atrocities were being committed?

CHAPTER

3

H aji walked next to Rebecca.
He felt safe with her.

She had not let go of his hand since they stepped into the church.

Haji's mind kept drifting. What would have happened if the soldier didn't come barging into the house? Would those soldiers have made him do anything to Rebecca? He did have a crush on her, as did all the boys in school, but oh my God, he would have died. Haji then started thinking about his parents.

He envisioned the soldiers laughing while waiting on line to rape his sweet dear mother.

One after another, as though she was an object, not a human being.

The more she cried, the more she begged, the happier the soldiers became.

The young barbarian who cut his mother open while she was still alive just to satisfy his curiosity of the sex of her unborn child will haunt him forever.

What kind of barbarian would do this?

His poor father stood there helplessly holding Mary's legs.

Haji can still see him crying in total helplessness. And the choice that his father made instinctively in panic by trying to save him during the chaos forced his sweet little sister's neck to snap as she swung from the rafters.

His father probably knew those barbarians were going to kill his whole family anyway. He must have just wanted to take out at least one of them. But he took out none. None. Not even one.

Don't worry Baba; I'll avenge our family's deaths, Haji kept saying to himself. *These savages will pay. I don't know how, but I'll make them pay.*

After fifteen minutes the gunfire got louder. The Turks no longer sounded as though they were in the distance. They sounded closer.

Suddenly they heard explosions.

Haji withdrew his hand from Rebecca and covered his ears. When Rebecca saw how frightened Haji was, she put her hand over his ear and pulled him close to her. She held him tight.

Haji can only imagine what was going through her head. She had to be thinking what could have happened to her back at the house. But for now she would not let go of him as they followed close to the back of the line. As safe as Haji felt with Rebecca, he found himself wishing that Fr. Demitri was next to them.

Suddenly they heard vehicles coming towards them from just around the bend. They all stopped in their tracks. Then Fr. Demitri turned around and yelled to everyone to get off the road and hide in the weeds and woods.

"Do not move until I tell you to. Understand? Nobody move until you hear from me."

That's exactly what they did as they ran into the woods and crawled on their stomachs. They buried their faces in the dirt. Haji felt Rebecca's arm around him. He felt protected. But who was he kidding? Who can really protect them? As the army vehicles passed they still didn't move. They all lay in the weeds waiting for Fr. Demitri's instructions. Every once in a while Fr. Demitri would crawl on his hands and knees to check on them.

"Stay down." Fr. Demitri said. "There are too many of them. We must wait until nightfall."

By now they were all starting to get hungry. Some of the little children were telling their mothers they wanted to eat.

Meanwhile Haji had to go to the bathroom. The only thing is; there was no bathroom. As usual Fr. Demitri sensed what they were all feeling so he told them to crawl deeper into the woods.

"We need cover," said Fr. Demitri.

By the time they were deep in to the woods nightfall approached. Fr. Demitri had them sitting around praying.

Finally he said, "You all know the story about Jesus feeding five thousand people with five loaves of bread and two fish, *(Mathew 14:13-21)*. Well, I'm sorry to inform you, I'm not able to do this. There is no food. But we do have the knowledge to stay alive. Our ancestors lived off the land. We must do the same. Look around. There are lots of wild fruit trees and berry bushes. Look, over there, there's a blackberry bush. Go. Go pick some fruit. This is the way our ancestors lived hundreds of years ago. And please, don't forget to help each other. Share what you find."

With this they started looking around for fruit. Within thirty minutes everyone returned with handfuls of fruits and berries. Although they lived on farms and ate meat every day, fruits and vegetables were part of their daily diets. Fr. Demitri tried to comfort everyone, but concentrated mostly on the children. He knew the children needed to keep quiet. If the Turkish soldiers heard them they would all be goners. Through all this, nobody saw Fr.

Demitri eat a single piece of fruit. Rebecca crawled over to Fr. Demitri and handed him a few figs, and berries.

"No thank you," Fr. Demitri said. "I had a big breakfast."

"You have to eat something Fr. Demitri," encouraged Rebecca. "I've been watching you. You're exhausted. You must eat something. We need you. We need you strong."

Fr. Demitri took a long look at Rebecca and then took a couple of figs.

"Get up everyone, follow me," said Fr. Demitri.

They all stood. Fr. Demitri led them in prayer. Again he asked God to look over them, to help survive this catastrophe. And again he prayed for the souls of the Turkish soldiers.

Not Haji.

He wanted them dead.

They stayed in the woods. They couldn't walk along the road; too many Turkish soldiers would have spotted them.

"Now, before we leave I want you to all walk away two by two with a partner into the woods, and go to the bathroom," said Fr. Demitri. "Don't be embarrassed. It's something that we must do."

They all did what they needed to do. The women walked a little further into the woods than the men.

"Come on Haji," Rebecca said. "Go to the bathroom."

Haji looked at her in embarrassment. He then lowered his head and walked into the woods. Haji felt Rebecca's protective eyes on him as he walked away. When he came back Rebecca gave him a little smile and asked; "Was that so bad Haji?"

Haji only smiled back. Then he watched Rebecca walk into the woods. This time he watched over her. They had to survive this together.

Suddenly Mr. Mousikou in a startled way asked. "Where's Fr. Demitri? Oh my God, what happened to him?"

They all looked around. Finally they saw him coming out of the woods.

"What, didn't you think priests go to the bathroom? Priests go to the bathroom just like everyone else," said Fr. Demitri with a smile.

When totally dark, they continued working their way up the hill towards the monastery. Some knew their way around the woods like the back of their hands. Fr. Demitri asked Haji to walk up front with him since he knew that Haji and all his friends hung out in the woods. But in the dark Haji had a hard time navigating his way around. He knew he had to focus on his footing and his direction. Rebecca was towards the back of the group. Most were praying and sobbing.

Haji was thinking about his family and his house. Then he thought of himself.

What will happen to me?

What will happen to all of us?

Will the monastery walls protect us? Those barbarians don't care about the sacredness of a monastery; Haji continued to think. He hoped they don't attack it, if they haven't already.

As they approached a meadow they heard sounds of others crying. Haji looked up but was unable to see in the darkness. But he heard them. They all heard them. It was not a pleasant sound. Mr. Mousikou whispered to Fr. Demitri to wait where they were. He wanted to investigate the cries.

Mousikou was about forty-years old. He lived alone at the far end of the town. His wife passed away from cancer about five years ago. His only child Nick was away at a university somewhere in England. Mousikou was as big as Fr. Demitri, about 6'-5" inches tall. Fr. Demitri insisted that he go with Mousikou. Haji asked if he can go too, but they told him to stay put. But by now Haji was not feeling sorry for himself anymore. He was thinking about the way his family was massacred. At twelve-years old he was the toughest kid in his grade and was even able to beat up some of the older kids in school. At 5'-7" and 175 pounds, he was ready to get revenge.

"Just wait here." Mousikou said. He seemed to be in charge now. Mousikou led the way with Fr. Demitri two steps behind. Everyone else waited. Rebecca was watching Haji. She sensed what he was thinking. She knew he wanted to follow them. She started walking toward him. But it was too late. Haji knew what he was going to do. "Haji, wait" she whispered. But Haji ignored her.

Haji followed Mousikou and Fr. Demitri into the woods. They seemed to be walking slowly towards the faint cries.

Suddenly they stopped.

They appeared to be whispering about something they saw and what they were going to do. Then they separated. As Haji watched them he realized they were planning their attack. All of a sudden they were holding sticks in their hands and simultaneously started to run. Haji ran behind them with the first stick he found.

There were five soldiers, and two sobbing women. One of the women could not have been much older the Haji. The other must have been her mother. They were in various stages of undress, and it was not by their choice.

Fr. Demitri grabbed the one closest to him and punched him in the face and knocked him down. Mousikou kicked another in the stomach and sent him against a tree and fell to the ground. Then the third soldier reached for his rifle but Fr. Demitri was able to grab it before he could touch it and hit him over the head, and all Haji saw was blood. Haji then looked over at Mousikou who had no trouble handling the other two. They were down in seconds. The two women looked around in amazement.

Then the woman yelled, "Look out!" and pointed at the first person that Fr. Demitri punched out. He was already standing on his feet.

Now it was Haji's turn. Haji hit him with his stick. The soldier barely moved. Then Haji pointed the stick toward his face and stabbed him in the eye.

"Take that you animal."

The Turkish soldier screamed as blood oozed out of his eye as he dropped to his knees. Then Haji completely lost control. He kept pounding him with the stick. Now it was the Turkish soldier who screamed in agony. Then Mousikou came running over and starting punching the soldier until he beat him into unconsciousness. Haji looked up at Fr. Demitri and saw tears in his eyes. The two women were indeed mother and daughter. The younger girl called the other woman Mama.

Mousikou then came over with a large rock and started to pound one of the soldiers on the head. Fr. Demitri went to stop Mousikou, but as big as Fr. Demitri was, he was in his late seventies and no match for the younger Mousikou. Mousikou just pushed Fr. Demitri aside.

"Stop it" cried Fr. Demitri. "In the name of God, stop it!"

"No way," Mousikou yelled back. "Look what these savages did. They have no respect for human life. Besides, if we let them live they will try to get revenge against us."

"If I allow you to kill these men we would be no better that they are," demanded Fr. Demitri.

"You don't believe that any more than I do," said Mousikou. Mousikou then lifted the rock once again and bashed the second unconscious soldier in the face.

"Hit him again," the mother cried out. "Kill them all," she screamed. "Right before they killed my husband and son they told them that they were going to bring us back to Turkey and sell us into prostitution. They don't deserve to live."

Fr. Demitri pleaded with everyone to calm down.

"You calm down," Mousikou said, and killed the other three. "Now we can leave!" yelled Mousikou with authority.

They walked away leaving five dead Turkish soldiers. But this time they were carrying five rifles, five hand guns, and five knifes. As they returned to the group Fr. Demitri had a difficult time comforting the still sobbing women.

Everyone noticed the two sobbing women. Nobody asked what happened to the mother and daughter. They seemed to figure that much out. But what happened over all, they didn't know. But they did see all the weapons. Fr. Demitri asked everyone to pray again.

"Enough of that praying shit," said Mousikou.

"Watch your mouth," scolded Fr. Demitri.

Everyone saw that Mousikou was prepared to speak. They gathered around to hear what he had to say. Mousikou did not give much in detail. But he did explain what kind of animals they are dealing with on their small island. By the way Rebecca comforted the two women, she somehow figured out most of what happened.

"All right everyone" said Mousikou. "We have five rifles, five hand guns, and five knifes. Who knows how to use them?"

CHAPTER

4

By now it was daybreak. Mousikou was now in charge. He convinced everyone that although it's still a good idea to continue praying, it's going to take more than prayers to survive.

"Listen up everyone," said Mousikou. "We're in a lot of trouble. Right now we're on our own. There is nobody to depend on but ourselves. I know you're hungry. I know you're tired. I know you haven't had a decent night's sleep. But I warn you. It may get worse. We have little food. We have no water. We have no change of clothes. But I'll tell you what we do have. We now have weapons. Weapons those Turkish motherfuckers don't know that villagers like us are capable, and willing to use."

"Watch your mouth I said," yelled Fr. Demitri.

"Sorry Father."

"Not sorry *Father!* Sorry *everyone!*" said Fr. Demitri. "Don't let the devil take over."

"Don't let the devil take over!" yelled Mousikou. "Take a look around! The devil has already taken over! Now Father, may I please continue?"

"Please do, but refrain from cursing."

"Like I said," Mousikou continued, as he looked at Fr. Demitri. "We must be careful. We are not an army. And there are very few of us compared to what's out there. For now we must stay put. We cannot continue to make our way up to the monastery in daylight. It's not safe to move around. Again I tell you. We must stay put. When nightfall comes, we'll continue our journey. Please, we must remain quiet. Do not wander off. Especially alone. Use the buddy system. Try to get as much rest, or better yet, sleep, as you can. The men will take turns staying awake. We have plenty of fruits and berries. They are a great source of nourishment. I'll try to grab a rabbit or any other animal."

"Come here and sit next to me," Rebecca said to Haji.

Haji no longer needed the comfort of Rebecca. He was too angry. He got a taste of retaliation and he liked it. He wanted to stay with Mousikou. He felt much safer with him after he saw what he was capable of doing. And he admitted to himself that he not only liked it, he enjoyed being part of it.

As they sat in silence Fr. Demitri motioned for Haji to come next to him. How Haji loved Fr. Demitri. He was like a grandfather to him, and had the utmost respect for him. Haji walked to where Fr. Demitri was sitting and sat next to him. Fr. Demitri never pulled any punches as he went right to work on Haji.

"Miss Economou told me what happened back at your house. I'm so sorry you had to experience such brutality. I assure you that God has a plan for all of us. It may not seem so right now, but I guarantee it."

"I know Father, but right now I'm sorry to say I don't feel God has a plan for us. I believe Mr. Mousikou when he says we are totally on our own. God's not helping us right now. We *are* on our own."

"You know Haji; you are a very confused kid who is being forced to grow up too fast. These last two days you were thrown into the deep end of the river and have already emerged as a lifeguard. I just wanted to let you know I saw what you did to the Turkish soldier last night and really understand. But I still have a problem with the killing. Especially when the soldiers were already subdued. Miss Economou also told me what almost could have happened between you and her back at your house. Luckily the soldiers had to leave in a hurry. Why this is happening are mysteries of God. And as much as we want to question God, it is not our place to question Him."

"I know Fr. Demitri. My family was in church every Sunday, remember? I listened to your sermons. Holy week, all you ever talked about was forgiveness. And I always forgave. Well, I forgave a lot. But this? What's happening now! I'm so sorry, but forgiving is not what I'm thinking about right now!"

"What *are* you thinking about right now my son? Please tell me."

"Father, I'm thinking that if I never opened my bedroom door my father would not have tried to save me from that Turkish soldier, and Mary would not have died."

"You cannot blame yourself. It wasn't your fault. Do you hear me? It wasn't your fault. Haji, look at me! I said look at me!" Haji slowly picked up his head and looked Fr. Demitri in the eyes.

"Yes Father?"

"It wasn't your fault."

"I know. At least I think that I know," he said in a faint voice.

Then he broke down and sobbed like a baby in Fr. Demitri's arms.

Haji now knew that he really wasn't such a tough guy like he thought he was becoming. But one thing for sure, he was going to survive this. He was going to do something to anyone who had anything to do with this. But for now he continued to cry in the comfort of Fr. Demitri's arms. When Haji walked away from Fr. Demitri he remained totally confused.

What am I? Am I still a little kid of twelve-years old, or am I that person who hit and stabbed the soldier in the eye and then felt nothing but complete satisfaction while I watched Mr. Mousikou kill all five soldiers?

Haji wanted to be alone. He found a rock away from everyone and sat. A day and a half had gone by since Haji's family was brutally massacred. He kept thinking about how he could have changed anything that happened. But deep down he knew what happened was, and will always be, a mystery of God. He must find the strength to go on with his life. He had no other family in Cyprus. He had nowhere to go. His mother had one uncle, Uncle Socrates who was killed. His father had a brother living somewhere in America.

What will become of me?

He was so tired.

He was so scared.

He felt himself drifting off.

He needed rest.

He needed sleep.

He felt emotionally drained. He drifted into a deep sleep.

Haji didn't know how long he slept. But he was awakened by the sound of his mother's voice. Or at least that's what he thought.

"Haji, Haji, wake up." Haji opened his eyes and saw his mother. Well, he saw his mother's dress on Rebecca. Then it all came back to him. He no longer had a mother. Again he felt all alone.

"Haji," Rebecca said. "I have some fruit. Here, take some. They're perfectly ripe."

"No thank you Miss Economou. I don't feel like eating."

The truth was; Haji *was* hungry. He wanted to eat. But he wanted to eat food. He didn't want any fruit. He wanted to bite into some meat.

"Haji, I know you feel lost. I also feel lost. I don't know what else is going on in Cyprus, but I'm sure it's not good. Right now, let's concentrate on surviving until we make it to the monastery."

Haji nodded several times, "You're right."

Rebecca sat next to him. She didn't say much after that. Haji just ate the fruit.

Not much happened for a few hours. Most everyone sat around sharing their experiences of the last day and a half. It was not anything in anyone's wildest imagination. The mother and daughter need not say anything. Everyone seemed to understand. Rebecca and Fr. Demitri spent most of their time trying to comfort them. But all they did was stare into the woods. At one point the mother started to walk over to Mousikou but the daughter started to sob again. Rebecca hurried to the daughter to try to comfort her, as the mother sat next to Mousikou.

Nobody knew who she was. All they knew was that she was from another village a few miles west of Vavla. They sat and talked a few minutes. Nobody was able to hear much of what they were saying, but there had to be lots of thank-you's from the mother. Mousikou didn't say much. He just held her hand and told her she had to stay strong for her daughter's sake. Then they sat in silence holding hands for a short time longer. The mother returned to where her daughter sat with Rebecca and the three of them sat holding each other with tears in their eyes.

There is a bond with women that only they can understand. It's as if they are able to read each other's minds. They looked at each other and felt what the other was feeling. Everyone envied the silent comfort these three women were feeling while communicating without saying a word. Just like the song: *Sounds of Silence.*

"People talking without speaking. People hearing without listening."

⇥⇤

"Haji, you feel like going hunting for some real food?"

Haji looked up and saw Mousikou. He couldn't wait to hunt with Mousikou. Haji hunted many times with his father.

"Let's go," Haji said and followed Mousikou into the woods. Mousikou was carrying a rifle and also had a knife tucked into the side of his pants. He told Haji they needed to keep the rest of the weapons behind. They heard a lot of movement in the woods, which had lots of game; anything from deer down to cottontails.

"Haji, do you hear the gunshots in the distance?" asked Mousikou.

"Yes I do."

"There's a war going on and we're right in the middle of it."

"Who's winning so far?"

"I don't know, but from what I have seen so far I would guess they are. But with all the shooting going on in the background we're now able to shoot and not worry about being heard. Have you ever hunted before?"

"Many times with my father."

"Good, I was hoping that you weren't afraid."

"Afraid? Me? Never! Yesterday I was a twelve-year old hunter. Today I'm a twelve-year old hunter and soldier."

"Glad to hear it," said Mousikou. "Stop!" Haji froze like a piece of ice.

Up ahead they saw about ten people they didn't recognize. They froze as they spotted Haji and Mousikou. Mousikou whispered to Haji that they looked friendly.

"Stay behind me," whispered Mousikou as he started walking towards them.

26

One of the men also started walking towards Mousikou. The rest of his group waited behind until he reached Mousikou. Everyone felt that they were both on the same side. Nonetheless, they all were cautious.

"Hi, my name's Steve Savas."

"Gus Mousikou," answered Mousikou. "This young man here is Haji."

"Hello Haji."

"Enough introductions! Call me Gus and I'll call you Steve."

"All right," said Savas.

Mousikou asked Steve; "Do you have any weapons?"

"No."

"Any food?"

"No."

"That's all right. We don't have any food either, but I'm sure that we're all equally hungry. We're out here hunting. Where are you guys from?"

"We were on a tour bus. We're from Aegean University in Greece. We were studying the northern part of Cyprus and all hell broke loose. I'm their professor, these are my students. What the hell is going on? We were on top of a hill admiring the hillside when we saw three jeeps pull up to the parked bus. The soldiers got out, opened fire on the bus with people inside, and then blew it up. Thank God all of my students were with me. We stayed put in the woods all night. Gus, you said you didn't have any food. What have you been surviving on?"

"Wild fruit and berries. Come with us, join our group. There's strength in numbers."

They all joined Fr. Demitri and the rest of Haji's group. Now there were nearly fifty of them.

Fr. Demitri immediately stood when he saw the newcomers and introduced himself. They surrounded him. They, like everyone else, felt safe around a priest. The closer you were to Fr. Demitri, the closer you felt to God. Mousikou then asked Savas if he knew how to hunt.

"Are you kidding? Hunting is my middle name."

"Good, here's a rifle."

"Thanks."

"Come on Haji," said Mousikou.

"I'm right behind you."

The three headed back into the woods. Two had guns; one twelve year old was carrying nothing. Once in the woods it was as though Mousikou and Savas had been hunting partners for years. They were quiet, and observing. They knew when to stand still. Haji followed along. When deep into the woods, Savas stopped short. He picked up his rifle, took aim, and fired. Haji looked up ahead and saw a deer dead as a door nail. They reached the deer and quickly dressed it and dragged it back to the rest of the group.

Savas' students were grossed out by the dead animal.

The villagers were looking at the dead animal as though they were prepared to eat it raw.

"Who's got matches?" asked ask Fr. Demitri.

"I do," said several people at once.

Thank God most of the villagers smoked. Even Haji smoked from time to time.

"Quickly, let's start a fire before it gets too dark; we all know that light travels 186,000 miles per second," said Savas like the college professor he was. "We don't want the fire to be seen by anyone but us. Quickly everyone, get some fire wood."

They gathered twigs and branches. Within ten minutes everyone returned with enough wood to make a bonfire. Mousikou and Savas cut the deer into tiny pieces to cook fast. They kept the fire small with the meat close to the flame. The meat burnt a little on the outside and rare on the inside. But they were starving. They would have eaten it raw.

Fr. Demitri gave the quickest blessing that anyone has ever seen him do as the meat was passed around.

As always, women and children were first.

"Slow down," said Fr. Demitri. "Remember, we have no water. Don't get thirsty. Next thing you know you're going to start to hiccup. Hiccups with nothing to drink are not fun."

"Fr. Demitri," Rebecca said.

"Yes my child."

"Father, you're not eating. How come you're not eating?"

"I'll eat when everyone else has eaten."

That's the way Fr. Demitri was. He put everyone else ahead of himself. After everyone ate, Savas put out the fire.

By now it was starting to get dark.

"Rest up my children," said Fr. Demitri. "In about an hour it'll be dark enough to start making our way up to the monastery. We will be safe there."

Savas asked, "What is it about this monastery that's so special?"

Fr. Demitri smiled. "You'll see when we get there."

CHAPTER

5

Once it was dark enough they continued the journey. Fr. Demitri led the way. Rebecca was with the mother and daughter. Haji wanted to stay away from them. He kept getting visions of what almost happened between Rebecca and himself. Meanwhile, gunshots were still being heard in the background. Most had difficulty walking the terrain. The older people had great difficulty and constantly needed to stop and rest. Haji was worried about Fr. Demitri. As indestructible Haji thought Fr. Demitri was, he knew that his getting on in years had to make this journey extremely difficult for him.

There were many rocks that most were slipping on. The terrain was getting steeper. Some of the elderly wanted to give up. Many didn't even know where they were. They couldn't see in the dark. Even if they could see, the woods were so thick that they wouldn't see much anyway.

Then Haji almost bumped into the person in front of him. It seemed that Fr. Demitri stopped up ahead. He wanted everyone to rest and eat some of the deer meat that some carried. After fifteen minutes they heard the whispers from the front of the line that Fr. Demitri wanted to continue. They needed to continue on to the safety of The Holy Cross Monastery.

As they were all getting up they heard gunshots from the front of the line with screaming right afterwards. Haji tried to see what was going on. He couldn't see anything from where he was. He started to walk to the front of the group. The closer he got the more crying and sobbing he heard. Nearing the front, he noticed Rebecca on her knees. She was leaning over Mrs. Argiriou. Mrs. Argiriou was the owner of the general store in Vavla. She was bleeding from the chest. She wasn't moving.

"Fr. Demitri, Fr. Demitri," cried out Rebecca.

"Where's Fr. Demitri?" some of the villagers cried out.

Then it hit them. What would happen if Fr. Demitri got killed? What would happen to them? Then Haji saw him coming towards Mrs. Argiriou. Thank God he's alive Haji thought. Mousikou followed right behind.

"What happened?" asked Haji.

"Eight Turkish soldiers came out of the woods towards us," said Mousikou. "I guess they thought we were just plain ole villagers that would never be able to put up a fight; let alone have guns to fight back with. Well, they had another thing coming. The Turkish soldiers came right up to us. Most had their guns at their sides demanding our women. Well, we opened fire on them. Unfortunately they got off a few shots. Haji, you should have seen Fr. Demitri shoot."

With that, Fr. Demitri looked up from Mrs. Argiriou.

"God," he said. "When will the killing stop? I'm pissed, I'm really really pissed!"

Everyone was now scared. Anyone who knew Fr. Demitri had never seen that side of him. What would happen if Fr. Demitri completely lost it? Fr. Demitri lowered his head towards Mrs. Argiriou, blessed her, and said; "There's nothing we can do for her anymore. Let's go. Let's get the hell out of here."

Haji couldn't believe it. Fr. Demitri said *hell*.

As they were about to continue their journey, Haji wondered if things would worsen. Then it happened. Haji heard more screaming. It was Savas. He was shot. He didn't move. Fr. Demitri quickly ran to Savas and kneeled beside him. Even Haji knew that it was too late by Fr. Demitri's reaction. There was too much blood everywhere.

"He's dead," said Fr. Demitri. "There's nothing we can do. He's with God now."

All of Savas' student's started to cry. The female students were hysterical.

"Oh my God, what are we going to do without Mr. Savas?" one of the girls cried.

"What will happen to us now?" another cried.

Haji thought...*What are we going to do without Mr. Savas? I'm twelve-years old. I witnessed my entire family being massacred. I saw my mother being raped repeatedly. I saw my mother's belly cut open while she was still alive to produce an unborn child just to satisfy their curiosity, and these girls are wondering what going to happen to them? What about me? Huh? What about me?*

And that's when Haji broke down and cried uncontrollably.

While Haji was crying, Fr. Demitri and Rebecca came over and held him.

"I'm sorry," Haji whimpered. "I just can't help it," he added as he continued to cry.

"I know, I know," said Rebecca with a motherly emotion.

"Come on Haji," said Fr. Demitri. "We need to continue moving."

Haji slowly stood and looked around. He wasn't the only one scared. Everyone looked scared.

Fr. Demitri took Savas' sidearm and said, "Come on," and everyone followed. After about an hour before sunrise they finally saw it. The Holy Cross Monastery. As many times as Haji's parents took him and Mary to the monastery, he had never felt the way he did at that moment as he looked at the doors to safety.

CHAPTER

6

"It looks like a fort," said one of Savas' students.

"It was never meant to be a fort," said Fr. Demitri. "Quickly, let's get to the doors."

As tired as they were, they ran like a deer fleeing a hunter. As they approached, the doors started to open and a monk stuck his head out. He looked at the stampede of villagers, and immediately started to close the doors.

"What are you doing?" yelled Mousikou, as he and others pulled the door wide open and ran into the safety of the monastery.

"You," said Fr. Demitri as he pointed to some of his group standing over to one side; "Secure the doors! Mousikou," he yelled. "Let go of the monk!"

"No way," Mousikou yelled back at Fr. Demitri. "He tried to lock us out. What's his problem?" he asked as he had the monk by the throat up against the wall.

"I don't know," said Fr. Demitri. "But as soon as he saw us he wanted to lock us out. I'll get to the bottom of this. In the meantime Mousikou, I said let go of the monk!"

Mousikou looked at Fr. Demitri and then the others and let the monk go, by throwing the monk to the ground.

"The enemy is out there," Fr. Demitri said to Mousikou as he pointed to the other side of the wall.

"Are you out of your mind?" screamed Mousikou. "He tried to lock us out."

"You're trying my patience," Fr. Demitri said with fire in his eyes.

"What's going on?" they heard, from about fifty feet away. They all turned to see who it was. Now they really felt safe. There he was…the highest ranking priest on Cyprus.

The Bishop. Bishop Emanuel.

"What's going on?" the bishop repeated as he walked towards everyone.

"Your Grace," said Fr. Demitri as he lowered his head. "Our island is being attacked. Our village was destroyed. Many people have been murdered. I cannot begin to repeat the atrocities that we have experienced. We traveled days to get here, and when your monk first opened the doors to let us in he suddenly changed his mind and attempted to lock us out."

"I have been listening to the radio," said Bishop Emanuel. "The Turks have taken over the northern part of Cyprus and are working their way south. It's very bad. As for why the monk changed his mind about letting you in, I'll give him permission to speak when I ask him."

Bishop Emanuel took a few steps towards the monk and hesitated. He turned around towards Fr. Demitri and said; "My dear

Fr. Demitri, I know why the monk tried to shut you all out. You
should have known. What's the matter with you?"

"What's the matter with me?" asked Fr. Demitri. "The question you need to ask is why did you try to lock these people out,
and the person to ask is the monk, not me," yelled Fr. Demitri.

"No," snapped the Bishop. "And need I not remind you Fr.
Demitri, that you better not forget who you are talking to, and
when you talk to *me*, remember the word obedience."

The Orthodox faith is like the military. The clergy call it
obedience, but it's more like slavery. All the Bishops outrank the
priests, which make the priests kind of like their slaves.

God forbid, if a priest questions a bishop.

"I'm sorry Your Grace," said Fr. Demitri as he lowered his head.

"I'll let it go this time, but don't forget your place."

"Yes Your Grace," Fr. Demitri said with his head down.

There has always been some kind of problem between Fr.
Demitri and the bishop. Every year during holy week the bishop
always served at St. George. As much as a holy man as the bishop
was; he always treated Fr. Demitri with disrespect. The whole village knew it. Nobody knew why. It was just a way of life.

Haji glanced at Mousikou and felt he was going to say something but changed his mind.

"As I started to tell you before Fr. Demitri," said the bishop.
"You should have known better. There are women here. You
know this is an all-male monastery. Do you understand? All-male
means no women. The monk was following the rules. The rules
you should have realized."

"But Your Grace, we're in the midst of a crisis. I couldn't leave
the women outside," Fr. Demitri said with a raised voice.

"Only I can make that decision," the bishop snapped. "Do you
understand me? Only I."

"I'll tell you what; I'll help you with that decision!" Fr. Demitri
snapped at the bishop.

"Fr. Demitri, must I remind you…?"

Fr. Demitri walked right up to the bishop and punched him in the face and the bishop went flying on his back.

"All right Fr. Demitri," said Mousikou with a smile. "I knew you had it in you."

Fr. Demitri then walked up to the much younger Mousikou, stood nose to nose with him and asked, "Do you want some?"

Mousikou was a hot head but knew when to back down.

The monk quickly ran to the bishop. The bishop laid there staring up at the sky. He didn't know what hit him. As the monk was helping the bishop to his feet Fr. Demitri ran over to help. The bishop was wobbling on his feet as the monk and Fr. Demitri were trying to help him stand. Fr. Demitri indeed still had it.

"I'll help you to your room Your Grace," Fr. Demitri said. "But before we go, can you be so kind as to ask the monk to help my flock. We need some food, water, change of clothes, and some beds. It's been a really rough few days." The bishop did not respond to Fr. Demitri, but told the monk to give Fr. Demitri whatever he asks for.

Within ten minutes the courtyard was full of monks. None spoke. But it didn't take a genius to follow their instructions. They all went many separate ways. Haji's monk had to be ninety-years old. He also smelled like he didn't take a bath in ninety-years. He was disgusting.

Rebecca went with Mrs. Lichou and Anna (the mother and daughter from the woods.) Their monk was about thirty-years old. Haji didn't like the way their monk was looking at Rebecca. Although Rebecca hadn't taken a bath in some time and wore the same dress since the invasion she still looked beautiful.

That monk better not try anything on her, because if he does he's going to be in a lot of trouble, Haji thought.

When they reached their destination Haji couldn't believe it. They were in another courtyard. There had to be a hundred rooms surrounding the courtyard. Haji had been to the monastery many times but never to this part. Many men have come here over the centuries from all over the world as a religious retreat. The monastery was a place to recharge their spiritual batteries. In the middle of the courtyard were two wells with hand pumps. *Well water.* It seemed that's the way the monks washed themselves.

Except Haji's Monk. Haji's Monk smelled like he never washed.

Haji then noticed the monk trying to explain something to Rebecca and some of the other women. At first Haji couldn't figure it out. Then he got it. He was trying to explain to them to remove their clothing, wash up, and put on some clean monk cloths. When the women finally figured it out Haji saw more monks come by and surround the well. They did an about face so the women could undress, wash, and put on the clean monk clothes with the monk's backs to them. The monks were very respectful. For a second Haji tried to peek, but his smelly monk noticed and slapped him in the face. Haji knew he deserved it.

After they all washed, they were escorted to the dining area. The dining area was a large room with many tables lined in rows. The women were escorted into the dining room first and seated in an entirely different section at the far end of the room. Bishop Emanuel was up on a loft reading from a prayer book. The food was already on the tables. Haji has been to the monastery every year for as long as he can remember. It was always done this way. Someone always read for twenty minutes while the food was right in front of you and you weren't allowed to touch it.

Obedience.

A few of Savas' students unknowingly went to grab some food. As quick as cats, a couple of monks stopped them. So, after twenty minutes of prayers they were given permission to eat. It made them appreciate the food that much more. After they ate and listened to the bishop for another twenty minutes of prayer, he informed everyone about the war outside the safety of the monastery walls. He said he heard on the radio the Turks have taken over the Nicosia Airport and that the Cypriot army was defenseless against the invaders. They were also informed that many of the Cypriot soldiers were in hiding. The bishop reassured everyone that they weren't alone, and that God was on their side. But once everyone heard the Cypriot soldiers were in hiding they immediately heard the sobbing; especially from the women and Savas' students.

They were then escorted to their rooms. Of course the men went first, and then the woman. Haji's room was as simple as it could have been. It contained a bed, a small dresser, and a lamp. Bathroom? Yes. It consisted of a very smelly outhouse with no window. Haji laid down on the bed and felt so alone as tears started rolling down his face. He was about to start sobbing when he heard a knock on the door. The door opened a few inches and he saw Fr. Demitri.

"Can I come in?" asked Fr. Demitri.

"Of course you can Father."

"I wanted to check on you."

"I'm fine thank you."

"Good, how does it feel to lie down on a warm bed?"

"It feels great."

"Haji, remember all those Holy Weeks when I always talked about forgiveness?"

"Of course I do Father."

"Well, what you saw in the courtyard was not the real me. I never should have punched the bishop. I never should have even talked back to him; let alone question him. I failed to follow obedience."

"Really Father? If you really truly feel that way, why don't you correct what you did wrong?"

"I did correct it."

"How did you correct it?

"I apologized to the bishop. I asked for his forgiveness."

"Did he forgive you?"

"Of course he did."

"Father, may I ask you something?"

"Of course you can my son."

"Well, remember every year during Holy Week when you told us that sometimes forgiveness is not enough and we must also, whenever possible, make it right?"

"Yes my child," he said with a smile feeling proud that at least someone was listening to his sermons.

"Well then, if you really truly feel that you were wrong; then make it right. Go get all the women and throw them out of the monastery."

Fr. Demitri lowered his head and walked out the door.

CHAPTER

7

That night Haji didn't sleep soundly. The events of the past few days kept awakening him. Then he started thinking about his life. Whatever was left of it; if any? His father served in the Cypriot army many years ago. He always told Haji that their army was nothing to brag about. They only had five planes. And since the bishop told everyone the Turks took over the Nicosia airport, Haji was sure the planes were grounded, if not destroyed. And since many of the Cypriot soldiers were in hiding, it didn't look good for Cyprus.

What will become of his island? He thought. They have done nothing wrong. Someone must help them.

Where is Greece?

Where are the Americans?

Greece and America are their number one allies.

Or that's what everyone thought.

Can these monastery walls protect them?

Again Haji fell into a light sleep.

Tossing and turning for most of the night, he saw a vision of his family. The thought of stray animals licking the wounds of his mother and father both half eaten by now by the stray animals that roamed around the village. His sister Mary still hanging by her neck in the kitchen with her body covered with flies. He hoped and prayed Fr. Demitri was correct when he said that all the deceased are in: "*a place where there is no pain, no sorrow, and no suffering.*"

As Haji lied on the bed staring out the window into the darkness, he heard a knock on the door. He dared not move. Who could it be, he thought? If the Turkish soldiers took over the monastery they would not knock on the door. Besides he would hear gunfire. *Maybe I'm hearing things. That's right. I'm hearing things.* Then the door opened. It was the monk. Haji's smelly monk. As usual, he didn't speak. But he did motion by using the international sign with his thumb for Haji to get out of bed. Where does he want to take me in the middle of the night Haji wondered? I'm a guest in his place so I should listen to him.

So Haji put on the monk clothes that were given to him the night before. His smelly monk waited for him outside his door. Using the international wave for Haji to follow, Haji did just that. As they walked across the courtyard Haji noticed other people in his group following *their* monks. Where could they possibly be taking us at this time of the night? They were brought into the chapel and separated. Men were on the right, and women on the left.

"You gotta be kidding," Haji heard Mousikou say. "You got us up at this ungodly hour to pray? It's four o'clock in the morning."

Then Haji remembered. On his many trips to the monastery, they were always told the monks wake up every morning at 4:00 a.m. to pray for an hour and a half, then return to bed for an hour.

"I was getting the first good night's sleep in days and you wake me up for this," Mousikou yelled out again.

Under the watchful eye of the bishop, Fr. Demitri walked out of the altar, right up to Mousikou, stood nose to nose with him and whispered, "Shut your mouth now, before I shut it for you."

Mousikou was a smart man. He knew just how far he could push Fr. Demitri, and when he should back down. This time he chose to back down.

Halfway through the liturgy (mass) Haji glanced towards the women and noticed Anna looking at him. Haji liked that. Anna was a very pretty girl. And it turned out she was a year younger than Haji but had the body of a fifteen-year old. But the real beauty was Rebecca. Even wearing the monk's clothes, she looked beautiful. As loose as the clothes were on her, he was still able to make out her gorgeous figure.

"Hey Haji, stop looking at the girls," whispered Mousikou. "Fr. Demitri is watching you."

Haji started to sweat. When he looked up, he saw Fr. Demitri and the bishop looking at him. Oh my God, I'm in trouble Haji thought.

The next hour was very boring. But they all got through it. They knew that doing this was better than being out there under the unmerciful Turkish soldiers.

After liturgy the bishop gave the most boring sermon Haji had ever heard. He talked and talked. He never even touched base on what was going on outside the monastery walls. They needed to hear something about what was going on outside those walls. The bishop had a radio. Didn't he listen to it? Haji thought. He should have had his ear glued to it all night. Instead he drags everyone into the chapel to pray. When it was over the men were escorted out first.

After the men left, the women were escorted out. But not Haji. Fr. Demitri wanted to talk to him. But when Fr. Demitri and Haji went into a smaller chapel off to the side to talk, the bishop was waiting for them. The bishop asked Haji to sit, but not before dismissing Fr. Demitri.

"Your Grace, if I may, I would like to sit in on your meeting with Haji."

The bishop picked up his head and glared at Fr. Demitri. As the saying goes, (if looks could kill, Fr. Demitri would be dead). Fr. Demitri didn't say a word. He lowered his head and walked out of the chapel. *Obedience.*

"My child," started The Bishop. "Do you know why you are here? I must inform you that what you were doing in the house of God, cannot, and will not be tolerated. Did you think what you were doing would go unnoticed?"

"What was I doing Your Grace?"

"If you don't remember, then I guess you need a little time to think and pray about it. Instead of going back to sleep, I'm leaving you here in the chapel. You need to do some soul searching. And Haji, don't forget. This is God's house. And God knows everything."

When the bishop left, Haji started to cry. "I'm sorry God," Haji said aloud. "I'm sorry I was thinking such sinful thoughts in Your house. God, please forgive me." Then he heard his voice.

"It's all right Haji, God forgives you."

Haji didn't have to turn around. He immediately recognized Fr. Demitri's voice.

"You're always in the right place at the right time," said Haji.

"You didn't think I would leave you my son, did you?"

"Well, the bishop did send you away."

"Yes he did, but I didn't go very far. But Haji, you must exercise obedience. You must stay here and pray. And another thing Haji; stop looking at the girls while here in the monastery. Especially inside the chapel. And if you do look, don't stare like you've been doing. I'm sure the women noticed. They just haven't said anything to you about it. But rest assured, they know. Now, start praying, and I'll sit right here besides you. When it's time for everyone else to wake up we'll go into the dining area and pray some more, and then we'll have breakfast with everyone, and remember, I'll never leave you. I'll never let anyone hurt you or allow anything to happen to you."

For the next ten minutes or so, they sat in the pew and prayed. After that Haji fell asleep. He was awakened by Fr. Demitri tapping on his shoulder. Haji looked up at him and said nothing. He was sure Fr. Demitri read his mind. He appreciated the fact that Fr. Demitri let him sleep.

"Come on sleepy prayer, let's wash up and get something to eat."

"Hey Fr. Demitri, you think if I ask the bishop for a pass to not pray for the next twenty minutes because I've been praying for the last hour, he'd give it to me? You could be my witness."

"Very funny wise guy," Fr. Demitri smiled. "Don't you think I'm in enough trouble with the bishop? Do I need to add lying to the bishop's list of reasons for him not to like me?"

Fr. Demitri and Haji went to the well and washed up. Then they went their separate ways to get a change of clothes.

"I'll meet you by the well in ten minutes," said Fr. Demitri.

"Yes sir," Haji smiled.

Of course when Haji reached the well Fr. Demitri was already waiting for him.

"Can you spare a few minutes before breakfast?" asked Fr. Demitri with a smile.

"Sure."

As they started to walk Haji realized where Fr. Demitri was taking him. Haji had been there before with his family. The place always sent a feeling of spirituality right threw him.

There it was, right before them, the grave of St. Helen.

St. Helen and her son St. Constantine were the ones who found the actual cross that Christ was crucified on. The cross was then brought to Cyprus and The Holy Cross Monastery was built around it.

The Holy Cross Monastery was the holiest place in Cyprus.

"Haji, do you feel like praying again?"

"I sure do."

"Good, do you think this time you can stay awake?" Fr. Demitri asked with a smile.

"This time I will," Haji smiled back. They kneeled together. Then Fr. Demitri started.

"My Dear Holy Mother of Constantine, we are here at your house. We need your holy protection. Please protect us from the evils outside these walls, and please forgive us of our sins. Come on Haji, the bishop awaits."

"I'm right behind you Father, I'm starved." They walked fast, almost a small trot. They were like two little kids hurrying back to school because they took too much time at recess. But there was no sneaking into the dining hall. They were still at prayer. They both walked in and took their seats. They did not go unnoticed, as all eyes were on them, especially the bishop's.

"Look Fr. Demitri, the women noticed us. I hope the women don't get into trouble for looking at us."

"Don't be a wise guy," said Fr. Demitri as he rubbed the top of Haji's head. As usual they ate in silence. Something about obedience and the purity of the souls keep control of emotions. They were still supposed to pray while they ate. This time they did pray. They prayed from their heart. Not because they were supposed to, but because they were still scared. They knew that the monastery walls cannot keep the Turkish soldiers out. They had tanks. They had guns. Many guns.

Themselves? They had a few guns but they weren't an army. Their army was in hiding. The only thing they did have was their faith and prayers.

After breakfast they were joined by the monks and escorted outside. As usual the men left first. This time while they were walking out Haji looked straight ahead. He didn't dare look around. He did notice the bishop and Fr. Demitri watching him. Haji had the feeling the bishop wanted to catch him, but Fr. Demitri was praying that Haji behaved himself. Outside they were taken to the garden. They spent the rest of the morning tending the garden. They picked lettuce, tomatoes, carrots, and fruits. Monks don't eat meat. They are constantly fasting.

When they finished picking fruits and vegetables they were instructed to weed. Sometimes the weeds were so large Haji couldn't tell the difference between the weeds and the plants. Haji was beginning to think the monks didn't do any weeding before he got there.

By lunch time they were exhausted. They were all escorted to the outhouses, then to the wells to wash up. Into the dining room they went. Again they sat starving with the food right under their noses waiting for the bishop to finish his readings. Finally, they were allowed to eat.

After Haji finished eating, he needed to stand and stretch his legs. He spent the entire morning bent over picking vegetables and weeding in the garden. His entire body was stiff. His back was killing him. When he stood all eyes were on him. He noticed the bishop lean over to Fr. Demitri and whisper something in his ear. Fr. Demitri then walked over to Haji.

"What are you doing?" asked Fr. Demitri.

"What?"

"Don't tell me what!"

"What did I do?"

"You got up without permission."

"You gotta be kidding me?"

"You know you can't do that."

"Do what?" Haji snapped back. "All I did was get out of my chair."

"Don't you know anything? You can't do anything without permission. You are starting to annoy the bishop."

"Annoy the bishop? He's picking on me. I'm not his slave! Tell him to get off my back!"

Fr. Demitri grabbed Haji by the arm and dragged him outside.

"Ouch, you're hurting me."

"Listen up Haji; there is nothing more important in this place than obedience."

"Come on Father, it's not that I asked to get up and was refused and then I disobeyed. I just got up. I'm stiff all over."

"Poor you," said Fr. Demitri. "You are the only one who's in pain. Why don't you go to your room and pray about it."

"All right, I'll do that."

"Good, you do that."

Before Haji went to his room he decided to walk back to St. Helen's grave again. When he got there he didn't want to say anything. Fr. Demitri always said; if you have nothing good to say, don't say anything. So, he sat there for about an hour not saying anything at all to her. All he did was hold on to The Holy Cross of Jesus Christ. With his hand on the cross, he felt that nothing can happen to him, or this holy place. Then he remembered his village church. That was a holy place. Look what happened to it. The Turks destroyed it. Then they humiliated the sanctuary by defecating on The Holy Altar.

Suddenly Haji didn't feel safe anymore. He again questioned if these monastery walls can protect him. On his way back, as he passed the garden, he noticed everyone working. He felt he should be feeling bad not helping out and considered helping everyone. But since Fr. Demitri ordered him to go to his room he asked himself; *who am I to disobey Fr. Demitri?* Obedience. Now obedience is working for me he thought. But as he noticed everyone working, they noticed him. Especially his smelly monk. Once his monk saw Haji he stopped what he was doing and started running to the bishop's building. That's it Haji thought. I'm done. So Haji continued walking past the garden. Rebecca waved to him. So did Anna. They're done too Haji thought. Nah, they can't be done, the bishop only picks on me.

In his room he took off his shoes, laid on the bed, and stared at the ceiling. It felt so good to rest. I've helped my father in the fields many times, but not like this, these monks can really work, Haji thought. Haji remembered falling on and off asleep while dreaming about his family. Then the dreams turned into nightmares of the past few days.

Then he felt like someone was staring at him. He opened his eyes and saw Mousikou standing over him holding a tray of food.

"Oh my God, you scared me half to death," said Haji.

"The way you've been acting Haji, I didn't think you scare that easily," laughed Mousikou.

"I'm guessing I'm in trouble."

"Nah, the bishop told me to bring you this food."

"What's that, my last supper?"

"Don't let the bishop get to you, he's just miserable."

"Yeah, I know."

"But you should have seen Fr. Demitri. I had to pull him off the bishop. The bishop started yelling at Fr. Demitri after your monk ratted you out. Fr. Demitri lost his temper again. He grabbed the bishop by his collar and lifted him up against the wall. Fr. Demitri kept yelling; he's only twelve years old, he's only twelve years old over and over again. You have no idea what he has experienced."

"Wow, I hope Fr. Demitri isn't in trouble."

"I don't think so. After it was all over the bishop told your monk to make you a tray of food and bring it to you."

"So what are *you* doing here?"

"I followed your monk out and took the tray from him and told him I would bring it to you. What was he going to do, kick my ass?"

"Nah, I don't think so," Haji said, as he took the tray.

Mousikou sat with Haji while he ate. They talked about the past few days, and also talked about what could happen to them in the next few days. Mousikou told Haji that Anna is pretty, but also told him that he's too young for girls. Mousikou and Haji sat on the bed for a couple of hours. They talked about everything, from girls, to Haji trying to find his uncle in America, and getting an education. It was good to talk to a non-priest, even though Haji wished Fr. Demitri was with him.

"Anyway Haji, I'm tired. Some of us worked in the fields today," Mousikou laughed.

"Yeah I know. See you in the morning, and don't worry, I'll be good tomorrow."

By now Haji was really tired. Mousikou gave him more things to think about. Anyway he thought; I'm safe for at least another night.

Little did Haji know that at 3:00 a.m. his life would change again forever by the way his door was broken down and a machine gun pointed at his face.

CHAPTER

8

Same day, Astoria, New York, 1974

At 5:00 a.m. Andreas started his daily ritual. He walked out of the bedroom into the kitchen. His wife Christine for some unknown reason was unable to have children. So since it was only the two of them they decided to live in a small apartment and save their money.

Save it for what? They didn't know.

Since they had a small apartment he couldn't just open the door to the kitchen and open the light without waking his wife. So he started each morning by turning on the oven light. It gave off just enough light without lighting up the apartment. He then heated the coffee Christine always prepared for him the night before. It was quicker this way. Next came the Maalox for his ulcer.

Andreas as always sat at the kitchen table and sipped his coffee as he ate a small piece of five day old Italian bread. He loved eating hard bread after the Maalox soothed his stomach. Every morning he would sit and think about the business of his small diner. He always started with the receipts of the day before. With pencil and paper he would figure his profit of the day before. He came home with a substantial amount of money every night. Business was good since he and Christine bought the diner. The money flowed in, but Andreas and Christine never spent much of it. There just wasn't enough time.

They opened at 6:00 a.m. every morning. That meant Andreas had to be there at 5:30 to start making the coffee, turn on the ovens, and crank up the heat in the winter. This way the customers can be waited on at 6:00 a.m.

That afternoon he was marching from St. Demitrios Greek Orthodox Church to the United Nations to protest the Turkish invasion of Cyprus. Then return to the diner, work through dinner, and lock up at 11:00 p.m. This was his life. 5:00 a.m. to 11:00 p.m. seven days a week. As he sipped his coffee and added the receipts from the day before, he noticed that his profits kept increasing.

"Business is great," he whispered to himself.

"Did you say something dear?" asked Christine from the bedroom.

"No, just talking to myself as usual, go back to sleep dear." Andreas stood from the table and put his dirty dish and coffee mug in the sink. One rule he promised himself was never eat at the diner. The diner was work, eating is something he did at home. Christine could never understand how he can own a diner and never eat there. Breakfast at home, for lunch he would pick at some food as he cooked during the day, but at 11:15 p.m. he would eat a small dinner at home.

Every morning as always, Andreas tiptoed back into the bedroom and slowly fondled Christine's breasts and kissed her on the head as to not wake her. As he left the bedroom she said; "Have a nice morning, and please be careful walking to work."

"I didn't know you were awake," he would say.

Christine just smiled. *I wasn't awake; you woke me like you do every morning.*

Andreas opened his door, stepped out into the hall, and double bolted the door. He walked down the four flights of stairs, out into the street, and turned left. Halfway up the block he saw Mrs. Misoulis coming out of her house with her dog Ouzo.

"Good morning Andreas, any news from Cyprus?"

"Good morning to you Mrs. Misoulis. No I haven't heard anything I'm sorry to say," Andreas said as he leaned down to pet Ouzo. "I'm going to St. Demitrios at 11:00 a.m. A bunch of us are walking to the United Nations to protest the Turkish invasion of Cyprus."

"You're going? So am I. Four of us are taking a taxi to the United Nations. It's too far for us old ladies to walk."

"I understand."

"Anyway Andreas, I'll see you later for breakfast," she says as Ouzo squatted down to do his business.

Andreas continued to Broadway, turned right, and started his ten block walk. He approached O'Malley's bar as Patty O'Malley was locking up.

"Morning Patty," Andreas said as he passed.

"Top of the morning to you Andreas, I heard what's going on in Cyprus," he said as he slurred his speech from all the whiskey he drank during the night. "Have you heard anything from your brother? I hope he and his family are all right."

"Thanks Patty, but no, I haven't heard anything. All the lines are dead. I'm sure they're fine."

Andreas felt sick to his stomach. Deep down he was worried. He knew his brother would have called if he could. Andreas prayed that the only reason his brother didn't call was because the phone lines were down.

As he continued the ten block walk he said good morning to two other bar owners closing up and to Mike, the hardware store owner who was parking his car on the corner of 44th Street and Broadway. Mike drove in from Long Island every morning. When he saw Andreas he rolled down his window and asked:

"Good morning Andreas, any news from Cyprus?"

"No, nothing so far Mike, thanks for asking."

"I'm sure they're fine. Let me know if I can do anything."

"Thanks Mike."

"I'll see you for breakfast in a little while."

"Great, looking forward to it."

Andreas crossed the street at the Salvation Army building on the corner of 46th Street and Broadway and looked at his diner. He's owned it for three years now and was as proud as always as he crossed the street onto his parking lot. As always there were three cars waiting in the parking lot waiting for Andreas to open. The first person to get out of his car was Joseph, the postal worker.

"Good morning Andreas, have you heard from your brother yet?"

"No, nothing yet, thanks."

"Hey Andreas," he hears, as Clyde gets out of his car. Clyde is another postal worker.

"Good morning Catman." Clyde always went by Catman. Catman stood 6'-6" tall. He played football in college until he blew out his knee, lost his scholarship and then became a postal worker. Andreas was always happy to see Catman. Many times in the early mornings there were drunks outside the diner waiting for Andreas to open. Sometimes it got rough. Andreas wasn't able to do much though he was solid as a rock. He only stood 5'-5" tall. Catman always handled it for Andreas.

"Andreas, hope all is well with your family. They outta send in the marines. America needs to throw out those Turks and then drop an atom bomb on Turkey. That'll send a message to the whole world. Especially the Russians."

"From your mouth to God's ears," replied Andreas. "From your mouth to God's ears," he repeated.

"Enough talk of violence so early in the morning," Yoyo the waitress says as she gets out of her car.

"Sorry Yoyo," they all said together. When Yolanda first came to the diner looking for a job, Andreas asked her three times what her name was. Three times she told him Yolanda.

"I can't pronounce that name. If you want to work here your name will be Yoyo," said Andreas.

"I'll take the job," she said. And from then on everyone knew her as Yoyo.

Andreas did his thing. He opened the door as everyone followed.

"Come on Andreas, let's crank up the coffee," said Catman.

"Hold your horses; let me turn on the lights first."

"No problem, I'll do it myself."

Catman on many occasions helped Andreas open the diner. He knew where everything was kept. He went into the kitchen every morning and made himself breakfast. He poured his own coffee, made his own eggs and bacon, and buttered his own toast. Andreas didn't mind, even if it did cost him a couple of extra slices of bacon, Catman was always great to have around.

Andreas went straight to work. He took the home fried potatoes out of the refrigerator that were prepared the night before and put them on the grill that was already being heated. He brought out the bacon, eggs and sausages and put them in the right spots next to the grill for the short order cook to fill the orders that Yoyo called into the kitchen. Everything was falling into place.

At 9:30 Christine walked into the diner and said her hello's to Yoyo and the customers. Andreas loved the way Christine came into the diner every morning and worked the room. They all loved her. And why shouldn't they? She knew most of them by name and she was exceptionably beautiful. So beautiful that growing up in Vavla with Andreas, Christine's mother tried to keep her away from Andreas when he started to take an interest it her. Christine stood 5'-7" tall and beautiful.

Christine walked into the kitchen and kissed Andreas. Then she acknowledged the two cooks and the dishwasher. Christine was nothing like her mother. She treated everyone with respect, no matter who they were, what they looked like, how much money they had, or what they did for a living.

Christine as always asked the kitchen help if she can bring them coffee or soft drink. The kitchen help as always respectfully declined. She then turned to Andreas and asked him what time he was leaving as they walked from the kitchen into the dining area.

"I'm leaving now," he replied.

"Please be careful," she said as she again kissed him on the lips and stepped behind the cash register.

Everyday Christine was the cashier for late breakfast, lunch, and into dinner. She was the face of the diner; the first to greet you, and the one who always thanked you for coming in.

Andreas walked out the door, through his parking lot, and started his fifteen block walk to 31st Street. As he walked down Broadway he nodded and said hello to many people he knew. He lived in Astoria for thirteen years. The year they married they decided that since Andreas worked at a diner they should open their own. So they bought the Broadway diner on the corner of 46th Street and Broadway.

CHAPTER

9

Vavla, 1961, thirteen years before the Turkish invasion.
Andreas was 5'-5" tall, not very handsome, and poor on top of it. Christine's mother wanted her daughter to go to America and marry a handsome rich man. As a teenager, Andreas walked Christine home from school almost every day. Christine's mother always called her into the house immediately.

"Hello Mrs. Alexander," Andreas would always say. Mrs. Alexander would sometimes nod her head but most of the time she ignored him.

"How many times must I tell you? I don't want that boy around you."

"I've told you many times Mother, he's a nice boy. He's always nice to me."

"Stay away from him. Do you hear me? I'm tired of telling you. You stay away from him or I'll tell him myself to stay away. Your brother Basil in America is going to send for you and you *will* go there. Basil will find you a husband. I don't want Andreas interested in you at all."

"But why Mother? I really care for him."

"Why? I've told you why. I've told you a hundred times why! He's short! He's ugly! And he's poor! What kind of life will he ever give you? Huh? Answer me! What kind of life will you have with him?"

"The way I feel about him I'm sure that my life will be beautiful."

Mrs. Alexander slapped Christine in the face. Christine started to cry and ran into her bedroom.

The next day after school Andreas noticed Christine's red cheek.

"What happened?" he asked.

"Nothing, nothing at all," she repeated as she broke down and cried hysterically.

Andreas held her close as she continued to cry. Christine told Andreas that her mother didn't want her seeing him anymore.

"I'll speak to her."

"Don't bother. She wants me to stay away from you. But I'm not. Let's go somewhere. Please, let's go somewhere where we can be alone."

"Where do you want to go?"

Christine took Andreas by the hand and walked him towards the back of the schoolhouse. By this time school had already let out. She opened the hatch to the basement and led him down the steps. They stayed there talking about how their lives would be if they could somehow escape Christine's mother.

As they were about to leave the basement Andreas asked, "Christine, will you marry me?"

Tears started rolling down her cheeks. She stared him in the eyes while gasping for her breath.

"Yes, I'll marry you. Let's run away together. Now."

"No no no. Not like that. Let's go tell your mother."

"Are you kidding? She's not going to allow it."

"I'm charming, she'll accept me. I'll tell her with the utmost respect that I love her daughter and I want to spend the rest of my life with you."

"It's not going to work."

"We won't know unless we try. And I want to try."

"All right," Christine said reluctantly.

They left the school house basement and headed towards town as Andreas held her hand.

"You two make a cute couple," they heard a familiar voice say as they simultaneously turned around.

There he was, standing behind them like a giant.

"Good afternoon Father Demitri," Andreas said as he quickly let go of Christine's hand.

"Good afternoon to you too, good afternoon to both of you," Fr. Demitri smiled.

Christine instantly approached Fr. Demitri and kissed his hand as it is traditional in the Orthodox Church.

"It's nice to see you," said Christine.

"Where are you two going all lovey-dovey?"

"We're going home. We just came back from school," said Christine.

"School? School was over an hour ago. Come with me my children. Let's go into the church and pray."

With the utmost respect Andreas and Christine followed their spiritual Fr. Demitri into the Church of St. George. They walked up the stairs and entered the church.

"Come sit up front. Let's pray together. Lord, please help guide all of your children, and please help them fight temptation."

Christine started to worry. What does he want with us? She thought.

"Well my children. I just never get a chance to speak to my children on a one to one basis. Sometimes I don't get a chance to tell all my children of the temptation of the devil. Please be aware that the devil *is* alive and well."

"Thank you Fr. Demitri," said Andreas. "I'll try to remember that."

"Christine, please wait for Andreas outside. I need to speak to him a moment alone."

"Sure Father, I'll be outside for as long as you need to keep Andreas."

"Thank you my child."

"Andreas, I'm not going to ask you any questions. I'm just going to tell you to be careful. I suggest you keep your distance from Christine. You know her mother. Her mother will never back down. Yes my son, I know everything."

"Thank you Father. I'll keep that in mind."

"Go in peace my son, and have a blessed day."

"What did he say to you?" asked Christine as soon as Andreas approached her.

"He didn't say much. He was talking about the devil and all that church stuff. We have nothing to worry about."

When Andreas reached Christine's house he took a deep breath and said, "Let's do this."

Together they walked into the house.

"Good afternoon Mrs. Alexander. May I speak to you please?"

"Get out of this house now. Do you hear me? Get out, and stay out. You," she pointed to Christine, "go to your room and don't come out until I tell you."

"Mother please, I love him, and he loves me."

"Mrs. Alexander, please. I love your daughter."

"Go find someone else's daughter to love. Get out of my house now and never come back. Do you hear me? Never come back," yelled Mrs. Alexander.

Andreas saw how quickly Christine ran into her room. He knew it. He knew that he and Christine can never be.

So, in 1961 at the age of seventeen, Andreas knew there was no future for him in Vavla. Christine was the only girl he had feelings for. He knew Christine's mother would never allow her to get involved with him. Besides, Vavla was a small village. There was no future for him there anyway. His father had a small olive growing business. As is tradition, his older brother Costas gets everything, from the house, properties, and the business. Andreas knew what he had to do. He not only had to leave Vavla, but he had to leave Cyprus. He would go where most Cypriots went.

He would go to America.

So, at seventeen-years old Andreas informed his parents he was leaving Cyprus. Andreas' parents knew that it was the best thing for their son. There was no way Andreas can stay with a broken heart. Besides, there wasn't much he could do to earn a living in Vavla.

So, Andreas walked away from Vavla and never looked back. It took him three days to get to the Mediterranean Sea. Once there he spent three weeks working on the piers. He took any job he could find.

He worked day and night, slept on the docks, saved all his money, and ate the scraps that the fisherman left behind. All he wanted to do was buy his way to Greece. From there he knew he would board a boat to America.

Those years it was easy to make your way to Greece from Cyprus. There were no passports needed. Well, not really. You did need a passport, but it was very easy to board a cargo ship and make it across the Mediterranean. That is exactly what

Andreas planned to do. He would bribe one of the cargo handlers to sneak him onto the ship.

But the Lord must have been watching. While Andreas was working on the docks the foreman instructed him to hurry up and load the crates onto the ship, or else he would fire him. Andreas now had a way to get on the ship without spending his money.

He must have loaded one hundred crates onto the ship. He was exhausted. By ten o'clock the ship foreman told everyone to go down below. Andreas went below and found a bunk. He put his head back.

As he was falling asleep he thought, *step one.*

I'm making it to Greece.

From Greece I'm going to America.

CHAPTER

Present day, Astoria New York, July 1974

As Andreas turned left on 31st Street and started walking towards St. Demitrios Greek Orthodox Church, he heard the chants of, "Turks out of Cyprus! Turks out of Cyprus! Killer Kissinger! Killer Kissinger!"

Approaching St. Demitrios, many of Andreas' Cypriot friends greeted him with hugs, kisses, and handshakes. There is something about all foreigners. For whatever reasons, they always feel most comfortable with their own kind. It's almost like family. They almost feel obligated to be among their own. Whenever they need any business dealings they use one of their own. At Andreas' diner he bought his supplies only from a Cypriot. The butcher, eggs and cheese, vegetables, etc., they were all Cypriot business owners. For the most part they did take care of each other. But yes, once in a while you would have a Cypriot take advantage of one of their own.

"Andreas," yelled Fr. Harry the presiding priest. "Any news from your brother?"

"No Father. Nothing yet."

"I'm sure it's going to be all right."

"I sure hope so."

For the next twenty minutes Andreas made small talk with many Cypriots. There were many Greeks there too. 99% of all Greeks and Cypriots considered themselves one. Although separate countries, they share the same language, religion, music, culture, foods, and national anthem.

Andreas looked up and noticed someone helping Fr. Harry stand onto the hood of a car. Fr. Harry stood on the hood for several minutes before it got quiet. When he started to speak; you were able to hear a pin drop.

Fr. Harry asked everyone to move close to him. Then he started:

"We are peaceful God loving people! Remember! Peaceful! I have the demonstration permits. Permits, for a peaceful demonstration! I do not want any violence! There is enough violence going on in Cyprus. We must show the United Nations that we are better than the Turks! We will march down 31st Street to the 59th Street Bridge. New York City has closed off the farthest right hand lane for us to walk across. There are police on every corner. Let's all behave ourselves! When we cross the bridge we are making a left on Second Avenue. We are then going to make another left on 42nd street. Then we will go to the front of the United Nations building and begin our protest. We *will* send a message! We *will* let our government know how upset we are. But we will do it in a *peaceful* way. Now, let us pray to the Lord."

Suddenly the train up above came to a screeching halt. It never fails. The elevated RR train of the New York City Subway line always comes at a time you need quiet most. But when you live in Astoria, the train is something you get used to. So, Fr. Harry waited for the train to leave the station and then continued his prayer.

"Lord our God, please help us in our journey to the United Nations and protect us, and please forgive our sins. Amen. All right everyone, let's go."

Everyone waited for Fr. Harry to lead the way. As Andreas was walking under the elevated train on 31st Street with his people, he felt most comfortable. He chatted with many of his own kind. Many of his friends introduced him to other Cypriots. Andreas wasn't the only person with uncertainty about his family's whereabouts.

31st Street rounded to the right as the demonstrators approached Queensboro Plaza. As they started to walk across the lower level their chants echoed. The 59st Bridge had an upper and lower level. On the lower level there was a single separate lane. This was the path the City of New York chose for the demonstrators; it was the safest way to walk across the bridge without any fear of traffic. The louder the chants, the louder everyone got. They all had goose bumps.

As Andreas reached center span he looked down and noticed a cargo ship. Then he started reminiscing.

He started looking back in time when the ship he was on docked in Greece.

CHAPTER

11

A thens Greece, 1961, thirteen years before the Turkish invasion. "Andreas, wake up," said Yanni, the man who slept in the bunk above Andreas. "The foreman wants everyone on deck."

"What time is it?" asked Andreas.

"5:00 a.m."

"I feel like I just fell asleep."

"Well, if you want to get paid you better get your ass out of the bunk."

Paid? I don't even work here.

Andreas left his bunk and made his way upstairs. People were already working. With a British accent the foreman was yelling at everyone.

"Hey you," the foreman yelled at Andreas.

"Yes sir."

"Get your ass over here on the double."

"Yes sir. What can I do for you sir?"

The foreman looked at Andreas and asked.

"What's your name kid?"

"Andreas Ioannou."

"How come I don't know you?"

"I'm new sir. I was hired the day we left Cyprus."

"All right then. Get this cargo off this ship as soon as you can. You know these Greeks are charging my docked vessel by the second. This country always gives Onassis a break. Me, they charge me by the second. So move your ass, and move it now!"

"Yes sir."

Andreas worked for three days unloading the ship and preparing the ship to be loaded for a trip to Italy then to America. During the three days he had three square meals. Nothing like his mom, but it was better than nothing. He even had a job. The only thing was; nobody knew him. It was a large ship, so it had to have a payroll department. At that moment Andreas didn't care. He was off Cyprus, in Greece, eating, and sleeping in a warm bed. On the day before they were scheduled to leave, the payroll whistle blew. Everyone got on line. Of course, Andreas' name was never called.

"Come on," said Yanni.

"Where are you going?" asked Andreas.

"Where we always go on pay day. To the whore house."

"I don't have any money. The payroll guy messed up my pay," he lied. "I didn't get paid."

"Come with me. I'll get you your money," said Yanni.

"All right, I'm right behind you."

An armed guard stood at the payroll door. Yanni knew him by name.

"Hey Bruno, is Barry inside?"

"Yes he is."

"I need to speak to him."

"Go ahead. Who's this guy?"

"This is Andreas, there's a problem with his pay."

Bruno looked suspiciously at Andreas.

"Don't worry; he's cool," said Yanni.

"All right, go ahead inside."

"Hey Barry, what's the deal with Andreas' pay?"

"Who's Andreas?"

"This guy right here. Don't you recognize him?"

"No, I've never seen him before in my life. Hey kid, what's your full name?" asked Barry.

"Andreas Ioannou."

"I never heard of you."

"Well I'm here and I didn't get paid."

"Leave me all of your personal information and come see me tomorrow."

"Yes sir, I'll see you then. Can I get some sort of an advance?" asked Andreas.

"Sorry kid, no advances."

Andreas and Yanni left the ship and went into town.

"Well Yanni, enjoy yourself."

"Where are you going?"

"Not where you're going. I'm outta here. My next stop is America."

CHAPTER

12

P resent day, Astoria New York, 1974
Andreas had tears in his eyes as he approached the United Nations. He never saw so many people in one place. As everyone chanted "Turks out of Cyprus, and Killer Kissinger," the tears rolled down his face. Unfortunately it did get a little out of hand and there were some arrests. But all in all it was a successful protest. Everyone rode the crowded subway back. Across the subway car, Andreas saw his brother-in-law Basil.

"Hey Andreas," called out Basil.

"Hey Basil," replied Andreas as he watched Basil wiggle in the crowd towards where Andreas was standing.

"Were you at the demonstration?" asked Andreas.

"Yes."

"Me too, sorry I missed you."

"You're full of shit," said Basil. "We made eye contact and you turned away."

"No, it wasn't me."

"If you say it wasn't you than it wasn't you. Anyway, how's my sister doing?"

"She's fine. I'll tell her you asked about her," Andreas said as he turned away.

"Andreas, what's your problem?"

"I have no problem. I don't know what you're talking about."

"Andreas, when are you going to get over it? It was a long time ago. When are you going to grow up?"

"Basil, not now, not here on the train if you know what's good for you."

"What are you going to do, hit me right here on the train?"

"If need be I will. Now get away from me before I knock you on your ass." Basil just walked away shaking his head.

When the train stopped at Broadway and 31st Street Andreas exited the train, walked down the stairs, entered a candy store, and bought a pack of Chesterfields. He needed a cigarette to calm his nerves after the confrontation he had with Basil. Besides, Andreas loved his no filter Chesterfields, even at .33 cents a pack.

When Andreas returned to the diner at 6:30 it was packed. It looked like another good dinner take. Christine stopped what she was doing and gave him a loving kiss. When things started to slow down at 8:30 Christine said her goodnights to the kitchen help and kissed Andreas again.

"Andreas, can I see you a minute?"

"Sure, I'll be out in a minute."

Christine sat with Andreas in a booth and explained the day's events. She told him about the business of the day, how much money she took in, and the deposit she made at the bank earlier in the afternoon. She seemed very happy. She even joked about the streets of Astoria and the bank being empty due to the demonstration at the United Nations.

Andreas was staring at Christine as she suddenly looked sad. She started to tear up.

"What's the matter?" he asked.

"Nothing, I'm fine."

"We're married too long for you to fool me. Again I ask; what's wrong?"

"I'm worried about you. I know you must be going crazy wondering what's going on with your family in Cyprus. I just love you so much. I want you now. I want you right now on this table," she smiled.

"Right here, right now, in front of everyone?" Andreas smiled back.

"Yes, but I guess I have to wait until you get home. Try to get someone to lock up for you and get yourself home early." She winked and then smiled.

"You know my love, I don't like anyone locking up but Yoyo, and she's gone for the day. But I'll try."

"I know I know, but please get yourself home as soon as you can."

"Yes ma'am."

Andreas reached his hands across the booth to her side of the table and she instantly leaned her breasts against his hands and gave him a ten-second kiss. She then broke the kiss and whispered, "How do they feel?"

"They feel great," Andreas whispered back.

"Good, because these babies will be waiting for you when you get home tonight. Don't keep them waiting too long. Now, I need to leave because I'm guessing you need five minutes or so for your pants to loosen up," she said with a smile as she got up and walked out the door. Andreas sat there looking out the window watching his beautiful wife walk down Broadway.

"Andreas, the cook needs to see you in the kitchen," said the dishwasher.

"Tell him I'll be there in a few minutes."

The rest of the evening everything went like clockwork. Customers came and went. Andreas locked the doors at 10:30. By 10:45 Andreas was out the door. Ordinarily he would keep the doors open until 11:00 p.m. But tonight his erection was leading the way. Andreas locked the doors and quickly made his way down Broadway. *I hope she's wearing the blue night gown.*

Andreas opened the door and found Christine sitting at the kitchen table drinking a glass of wine wearing her flannel pajamas. Okay he said to himself. No blue nightgown but she looks like she's getting in the mood with the wine.

"Where's mine?" he asked.

Christine looked at him.

He knew that look.

She was pissed.

"What's the matter sweetheart?"

"Don't sweetheart me. What happened today?"

"What are you talking about?"

"On the train!"

"What train?"

"Don't play dumb with me. I'll give you a hint. My brother called."

"Oh, that's it."

"Yes, that's it."

"You know what? I'm tired of this. Your brother comes over to me on the train all nicey-nice and caring asking me how I'm doing. I'm tired of his phony bullshit. That man doesn't like me and never will. He's no different than your mother. When did they invade Cyprus? A week ago? Did he call me to ask about my family in Valva? No! Not once! I saw him on the train and he didn't even ask. When he called you tonight, did he once ask you about my brother? Let me guess. He never asked. He never wanted me to marry you just like your mother didn't want me!"

"When are you ever going to let it go? Let it go! Do you hear me? Let it go! They didn't want you! So what? I wanted you! I love you! Isn't that enough?"

"No, it's not enough!"

"Well, what do you want me to do?"

"What do I want you to do? I'll tell you what I want you to do! I want you to let your brother know that he can't fool us into thinking he cares anything about me! Because you and I both know that he doesn't give a damn about me! That's what I want you to do!"

Then Andreas stormed out of the house.

CHAPTER

Greece, 1961

When Andreas walked away from Yanni he had no idea where he was going. He walked around the docks in Greece for two hours. The place was a mess. There were people of all sorts.

Homeless people begging for money.

Prostitutes looking to make money.

When Andreas left Cyprus his parents gave him $300. He divided the money in all four of his pockets, and his shoes and socks. He needed a place to sleep. He didn't want to sleep on the docks, but was afraid to wander into the outlying streets. So he took his chances. With the water on his right he turned left. He walked two blocks and turned left again. The area was deserted. He felt he made a mistake. He was not only growing tired but was also a little scared although exceptionally strong for someone his size. He knew he was out of his element. As he walked he noticed what looked like a cheap motel. He had money but he didn't want to start spending it without any form of income. But he realized he did need a good night's sleep. Besides, he had nowhere else to go. He figured in the morning he could look for a job and a room to rent.

So, he entered the lobby of the motel. As soon as he did a young lady approached him and asked him if he wanted a date. Even at 17-years old, living in the mountains of Cyprus, he knew what that meant. He smiled and said no thank you. He went to the front desk to ask for a room.

"Do you want the one or two hour rate?"

"I'm sorry, I don't know what you mean?" replied Andreas.

"How long do you want the room for kid?"

"I want it until morning."

"You mean you want to sleep overnight?"

"Yes sir, if I may?"

"Oh, I didn't know, that'll be $10."

Andreas took out the money from one of his pockets which immediately brought attention to himself. He then walked up three flights to get to his room. When he opened the door the first thing he noticed was that the bed wasn't made. He put his small overnight bag on the bed, opened it, took out a clean underwear, and entered the bathroom to shower.

It was a warm night so Andreas lied down on the bed in his underwear. He wasn't asleep very long when he heard a knock on the door. He cautiously opened the door two inches.

"Hi," said the young girl who approached him in the lobby.

"Hi, can I help you?"

"I hope so, my name is Voula and I was wondering if I can sleep on the floor in your room. I have no place to stay and I won't be a bother to you. All I need is a corner in your room to sleep."

"Well, I don't know." replied Andreas nervously.

"Oh please, I really need a place to stay."

Nervously, and reluctantly Andreas let her in, but not before asking her to wait so he can go into the bathroom to wrap a towel around his waist. Andreas noticed that she was very young. Voula couldn't have been more than 15-years old.

"Thank you so much," Voula said as she entered the room. "I can sleep right there," as she points to a spot on the floor.

Andreas felt embarrassed to let her sleep on the floor. That's not the way he was brought up. He was Cypriot. He looked at Voula as someone who needed help and was kind of a guest in his home. Even when his mother and father had overnight guests in their house his mother and father always gave up their bedroom. It's the right thing to do. As tired as Andreas was and as much as he needed to sleep in a bed he told Voula she could have the bed and *he* would sleep on the floor.

"Thank you," said Voula. "Is it all right if I take a shower?"

"Sure you can, where's your change of clothes?"

Voula started to stutter. She didn't know how to answer. Finally she says; "It was stolen. You must be very careful with your stuff. I'll just put my same clothes back on. At least my body will be clean. Why don't you lie down on the bed until I come out of the shower?"

"All right."

Andreas went straight to the bed to lie down. He was hoping to fall asleep at least for a little while. He was dead asleep when he felt Voula's presence. As Andreas opened his eyes he couldn't believe what he was looking at. There was Voula standing next to the bed looking down at him completely naked. Andreas didn't know what to do. He didn't move. Finally he spoke.

"What are you doing?" he asked nervously.

"I decided to wash my clothes. I have them drying in the bathroom. Don't worry, there'll dry overnight. Please move over. I'm starting to get cold."

Andreas moved over to the other side of the bed. As he moved over he instantly felt the need to adjust the crotch part of his underwear. Voula noticed him doing that. She smiled at him and said:

"I'll do that for you."

"Do what?" Andreas replied embarrassed.

"Do this."

Voula put her hand on Andreas' crotch and held it firmly. Andreas didn't know what to do. Then it happened. A few little shakes and he released his manhood fluids.

"Don't be embarrassed," she said. "I'm sure you can sleep well now. Goodnight," she said, as she held her hand exactly where she had it.

Andreas instantly fell asleep. During the night he felt Voula's hand stroking him again, as he instantly released his fluids a second time. It exhausted him. This time he felt himself fall into a deeper sleep.

The sounds of seagulls woke Andreas in the morning. At first, he didn't know where he was. Then he realized the motel room. Then he felt the dampness in his underwear and looked over towards Voula. But there was no Voula. Voula was gone. Where could she have gone? Why did Voula do what she did to me? Andreas thought. Where was she?

Andreas went into the bathroom for a hot shower. When finished he dressed and decided he needed to figure out the rest of his life.

Then he realized something was wrong. His money. Where was it? It was missing. It was gone. She took it. Voula took it. Andreas panicked. He needed his money. He knew he couldn't go to the lobby to complain. They wouldn't believe him. I'm finished, he thought. He was in a faraway land without knowing anyone. He had nowhere to turn. How will I survive? He thought.

He quickly gathered his stuff and put them in his bag. He hurried downstairs to look for Voula. He went to the front desk and asked if anyone knew her. The man at the desk was a different person than who rented the room to him the night before. Andreas asked him if he knew a woman named Voula.

"Voula? I know a Voula. I have an aunt named Voula," he laughed.

"No, not your Aunt Voula. A young girl named Voula. Do you know her?"

"Sorry kid. I know nobody else by that name."

Andreas felt a weight on his chest. *What will I do, where will I go?*

Andreas knew that Voula must have somehow known he had money. A date he thought. She asked me if I wanted a date last night. She's a prostitute, he thought. She tricked me. She had to have known I had money. Now I remember. She was in the lobby when I paid. She had to have seen me take out my money. I'll find her. I'll get my money back.

Andreas stormed out of the motel thinking he would see Voula as soon as he stepped outside. No such luck. *Where do I go now?*

He quickly went back inside and asked some of the other women sitting around the lobby if they knew Voula. They all laughed. They all knew what happened to him. *I don't believe that this is happening to me.*

Andreas left the motel and started walking. He had nowhere to go. He decided to return to the docks. He would have to find a job. *There had to be plenty of work on the docks.* Ships going in and out of port, someone would hire him. When he got to the port he heard someone calling his name.

"Hey Andreas, where've you been all night?" Andreas turned around. It was Yanni. The closest thing to a friend he had.

"Yanni, I'm so glad to see you."

"Are you back from America?" Yanni laughed.

"Very funny. I'm in a lot of trouble."

"What kind of trouble?"

"I got robbed."

"Robbed? Are you all right? Did they hurt you?"

"No, I'm not hurt. But I got robbed."

"What happened?" Yanni asked with a concerned look.

For the next few minutes Andreas told Yanni the whole story. The motel. Voula. The knock on the door. Coming out of the shower completely naked. With embarrassment, he even told Yanni about the rubdowns that Voula gave him.

"Holy shit Andreas. You got taken. That girl saw you coming. It's a scam. That happens every day. Forget about it. You're lucky they didn't hurt you."

"Hold on a minute. What do you mean I'm lucky *they* didn't hurt me? There were no *they*. It was only Voula. Nobody else was involved."

"Kid, you were scammed. That's the oldest trick in the book. They saw you coming. The girl asked if you wanted a date. Don't you know what asking you for a date meant?"

"I did. But when she came up to my room I figured I was wrong, and she really did need a place to stay."

"Forget it Andreas, chalk it up as experience. By the way, how much did she take you for?"

"Three hundred dollars."

"Holy shit. That's a lot of money. Forget it. Do you hear me? Forget it. Now, come with me. Barry's looking for you. He has your money."

"Has my money? What are you talking about? I came to Greece illegally. I have no passport. How can he have my money?"

"Welcome to the real world."

"What real world?"

"The real world of nobody has a passport. Your pay that's coming to you is $40. Give it back to Barry and he'll have a passport for you by the end of the week."

"You mean I can stay on the ship as a worker with the correct paperwork?"

"Yes you can. Now, forget Voula. Besides, I'm sure Voula isn't even her real name."

Andreas followed Yanni back to the ship. They immediately went below to see Barry. As usual Bruno was standing outside Barry's door with his shotgun.

"Barry inside?" asked Yanni.

"Go ahead," this time motioning to Andreas to follow.

They walked into Barry's office. As soon as Barry saw them he motioned to them to sit down while he was on the phone. Barry talked on the phone for fifteen minutes before hanging up. When he finally hung up he stared at Andreas for a few seconds. Then he started.

"Mr. Andreas Ioannou. You need a passport. It seems you somehow worked your way onto my ship and made it all the way to Greece. Congratulations. You made it. Now, what do we do with you? I can turn you over to immigration to be deported back to Cyprus, but not before spending a week or so in an immigration jail. Or I can help you. But keep in mind that I don't like people coming aboard my ship uninvited like you did. So, Mr. Andreas Ioannou, what do you have to say for yourself?"

Andreas was scared. Barry had him dead to rights. But before they saw Barry, Yanni coached Andreas on what to say, and how to say it.

"Well Barry, I have a lot to say. First I want to apologize for coming onto your ship uninvited. I also want to thank you for the opportunity to work for you on your ship. Yanni tells me you can get the legal documents that I need to stay aboard. For all this I'm gratefully indebted to you."

"Not bad," said Barry. "Not bad at all. But this is the way it's going to be. The pay is $80 a week at sea. Every week that you are entitled to get paid you will owe me half.. Every week. Do you understand? Every week! No need to answer me now. I'm going to need only one yes when I'm finished. You will continue working for the remainder of the week before we set out to America. When we are at sea in route to America there will be no weekly pay for anyone. When we dock in America everyone gets their checks and goes to an American bank and either cashes or deposits their check." The moment Andreas heard the word America his eyes lit up. "By the end of the week you will have your passport. All legal. It's going to cost you one hundred dollars. That's why I need to hold back half your pay. If you try to do the numbers in your head don't bother. I can give you the exact numbers. I know what you're thinking. The numbers don't add up. But they do. They always do, in *my* favor. The rest is my profit. That's the deal. You either take it or I call immigration."

Andreas hesitated a little too long. Barry instantly picked up the phone and called Bruno. Bruno was inside Barry's office within a second.

"Bruno, please escort Mr. Ioannou to a holding cell."

"I'll take it," Andreas said.

"I thought so, now please go to work."

Andreas immediately went to work. He was the happiest person on the ship. The first week went by quickly. Andreas was happy to be working. He really didn't care if Barry took half his pay. He was going to America.

Barry was true to his word. One week after their talk Barry sent for Andreas and gave him his passport. Who had it better than Andreas? He had his passport but no money. He didn't care.

Their ship set out to America on schedule. Andreas was very excited, although the thirty day trip was exhausting. Andreas never worked so hard. At times he thought extra work was given to him because he was young, strong, and a rookie. It didn't matter. The more they gave him the more he did. He was looking forward to starting a new life in America. One morning, Andreas was standing on deck and he thought the ship was going sideways. The land was closing in on him. He thought something was wrong. Then he noticed people waving. Then he realized what it was.

Gibraltar.

The Strait of Gibraltar.

He had heard of it. Once they were through, there was no turning back. Right into the Atlantic Ocean.

For the most part, the trip wasn't too bad. Many of the men had brought whiskey. They were drunk every night. Barry through his connections also added seven women to the ship. All were given passports. All needed to keep the men happy. Besides, Barry as usual, got his cut. And of course, Barry's own relaxation therapy from the women was always free of charge.

AMERICA

CHAPTER

14

"Listen up everyone," yelled the foreman. "I know you feel like caged tigers with the need to run and be free. But as you know, it doesn't work like that. There's still a lot of work that needs to be done. We will be in America for one week. If you are lucky, you'll have a day or so to go out there and have some fun. But come on, it wasn't too bad these past 30 days. You had your booze and the occasional woman. So come on, it hasn't been that bad.

"First and foremost I know you want your money. It's yours. You're entitled to it. I'm going to send you to payroll to get your checks. Hold on; hold on, not so fast. You'll get your money but not all of you at once. Come on, you know the rules. I'm going to send you to payroll in alphabetical order."

The foreman started rattling off the alphabet. When he reached the letter I, Andreas went. At the payroll window, the man recognized Andreas immediately.

"Mr. Ioannou. Barry has your check. Do you know where his office is?"

"Yes I do."

"Good. Please go there. He's waiting for you."

Andreas went directly to Barry's office. He couldn't believe it. There had to be at least thirty people waiting for their checks. Barry had total control.

Andreas spent half the day waiting for his money. Bruno and other security personal escorted one or two at a time to the bank on the west side of Manhattan. They escorted them directly back to Barry. Security then collected what was coming to Barry. Finally it was Andreas' turn.

"Come in Andreas," said Barry. "Are you ready to get paid?"

"Yes sir, I'm ready," Andreas replied as he recognized two of the women that were hired to keep everyone from getting lonely.

"Did you meet the ladies?"

"No I have not."

"You're kidding? You mean to tell me for the last thirty days you haven't spent any time with my beautiful guests?"

"No I have not," repeated Andreas.

The truth was, Andreas had no desire for those kinds of women. After meeting Voula he never wanted to have anything to do with women of that type.

"Your loss, not mine."

"I'm here for my pay sir."

"I'm sure you are."

"Bruno, here's Andreas' check. Please escort him to the bank. Now if you please, leave now, I need to have a meeting with my ladies."

Bruno and Andreas walked out of Barry's office as Barry's two lady friends started to approach Barry.

"He does all right for himself," Andreas said to Bruno after they left the office.

"Yes he does. A lot better than you can ever imagine."

As they were approaching Twelfth Avenue, Bruno explained to Andreas how the check cashing was going to work.

"These are the numbers. Four weeks at sea. One week at port before we left. That's five weeks pay at $80. That comes to $400. $100 for your passport. That leaves $300, and half of that leaves you $150. You will go into the bank. You will hand them over the check and ask them to cash it. They will ask you for identification. You will show them your passport. They will then hand you over $400. You will come out and meet me across the street in the coffee shop over there." Bruno points to the coffee shop across the street. "I will be sitting at the counter eating lunch. You will come in and sit next to me. There will be a cute little redheaded waitress who will ask if she can help you. I suggest you order the beef goulash.

"We will sit together and eat. When we are done you will hand me over Barry's $250. When the cute redhead brings us the bill I expect you to tell her to give it to *you*. I will then get up and leave. You will pay for both lunches and then you are on your own to go discover America. I know what you're thinking. You're thinking that Barry owes you money from the time you left Cyprus. Forget it. That was on you.

"And another thing. Make me look good. Leave the cute red-head a good tip. By the way; if you're thinking of running with Barry's money, try it. I *will* chase you. I *will* catch you. I *will* beat the living shit out of you, and then I *will* take all your money and leave you in the street penniless."

Andreas felt dumfounded. He felt his life wasn't his own. He knew what he had to do. There was no way he can physically beat up Bruno.

"All right, I'll do it. I'm a man of my word. I would never try to cheat anyone out of anything that I agreed to do."

"Yeah, whatever you say. Just remember what I said," as he stepped off the curb and started crossing the street.

Andreas stood on the sidewalk in front of the bank and watched Bruno walk into the coffee shop. He then turned around and looked at the largest building he has ever seen. He looked at the massive double glass doors as people walked in and out. Well, here I go he thought. He opened the door and was immediately approached by a uniformed guard with a visible gun at his side.

"Can I help you young man?"

"I like to cash a check please," Andreas said nervously.

"Over there," the guard said as he pointed to the lines to see the tellers.

"Thank you."

Nervously Andreas gets on one of the teller lines. After five minutes Andreas approached the teller.

"Welcome to the Bank of New York. How may I help you?"

"I'd like to cash this check please."

"Do you have an account with us?"

"No," replied Andreas nervously.

"I'm sorry, but I cannot cash a check without you having an account. You're going to have to see someone on the platform," she said as she pointed to the many employees sitting at their desks at the far end of the bank. "Go over there and someone will help you," she said with a friendly smile.

As soon as Andreas walked to the platform area a gentlemen stood and introduced himself as Mr. Johnson and asked Andreas if he could help him. Andreas explained that the teller send him to his section. She couldn't cash his check because he didn't have an account.

"Well, let's see if we can help you. Have a seat right here." Mr. Johnson then sat behind his desk and looked at Andreas.

"What is your name sir?"

"Andreas Ioannou."

"Mr. Ioannou, do you have any identification?" Andreas handed Mr. Johnson all that he had. "Let's see now. You have here your ships I.D. and passport. Everything looks fine. Your shipping company has an agreement with the Bank of New York. I can cash your check with no problem. But let me ask you a question Mr. Ioannou. Would you like to open an account today, or are you going back at sea? Even if you're going back at sea, many of your co-workers have accounts with us. Always remember, your money is safer in the bank than tucked under your bunk."

Andreas thought for a moment. He knew American banks were safe. He had no idea where he was going and started to think of Voula. He was a stranger in this foreign land. He needed to lay down roots. He started calculating in his head how much money he would need right away. Of the $150 he would have left and after buying Bruno lunch he knew what he had to do.

"All right Mr. Johnson, I would like to open an account. I'll start with $130."

"That's fine Mr. Ioannou. Let's fill out the paper work." Mr. Johnson produced the forms and helped Andreas fill them out. Andreas was happy he learned English in his village. As an address he put the ship's name.

Andreas walked out of the bank a happy man. Here he was, in America. Legally. Even with a bank account. He quickly walked across the street, entered the coffee shop, and sat next to Bruno.

"Got my money?"

"Yes I do." Andreas then hands it to him and says, "Pay for your own lunch."

Andreas left the coffee shop and never looked back. He was tired, depressed, and scared. But knew he had to move on. He walked to 11th Avenue looking for a place to eat. He saw a man selling hot dogs and approached him. The man asked Andreas how many hot dogs he wanted with a very recognizable Greek accent.

"Are you Greek?" Andreas asked the hot dog man in Greek.

"Yes I am, my name is Poppas," he replied in Greek.

Andreas stood talking to Poppas eating his hot dogs for almost an hour. Andreas gave him his life story. He talked mostly about him leaving Cyprus, his short time in Greece, on the ship, coming to America, and up to opening an account in the bank.

"Sounds like you're all alone here. Where are you going to stay tonight?"

"I don't know. Do you know anywhere I can stay?"

"Not really unless you want to sleep with the hot dog wagon."

"What do you mean?"

"Well, a bunch of us rent a spot a few blocks from here and keep our hot dog wagons there over night. There's really no place to sleep there but at least it's indoors."

"I'll do it."

"Good, maybe you can help me?"

"Sure thing, just tell me what you need me to do."

"All right. It's quitting time. I'll teach you the business. See that valve down there?"

"Yes I do."

"Good, turn it to the left." Andreas did exactly that. When Andreas turned the valve the water started emptying out. When all the water emptied Poppas had Andreas push the hot dog wagon six blocks to the store front where Poppas shared rental space.

"This is what we do at the end of our day. I take all the unused hot dogs and put them into that refrigerator with my name on it. Along with the onions, sauerkraut, mustard, ketchup, and leftover hot dog buns. Lock it up and I go home."

"You know what Andreas; you look like you could use a good night's sleep. I'll make a deal with you."

"What's the deal?"

"You come home with me tonight. You can sleep in the basement until you get your own place while you work for me."

Andreas couldn't believe it. He was being offered a job and a place to stay.

"Poppas, I would love to."

"Great, it's a deal."

Andreas and Poppas finished securing the hot dog wagon.

"Where do you live?"

"Greek town USA, Astoria New York," answered Poppas proudly.

"Wow, I've heard of Astoria. I understand many Greeks end up there when they come to America."

"Yes, many Greeks do. Greeks like yourself will not only end up there, but will probably spend the rest of your life there."

Andreas was now very excited. He had never heard of the subway before today. This was an experience he would always remember. They changed at 59th Street and Lexington Avenue. The RR subway train was very crowded. Andreas looked around in amazement at all the people. Some were sleeping, reading, talking, or just looking around. He couldn't believe it. Most were talking Greek. Poppas looked at Andreas and smiled.

"Starting to feel at home?"

"Right now I don't really feel at home, but I do feel like Astoria is going to be my *new* home."

Andreas watched in amazement as the subway came out of the ground and was elevated above the street and pulled into the Queensboro Plaza Station. After a few stops they reached their destination. They heard the conductor say, "Last stop, Ditmars Boulevard."

Andreas followed Poppas down the elevated platform steps. Poppas walked along Ditmars Blvd with Andreas next to him. Andreas couldn't believe all the Greek shops. There were news-stands selling Greek newspapers. Coffee shops with Greek names like Athens and Crete. Then he couldn't believe his eyes, The Cyprus Coffee Shop. Now he really felt at home. They reached Steinway Street and turned left. After one block Poppas said; "Here we are."

"You live here?"

"Yes, this is it. I bought the house two years ago. It's a three family house. I rent out the top two floors and I live on the main floor with my wife and son. Come on inside."

Andreas followed Poppas up the six steps to the front door. As Poppas opened the door he was instantly welcomed by his son running to him.

"Ba-Baaa, Ba-Baaa," yelled his son as he ran to Poppas. Poppas squatted down as his five-year old son Philippou ran into his arms as Poppas lifted him up. Poppas hugged Philippou tightly and told him that he loved him and missed him.

"Who's that?" Philippou asked as he pointed to Andreas.

"This is my new friend. His name is Mr. Andreas." Andreas gave Philippou a smile and said hello.

"Poppas, is that you?" Kassinai asked as she walked into the room.

"It's me. I have a guest with me." Kassinai gave Andreas a warm smile. Andreas politely smiled back. He was also careful not to stare. Kassinai was not an attractive woman. She stood at about five-feet tall, but weighed about 200 pounds. But where she lacked in looks Andreas could see she more than made up for it by her warm hospitality. She instantly extended her hand to welcome him.

"Andreas just came to America today. I'm the first person he met. I told him since he had no place to go he can stay with us for a while. I'm going to bring him to work with me tomorrow and teach him the hot dog business."

"That's wonderful," said Kassinai. "You two go wash up and I'll get dinner on the table."

Poppas showed Andreas around. When they finished washing they sat at the kitchen table and Kassinai served them a traditional American dinner with a touch of Greekness. Poppas, who came from a poor family on the island of Crete was happy to have a steak dinner almost every night. Steak was a rarity in his family. But every night he had to have his greens. It didn't matter whether it was string beans or dandelions. And of course lamb was at least once a week.

After dinner Kassinai put Philippou to bed and then sat with Poppas and Andreas. They talked about everything from America and the wonderful opportunities for anyone who wanted to succeed, to their island of Crete, and of course Cyprus.

Andreas filled them in about his life in Cyprus and his love for Christine and how her mother didn't want him for her. He told them everything up to the part of opening a bank account. Of course he didn't mention Voula.

Andreas felt welcomed and comfortable, but extremely lonely for his family.

"Well," said Kassinai, "I'll go downstairs and make up the couch."

"Thank you very much," said Andreas. "I really appreciate everything you're willing to do for me. I hope one day I can pay you back."

"Don't worry," said Poppas. "Tomorrow you will start by selling hot dogs."

CHAPTER

The next morning Andreas was excited to start the day. He was up at 6:00 a.m. Kassinai told him to make himself at home and to take a shower. She had a new bar of soap, a clean wash cloth, and a fresh towel.

"Put your dirty clothes in this plastic bag," she said. "I'll wash them for you."

Kassinai made a hardy breakfast for everyone as she ran around serving like a good Greek wife.

"Ready to go to work?" asked Poppas.

"You bet I am."

It was only his second day in Astoria but Andreas already loved walking around Ditmars Boulevard. He was proud that he knew his way around, even if it was only between the RR train station and Ditmars Boulevard.

Poppas explained the New York City subway system; how he had to cross the street to get to the downtown train and how he can get to any place in NYC for fifteen cents.

When they reached the storage place where vendors kept their hot dog wagons Poppas started to teach. Poppas made Andreas do everything so he can get real hands on experience. When ready to go, Andreas pushed the hot dog wagon to the corner of 11th Avenue and 37th Street.

"Now we're open for business," said Poppas. "I'm going to sell the first few hot dogs. You watch me."

Andreas watched Poppas work for an hour before he was able to take over. Poppas first had Andreas practice by putting the hot dogs in the bun and so on. Finally the moment came.

"Ready to be on your own?" asked Poppas

"What do you mean?"

"I'm leaving you alone. I'm going home. You stay here and sell my hot dogs. I'll be back at 8:00 p.m. Don't worry. Just keep doing what you're doing."

Andreas was in his glory. He was happy to be working. Poppas trusted him with his hot dog wagon and his money. Before you knew it Andreas was getting up every morning by himself and taking the subway into Manhattan alone. Poppas trusted Andreas. He knew Andreas would never steal a penny from him.

After a few months Poppas bought another hot dog wagon. He had Andreas work one and he worked the other. But Andreas didn't like the hot dog business. He didn't like the rain. Winter was approaching and he kept hearing about the 20-degree temperatures. Besides, he felt it was time to move on.

He ended up moving out of Poppas' house and rented an apartment upstairs from The Cyprus Coffee Shop on Ditmars Boulevard. When the owner of The Cyprus Coffee Shop discovered that Andreas was from Cyprus he immediately offered him a job. Poppas was okay with it. He knew that Andreas wouldn't sell hot dogs for him forever.

So now Andreas was living upstairs from where he worked. He was happy not to spend forty-five minutes a day commuting, and he was saving thirty cents a day on the subway.

CHAPTER

16

Ten years later. 1971

By now Andreas was a head chef at the luxurious Neptune Diner on the corner of 31st Street and Astoria Boulevard. It's been ten years since he came to America. He had many friends and money in the bank. Everything was falling into place for him. The only thing he wanted now was to settle down. At age twenty-seven it was time to get married.

He was always too busy to meet someone. So finally when he heard about an American Cypriot dance at the Crystal Palace on Broadway in Astoria he decided to go. It's time he said to himself. It's time to settle down. He walked to Steinway Street and bought a couple of new suits. You need to spend your money if you want to impress the ladies he thought.

Andreas showed up at the Crystal Palace in his new blue suit. As soon as he walked in, he was greeted by several people he had acquainted over the past few years. At the bar he ordered a popular Greek brandy called Metaxa. After an hour or so of small talk with various people he headed to the buffet. He picked up his paper plate and plastic knife and fork. Women were behind the hot plates serving. There were keftedes, (Greek meatballs), dolmades, (stuffed grape leaves), tava, (lamb with rice) along with several other dishes. As he approached the end of the line the woman asked if he wanted some tava.

"Are you kidding? Tava is my favorite," Andreas said as he looked up at her.

Suddenly he froze.

He couldn't believe his eyes.

He almost dropped his plate.

"Christine?"

"Andreas?"

He couldn't believe it. After ten years, there she was, standing right in front of him. Her eyes instantly became watery as did his. They stood there a few seconds just looking at each other when the person behind Andreas broke the silence by saying excuse me. It was another way of saying move along.

"Maria," said Christine to the women to her right. "Please cover for me. I need to speak to my friend."

"Sure Christine, take your time."

Christine hurried to the other side of the serving table and wrapped her arms around Andreas.

"It's so good to see you," she said. "How have you been? What have you been doing with yourself? I've often thought of you. I've wondered what happened to you. Why haven't you written to me?" Christine rattled on and on. She couldn't catch her breath.

"Christine, you're as beautiful as ever. I also haven't stopped thinking about you. But to answer some of your questions; I'm fine. I've been in America for about ten years now. I'm the chef at the Neptune diner. As far as writing, you need to remember I left Cyprus with a broken heart. Remember?"

Andreas spent the entire evening with Christine. They talked about the last ten years. They danced most of the slow songs. He loved feeling her body against his. Christine explained to Andreas that her brother Basil did send for her. Basil had tried for the last several years to marry her off to some of his rich friends. But Christine wasn't interested. If she wasn't in love, she wasn't in love.

She was living with her brother Basil and his wife Athena in the suburban town of Valley Stream since he sent for her five years ago. She hated it. Her brother was very controlling.

"Basil dropped me off at the dance and went to visit his friends at some men's club to play cards. He's picking me up at midnight. Would you like to meet him?"

"Yes, I would love to meet him."

The rest of the evening was like heaven for both of them. They talked and danced. They caught up on their lives since they last saw each other. At 11:30 Christine helped clean up. Then the moment came.

"Well," she said. "It's 12 o'clock. I'm sure Basil is waiting downstairs."

"I'm with you," said Andreas. "I can't wait to meet him."

"Be careful what you wish for," she smiled. "If you think my mother thought the world revolved around money, wait until you meet my brother."

As they walked down the stairs Christine stopped, turned around, and kissed Andreas on the lips. She wrote her phone number on a piece of paper and asked Andreas to call her.

"Basil," this is Andreas. "He's from the same village as us."

Basil had to be at least twenty years older than Andreas. He looked successful, wearing a big gold watch and driving what looked like a new Cadillac. But all in all Basil was very nice and respectful to Andreas.

"I'll give you a call tomorrow," Andreas said to Christine as she got into the car.

"I'll look forward to it."

Andreas almost skipped home. He couldn't believe it. He saw the only true love he had ever known. He couldn't wait until tomorrow to call Christine. He felt like a teenager with puppy love.

The next morning was Sunday. His days off were Sunday and Monday. Andreas was up at 7:00 a.m. after tossing and turning all night. He couldn't wait to call Christine at twelve o'clock. He went downstairs and bought the Greek newspaper. When he returned to his apartment he made himself a cup of coffee and toast. After breakfast he decided to go for a walk.

Whenever Andreas had things on his mind he always went for a walk to his favorite place, Astoria Park. He spent a few hours there admiring the Manhattan skyline. He ran into Philippou, Poppas' son who was working one of Poppas' many hot dog wagons. Andreas spent a few minutes talking to Philippou while eating a couple of hot dogs. They said their goodbyes and Andreas returned home. It was now twelve o'clock. Do or die. He picked up the phone and dialed Christine.

His heart raced when he heard her voice. They talked for an hour. Finally, he asked if he could see her tomorrow. She excitedly said yes. The next day Andreas borrowed Poppas' car. They were still good friends. Poppas didn't mind lending Andreas his car because he knew Andreas would do almost anything for him.

Andreas drove up Steinway Street and turned left on Astoria Boulevard. Going east on Astoria Boulevard Andreas he entered the Grand Central Parkway to the Van Wyck Expressway to the Belt Parkway to the Southern State Parkway. He exited at the Franklin Square exit and followed the local streets that Christine gave him.

When he pulled up to Basil's house he was amazed. What does this guy do for a living he thought? This house was not only beautiful but enormous. Andreas got out of the car and admired the beautiful landscaping. He looked around and noticed that each house on the block was better than the next. What a neighborhood he thought.

He rang the bell and Basil answered the door. He shook hands with Andreas and took a long look at Poppas' five year old Chevy with a dented fender which he thought belonged to Andreas.

Andreas walked into a beautiful foyer. He was greeted by Athena who was very pleasant to Andreas. But she did seem a bit of high maintenance by the way she kept adjusting her jewelry. Basil told Andreas that Christine would be down in a few minutes. Andreas knew that was bull. Basil just wanted to interrogate him.

Basil asked Andreas what he did for a living, and about his car. Basil's face dropped when Andreas told him that it wasn't his car. He didn't even own a car. Then almost on cue Athena called Christine downstairs. Andreas saw the loving look on her face and she saw the same look in his. He knew he still loved her and she loved him. But that wasn't enough. He needed to rescue Christine from her brother.

"Good morning Christine, ready to go?" He had to take control immediately before Basil did.

"Wait a few minutes," said Basil.

"We need to get going," said Christine

"Yes, we need to get going," added Andreas.

"Where are you taking my sister?"

"I have a full day planned. First we're going into Manhattan for lunch. I've been in New York for ten years and I've never been to the Statue of Liberty."

Andreas stopped talking. He walked up to Basil and shook his hand. Basil towered over Andreas; at six-feet tall he had seven inches on Andreas. But Andreas was built like a bowling ball. Andreas extended his hand and told Basil it was a pleasure to see him again. He turned to Athena and showed his pleasure to meet her and thanked her for her hospitality. Then he took Christine by the hand and walked out the door.

"You were right about your brother. He interrogated me. You should have seen his face when I told him that I didn't even own the car."

"That's my brother," she said. "But Andreas please do me a favor?"

"Sure Christine, anything you want."

"Let's just enjoy the day and not talk about Basil. Let's try to enjoy each other's company."

"Nothing would make me happier."

Andreas and Christine spent the entire day walking around Manhattan. They visited many popular sites. They even climbed to the top of the Statue of Liberty. He didn't get her home until 11:00 o'clock.

Andreas walked Christine to the front door and told her he had a wonderful time and was so happy they reconnected. She expressed the same feelings. They were standing at the front door facing each other when Andreas put his arms around her waist. She instantly put her arms around Andreas' neck and then they touched lips. But as soon as their lips touched the outside light went on as Basil opened the front door.

"What's going on? What do you think you're doing?" he yelled at Andreas.

"Please Basil stop," said Christine. "There's nothing going on. Go back inside."

"Yes Basil, go back inside," said Andreas. "She'll be in in a minute."

Reluctantly Basil went inside. Andreas gave Christine a kiss and told her that he would call her tomorrow.

The next day Andreas went to work but thought about Christine the entire day. At home he called her immediately, but this time Basil answered the phone.

"She's not home right now," said Basil.

"Who's not home?" Andreas heard Christine yell in the background.

Andreas then heard Christine start to cry.

"Basil! Basil, do you hear me? I'm talking to you Basil. Basil, don't make me come out there."

"What are you going to do, walk here? Do you think you're friends old Chevy will make it again? Or did some miracle happen and you turned into a man and bought your own car?"

Andreas hung up and quickly walked to Poppas' house.

"Andreas, is everything all right?"

"I need to borrow your car."

"It's nine o'clock. What's wrong?"

"It's Christine. Her brother won't let me talk to her and she's crying."

"Come on inside. I'll get the keys."

Andreas went inside and was greeted by Kassinai walking to the door with a nightgown while closing her robe. He instantly hoped that she didn't notice his staring at her braless breasts hanging down to her waist. Gross, he thought.

"Andreas, is everything all right?" she asked.

"Go back to sleep," said Poppas. "Everything is fine."

"Here's the keys, and drive safe."

"Thanks."

Andreas went through three red lights on Steinway Street before he turned left on Astoria Boulevard. At 9:30 there wasn't much traffic on the Grand Central Parkway. He made it to the Cross Island Parkway in no time at all. Doing 65-70 mph was a little too much over the 50 mph speed limit, but Andreas didn't care. He almost lost control rounding the 20 mph exit ramp from the Cross Island Parkway to the Southern State Parkway. When he got off the Franklin Square exit he went through another red light. When he pulled up to Basil's house he noticed the house was completely dark. *I drove here like a maniac and they're all asleep,* Andreas thought as he ran up the steps and rang the bell several times. A moment later, Basil opened the door with Athena and Christine behind him in their robes.

"I must admit, you got balls," said Basil.

"Basil, I'm here to see Christine. Christine, I'll be waiting by the car. I'd like to speak to you if I may."

"Sure Andreas. Give me a minute to change."

"You're not going anywhere," Basil ordered his sister, as she ignored him and ran up the stairs to change. "The only person that's going anywhere is Andreas. And if he knows what's good for him, he would turn around, walk back down those same steps he walked up, back into that piece of junk he rolled up in, and drive away. That's if it starts," he smiled.

"Basil, remember what you said to me about having balls? Well, I'll tell you what. Why don't you use *your* balls and make me go down those steps."

"Who do you think you are coming to my house and disrespecting me in front of my family? Do you know who I am?"

"Listen to me, and listen to me good. I came here with the utmost respect. It's you that disrespected me. It's you who thinks you're better than me. So, if there's anything you want to do, I'm here."

Before Basil was able to open his mouth Christine came running down the stairs.

"Come on Andreas, let's talk," Christine said as Basil just stood there speechless.

Christine and Andreas spoke for thirty minutes. When they were done talking they agreed to go out on Saturday night. Andreas then walked Christine to the door and said good night.

"Wait a minute, aren't you forgetting something?" Christine asked.

"What did I forget?"

"You forgot to kiss me."

Andreas then took Christine in his arms and held her tight.

"Christine, first of all, I didn't forget to kiss you. I'm dying to kiss you. I'm just not a trouble maker. Your brother was starting to back down. I don't want to throw it in his face. So please don't think for a minute that I don't want to kiss you. But listen to what I'm about to *not* tell you, and to what I'm *going* to tell you. I'm not going to tell you that I'm in love with you. I'm going to tell you that I'm *still* in love with you. I haven't stopped loving you since the days I walked you home from school. I haven't stopped loving you since I left Cyprus ten years ago."

Christine started to cry as she wrapped her arms around Andreas.

Then they did kiss that long passionate kiss.

"I love you too. I never stopped loving you. When you left Cyprus I didn't speak to my mother for weeks. I've always thought of you. I always prayed I'd somehow find you. And now that I've found you I'm never going to let you get away ever again."

━┽┾━

Three months later Andreas and Christine were married at the Crystal Palace. Basil paid for the entire festivities. He played the big shot like a pro. Andreas let him. He didn't want to stand in the way of an older brother taking care of his baby sister. Besides, it was the bride's day. Andreas wanted her to be happy. As Andreas stood watching the most beautiful woman in the world being escorted up the aisle by her brother, Andreas knew he needed to stay alert with Basil.

Basil was the type of person that if you let him, he would totally control you.

CHAPTER

Astoria New York, present day 1974

After Andreas stormed out of the house when Christine yelled at him for arguing with Basil on the subway he walked back to the diner. He unlocked the door and went straight to the dining room and sat in one of the booths. He kept all the lights closed. He didn't want anyone to see him, or to think he was open for business.

What else can go wrong he thought?

My brother and his family were unreachable.

My wife is upset with me for arguing with her brother.

The beautiful plan of love making with the woman who is so beautiful, she could have married anyone of her choosing but chose me, is upset with me.

Maybe she's right. Maybe I should let bygones be bygones. After all, Christine is right when she said that she married me, not any of Basil's friends.

Two hours later Andreas decided he should go home. Maybe he should try to make up with Christine. All he knew was he couldn't bear to live without her. Maybe I should give Basil a chance. Maybe I never gave him a chance. I'll try to make it right with Basil, but first I need to make it right with Christine.

He quickly locked the diner for the second time in the evening and almost ran home. When he reached his building, he quickly took two steps at a time. When he opened his door he expected to find Christine at the kitchen table still drinking her wine.

She wasn't there.

He walked into the bedroom to give her a hug. All he wanted to do was give her a hug. He needed to let her know how much he loved and needed her. To his surprise she wasn't in bed. He ran back through the kitchen to look in the bathroom.

The bathroom was empty.

Then he saw it.

It was a note on the table. He picked it up and read it:

"Andreas, I asked Basil to come pick me up. Please don't come by or call me. I have a lot of thinking to do. Christine."

Andreas sat down and cried.

"She's gone. She's gone. What am I going to do? She's gone."

CHAPTER

18

Cyprus, present day, 1974
Haji froze. What else could he do, as he stared into the barrel of a machine gun?

"Get up," the Turkish soldier said. "Let's go! I said get up!"

Haji remained still. He couldn't move. Then the soldier helped him move by sticking the barrel of the machine gun in his mouth.

Then Haji heard shots.

Machine gun shots outside.

Slowly Haji stood. But it wasn't easy with the barrel still in his mouth. He couldn't even cry. He was too scared.

"Start walking."

The solider pulled the barrel out of Haji's mouth and pushed it into his chest as Haji went up against the wall.

"You're going to walk out into the courtyard and you're not going to say a fuckin word. You hear me? You open your fuckin mouth and you're dead."

"Yes sir, I hear you."

"Good, now move, before I blow your fuckin brains out."

Haji walked out into the open courtyard. Many people were already outside; all lined up like a firing squad. Of course most were crying. Haji was instructed to join the group. Everyone was in various stages of undress. How else would they be? They were woken up in the middle of the night. Most of the women were crying hysterically. The uncertainty of what was going to happen to them couldn't leave their minds.

"Good morning everyone. Sorry for the intrusion. My name is General Ilhan, but you can call me General. I am not only in charge of my troops, but I am now in charge of you. That's right. You. This beautiful island you call home is no longer your home. You are now a guest in Cyprus. Why you may ask, are you a guest? It's because Cyprus is now owned by Turkey. Up to a week ago your lives belonged to yourselves. Not anymore. Your lives now belong to me. That's right. You are mine. Mine to do whatever I want to do with. I'll show you. You, come over here," he said to one of the monks. The monk stood still. The General didn't flinch. But you can see in his eyes he wasn't happy.

"That's all right, I'll come to you." The general walked right up to the monk and shot him in the leg. Everyone looked on in horror. Bishop Emanuel immediately went to the monk. Two soldiers quickly ran to Bishop Emanuel and pulled him away. At the same time many of the other soldiers started shooting into the air as everyone hit the ground in fright. The general then lifted his arm and the shooting stopped.

"Get up everyone. If you follow my instructions you will not get very hurt. Keep in mind you will get hurt. How hurt you get will depend on you and me. But mostly it will depend on me. If you follow my instructions it won't be as bad. The reason I didn't shoot the monk in the head but only in the leg is because I want you to watch him suffer. He will die a very slow death. You will watch him bleed to death. Why? Because I said so."

The general walked up and down the line and looked the prisoners in their eyes. He saw their fright. He loved it. He knew what he was going to do. He just hadn't decided the order of the atrocities he planned.

"All right everyone, listen up. My soldiers will escort you to your dining hall. There you will learn the rules. The new rules. My new rules."

Haji was standing next to Rebecca. She had her head down. She looked scared. Haji took her hand. He knew he couldn't do anything to protect her, but he felt if he held her hand he would give her some comfort. Besides, he felt safer holding her hand.

"Hey kid, what are you doing?" asked the general. There was silence. "Private Akman, bring me the boy."

Haji couldn't believe it when he saw Private Akman. Private Akman was the one who cut his mother's belly open to produce his baby brother right after he raped her.

"Yes sir General," replied Private Akman.

Private Akman was not much older than Haji. He couldn't be more than sixteen years old. Private Akman hit Haji in the back of his head with the butt of the gun.

"Let's go, you heard the general. Move your ass. Hey, I remember you. I cut your mothers belly open right after I fucked her."

The blow to the back of Haji's head almost knocked him down. Haji let go of Rebecca's hand and stumbled towards the general.

"Who gave you permission to hold someone's hand? I don't remember telling you to hold someone's hand? Listen up everyone.

Nobody does anything without my permission. What's it going to take to make you understand?"

The general put his hand on top of Haji's head. Then grabbed him by his hair and shook him.

"Get your hands off the boy. Do you hear me? I said get your hands off the boy. He has done nothing to you. Nobody here has done anything to you. You have no right."

Haji picked up his head and couldn't believe it. It was Bishop Emanuel who started to walk towards the general. Three soldiers ran to stop him. Fr. Demitri and Mousikou started to move and another five soldiers surrounded them with machine guns.

"Let the old man through," said the general. "Come forward old man."

"You two big guys, come over here too," he said to Fr. Demitri and Mousikou.

They both hesitated. But not for very long. They had help from the five soldiers who stopped them. Fr. Demitri led the way.

"Identify yourselves," ordered the general.

"My name is Fr. Demitri."

"What is your title here?"

"I have no title. I'm assigned to the St. George Greek Orthodox Church in Vavla."

"Ahh, Vavla. I know the place. That's the place that was in need of a toilet on the Altar. You needed a toilet. I had no place to shit. But I hear you now have one. Why are you here?"

Fr. Demitri almost died. He wanted to strangle the general. But he thought this is not the time.

"When Vavla was destroyed I led the villagers here for safety."

"Ahh, safety. Do you feel safe right now?"

"I always feel safe with God."

"That's good. I'm going to need you to help keep this place safe. Go back to where you were." Fr. Demitri followed his instructions.

"You, big guy," the general motioned to Mousikou. "Come here." Mousikou took a few steps toward the general. "I see fire in your eyes. Is that fire in your eyes I see? I think it is. I cannot tolerate this sort of thing."

With that the general took out his side arm and pointed to Mousikou's leg, then lifted it higher and shot Mousikou right between the eyes. As soon as the general fired the gun there were screams all over the place. Mr. Savas' students were the loudest. After all, all they thought they were going to do this summer was a little history on the island of Cyprus for a week and then enjoy another week at a resort in Larnaca, the resort capital of Cyprus.

"You animals," yelled Bishop Emanuel. "You stop this violence now. Your killing must stop."

The general grabbed Haji by the hair and started to shake him. "Come on old man. Come on. Come help the boy."

Then the General threw Haji on the ground and pointed his side arm at Haji as he laid there looking up at him. The general then motioned to some of his soldiers to pick him up.

"Old man, come here," the general said to the bishop.

With no emotion the bishop walked right up to the general, stopped a foot in front of him, and stared him in the face.

"Old man, with your arrogance you are going you get this boy killed. Then you're going to live with the fact that the boy died because of you."

"Leave the boy alone," said the bishop. "He's a good boy. He has done nothing to you, neither has anyone else. Leave here now. Leave this place at once."

The general once again pointed at Haji's chest. The bishop watched. He kept his eye on the general's trigger finger. The second he saw his finger move a fraction he stepped in front of Haji and the bullet hit him in the chest. The bishop fell to the ground dead. A second later everyone started screaming. The general and the soldiers started shooting into the air again.

The prisoners immediately settled down. Then the general started to yell.

"That's it! I'm tired of playing games! You are going to obey me or die! Period! Now this is what's going happen! My men will divide you up! I want women on the right, and men on the left! Let's go, move!"

"Let's go everyone," said Fr. Demitri. "Let's follow their instructions. We will be all right. God is on our side."

The soldiers didn't give them a chance. They divided everyone up by pushing them around. There was lots laughter and gun fire. The women were crying as were some of the men.

Then it happened.

The soldiers started groping some of the women and tearing at their clothes. Most of the soldiers had their guns pointed at the men. The men stood there helpless. The women were crying. But there was nothing they could do.

There wasn't anything anyone could do, as they watched in horror as Private Akman tore off Rebecca's clothes and raped her.

CHAPTER

19

The next morning everyone woke up from an evening of hell. The night before, all the men and women were separated. The men were locked in the dining hall, and women in the chapel. But who could sleep? The men were all lying on the floor listening to the women scream. Haji could hear them begging the soldiers to stop. The only other sounds were the soldier's laughter. They all took turns. When the rapists finished with the women they relieved the ones guarding the men. Then it was their turn to have their way with the woman. It was an endless cycle. Nobody slept that night. At one time, Fr. Demitri started praying. Once the soldiers heard him pray they almost beat him unconscious with the butts of their rifles.

"Good morning everyone, I hope you slept well last night," the general said as he walked into the dining hall. "I myself slept great. My evening did start out a little lonely but then three of your women kept me company. They made me feel like a king instead of a general. And the music they were making the entire night was so soothing. I loved it. I can't wait until tonight.

"By the way, were the women singing loud enough for you? What? No answer? Tonight they will be singing much louder. Now, listen up you big strong men. There's lots of work to be done here today, and every day. But please, do not worry about the work. You will have lots of help. By the end of the day there will be another five hundred more of you. I love it here. This place is built like a fort. I will command the entire Turkish Army from here. It will be a command center and a working prison.

"But do not worry, you will be rewarded. You will get fed, and maybe, just maybe, if you get lonely during the night I can get someone to sing to you like they sang for me and my soldiers last night. But for now, get up and follow me."

Terrified, they stood. Outside they couldn't believe what they saw. There had to be a thousand soldiers. There were jeeps, tanks, and men setting up commutation systems. There was a large truck with a flatbed cage with sheep and pigs on it. The smell coming from it was unbearable. Haji was standing next to Fr. Demitri. But this time Haji wasn't looking for comfort *from* Fr. Demitri. Haji was looking to *comfort* Fr. Demitri. He couldn't understand how Fr. Demitri was able to stand after the beating he took the night before.

Haji noticed the women being escorted to his group
They were completely naked.
A dominant sign of total humiliation.
They looked exhausted, and emotionless.
Why shouldn't they?
They lived a night from hell with no means of ending.

When they grouped with the men the general instructed them to go to the table and eat the stale bread and water prepared for them.

"Eat up everyone," said the general. "Make if quick. There's work to do."

They ate and then were led by Private Akman for a walk with other soldiers.

The women were still naked.

Within minutes they knew where they were going. They were walking to the highest point of the monastery. They were going to the Holy Cross of Christ.

"Gather round everyone," said Private Akman. "We have work to do. Before we install our communication system we must remove the ugly eye sore. You two," he said as he pointed to Haji and Rebecca. "Pick some of your friends and go bring me some small sticks. We need to start a fire."

"Hold it right there," yelled Fr. Demitri. "This is The Holy Cross. Do you have any idea what that Cross represents? It held the body of the Son of God. Do you understand? It's the actual Cross that Christ was crucified on. It's also the holy burial ground of St. Helen, the one who found the Cross with her son Constantine. You cannot do what you plan on doing. It's not right. I will not allow it."

"Shut up old man. I'll do anything I want. If you don't believe me just ask some of your lady friends. Just ask them about last night. They'll tell you what I can or cannot do. You! Get your ass over here," he said to Rebecca.

Rebecca lowered her head and walked to Private Akman. As she approached him he started to beat her up.

"Now bitch, go get me some wood," he said as he groped her.

Rebecca limped away crying while others followed her to help. When they returned with the wood Private Akman instructed them to place it at the base of the Cross. Private Akman pulled out his side arm and walked up to Haji and put the gun to his head.

"Come on, I need your help. Move your ass," he said as he pushed Haji with his gun. "You see those gallons of gasoline? Dump it on the wood. Let's go! Move! Are you deaf? I said move!"

Haji had no choice. He wasn't able to do anything. He had to follow instructions or die. He knew if it was Fr. Demitri he would have died *for* the Cross as did Jesus *on* the Cross. But not Haji, he was too scared. He was too scared of dying, and even a little scared of living. Fr. Demitri sensed it. He knew Haji was good a boy, but was not quite ready to become a martyr. Haji looked up at Fr. Demitri. Fr. Demitri knew he had to decide for the boy, so he gave Haji a slight nod of approval. Haji then dumped two gallons of gasoline onto the wood at the base of the Cross.

"Very nice, you're doing a great job so far," said Private Akman. "Now you little shit. I'm going to light this torch and you are going to light up the Cross. And let's see if your Jesus can protect you."

Private Akman lit the torch and handed it to Haji. Haji didn't have to look for Fr. Demitri's approval this time. He knew what he had to do. With tears in his eyes he slowly walked the entire circumference of the Cross as he lit it into flames. Within minutes the Cross was one burning torch. Everyone stood around in silence. There was no crying; only shock and sadness in everyone's face, except for the Turkish soldiers. The soldiers didn't care one way or another. They were there to do a job.

But not Private Akman.

He loved every minute.

For a sixteen-year old kid, he was already nothing but a barbarian.

He had the look of the devil on him as he watched the Cross burn.

"You, come over here," Private Akman yelled to Anna. Anna hesitated. But the hesitation didn't last very long. One of the soldiers grabbed her by the hair and dragged her to Private Akman as Anna's mother tried to hold onto her daughter. But she was pulled back by another soldier.

"Please, please, leave her alone. She's only a child. Didn't you do enough last night? Please, take me. Please leave my baby alone," cried Anna's mother.

"Baby?" said Private Akman. "She fucked me like a woman last night. Then again she did cry like a baby."

Private Akman told the soldiers to prepare to shoot if anyone tried to stop him as he forced Anna down on her knees and instructed her to do what she learned last night. Within seconds Private Akman was finished.

"Not bad bitch. Now go back to your mama. By the way mama, I *will* take you, but not until tonight. I want to give you something to look forward to."

Anna cried all the way back to the main courtyard as her mother had her arm around her.

Fr. Demitri felt helpless.

Why wouldn't he?

He was their spiritual leader.

Everyone looked up to him, and he felt he failed them all.

But deep down inside he knew his flock knew there wasn't anything he could do. Then it hit him. He had to keep control of his emotions. He was going to pray non-stop. But what he would pray about is fighting back.

He decided not to *turn the other cheek* anymore.

⟫⟩ ⟨⟪

When they finally reached the main courtyard, they noticed at the far end next to the wall the bodies of the monk who bled to

127

death and Mousikou. As for the bishop, the Turks made a cross and nailed him to it. Fr. Demitri's anger grew worse. These savages must pay. Mousikou helped out so much with their trip to the monastery. Who knows, maybe none of them would be alive if not for him. He didn't deserve what the general did to him.

"General," said Private Akman. "As you can see from here the Cross is still on fire. It took a little convincing but we got the job done. I even had a little celebration with one of my new lady friends."

"I'm proud of you. You really are the son of my brother. I can see you working your way up the ranks in no time at all. You know what? By next month I'm going to make you a sergeant. Not bad for a sixteen year old. What do you think of that?"

"I think I'm going to celebrate tonight with two of my lady friends."

"Celebrate with as many as you want. In about an hour you will have more lady friends than you can handle."

Fr. Demitri wanted to vomit. How could God's creations turn out these animals? He thought. Right there he knew he had to stop Private Akman, because he was going to turn out to be worse than his uncle.

"Fr. Demitri, parish priest of the newly installed toilet of The Holy Altar," the general called out. Reluctantly, Fr. Demitri approached. "I have a job for you. I was in the chapel and noticed it was in need of cleaning. Why don't you take one of your friends and go clean it. I would take it as a personal favor if you did that for me. But please, leave the women here. I have other plans for them," he said with a smile as he put his arms around Anna and her mother.

Fr. Demitri didn't want to leave his flock. But he knew what he had to do to stay alive for a little bit longer.

"Yes sir General," replied Fr. Demitri with a heavy heart. "I'll do what you ask."

"That's very smart of you."

"Thank you General."

Fr. Demitri asked Haji to go with him. They walked together slowly. They didn't talk. There was nothing to say. Everything was already said. All the praying was prayed. They knew they were in hell. But Fr. Demitri knew that God would free them one way or another.

Dead or alive, they will be saved.

As they approached the chapel, they saw Private Akman standing at the front door with the biggest grin Fr. Demitri had ever seen. As they got closer to the chapel they started to smell something. The smell was coming from Private Akman. How can such a strong odor come from him? Fr. Demitri thought. He didn't smell like that a few minutes ago. Then it hit him. The smell was coming from the chapel. Fr. Demitri started to run towards the chapel. Haji followed behind along with their five escorting soldiers. Fr. Demitri started to run up the steps. When he was three steps from the top he was eye level with Private Akman when he hit Fr. Demitri square in the face with his side arm. Fr. Demitri fell back down the steps and didn't move.

"Fr. Demitri, Fr. Demitri," cried Haji. "Are you all right? Fr. Demitri, don't try to get up," Haji continued to cry as Fr. Demitri was opening his eyes. "Just lie there a minute."

"Get your ass up you holy asshole," yelled Private Akman. "You guys, get him up now. Bring him in the chapel now."

Four soldiers lifted Fr. Demitri while another grabbed Haji by the hair and dragged him into the chapel as Private Akman opened the door laughing. With Fr. Demitri it was a little slower. It took four soldiers to drag him up the steps and into the chapel. When they finished they closed the door and locked it from the outside.

By now it was starting to get dark, but not dark enough to not see what happened inside the chapel. Every one of the beautiful stained glass windows was broken. The Holy Altar was destroyed. All the icons were taken down and thrown on the floor. The smell, the awful smell was coming from the animals. They turned the chapel into a barn. All the pigs and sheep were urinating and defecating on the icons. Fr. Demitri instantly vomited, as he broke down and cried.

"How can anyone take holy items and do this?" Fr. Demitri cried out loud.

"It's all right Fr. Demitri," whispered Haji. "Remember what you said to the general? You said you feel safe with God. I feel safe right now. I feel safe because I'm in God's house with my spiritual father. There is nothing anyone can do to hurt us spiritually. Isn't that what you always taught us?"

"Haji, you are growing up very quickly these past few days. No, I stand corrected. You've grown up. Period. Here I am, the one who should be teaching you, and instead, it's you who's teaching me. I'm so very proud of you. I just can't stop feeling that I have failed you. That I have failed everyone."

That evening was the same as the night before. The crying and screaming from the outer buildings were unbearable. The soldiers were treating the women worse than anyone would treat an animal. Fr. Demitri didn't know what was worse, the cries from the woman or the laughter of the soldiers. They didn't know what time it was when things were finally either simmering down, or if it was the pain and humiliation that was becoming a way of life for the women. Either way, it got quiet. Haji sensed that Fr. Demitri wanted to talk about something. He didn't know how to ask so he just asked.

"Fr. Demitri, I'm getting the feeling there's something you need to talk about. What is it?"

"Haji, you are an incredible young man. With all you've been through you seem to be holding it together. I don't know how you are still keeping your sanity, and yes, there is something I need to talk to you about now that we are alone. Who knows? Maybe this is why God put us in the chapel. Look around. Listen around. There's a hundred times more suffering out there than there is in here. It must be a sign that I must speak to you."

"What is it Fr. Demitri? You can talk to me. Tell me what it is. I also believe that there must be a reason we're locked in here alone. Is this one of those mysteries of God you always tell us about?" Haji said with a faint smile.

"Yes it very well is a mystery of God, and as I have said many times, it is not for us to judge. God has a purpose for us. He has a purpose for all of us, including those barbarians out there."

CHAPTER

"Haji, I'm now going to tell you a story. I need you to pay close attention to me. I'm going to tell you about your Uncle Andreas who lives in America."

"Yes Father, I know I have an Uncle Andreas somewhere in America. I don't know anything about him. All I do know is he left Cyprus a long time ago."

"It wasn't that long ago. He left Valva in 1961. He left with a broken heart. You see Haji, when your Uncle Andreas was seventeen-years old he was in love with a sixteen-year old girl named Christine Alexander. Christine was a beautiful girl, but her mother wanted nothing to do with your Uncle Andreas."

"Why not, was he not a good person?"

"Oh no, he was a wonderful person. It's just that Mrs. Alexander wanted someone who would be able to give Christine a much better life than the ones we live here in Valva."

"What's wrong with the life that we live here?" Haji asked confused.

"Nothing. Nothing at all. It's just that some people are not grateful of God's blessings. Please, let me continue. Christine was tall; she could have been a model, that's how beautiful she was. Andreas was an average looking young man who was shorter than Christine with nothing to offer but his love, and let me tell you Haji; love he had. But love wasn't enough for Mrs. Alexander. Mrs. Alexander wanted prestige. She wanted money for her daughter. Your Uncle Andreas could not offer Christine any of that. All your Uncle Andreas could offer Christine was his unconditional love. Mrs. Alexander and your uncle would come to me separately, not knowing the other was coming to me too.

"I've always had a close relationship with your family even back then, and Mrs. Alexander knew it. That's why she'd come to me for help keeping your uncle away from Christine. At the same time your uncle would come to me asking how he can get Mrs. Alexander to accept him. I kept telling him that all he needed to do was to continue being himself, and Mrs. Alexander would eventually come around. But I always knew she would never let it happen. I've even had many conversations with Christine. She had expressed nothing but love for your uncle. She tried on many occasions to talk to her mother but her mother would refuse to hear a single word of what Christine had to say.

"Christine had an older brother named Basil who lived in America. Basil was a very successful business man. He lived in a big house and had a few restaurants and lots of properties in New York."

"We have properties. We have many acres. How many acres did Basil have?"

"Acres? Not many. In New York, properties mean buildings. Basil owned buildings. Today he owns many buildings. So Mrs. Alexander wanted to keep Christine away from not only Andreas, but all young suitors until she reached eighteen-years old. Then her brother Basil would send for her and find her a suitable husband. Of course suitable, meaning rich. But Andreas frightened Mrs. Alexander because she knew that Christine was in love with him, and as you will one day find out, love, like faith, is a very powerful source.

"It got real bad one day," Fr. Demitri continued. "Andreas and Christine decided they were going to tell Mrs. Alexander the way they felt about each other. Andreas was prepared to spend the entire day convincing Mrs. Alexander of his unconditional love for her daughter. Well, it didn't work out that way. Mrs. Alexander became furious at Andreas.

"How dare you come to me with this?" Mrs. Alexander yelled. "How many times have I told you to stay away from my daughter? Get out of this house now! Never come back! Do you hear me? Never come back! And you," she yelled at Christine. "Go to your room and stay there until I tell you to come out!"

"As you might imagine, Andreas lowered his head when he saw Christine run into her room. He knew what he had to do to mend his broken heart. He had to leave Vavla. He had to leave Cyprus. There was only one person he loved and knew that it could never be."

"Wow Father, that's some story. Thanks for telling me about my uncle. Why my parents hardly spoke about him I don't know. I think I might have heard his name mentioned maybe five times in my life. We don't even have any pictures of him. It's nice to know that I have an uncle out there somewhere. Thanks again for telling me about him. By the way Father, where did my uncle go, and what ever happened to that girl Christine? What happened to her mother? I don't know any Alexanders here in Vavla."

"Those are very interesting questions you asked. I'm glad you asked them. It shows that you are paying attention," Fr. Demitri said with a smile, while he pushed a pig away from him. "Your uncle went where most people want to go. He went to America. He worked very hard at various different jobs. He ended up opening a small diner in Astoria."

"Where's Astoria?"

"It's part of New York City. Now, please, let me finish."

'Sorry Father. Hey Father, stop talking while I'm interrupting," Haji laughed.

"Some years later," Fr. Demitri continued. "Basil sent for Christine and her mother. They went to live with Basil in the suburban area of New York called Long Island. Mrs. Alexander and Basil thought they could go husband shopping for Christine. Basil took Christine to many parties and get-togethers. He introduced her to countless men. Very successful men. But it didn't matter. Christine wasn't interested in any of them. A year or so later Mrs. Alexander passed away. Basil was now getting ready to get married himself, so he needed to find a husband for Christine now more than ever so he could get on with his own life with his new bride.

"Nothing worked. Christine wasn't interested in anyone. Basil was now a father image for Christine since her own father died when she was very young. After a while Christine felt like a prisoner in Basil's house.

"One evening Basil was going to Astoria to play cards with some of his friends. As always, whenever he had a chance to find a husband for Christine he took her. Well, Basil dropped Christine off at some American Cypriot dance and she met the love of her life. Let me rephrase that. She again met the love of her life. She saw your Uncle Andreas after ten years. She couldn't believe it. She found the only love she ever wanted, and so did Andreas. Shortly after that they were married."

"Wow, that's some story. I wonder why my parents never told me."

"Well Haji, it doesn't end there."

"Where does it end?"

"Listen carefully. Remember when I told you that your Uncle and Christine went together to talk to Mrs. Alexander?"

"Yes."

"Well, before they went they didn't know it but I saw them coming out of the basement of the school house. They did something that they should not have done."

"I don't know what you mean."

"Your uncle made Christine pregnant that day. That's what I mean. So when they both went to speak to Mrs. Alexander neither one of them knew it yet. So when your uncle realized that he and Christine can never be, he left Cyprus forever without knowing that he was going to be a father."

"Father, there's something I don't understand. What happened to the baby?"

"Well, when Christine realized she was pregnant she had no choice but to go to her mother. After a week of yelling and screaming, Mrs. Alexander decided to bring Christine to me. Christine wanted to keep the baby but her mother didn't allow it. I'm sure it had something to do with Mrs. Alexander thinking that no man in America would be interested in a woman who was never married but had a baby. It would have left a mark on Christine for the rest of her life. Christine didn't care. She wanted to have her baby but her mother forced her to give it up for adoption."

"That's a really sad story Father."

"I'm not finished yet. I escorted them right here to this very monastery. Remember, this is an all-male monastery and Bishop Emanuel made the exception because of the circumstances. When the Archbishop found out that the bishop made the exception without first consulting with him the bishop got into a lot of trouble. Remember? It's all about obedience. That's why the bishop was reminding me that this is an all-male monastery. I got him in trouble last time and he never forgot about it.

"So Christine and her mother spent the rest of the pregnancy right here on this mountain. When the baby was born they went back to the village, packed up and moved to Greece."

"What happened to the baby?"

"Haji, how many times have you heard me use the phrase; *mysteries of God*?"

"Many times Father."

"Well you're going to hear it again. Sometimes when a man and a woman get married they want to have a child but for whatever reasons known to man they cannot produce a child. So they are forced to adopt. And when they adopt that baby they love it like it was their own. Other times after a couple adopts a baby the wife gets pregnant. Sometimes immediately or years later. Those are mysteries of God. When your mother and father first got married they were unable to have a baby. They tried for years."

Haji's face dropped. He sensed what was coming.

"Your mother and father adopted the baby. The baby is you. You were adopted. Your parents wanted to tell you when you reached sixteen-years old. Five years after you were adopted, your mother was able to get pregnant."

Haji started to cry. Fr. Demitri held him close.

"It's okay Haji, it's good to cry. I know you're confused. But you must realize that your mother and father loved you very much. They knew that your uncle was your biological father. Nonetheless you were just like their real son. You *are* their real son. Your Uncle Andreas does not know that you were born and your mother Christine thinks that some unknown family from Greece adopted you. Christine never told your uncle about you. She was afraid. You must escape this place. You must find your way to the American Embassy and tell them that your parents are in America.

"You must go to America. You must go to Astoria in New York."

CHAPTER

21

The next morning, Fr. Demitri and Haji were awakened by the sound of gunfire.

"Looks like we're going to have another day from hell," Fr. Demitri said to Haji. "Quickly, come with me. I want to show you something if those barbarians didn't find them already."

Intrigued, Haji followed Fr. Demitri into The Holy Altar. Ordinarily only an ordained priest or deacon can walk up the steps into The Holy Altar. Haji didn't question Fr. Demitri. He knew if Fr. Demitri asked him to follow, he would ask no questions.

"Good, they didn't find it."

"Find what?"

"This hidden compartment under the floor behind The Holy Altar."

"What's inside it?"

"Quick, take a look."

Haji couldn't believe it. Gold coins. There had to be at least a hundred of them.

"Here, put some in your shoes. Not too many. You don't want anyone to see you walking funny. Also put only one in those two oversized pockets of your monk clothes. We don't want them clanking against each other. You're going to need these gold coins to sell when you escape this place. Okay? You *will* escape this place."

"What about you? Aren't you coming?"

"No, I'm too old to escape. But I'm not too old to help *you* escape. I just haven't figured out how to do it yet. But step one is you having money to get to America. Now, listen up Haji. There's something you need to know about me."

"What? What is it Father?"

"Quiet, don't ask questions. You need to listen. When I was a kid growing up in Greece I was not the same person that I am now. I was a tough kid. A tough trouble maker of a kid who was doomed to hell on my judgment day. I didn't find God until I was twenty-five years old. But like the old saying goes; a monkey dressed in silk is still a monkey, and a tough kid from Greece dressed in a collar is still a tough kid from Greece. You will soon see a side of me that I thought didn't exist anymore. I know it's going to blow up in my face. I'm hoping it doesn't blow up in yours."

Meanwhile the gunfire continued. Yelling, screaming, and crying was all they heard.

Suddenly the front doors of the chapel opened and in walked in Private Akman followed by three armed soldiers.

"What are you two doing back there? Praying?" Private Akman laughed. "A lot of good that's going to do for you. Now, let's go, move, get outside and join the party."

Reluctantly they followed Private Akman out into the sunlight. Never in their wildest imagination did they expect to see what they saw. There had to be three hundred more prisoners outside held at gun point. Off to the side were dead bodies. Dozens of them piled up like sacks of potatoes. But directly in front of them were ten women on their knees completely naked with their hands tied behind their backs with their heads down in fear and humiliation. The general walked right up to Fr. Demitri with the biggest smile and arrogance.

"Fr. Demitri, parish priest of The Holy Altar with a recently installed toilet. I hope your sleeping accommodations were acceptable to you. Take a look at these ten lovely women. They are already on their knees for you. Pick one, any one, or I'll pick one for you."

"Pick this one," Private Akman said as he grabbed Rebecca by the hair. "I already warmed her up this morning. She's really good." Then he kicked her in the back of the head and laughed as she landed face first onto the stone ground as she started to bleed.

"You savages," raged Fr. Demitri as he took the sidearm he still had in his oversized pocket that he took from Savas' dead body. He shot the general in the heart, and then shot at Private Akman but missed. By then it was too late. Several soldiers put at least a dozen bullets through Fr. Demitri as he dropped to the ground.

After that there was nothing but screaming and crying. With the general dead nobody knew who was in charge. Private Akman was yelling the loudest. He was now totally lost. With his uncle in charge he had free rein to do whatever he wanted to do. The soldiers feared him and hated him at the same time because of who his uncle was. Now it was Private Akman doing most of the crying. Private Akman picked up his head and saw Haji holding on to Fr. Demitri's lifeless body and freaked out. He ran over to Haji and started kicking him. He kicked him, and kicked, and kicked him until he was unconscious.

Nobody helped Haji.

Nobody stopped Private Akman.

It turned into a free-for-all.

No one was in charge.

No one knew what to do.

The next day everyone was just hanging around. With the general dead there was no one to set up the communication systems. There was no order. The only thing the soldiers did was abuse the women. Private Akman was the worst. He went around beating up anyone and everyone. The women feared him more than any of the other solders. He seemed to enjoy humiliating them. The more people around the more it excited him. He was one sick sixteen-year old.

With all the confusion after the death of the general the Turkish command center never continued. There were no leaders, only a bunch of soldiers who didn't know how to take charge. The Cypriot prisoners outnumbered the Turkish soldiers but the prisoners had no guns.

It took Haji three days before he was able to walk after the beating Private Akman gave him. He wasn't able to eat much because he was bruised all over. But there wasn't much to eat besides bread and water.

Private Akman saw to it that the women cooked the sheep and pigs for the soldiers but didn't allow the prisoners to eat anything but bread and water. He especially enjoyed eating a great meal in front of them while they watched.

Haji knew he had to somehow make Private Akman pay for his evilness. The worst part besides watching him rape and then cut his mother's belly open was when he held back food from the young children just so he could have his way with their mothers. At times he made the women beg him for sex if they wanted to have food for their children.

⊷⊶

After two more weeks of suffering Haji was awakened by the sound of tanks breaking down the monastery doors.

He couldn't believe it.

They were being rescued.

It was the United Nations Security Force escorted by American soldiers. Many Turkish soldiers scattered. They didn't know who they were. But Haji knew. Haji recognized the tanks from years ago when his father took him to the American Embassy to visit a friend.

All the prisoners started to embrace one another with the joy of freedom. Many broke down crying. It was all coming together. Rebecca hugged Haji. Some cried from happiness, but above all, they were crying about the last month and a half of living hell.

That night there were cries of sadness. The abuse had finally stopped. The Turkish soldiers were ordered to leave. The Americans, the Turkish government, and the Cypriot government along with Archbishop Makarios worked out a deal. The entire northern part of Cyprus now belonged to Turkey.

The soldiers were not charged with the atrocities. The killings were nothing but a mere plan for the northern part of Cyprus. It must have been well worth it for many, but life changing for many more. There were so many left homeless. Mothers were now alone with their children without knowing whether their husbands were dead or alive. But they sensed that somewhere out there their husbands lay dead.

For the next few days, the United Nations Security Force interviewed everyone. They were horrified by the atrocities. They were told they could leave the monastery and go home if their home was in the southern half of Cyprus. If their home was in the northern part of Cyprus, they no longer had any rights to their land.

⟨⟩

Twelve year old Haji begged to partake in the burial of Fr. Demitri and Bishop Emanuel. They were buried under the charred Holy Cross, directly next to St. Helen. The bishop of course on the right side of St. Helen and Fr. Demitri on her left. Haji felt tremendous guilt for the things he said about Bishop Emanuel. In the end, the bishop took a bullet for Haji.

As the days passed, people were leaving the monastery. They either went back to their own homes or to their relatives.

But it didn't matter where they went; their lives had been changed forever.

Rebecca decided to stick around the monastery with Haji and help some of the people. Haji was sad to see Anna leave with her mother. They were going to Anna's grandparents' house in the most southern part of Cyprus. They wanted to try to somehow restart their lives.

They had been through so much.

How will they survive the atrocities?

As happy as everyone was to be free again, you could see the stare. Those long drawn out stares of sadness.

Nobody would ever be the same.

No justice would be done to the barbarians who committed those unthinkable unthinkables.

Haji and Rebecca stuck around the monastery for several days, while the United Nations Security Force continued to interview everyone and tried to find placement assistance to anyone whose village was now in the occupied northern part of Cyprus.

"Listen up everyone," said General Franklyn from the United Nations Security Council who was from America. "I just received a wire from the United Nations Security Council. I was instructed to inform you that this monastery is right in the middle of the island. Which means; there will be a twenty-foot wall built right through this place. You have twenty-four hours to pack up your belongings and leave towards the southern region."

"Which part of the monastery will be the southern part?" asked Rebecca.

"I don't know ma'am, but I do suggest you get as far south as you can to be on the safe side. Because once you get caught on the north side there isn't much we can do to help you."

"This is a very Holy place, isn't there anything you could do?"

"Lady, I just take orders. Leave before you can never be helped."

"Come on Haji," whispered Rebecca. "We need to get out of here. We need to go south. There wasn't much left of our village. We need to find some place as far south as we can go. Let's see if there are any other survivors from Vavla besides us."

"All right Miss Economou, we'll go. But there are a couple of things that need to be done."

"Like what?"

"Follow me."

Rebecca followed Haji towards the chapel.

"Fr. Demitri taught you well. It's always good to pray."

"I'm not going to pray," Haji said as they walked up the five steps to the chapel's open doors.

"Oh my God Haji, it stinks in here. Look at this place. They turned God's house into a stable. Look at all the icons on the floor with all the animal poop all over them."

"I know, remember I spent a night in here with Fr. Demitri?"

"It's disgusting. But it's still God's house."

"No it's not. God doesn't live here anymore. Follow me Miss Economou and don't say a word."

Rebecca followed Haji towards what was left of The Holy Altar.

"What are you doing? You know that you are not allowed to walk up the steps of The Holy Altar. Only a priest can do that."

"I had Fr. Demitri's blessing. Come up here, I need your help."

"Are you kidding, women are not allowed back there."

"Please Miss Economou, it's very important."

Reluctantly, Rebecca did her Sign of the Cross and followed. She almost vomited as she stepped on animal feces.

"What is it?" Rebecca asked as she watched Haji get on his knees and start to remove the small piece of wood from the floor. "Oh my God, is that what I think it is?"

"Yes it is. It's gold. Fr. Demitri showed it to me. He gave me some to take with me if I escaped from here to use to buy my way to America. Now that we are free and this place might fall to the Turkish government we're going to take it all. Don't you agree?"

"God forgive us, but yes, we need to take it all. But please keep in mind that the gold still belongs to the monastery. If this building falls into Turkish hands the rest of the monastery may fall just south of it. Then it still owns the gold, and we must give it to back. But for now let's take it all."

"Miss Economou, do you know why I need to get myself to America? Fr. Demitri told me…"

"Stop right there Haji. I know the story. Fr. Demitri told Mr. Mousikou and me the story of your adoption."

"When?"

"When we were in the woods Fr. Demitri was concerned that if something happened to him he would never get the chance to tell you. So he told us just for insurance. So, I'm in agreement with him. You must get to America. You must find your parents. You now have the money to get there. Take it all. I know that someday you will give this money back to the monastery. But for now the money is better with you than the risk of it falling into Turkish hands."

"Miss Economou, what about you? You have nowhere to go. You can't go back to Vavla. Why don't you come with me to America?"

"America? I don't know anyone in America. Where will I go? How would I get there?"

"We have the money right here in gold. There's plenty here. We can cash in some of the gold and buy plane tickets. You have no family here since your parents died. Please, come with me. I'm afraid to go alone. Right now you are the only person in the world that I know. We can go to the American Embassy and tell them that we are brother and sister and our parents are in America."

"Do you think we can get away with it?"

"Yes I do. I'm just a kid. They might not believe you, but they'll believe me. I'm too young to lie."

Rebecca thought for a moment.

"All right, this is going to be our plan. Everything that happened back at the house happened to your aunt and uncle and little cousin at your aunt and uncle's house, which by the way is really the truth. I'm going to convince them that we were here at the house that our parents still own from the time we moved to America. What happened to your family was really at your aunt and uncle's house while you were visiting. Got it?"

"Got it."

"By the way, if we're going to be brother and sister, start calling me Rebecca. My new name is Rebecca Ioannou."

"Okay Rebecca," Haji smiled.

CHAPTER

22

The next morning Haji and Rebecca sat down with General Franklyn in his command center which was nothing more than a glorified tent. Rebecca explained to General Franklyn that Haji was her younger brother and they were the son and daughter of Andreas and Christine Ioannou who lived in America.

"Okay, let's see what we have here," said General Franklyn. "First of all, what part of Cyprus are you from?"

"Vavla."

"Vavla? Never heard of it. Let's see what my map says. Vavla, Vavla, Vavla. I can't seem to... Oh, here it is. It's barely on the map. Sorry to tell you this, but Vavla is now owned by Turkey."

"Are you sure?"

"Yes I am. The line will zigzag across the middle of the island. I also just received word that this entire mountain is going to now fall on the north side. It seems this monastery is the highest point of Cyprus. They're going to convert this place into a military communications base. Now, what business did you have in Vavla?"

"The house we have in Vavla belongs to my parents. When we moved to America my parents didn't know if we were going to stay there or not so they decided to keep the house in Vavla in case it didn't work out for all of us in America. We needed a place to come back to if necessary. My brother and I have been coming here every summer. This summer I was supposed to put the house up for sale and then all of this happened."

"Let me see what I can do. Do you have any identification? Passports?"

"No, everything was in the house. We left the house with nothing."

"What's in the bag you're holding?"

"The only thing I have is a few gold coins that my father had always kept hidden in the barn in case of an emergency. I plan on cashing them in to purchase two tickets so we can get home."

"So, let me get this straight. You were able to get to the barn and get the gold coins but not your passports. Is that correct?"

"Yes"

"That makes no sense."

"Sir, why doesn't it make any sense?"

"You were able to go into the barn but not the house to get identification. That makes no sense to me."

"Please sir. You have no idea what we've been through. We need to get home."

"My job is to get you home. I just need to know where home really is. Why don't you tell me your story?"

"I'm going to tell you, but please be patient. The night before this happened my brother and I were visiting my aunt and uncle. It was late at night when I decided to let my little brother sleep at their house since he fell asleep on the couch. I went home. The next morning I was awaked in the middle of the night by the gunfire. I didn't move. I was much too afraid. But I knew. I knew what it was. My father didn't want us to come to Cyprus this summer because he kept hearing about a possible Turkish invasion. But my little brother wanted to come. My brother loves it here.

"In the morning I started to walk to my aunt and uncle's house to get my brother. As I approached the house I was grabbed by my hair by a Turkish soldier and dragged into the house. I couldn't believe it," she said as she started to sob uncontrollably.

"It's all right ma'am, take your time. Here, have a glass of water," he said as he started to pour.

"Thank you. Please give me a moment."

"Take your time, there's no rush."

"The man dragged me into the house and I couldn't believe my eyes. My six-year old cousin was hanging by her neck from the ceiling. My Uncle was lying on the floor dead. My Aunt who was pregnant lay dead with her belly cut open with her unborn child on top of her. My poor little brother witnessed all this. Then these animals started ripping off my clothes right in front of my brother. Sir, do you know how many times I have been raped these past few weeks?" she said as she again broke down uncontrollably. "I can't even answer that question. Please, let us go home."

General Franklyn sat there watching Rebecca and Haji cry. All this only made Haji relive the resent atrocities.

"Fill out these papers. Don't worry about the bottom half. I'll fill that part out for you. I need the correct spelling of your names for your new passports. First thing in the morning you and your brother will be taken to the American Embassy in Nicosia. Once there you can cash in your gold coins at the International Money Exchange. Then you're on your own. Haji, please do me a favor.

It's getting late. Why don't you go into one of the rooms and go to sleep? We all have a busy day ahead of us tomorrow. Rebecca will fill out the paperwork."

"Yes sir, and thank you sir," Haji said as he walked away sobbing.

"Rebecca, I believe your story, well, maybe part of it, or maybe most of it. I know that you had to have been through hell and back these past few days. But somehow I don't believe your entire story. Let me ask you something. Where in America are you from?"

"New York."

"Where in New York?"

"Astoria."

"Where in Astoria? What's your address?"

Rebecca fell silent.

"Cat got your tongue? Did you forget?"

Now tears restarted to drip down her cheeks. She started to stutter.

"It's all right, don't worry. If you play your cards right I'll get you to America. The first thing I need to know is how much gold you have?"

"I don't know."

"Put the bag on my desk."

Reluctantly Rebecca put the bag on his desk.

"Open it."

Rebecca started to look around. She knew she had no choice.

"Don't bother looking around. Nobody can help you here but me. Open the bag."

As Rebecca opened the bag General Franklyn's eyes almost popped out of his head.

"That's a lot of gold you have there. This is how it's going to work. I'm taking half. The rest is more than enough for you to buy two tickets to Kennedy Airport. That's in New York in case you forgot. Now, get up and close the curtain of my tent."

Rebecca knew what was going to happen next. What choice did she have? She closed the curtain and turned right back around and faced General Franklyn.

She's been raped so many times. *What's one more time?* She thought. She just hoped that it will be done quickly and without a beating that always came with the rapes.

"Take off your clothes."

Rebecca started undressing without a thought. When she stood there completely naked General Franklyn looked at her in shock. He couldn't believe the bruises all over her body.

"Oh my God. What did they do to you? I'm so sorry. Please get dressed. Please forgive me. Go, go to your brother. Get a good night's sleep. Tomorrow you will have a new passport with your new address in Astoria, New York. Good night Rebecca, and please forgive me."

Rebecca quickly dressed, took her half of the gold, and went to go find Haji. Outside, she saw Haji sitting on the chapel's steps.

"What's the matter?" she asked.

"Nothing, Miss Economou, I'm just thinking about my family in Vavla that's still in the house."

"Their bodies are still in the house. Their souls are with God. Don't ever forget that. Understand?"

"Yes, I understand."

"Haji, another thing. This Miss Economou thing stops. It stops right now. I don't ever want to hear you calling me that again. For now on I'm your sister Rebecca. Got it? Rebecca. Don't forget."

"Got it Rebecca. I won't forget."

"Good, now let's get some sleep. We have a busy day ahead of us tomorrow."

CHAPTER

23

The next morning everyone was up bright and early with excitement.

"Come on Rebecca, let's get up. I'm getting tired of this place."

"All right little brother. I'm getting up."

Once outside they saw lots of activity. Buses were everywhere. Trucks were being loaded and soldiers making notes. Everyone was getting ready to leave.

"Rebecca, can I see you a minute?" yelled out General Franklyn as he opened the curtain of his tent while a student of Savas' walked out with her head down.

"Sure, General Franklyn," *you piece of garbage*, she thought.

"These are your passports. It's all good. I have your names and address in Astoria, New York. The address is fake. It's an empty lot. Don't worry, it's all official. So get going. Your brother goes to P.S. 7 on 21st and Astoria Boulevard in case anyone asks. That bus over there will take you and your brother to the American Embassy. It's leaving in ten minutes. So go get your brother or whatever he is and get out of here."

"Thank you sir."

"Rebecca."

"Yes sir?"

"You're a very beautiful woman. Please be careful."

"Yes sir. And thank you for everything."

CHAPTER

24

Rebecca and Haji were the last ones on the bus. They had the gold split between themselves in different parts of their bodies. They took the time to memorize their address in Astoria even though it was an empty lot. Their bus was in the middle of the convoy of seven buses as it headed north towards Nicosia. Six were being escorted to the safety of the south, and only one was going to the American Embassy. Jeeps were in front and behind them. Everyone on the bus was filled with emotion. Even with the military escort, they were still afraid. Some were Americans on vacation. Others had dual citizenship. But most were from Greece. It didn't matter to Rebecca and Haji. All they cared about were themselves at this time.

During the hour drive to the American Embassy everyone was in shock. Everything they passed was destroyed. Bodies were everywhere. Local villagers were being held at gunpoint as they were begging the United Nations Security Council to stop and help them. The United Nations Security Council was under strict orders not to interfere with anything going on in the northern region.

Then they saw it. The large sign. American Embassy.

American soldiers were everywhere as they approached. General Franklyn exited the lead jeep and spoke to the head guard at the gate. For the next five minutes everyone was on pins and needles. Finally, they were waved in.

As they crossed onto American soil no one cheered. Everyone cried. Some cried for joy, some cried for the dead they left behind, some cried for the uncertainty of their missing loved ones, but most just cried from the hell they had been through.

They were brought directly into a reception room and welcomed by all sorts of people. There were doctors to tend to their wounds, military personal ready to take statements, psychologist's to help anyone who needed to talk, and plenty of food and drinks.

"Good morning everyone. My name is Sergeant Johnson of the United States Marine Corps. I want to take this opportunity to welcome you to the American Embassy. Keep in mind, you are now safe. The American Embassy is on American soil. So in essence; welcome to America." Everyone cheered and cried at the same time. "I'm sure everyone's hungry. If you need the rest rooms to wash up before eating they are down the hall. So go, take care of your needs. You're free to do as you please."

"Haji, I need to go to the ladies room."

"All right Rebecca, you go. I don't have to go. I'm very hungry. I want to eat."

"Listen up little brother. Go wash up. You're going to start listening to your big sister."

"All right."

Haji was out of the bathroom in a couple of minutes. Rebecca was in there for a little while longer. The women all looked like they were in a daze as they walked around like zombies.

When Rebecca caught up with Haji he was eating a sandwich. She then grabbed a plate and put in a few pieces of fruit. She needed to cleanse her insides.

"Excuse me everyone. My name is Doctor Stone," a gentleman of about fifty announced. "Down the corridor over there are the locker rooms. Men on the left, and women on the right. There are attendants there waiting to help you with any personal needs. By now I'm sure you can use a shower. In the locker rooms there are changes of clothes. It's all military I'm sorry to say. Tomorrow morning you can go to the base shopping mall and purchase new clothing of your choice. If you don't have any money, don't worry. Uncle Sam will pay. So please, take a shower, get dressed and come back out here. Each of you will see a doctor. Any type of medical attention you may need can be done here. Any medication you need we have. The American Embassy is a country within a country."

Rebecca stayed under the hot shower for fifteen minutes. The hot water felt good on her wounds. She wished she could stay there all day. She washed her hair three times. Even Haji stayed under the shower longer than he ever did. When they all left the locker rooms they stared at each other with faint smiles while admiring the uniforms. Haji was already the size of a young man. Rebecca admired the way he looked in the uniform.

The American uniform.

It's going to happen. It's really going to happen.

We're going to America she kept thinking.

The next morning everyone saw a doctor. Haji had several bruised ribs, and was given antibiotics for the open wounds he received from the beating that Private Akman inflicted.

Rebecca as she suspected, was pregnant.

"Miss Ioannou, what do you want to do about your pregnancy? This is a military hospital. We can terminate the pregnancy. Do you know who the father is?"

"It can be any one of a hundred different men," she said as she broke down hysterically.

The doctor handed Rebecca a tissue while informing her that she's only a few weeks pregnant. "The baby isn't formed yet," he continued. "We'll just give you a scrapping. You're in good health. You'll be able to have more children in the future. No one will know anything."

Rebecca didn't want the genes of any of the raping barbarians to be extended into another human being.

Especially if it was Private Akman's.

"Do what you need to do. I don't want this child. I'll never be able to love it."

"Fine, and Rebecca, I'm not allowed to tell you this but you're doing the right thing. If you were my wife or daughter I would want them to have the courage to do exactly what you're doing," he said with his eyes watering.

"Thank you Doctor."

CHAPTER

By the next day, Rebecca was starting to feel better. She knew her bruises would eventually heal. Haji's bruised ribs were already healing nicely. The real factors were the broken hearts that would probably never heal.

Rebecca escorted Haji to the money exchange to cash in the gold. As nervous as she was, no one questioned her. Surprisingly, many people were cashing in their gold. Many were American tourists who came to Europe to buy gold a little cheaper than in America. Many others felt that gold was the only international currency, and carried it in case of an emergency. Others were cashing in their jewelry.

"Can I help you ma'am?"

"Yes please. I'd like to cash in my gold coins."

"Sure, how many?" Rebecca handed the women the coins under the bulletproof glass.

"All of these please."

"Let's see what we have here." It took the women several minutes to examine the coins to make sure they were authentic. She then pounded away on her calculator. "All right ma'am, at $159.26 an ounce, multiplied by your sixty-one, one ounce coins; your total is $9,714.86. How would you like that?"

"I don't know what you mean?"

"Would you like it all in cash, or would you like a certified check?"

"I don't know, I need to purchase two tickets to America and I do need some cash to hold."

"Where in America are you going?"

"New York. Kennedy Airport."

"Is it you and this young man?" she said as she looked at Haji.
"Yes."

"Why don't you do this? Purchase the two tickets. I can also help you with that. Let me see here," she said as she looked at the plane schedule. "There's an Olympic Airlines Flight 758 leaving tonight that I can still put you on. Most everyone here will be on that flight. You will have a two-hour layover in Greece. Then you will board a non-stop flight to Kennedy International Airport on TWA Flight 547. The reason I'm saying this is that that's a lot of money for you to carry; you being a woman and all. The two tickets are $1,118.72. I don't recommend you carrying that much cash. Why don't you do this? Carry $1,000 in cash and take a certified check for the remainder. Or I can wire the rest to your account in America. But since everything that has been going on around here I'm sure you don't have any of your American bank account numbers with you. Correct?"

"Correct."

"You can open an account with Chase Manhattan Bank with me now and withdraw the money when you get to America. I know there are several branches in Manhattan. I'll mail the copies of the signature cards to the main office in Times Square. It will take about a week by air mail for them to receive the signature cards."

"Okay then, why don't we do this? Give me the tickets and $2,000 in cash. We need to purchase some clothes and other items. Then I'll open an account with the Chase Manhattan Bank. That will be the best way. Thank you for your advice."

"You're welcome, glad to be of assistance to you. Your account balance is $6,596.14. Here's your receipt. Is there anything else I can help you with?"

"No thank you, that'll be it."

Fifteen minutes later Rebecca and Haji had two plane tickets and were buying clothes at the embassy store. She was careful with the money. She knew it had to last. She bought a pocket-book along with five outfits for each of them along with proper undergarments, and two small travel bags.

"Haji, we have what we need. Let's go get something to eat and rest up a little before we leave for the airport."

"All right Rebecca, but I want to let you know that I'm afraid."

"I'm afraid too. But we cannot let our fear stop us. We've been to hell and back already. We're going to be fine."

"I hope so."

At nine o'clock that evening they all boarded a bus to the Nicosia International Airport. Just like the bus ride to the American Embassy, they had a large military escort. The airport was now under Turkish occupation but they knew the United Nations Security Council was off limits. Besides, The United States Marine Corps were escorting the United Nations Security Council.

The scenery of the fifteen minute drive to the airport was no different than the drive from the monastery. It was a war zone. Although it was nighttime you were still able to see the burnt down buildings. The little bit of normalness that everyone felt the last couple of days brought them back a few weeks.

When they finally reached the airport the bus was met with a blockade. The United Nations officials on the bus informed everyone they had nothing to worry about. It's just a formality. They'll let us through.

After thirty minutes the driver was informed that they would be moving shortly.

Rebecca was sitting next to the window looking out and remembering all the rapes that she went through. No matter how hard she tried, she couldn't get them out of her mind.

Then suddenly she almost vomited.

Suddenly she felt a chill go down her spine.

She couldn't believe it.

There he was, standing directly under her window. Private Akman. He was holding his crotch and smiling at her. She wanted to scream. As she was starting to hyperventilate, the bus started to move again. She wiped the tears from her face as she started to breathe normally again. *Will I ever be free of him?*

The bus proceeded directly to the Olympic Airlines plane. Everyone was then quickly ushered off the bus and directed up the steps into the plane. Once inside they were told to find a seat quickly and put on their seatbelts. Haji and Rebecca grabbed the first two adjoining seats and connected their seatbelts.

"I've never been on a plane before, I'm scared," Haji whispered to Rebecca.

"Neither have I, but remember, we're from America and we've flown many times."

"I know."

Within minutes the door closed. The stewardess instructed every one of all possible emergency situations as the plane approached the runway. The next thing they felt was the plane leaving the ground. Haji had his eyes closed as he held onto the arm rests. Rebecca was looking out the window with amazement.

An hour and forty-five minutes later Olympic Airlines Flight 758 touched down at Athens International Airport.

⇒⟨+ +⟩⇐

"This is your captain speaking. I want to take this opportunity to welcome you to Athens International Airport. Since we were delayed in Cyprus you will need to quickly depart to make your connecting flights. Those of you connecting to TWA Flight 547 to Kennedy International Airport need to quickly get to gate 17."

"Let's go Haji. Grab your bag. We don't want to miss our connecting flight."

"I'm right behind you."

When they exited the plane, the size of the airport amazed them.

"Haji, look at the difference between this airport and the one in Cyprus."

"Yeah, look at the place. Look at all the restaurants. Do you think we can get something to eat?"

"Not now. They'll give us food on the plane. I don't want to miss our connecting flight. Let's go, this way," she said as she read the sign directing them to gates 10-20.

At their gate Rebecca held Haji close to her.

"Stay next to me. I don't want you getting lost. All right little brother?"

"All right big sister."

About ten people were in front of them. But before they knew it there were another thirty behind them. Rebecca recognized many from their flight from Cyprus.

Finally it was their turn.

"Ticket's please."

Rebecca handed their tickets and passports to the woman.

165

"I don't need your passports. You won't need them until you go through customs in America. I just need your tickets."

"Sorry."

"Everyone does it," the woman said as Rebecca put the passports back into her pocketbook. "Everything here seems to be in order. You two enjoy your flight. I hope you enjoyed your stay here."

"We did. Thank you."

Haji followed Rebecca down the long corridor to the plane. When they boarded the plane they were amazed by its size. Unlike Olympic Airlines out of Cyprus, with two seats on each side of the plane, this plane was a brand new Jumbo 747. It had three seats on each side and five seats across in the middle. The stewardess directed them both to center aisle seats. Rebecca was disappointed that she didn't have a window seat but was happy to be there, considering everything she had been through. Haji didn't care much about a window seat. All he wanted to do was have something to eat and to sleep.

When everyone was seated the stewardess went through her ritual of safety exits and seatbelts.

"Good evening everyone. This is your captain speaking. I want to welcome you aboard TWA flight 547 to Kennedy International Airport. Our flight will take approximately nine hours and twenty-two minutes. We will be taking off shortly. As a reminder, smoking is only allowed in the last twelve rows. Please obey the no smoking sections."

Within a few minutes, the fasten your seatbelt sign flashed as the plane started to move. It took another ten minutes until the plane reached the runway and stopped. Then they heard the engines roaring. Then the plane started to go forward with such great force and speed all the passengers were pushed back into their seats as the plane started to take off down the runway. Within seconds the plane lifted off the ground. Haji held on to Rebecca's hand this time for dear life as she smiled at him. After about thirty minutes, the stewardess' started rolling out their food wagons. By now, Rebecca was hungry too. They both finished their meals of chicken and rice, along with apple sauce and potato chips.

"Haji, are you all right?"

"Yes, I'm fine."

"Good, I'll be right back."

"Where are you going?" Haji asked concerned.

"To the ladies room," she smiled. "I'll be right back."

In the ladies room Rebecca started to cry when she saw her face in the mirror. She felt she aged in the past few weeks. She quickly washed her face and took a deep breath and headed back towards her seat. As she walked to her seat, she noticed Haji looking back towards the restrooms. The poor boy is really scared to be alone she thought. I must protect him. For a quick second they made eye contact and Haji quickly turned around and faced forward in embarrassment.

"I'm back."

Haji just smiled.

"Why don't you try to get some sleep," she said to him.

"I think I will. I'm very tired."

Rebecca put her head back and stared at Haji and started thinking. What's going to happen to this poor boy if he cannot find his parents? He's such a tough brave kid, and yet a really scared kid. What would he have done without me? Could he have made this trip alone? I don't think so. What are we going to do when we get off the plane? Where will we go? Thank God we have money. The first thing we'll have to do is check into a hotel and collect our thoughts.

And what about me? What am I going to do when we finally find Haji's parents? Where will I go? What if we don't find his parents? What will we do?

Right now I'm the only person he knows in the world.

I'm responsible for him.

Suddenly she felt the tears rolling down her cheeks again as she drifted off into a deep sleep thinking about the hellish days with Private Akman.

CHAPTER

26

"Ma'am, please move your seat in the upright position. The pilot is going to start his descent."

Rebecca opened her eyes and saw the stewardess looking into her face.

"We're going to be landing in fifteen minutes."

Rebecca rubbed the sand from her eyes and looked around. For a split second she didn't know where she was.

"I'm sorry. I'll get my brother up too. Haji, get up. It's time to get up. We're here. We'll be landing in a few minutes."

"What? When? Now?"

"Yes, now. Sit up."

"Ladies and gentlemen, this is your captain speaking. I'm starting my descent. Please make sure your seats are in their upright position and your food tray is closed. There will be no more smoking, and please keep your seat belt on until the seat belt sign has been turned off."

Ten minutes later the wheels touched down. Everyone clapped as they heard the engines screaming to slow the plane and taxi toward the gate. When the plane stopped the flashing *fasten your seatbelt* lights shut.

"Ladies and gentlemen, this is your captain speaking. On behalf of TWA I would like to welcome you to Kennedy International Airport. Please have a safe trip to your final destination; and please don't forget any of your personal belongings. Your luggage will be at carousel 18."

"Come on Haji, I want you directly in front of me so I can keep an eye on you. Under no circumstances do I want to let you out of my sight."

Rebecca kept a hand on Haji's shoulder as they walked off the plane to avoid anyone cutting between them. Most everyone followed the directions to the carousel to pick up their luggage. Since Rebecca and Haji had no luggage, only carry on travel bags, they went directly to customs.

"Just stand next to me right here," Rebecca said to Haji. "Remember our story. I don't think that there will be a problem."

Within minutes Rebecca heard the words that made her heart stop.

"Next."

"Good morning," Rebecca offered a smile at the customs agent.

As tired and ugly as Rebecca felt, she noticed the way the agent was admiring her. He was about thirty-five years old, fifty pounds overweight, and not very handsome. She then remembered what General Franklyn said; *you are a beautiful woman, be careful.* So she decided to see just how beautiful she really was.

"How are you today?" she smiled.

"I'm fine," he smiled back. "Welcome to America."

"Well actually, I'm home. We were away on vacation."

"My apologies then, welcome home," he smiled again.

Rebecca knew he was staring at her. Every once in a while he lowered his eyes to catch a glimpse of her breasts. Rebecca continued to look the agent in the eyes while she kept smiling at him.

"Passports please."

"Sure, here you go," she said as she took them out of her pocketbook.

The agent examined the passports but didn't pay much attention to what he was doing. He kept looking up at Rebecca.

"Well Rebecca Ioannou, everything looks fine. Again, welcome home."

"Thank you sir, it's good to be home," Rebecca said as she smiled at him. "Come on Haji."

Once they passed through customs they both went to the restrooms to wash up.

"Wait for me right here in front of this water fountain. Don't wander off. And don't talk to anyone."

"All right big sister."

When Rebecca exited the rest room, she found Haji waiting exactly where she instructed him.

"Are you hungry?" she asked.

"I'm starving."

Rebecca bought Haji a hot dog and a soda. As they walked through the airport Rebecca noticed a tourist booth. She selected several pamphlets on tourist attractions. She sat for fifteen minutes looking for anything on Astoria while Haji ate another hot dog. Nothing mentioned Astoria. She decided to stay near the airport. She chose the International Hotel, right outside the airport. They boarded a taxi and reached the hotel in ten minutes. Rebecca went directly to the front desk and paid for two nights at seventy-five dollars a night. It was a little steep but the name of the hotel made her feel like they would blend in. After given the room keys, she went to the hotel's tourist information booth and picked up several area pamphlets.

When they entered their room, Rebecca's breath was taken away. When she asked for two beds, she never expected two queen size beds with a beautiful view of the airport.

"Rebecca, look at the bathroom. I've never seen a bathroom so big."

When Rebecca went into the bathroom her breath was again taken away. She couldn't believe it. She had never seen a bathroom with two sinks and a shower separate from the biggest bathtub she has ever seen.

Rebecca double locked the door and called Haji away from the window and sat him down on the bed next to her.

"Haji, listen to me. There's a lot of work to do. We need to go through all these pamphlets. Look for anything that says Astoria, or diner. I'll be out in a bit. I need to take a shower. Do not open the door for anyone, and don't answer the phone. Do you hear me?"

"Yes."

Rebecca grabbed her change of clothes and entered the bathroom. When she undressed, she stood and looked at her naked body in the full length mirror. She still had some wounds. Some started to heal as the black and blues were turning yellow. The bruises on her face from Private Akman, when she landed face first on the stone ground, were almost gone.

Although she lost some weight, she felt she was getting some of her strength back, even after the scraping the doctor did to terminate her pregnancy.

She stood in the shower for such a long time that Haji started to get worried. But even at twelve-years old he was a little embarrassed that Rebecca was on the other side of the door naked.

When Haji heard the bathroom door open, he instantly picked up his head. Rebecca walked out of the bathroom wearing a new pair of tight jeans with a knitted light colored yellow V-neck top that clung to her breasts.

Haji noticed her beauty.

"Any luck Haji? Did you find anything in Astoria?"

"I don't know."

"What do you mean you don't know?"

"I don't know. I didn't see anything."

"We have a lot of work to do today. I know you're tired from jet lag but we need to get busy."

"Busy doing what?"

"Busy doing what?" Rebecca snapped. "How about busy finding your parents? How about this one? Busy trying to figure out the rest of our lives. Is that busy enough?"

Haji looked up at Rebecca and started to cry.

"I'm sorry, I'm just so scared."

"Haji, come here. I'm sorry. I'm scared too," she said as she held him tight. "I didn't mean to snap at you. Why don't you take a shower and put on a clean change of clothes? You'll feel a lot better. There's a white plastic bag in there for your dirty clothes. I'll have to figure out where to do laundry tomorrow, and please don't worry; I'll look at this material. We're here, we're here in America. Everything's going to be all right. We'll find your parents."

Haji carried his travel bag into the bathroom. Like Rebecca, Haji lingered in the shower. They weren't used to an unlimited supply of hot water in Vavla, but it's something they knew they would get used to.

While Haji showered, Rebecca looked through all the pamphlets. She saw lots to do in Manhattan and other parts of New York but nothing in Astoria. She walked to the big window and looked outside and thought. *I know they're out there somewhere. God, please help me find them.*

When she turned to look at the pamphlets again she noticed the telephone book on the desk. She ran to it, sat on the desk, and started flipping the pages in excitement.

I-I-I-I-I, where are you I? There you are I. O? I found you O. A, there you are. Come on N where are you N? N-N, I got you. All of a sudden it was right in front of her, *'Ioannou, Christine Andreas 102-05 36st Astoria AS4-5555.'* Rebecca quickly wrote the address and phone number using the pen and pad on the desk. Switching to the yellow pages, she looked under the letter D for diners. There were many diners in Astoria. So she started from the beginning in alphabetical order. The first diner was the Belair Diner on 21ˢᵗ street. She dialed the number; AS2-2222 and was ready to ask for Andreas or Christine Ioannou. If by chance one of them answered she would hang up.

"Belair Diner, may I help you?"

"Yes, may I speak to Andreas or Christine please?"

"Sorry, no one here by those names, you have the wrong number."

"I'm sorry," Rebecca said as she hung up.

The next was the Broadway Diner. She dialed the number; AS4-1441.

"Broadway Diner."

"May I please speak to Andreas or Christine please?"

"I'm sorry, Christine is not here right now, but Andreas is in the kitchen. Let me see if he's busy. Who's calling please?"

Click, Rebecca quickly hung up. She sat there on the chair feeling the sweat dripping down her spine. At the same time Haji was coming out of the bathroom.

"Haji, I found them."

"Where? Where are they?"

"Right here, look. The Broadway Diner. 46-02 46th Street in Astoria. I just called the diner and asked to speak to them. Your father was there."

"What did you say?"

"Nothing, I hung up. But I now know where they are. Get ready. We're taking a taxi there."

"Now?"

"Yes, now."

Rebecca quickly wrote down the address of the Broadway Diner and double checked it. She called Haji over and explained what she planned on doing.

"Haji, we still have about $1,500.00 in cash left. We need it to last. I don't want to touch the money in the bank yet. I know you're nervous. But look at what happened already. We're in America less than four hours and we know where your parents live and work."

Rebecca and Haji walked through the lobby toward the triple glass doors. Haji couldn't help noticing the way many of the men were looking at Rebecca, as did Rebecca. Why not, she was tall, beautiful, had a gorgeous figure, and walked with gracefulness. Once outside Haji followed Rebecca into a taxi.

"Where to ma'am?"

"46-02 46th Street, Astoria."

"You got it."

Rebecca knew she needed to become as American as fast as she possibly could. She whispered to Haji to keep looking around to familiarize himself with the area. She watched as the driver entered the Van Wyck Expressway. She studied the exit signs. Jamaica Avenue, Liberty Avenue as she watched the driver stay on the Van Wyck Expressway, not going left onto the Interboro Parkway. Within a few minutes they exited towards the Grand Central Parkway, Triboro Bridge. On her right was the marina next to La Guardia Airport. She wondered why they didn't land there instead of Kennedy. She could have stayed at the Traveler's Hotel directly across the street. She would have been that much closer to Astoria. But that didn't upset her. She loved the International Hotel. She couldn't wait to get back and take a long hot bath.

Passing La Guardia Airport they exited at Steinway Street. Then she saw her first sign of Astoria. They were on Astoria Boulevard. They rode along Astoria Boulevard. Rebecca had never seen so many cars in her life. When they reached Steinway Street they turned left and took it to Broadway and made another left.

"Haji," she whispered. "Look at all the stores with all the Greek names."

"I know, some of the store signs aren't even in English, they're in Greek."

"Okay lady, 46-02 46th Street. Looks like it's this diner on the corner here. That'll be $9.00 please."

Rebecca and Haji sat there unable to move. They both stared at the diner.

"Lady, I ain't got all day. I said that'll be $9.00."

"I'm sorry sir, here keep the change," as she handed the man a ten dollar bill.

When the taxi left, Haji stared at the diner while Rebecca took notice of the surroundings.

"Let's go see what your father looks like. Remember, don't say anything."

"I'll remember."

They nervously walked up the steps and into the diner.

"Hi, good afternoon," Yoyo said to them. "How many, just the two of you?"

"Yes, thank you, just the two of us," answered Rebecca.

"Would you like to sit in the dining room or out here?"

Rebecca quickly looked around. She wanted to sit where she could observe everyone.

"Right here will be fine," she said as she pointed to a table that overlooked everything.

Rebecca sat facing forward as Haji faced the restrooms. Yoyo came back and dropped off two menus.

"Are you hungry Haji?" Rebecca asked.

"I'm starving."

"Me too. Let's look at the menu."

By now it was 9:00 p.m. They were both hungry and tired. It had been a long day. Again Rebecca thought about taking a long hot bath and falling asleep on the queen size bed that waited for her back at the hotel. They both ordered cheeseburgers and French fries. Haji ordered a coke while Rebecca ordered coffee.

For the next fifteen minutes there was lots of noise of clattering of dishes. Yoyo brought out their food and was refilling Rebecca's coffee when she saw him coming out of the kitchen. He was shorter than Haji's father but she noticed the family resemblance. Haji didn't notice anything because his back was to him. Andreas noticed Rebecca looking at him as she quickly put her head down to take another sip of her coffee. He gave her a quick professional smile. For the next half hour Andreas went in and out of the kitchen many times, but always glanced toward Rebecca.

Rebecca saw that he ran the place. Yoyo also looked like she was in control of everything, even wondering if maybe the Yoyo name tag was only a nickname and she could possibly be Christine. But for some reason she didn't think so. Rebecca couldn't figure what it was, but Andreas had a concerned look on his face. She felt something was wrong.

"Haji, I'll be right back, I'm going to the ladies room. Don't go anywhere, and don't talk to anyone. Understand?"

"Yes."

When Rebecca walked across the diner to the restroom she felt all eyes on her. A few of the men even smiled at her. She admitted to herself that she liked it.

At least here, if anyone wanted me they didn't have the right to just take me, she thought.

As she walked back to the table, she noticed Haji eating ice cream.

"Where did you get the ice cream?" asked Rebecca.

"That man gave it to me," answered Haji, as he pointed to Andreas.

"He just came over and gave it to you?"

"Yeah, I mean no. He came over and asked me if I like ice cream. I told him yes. Then he brought it to me."

"Did you say thank you?"

"Of course."

"Did he say anything else? Did he ask you any other questions? Did he stare at you?"

"No. Is that him?"

"I'm not sure, but I think so."

Rebecca noticed Andreas coming out of the kitchen again and walk over to their table.

"Hi, I hope you don't mind me giving him some ice cream."

'No, not at all," Rebecca smiled.

"He had that look of all teenagers needing to satisfy a sweet tooth."

"I know what you mean. The only thing is he's not a teenager yet. He's only twelve."

"Really? He's big for his age."

"Yes he is. He's also very mature for his age too."

Haji ate his ice cream and smiled nervously while he kept glancing at the man who was probably his father. Then Rebecca felt like she got hit with a ton of bricks.

"What part of Cyprus are you from?"

"Excuse me?"

"What part of Cyprus are you from? I can read your accent a mile away. I'm also from Cyprus."

"We're from the north. My family came to America two years ago. It's a good thing we left. Our village is now under Turkish occupation. What part of Cyprus are you from?"

"Me? I'm from the central part of the island. It's a small village in the hills. I'm sure you've never heard of it. I came to America thirteen years ago."

"I have family in central Cyprus. I might know your village. What's the name of it?"

"Vavla. Ever hear of it?"

Rebecca hesitated a second.

"Can't say that I have, you're right; it must be a small village."

"Small it is. I've been trying to get in touch with my brother since the invasion. Most of the phones are still out from what I'm told. I'm thinking of flying there but the airport is still under Turkish occupation."

"I'm sure they're fine."

"I hope so. What's your name?"

"I'm Rebecca, and this is my brother Haji."

"It's nice to meet you both. I'm Andreas. Andreas Ioannou."

"Is this your diner?"

"Yes, I own it with my wife Christine."

"I see, it's a nice place," Rebecca said nervously as she looked at Yoyo.

"Thank you."

"Is that your wife?"

"Yoyo? No, she's not my wife. She works here. The best worker I've ever had. She's been with us a couple of years now. She's very dedicated. She works here like it's her own place. She's the only employee I trust with a key. My wife's not here now. She's on

Long Island visiting her brother. It's a lot of work. I couldn't do it without my wife and Yoyo. Yoyo usually leaves at three since she opens with me in the morning. But today her relief called in sick so she's staying till closing. It's a good thing I only live ten blocks away," as he pointed towards the direction of where he lived.

Andreas sat and talked awhile. Rebecca and Andreas did most of the talking while Haji ate another two scoops of ice cream. They primarily talked about the politics of Cyprus. Rebecca made up some story about living near Kennedy Airport and just recently moved to Astoria. The only thing she knew about Astoria was the diner and Steinway Street that she knew the taxi took. So she told Andreas she and Haji now lived on Steinway Street with their parents. By now they were all comfortable with each other, as all Cypriots usually are with their own. But it was getting late. Almost ten o'clock. They said their goodbyes while Andreas again welcomed them to Astoria.

"Who's that," Yoyo asked Andreas as they walked out the door.

"New Cypriots, you better watch out, we're taking over."

"Looks like she was taking you over the way you were looking at her. She's very pretty. Almost as pretty as Christine. By the way, have you heard from Christine?"

"Leave me alone."

CHAPTER

"Are we going back to the hotel?" asked Haji.

"No."

"I'm tired, I want to go back, and I'm cold too."

"I'm also cold. Let's get going. We have a few stops to make."

"Where are we going?"

"Andreas, whoops, I mean your father said he lives ten blocks up this way. I need to see where he lives. I have his address written down."

She needed to walk the ten blocks to 36th Street. So they started to walk down Broadway. As they crossed over Steinway Street Rebecca noticed a small variety store with a flashing sign, '*open till midnight*'.

"Look Haji, '*open till midnight*,' that's where we'll buy ourselves something to keep us warm."

"Good, let's go."

"Not now."

"Why not?"

"Because I said so. I need to see something first."

"See what?"

"I need to see where your father lives before he gets home. Trust me little brother."

"All right big sister."

When they reached 36th Street she didn't know which way to turn, left or right, so she guessed. She turned left and followed the numbers. She found the house. It was a small building four stories high. She walked to the front door and was happy to find it open. She looked at all the mail boxes for Ioannou. Apartment #16.

"Let's go Haji."

"Where?"

"I want everything to be perfect. I want to see the door with the number 16 on it before we come back." They quickly followed the numbers to the fourth floor. There it was, a large 16 on the door.

"Let's go, we'll come back later."

"Where we going?"

"You said you were cold, didn't you?"

"Yes."

"Well, let's go shopping."

When they reached Steinway Street Haji followed Rebecca into the variety store. They took their time looking around. Rebecca knew the diner closed at 11 o'clock from the sign on the door. She figured Andreas would be home by 11:20. She needed to time it right.

"Haji, see anything you like?"

"Yeah, I like this sweatshirt."

"Good, we'll buy it. Blue was always your favorite color. How do you like this jacket?" she asked as she put it on.

Now Rebecca was standing in front of him wearing a short unzipped imitation leather jacket that only emphasized her gorgeous figure.

"You look nice."

"Well thank you little brother. I agree," as she admired herself in the full length mirror. "We've been wearing the same shoes since we left Cyprus, maybe we both need a new pair. How about we treat ourselves to a new pair of sneakers?"

"Okay."

They tried on several pairs before deciding on what they wanted. Rebecca looked at her watch and saw it was already 11:30.

"Let's go Haji, its 11:30. We need to hurry."

Haji started to take off his new sneakers to put them back into the box when Rebecca stopped him.

"Haji, keep the sneakers on. Put the old shoes in the box. Let's wear our new sneakers."

"Is it all right if we throw away our old shoes here?" Rebecca asked the cashier. "We want to wear our new sneakers home."

"Sure, no problem."

"Thanks, do you have a scissors to cut the tags off the jacket and sweatshirt? It's getting cold outside, we're going to wear them home too."

"Absolutely."

They walked out of the variety store wearing their new stuff. The shoes they threw away were the last items from the world that they left behind; *out with the old, in with the new.* Again, they hurried back to 36th Street and turned left. Halfway down 36th Street they stopped in front of Andreas' building.

"Come on Haji, let's do this."

She walked in the front door, this time knowing exactly where she was going. She went directly to the stairs and started climbing as Haji followed. As they approached the top of the stairs, Rebecca noticed the light coming through the bottom of the door.

She didn't hesitate.

She knocked.

Within seconds the door opened.

"Rebecca? What are you doing here?"

"I need to talk to you."

"What? What are you doing here? It's almost midnight. Did you follow me home? How do you know where I live? What are you doing here? What's going on?" Andreas rattled on and on. He didn't know what to think.

"Can we come in?"

"No, what are you doing here?"

"I lied to you. We just came to America today. We checked into the International Hotel by Kennedy Airport and then looked you up. You weren't hard to find. You're listed in the phone book. Your diner is listed in the yellow pages."

"My diner? How did you know the name of my diner?"

"I didn't. I started calling all the diners in Astoria and asking for Andreas or Christine until I found you."

"Yoyo did tell me that someone called looking for me or Christine."

"That was me. Once I knew which diner it was we jumped into a taxi."

"I still don't understand. What are you doing here? Why me? Why did you seek me out? Who are you? Who told you about me?"

With tears dripping down his cheeks Haji stepped in front of Rebecca and took over.

"We're also from Vavla," he said.

"I don't believe you. You said you never heard of Vavla."

"We lied."

"Who told you about me? Who are you?"

"Fr. Demitri from St. George in Vavla told us about you. My name is John Haji Ioannou. My mother's name is Panayiota. My father's name is Costas. My sister's name is Mary. They're all dead," as he started to cry uncontrollably. Rebecca held Haji tight as Andreas, stunned, slowly walked backwards and sank onto the couch.

Rebecca and Haji followed Andreas into the apartment and closed the door.

"Haji quick, get a glass of water."

Haji ran into the kitchen and brought back some water.

"Here, drink this," said Rebecca. "Slowly. Not so fast."

"I'm all right, I'm all right. Give me a minute. Let me breathe."

"It's okay, take your time. Take slow deep breaths. Haji, wet a towel and bring it here. He's sweating like crazy."

"Haji started walking to the kitchen again and out of the corner of his eye he noticed something that almost made him pass out. On a small end table were three photographs. It was his family. One was a picture of Haji at about three years old with his mother and father. He had the exact same picture in his house in Vavla. *My parents must have sent it to him,* he thought. The other was a picture of his little sister Mary when she was a baby. It was the same picture that he had at home. The other was a wedding picture of Andreas and Christine. Haji walked closer and stared at them. Rebecca and Andreas noticed him looking at the photographs. The next thing Haji did was pick up the two photographs of his family, held them both to his cheeks, sat on the floor, and started crying again.

"They killed them, they killed them. Why did they have to kill them?"

Andreas still couldn't figure out what was going on. Could this really be his nephew? He had to be. How else would he know his brother and sister-in-law's names? And Fr. Demitri, they knew Fr. Demitri from St. George.

"Oh John, my nephew John," cried Andreas as he tried to stand but fell back onto the couch. "Rebecca, please, bring him to me."

Rebecca was already on her way to comfort Haji before Andreas asked her to bring him to him. Rebecca sat cradling Haji in her arms. Andreas watched the bond that Rebecca had with his nephew. What happened, what happened to these two poor souls? He thought.

"Please Rebecca, bring him to me."

Rebecca helped Haji to his feet. She held on to him as she brought him to Andreas.

"Sit here next to me my brother's son. Sit here next to your uncle. You're here now. You're safe now. No one will ever hurt you again. I'll never let anyone hurt you. You're safe here. You're with family."

For the next ten minutes Rebecca watched uncle and nephew cry in each other's arms.

One of them not knowing the other was really a son, as tears were rolling down her own cheeks as she remembered the atrocities of her recent life.

"Rebecca, talk to me. What's going on? What happened? I need to know. I really need to know," Andreas kept saying as he held Haji tight.

"Andreas, I'm really sorry to show up like this. I didn't know what else to do. I didn't know any other way. I couldn't show up at your place of business like this. I had to come to your home."

"No no no, don't worry about that. You're here now. Both of you are here. You're both safe. Rebecca. Who are *you*? I don't even know who *you* are."

"Andreas, please, it's very late. I'm, I mean, *we* are both very tired right now. We need a good night's sleep. Especially me. I'm so tired. I'm so drained. I cannot even begin to explain what has happened to us. How we've even gotten here. The things Haji has witnessed at such a pure young age and survived is nothing less than a miracle. Please, do you have a car? We need to get back to the hotel. We'll talk tomorrow. I promise, tomorrow you'll know everything."

"Nothing doing. You're not leaving. Not now. Even though this is America, you're still in a Cypriot household. You're staying here."

"Listen Andreas, I paid for the room. There are two queen size beds waiting for us. We don't have a change of clothes. I need a shower. Can you please drive us?"

"In the bedroom is a queen size bed. I'll change the sheets. You can sleep in there. John can sleep on the couch and I'll sleep on the chair. It's a recliner. As I told you earlier at the diner, my wife is visiting her brother. You're about her size. You can wear some of her clothes when I take you both shopping tomorrow."

"I don't know."

"For God's sake, he's my nephew. I can't let him leave."

If you only knew, Rebecca thought, if you only knew.

"All right, we'll stay. Are you sure Christine won't mind?"

"I'm sure."

"When is she coming back?"

"I'm not sure."

"Is she over Basil's house?"

"How do you know about Basil?"

"Fr. Demitri told us everything."

"Exactly what *did* Fr. Demitri tell you?"

By now Haji was falling asleep on the couch. He was all cried out. The twelve-year old boy that had quickly became a man turned into a twelve-year old boy again. He needed his family that was gone forever. The only things he had were his memories, and the two photographs that he was now holding under his arm. Rebecca worried that Haji's memories might not be of his wonderful childhood, but will only be of the recent tragedies.

Within twenty minutes Rebecca had helped Andreas change the bed sheets while Haji was asleep. Rebecca didn't want to stay at Andreas' house. She wanted to go back to the hotel and sit in the large bathtub for an hour. For now it would have to wait until tomorrow.

"Rebecca, Christine's clothes are in the dresser in the corner. Please help yourself to anything you need to sleep in. Tomorrow we can go to your hotel and pick up the rest of your things. Then we'll figure out what you're going to do next. I'm going to call Yoyo and ask her to open the diner tomorrow. I'm going to take as much time off from work as I need to help John. If you please, after you change can you come out and talk just a little bit?"

Andreas was a gentleman. He didn't wait for Rebecca to answer. He walked out of the bedroom and closed the door behind him. As soon as the door closed Rebecca went through Christine's drawers to look for something to sleep in. To her amazement she discovered the drawers were all empty. Empty, except for a sexy blue nightgown. She wasn't going to wear another woman's sexy nightgown while her husband was on the other side of the door. So she took off her new sneakers and socks and crawled under the covers and sat up.

Andreas was sitting in his recliner staring at Haji. He still couldn't believe his brother was dead. What happened, he thought? How did my brother, sister-in-law, and niece die? How did John survive? He needed answers. What will Christine say? This poor kid has no one in the entire world.

Would Christine be all right with keeping my nephew?

Will Christine even come back?

She came back once to take the rest of her clothes. Shit, I don't think there's anything for Rebecca to wear.

"Andreas, can you please come in here?" Andreas entered his bedroom and saw Rebecca sitting under the covers with the same yellow top. He sat on a small chair and looked at Rebecca for a few seconds before she started.

"I'm not going to ask you where Christine's clothes are. I won't get into your personal business. But Haji and I need your help."

"Anything, anything you need. Anything you both need if I can, I'll help you with. But for now please tell me what happened."

"John, by the way always goes by Haji. For some reason he likes his middle name. Everyone in Vavla called him Haji."

"All right, I won't call him John anymore."

"Haji's parents and his six-year old sister were tortured in front of him. Tortured in a way that was torture for Haji to witness. Those savages that invaded Vavla took pleasure in making him watch."

"How, what did they make him witness?"

"Please, not now. Maybe never. No, I'll tell you, but not now. We have more important things to discuss. Please, just listen."

"I'm sorry."

"Fr. Demitri, God bless his soul. For three days we hid in the woods by day and hiked by night to The Holy Cross Monastery. With all the killing and atrocities that we witnessed, Fr. Demitri never lost his faith in God, and insisted that we did the same. We never would have made it without him. He was truly a Spiritual Father to us, especially to Haji."

"Was?"

"Yes, was." Rebecca nodded sadly. "Haji as you can imagine was like a zombie at first. He's a very brave young man. He ended up turning into a young soldier at times, and other times he was just the twelve-year old kid that's out there right now. When we finally made it to the safety of the monastery we were safe for a couple of days. Then the monastery was taken over in the middle of the night by the Turks. That's when we were nothing less than enslaved. Right now I cannot and will not get into details. But as you can imagine it was worse for the women. It got so bad that I wouldn't wish what happened to us to happen to the people who did all that to us." Andreas nodded his head as Rebecca continued with tears in her eyes. "Because of the bond Haji had with Fr. Demitri the Turks turned the chapel of the monastery into a barn with animals and locked the two of them inside one night."

"Oh my God, that must have devastated Fr. Demitri."

"Yes, I agree. It must have. But believe me when I tell you. The women would have welcomed that devastation over the devastation *we* went through."

"I'm sorry," added Andreas with a heavy heart.

"That evening Fr. Demitri told Haji a story that he told me during our three days of travel to the monastery. He explained to Haji that he must escape from here and go to America to his Uncle Andreas. By the end of the night Haji knew your story. Your entire story. All of it. From the times you walked Christine home from school to the time Mrs. Alexander told you to leave and never come back because Basil was going to find her a rich husband in America."

"Why would Fr. Demitri share that with my nephew? Why would he share that with you? I don't understand."

"You will, trust me, you will. You see, since Haji's parents and sister were killed, the two closest people to him since he had no other relatives could only be his priest and his school teacher, which was me. I believe Fr. Demitri knew he was going to get killed. I was probably an insurance policy for Haji."

"I still don't understand why my relationship with my wife prior to us getting married was discussed with my nephew, or especially with you."

"Just listen. On the day you went to Mrs. Alexander's house to ask for Christine's hand in marriage, she was sent to her room and you were thrown out of her house. Remember? Of course you remember. But before you went to the house do you remember what happened?"

"I'm not sure what you mean."

"Fr. Demitri came up from behind you both as you were holding hands and asked you both to go into the church with him to pray." Andreas stared at Rebecca as he remembered. "What you didn't know was that Fr. Demitri saw you both coming out of the schoolhouse basement. The other thing you didn't know was; the day you left Vavla; you left a pregnant Christine behind."

"What? What are you talking about? How do you know?"

"Keep listening. When Christine told her mother she was pregnant, Mrs. Alexander took her to Fr. Demitri and they discussed what to do. Christine wanted to keep the baby. Mrs. Alexander insisted on putting the baby up for adoption. So they both moved to the monastery until the baby was born and then Christine and her mother moved to Greece, and eventually here to America. No one ever saw them again.

"As you probably may not know, your brother and his wife were having a difficult time conceiving a child so Fr. Demitri arranged for them to adopt a baby. That baby is now sleeping on your couch. When your brother and sister-in-law brought the baby home only they knew it was your baby.

"Six years later, by the grace of God, Panayiota got pregnant and Mary was born. The plan was, your brother and sister-in-law were going to tell Haji on his sixteenth birthday that he was adopted and you were his father. Haji had to know."

"I don't believe it. I mean I believe it, I just can't believe that all this is happening right now. Haji's tall for his age. Christine's family is all tall. We Ioannou's are all short. Besides, he looks a little like Christine. Does he definitely know that I'm his father?"

"Yes."

"I can't believe Christine never told me."

"Christine thinks her baby was adopted by some family in Greece. She has no idea your brother adopted her son."

"He's my son too."

"Yes he is. And he needs you now more than ever."

"I can't believe my brother never told me. Why wouldn't he tell me?"

"I cannot answer that question. Unfortunately neither can your brother anymore."

"Excuse me. I have to make a phone call."

"Who are you calling this late at night?" Rebecca asked as she watched Andreas get out of the chair."

"Who do you think I'm going to call? I'm calling Christine. I'm going to let her have it."

"Andreas sit down. Sit down I said. And keep your voice low. You're going to wake your son." Andreas looked down towards Rebecca sitting on the bed as she uttered the words *your son.* "Keep calm. Remember your son. He doesn't need to hear you yelling and screaming. That will confuse him even more. And I won't allow you or Christine to do that to him. Do you hear me? I don't care who you are. I will not allow you to do that to him. He's been through enough. Now sit down and listen to me." Andreas slowly walked back to his chair and sat.

"I know you're upset. But calling Christine now and yelling at her isn't going to help. What do you think will happen when she finds out that you know she gave up the baby for adoption? Don't you think she wonders what happened to her child? I guarantee you there isn't a day that goes by that she doesn't regret giving up the baby. Why is it you and Christine never had any children after you were married? I'm sure it's because she can't have another. Why? Probably because the monks that delivered your son did a real butcher job on her. It wasn't her fault. You weren't around. You left. You left her with her mother to make all decisions for her."

"Don't pin this on me!" Andreas snapped. "I didn't know she was pregnant! If I knew, I would have stuck around!"

"I know you didn't know, but now is the time to fix it. It's the time for both of you to fix it. Look Andreas. I know you're upset. You have every right to be upset. But what would you have done if Christine told you the truth about her pregnancy after you guys reconnected here in America.

"What rights do you think you might have had towards the baby? You wouldn't have known the first place to look for him. You would have started in Greece and you would still be going crazy looking for him. But he's right here sleeping on your couch. I guarantee you; Christine has been living the pain for both of you. Keep in mind. She always loved you. From what I've been told she could have had anyone she wanted. But she chose you. It was you she loved. It was you she married. Let her know how you feel but forgive her. Do you hear me? Forgive her! If not for yourself, do it for your son!

"For God's sake Andreas, do it for your son!"

CHAPTER

28

The next morning they were up bright and early. Andreas told Rebecca to make herself at home and left for a local deli. He bought all sorts of breakfast items. When he returned he insisted on making breakfast. With great difficulty, Andreas chose his words very carefully while talking to Haji. Haji did mostly small talk, usually speaking when he was spoken to. Rebecca always tried to keep the conversation going.

"Haji, do you like baseball?" asked Andreas.

"I guess. Sometimes we would play back home."

"I bet you were pretty good."

"I was. I'm a good hitter."

"Good hitter?" Rebecca chimed in to keep the conversation going. "Don't be so modest. I watched the kids play at recess. Whenever Haji got up to bat everyone took a step back. He was almost always guaranteed to hit the ball over the outfielder's head."

"I'll bet he's a good hitter. Haji, have you ever been to a real baseball game?" Andreas knew Haji had never been to a real game being from Vavla.

"No."

"Neither have I. How about we go together some time?"

"I think that would be great." Rebecca jumped in.

"So do I," said Andreas. "How about it Haji?"

"Okay, I guess."

"Good," said Andreas as he got up to clear off the table. "You two relax, I'll do the dishes. I have a busy day planned for the three of us."

"Andreas, can you sit down for a moment please?" said Rebecca.

"Sure."

"I don't know what your plans are but there's a lot that needs to be done."

"I know there is. Can I at least spend a little time with my son?"

"Hopefully the rest of your life, but for now, this is what I want to do. I need to do some shopping. That Steinway Street seems to have a lot of stores. I'm going shopping alone while you two get acquainted."

"Nothing doing. I'm taking you both. It sounded like you got out of Cyprus with your lives. I have money. I'm paying."

"We have money too. But you can buy Haji anything you want so he doesn't have to spend his money."

"How did you ever get money out of Cyprus?"

"That's another long story."

"It's only nine o'clock," Andreas smiled.

Rebecca explained the story about the gold. And how Fr. Demitri showed Haji where it was hidden, and how Haji had the brilliant idea to make up the story that Rebecca was his sister, and wanting to share it with her. And the way General Franklyn from

The United Nations Security Council didn't believe her and took half, in exchange for two passports with their names on them. She explained how she cashed in the gold at the American Embassy and opened an account with the Chase Manhattan Bank.

"By the way, where's Manhattan?" asked Rebecca.

"Why?"

"That's where the Chase Manhattan Bank is."

"Don't worry about it. There's a Chase Manhattan Bank on the corner of Steinway Street and Ditmars Boulevard.

"I know where Steinway Street is. Where's Ditmars Boulevard."

"It's right here in Astoria. Greek town USA. How much money are we talking about?"

"Right now I have about $1,500 in cash in my pocketbook. The bank account has over $6,500."

"That's good money. You keep it all. I'll take care of Haji. I'll take care of both of you."

"No, it's half Haji's money."

"We'll talk about it some other time."

"Fine, but for now Haji and I need to buy some clothes. I need to go back to the hotel. I need a job, and an apartment. I'm not going to live here with you two or three. Is your wife ever coming back? Her drawers are empty."

"I'm sure she'll be back," Andreas said as he took $500 from his pocket which was part of the diner's receipts and handed it to Rebecca. "Please, both of you go shopping on me. I won't take no for an answer. Right now I need to go see Christine. Haji, I'm afraid to let you go but I need to speak to your mother alone."

"I understand Uncle Andreas."

Andreas looked at his son after he called him Uncle Andreas. He wanted to be his father, but he understood that the only parents this poor kid ever knew were dead. Both Rebecca and Haji noticed the awkwardness so Rebecca quickly jumped in.

"Andreas right now you are his uncle. In time I'm sure you and Christine will become his second parents."

"Thank you Rebecca, and especially thank you Haji for finding me," said Andreas as his eyes glistened.

"We're leaving now," Rebecca said. "We're going to Steinway Street and then we'll take a taxi back to the hotel."

"All right, you two do that. I have a few things to take care of before I see Christine."

"No Andreas, you need to see Christine first. Don't keep all this news waiting."

"All right, I'll walk with you to Steinway Street. I need to rent a car. I'm also going to stop at the real estate office to make an appointment to see apartments for you and for me. You need a place to live and I'm going need a two bedroom apartment so Haji can have his own room. Rebecca, would you like me to contact Fr. Harry at St. Demitrios and ask him if he needs a teacher? St. Demitrios also has a school up to the eighth grade. That's where I would like to enroll Haji before he goes to high school next year."

"Yes please. That will be perfect. An apartment and a job is exactly what I need."

"Good, I will also see a lawyer friend of mine to make sure all your paperwork is in order. Because if it's not, we'll have to fix it. For now let's go. I'll drive directly to Basil's house and tell Christine. After that I'm sure we'll go straight to your hotel. I know where it is. What's the room number?"

"Room 407. Don't come straight up. Call us from the lobby."

"That's a good idea. It'll give you both extra time to get ready."

All three left the apartment together. Andreas tried to make some small talk with Haji as he tried to explain the neighborhood. Rebecca was like a hawk scanning the area trying to familiarize herself with what she knew would be her new home.

"All right, here's the rent a car place. Steinway is one block up. Good luck. Haji, come over here please."

"Yes sir," Haji answered awkwardly.

Andreas embraced his son and said; "I'm afraid to leave you. Thank you again for finding me. I promise you I'll try my best to be the father that my brother was to you." After that Andreas gave Rebecca a hug and they parted.

Andreas rented a full sized Chevrolet Impala sedan with the hopes of bringing home Christine and Haji.

As he drove, he kept repeating in his head what he was going to say.

How shall I tell her?

What shall I tell her?

What if she doesn't want to talk to me? She moved out. I didn't ask her to leave. What if Basil gets in my face? Should I knock him on his ass or should I just walk away and not tell Christine anything. That's one way of getting even. Then I'll just go home and live happily ever after with my son, and Christine won't know a thing. Yeah, why not, maybe I'll do that. She never told me that I had a child out there somewhere. Maybe I'll do the same to her. Maybe I'll turn this car around and tell Haji that his mother ran away with another man or that she doesn't want to see him. That'll fix her.

Who was Andreas kidding? He loved Christine. He could never hurt her no matter how upset he was. He needed Christine now more than ever.

He was lost without her.

Now, with his son, with their son, he needed to be a family.

They needed to be a family.

Haji needed to be part of a family again.

When Andreas pulled in front of Basil's house, Basil was outside raking leaves. When Basil noticed Andreas, he stopped raking and greeted him as he exited the car with an extended hand to shake. Not quite the confrontation Andreas expected.

"Andreas, believe it or not, it's good to see you. Christine's inside. I'm telling you, she misses you. She's been miserable ever since she got here. She's concerned, and scared. She called the diner this morning to speak to you and was surprised when Yoyo told her that you were taking some time off. She called your house a few times this morning. The no answers worried her. She worried that maybe you went to Cyprus to try to find your brother. We watched the Greek channel and they showed the map of the Turkish occupation. We saw that Vavla falls just north of the line. I'm glad you're here. For what it's worth, I'm glad you didn't go to Cyprus. Have you heard from your brother?"

"He's dead. They're all dead," Andreas said as he started to cry.

Andreas was shocked by the way Basil just embraced him. It was totally out of Basil's character. But at that moment Andreas needed all the hugs he can get.

"You said Christine's inside?"

"Yes she is. She's packing. She wanted to go home and wait for you in case you went to Cyprus. I planned on driving her tonight."

"Is Athena inside with her?"

"No, Athena is visiting her sister in New Jersey. She's coming home tomorrow."

"Basil. Can you give us some privacy? I need to talk her alone."

"Sure Andreas, take all the time you need. I'm leaving now to go to the hardware store. Do me a favor; please lock the house when you leave. I'm going to be gone at least an hour."

"Sure, no problem."

Andreas entered the house and saw the two suitcases in the foyer. He walked into the kitchen where he heard water running and saw Christine facing the sink with her back to him. He couldn't help admiring his wife's figure from behind. He could have stood there all day looking at her. She just made him melt. Finally he spoke; "I see you're going on a trip. Where are you going?"

Christine quickly turned around.

"Andreas, you're here. I'm so glad you're here. I was coming home. I'm so sorry. I really mean it. I'm so sorry I left. I never should have. I was so worried this morning when I called the diner. Yoyo told me that you were taking time off. I thought you went to Cyprus."

"Don't you think if I was going to Cyprus I would have told you?"

"I don't know what to think; all I know is I'm glad you're here. Take me home. Please take me home."

"I will," Andreas said as his eyes watered. "I will. Let's sit down and talk for five minutes first."

"What is it? Your brother? Is it your brother? I was watching the Greek channel. I saw the way they drew a line across Cyprus. I was so worried that you would go there," she cried as she wrapped her arms around him.

"Yes, it is my brother. He's gone. His whole family is gone. They're all dead. The town was invaded. I don't know much more about Vavla. The other person I do know that was killed is Fr. Demitri."

"Oh my God Andreas, I'm so sorry. I wish I was there when you found out. I'm so sorry I made you learn all this alone. I love you so much."

"I love you too. I've always loved you. And I'm also sorry for the way I acted. I'm sorry for the way I've always acted towards your family. Will you forgive me?"

"Only if you forgive me," she said as she kissed him on the lips.

"Let's go in the living room and talk a bit."

"No, let's go home and talk. I want to go home. I don't want to stay here anymore. We belong home."

Andreas took Christine by the hand and led her to the kitchen table.

"Sit down. I need to talk to you about something."

"Can't it wait until we get home?"

"No, now listen." Andreas knew that there would be no yelling. He had forgiven Christine. "Christine, remember the day when we were going to your mother's house to tell her we wanted to get married?"

"Please Andreas don't bring up the past. That was a long time ago."

"Shh, quiet. Just listen," he whispered as he guided his finger on her lips and then kissed her as he fondled her breasts. "I miss them."

"They miss you too. Let's go home so you can get reacquainted with them."

"All in due time, all in due time. For now I need you to listen."

"All right. Please hurry. I want to go home."

"Remember before we went to see your mother Fr. Demitri came up behind us as we were holding hands?"

"Yes. I was so scared."

"I was also scared. Remember when he took us into the church to pray and told us about the devil?"

"Yes. What are you getting at?"

"What we didn't know was that he saw us coming out of the schoolhouse basement." Christine fell silent. "After Fr. Demitri's prayers and talk we went to see your mother. Remember? I told her that I was in love with you. All she did was send you to your room and you obeyed. You left me there with your mother to get thrown out."

"Andreas, please, why are you bringing this up? I thought you finally wanted to put all this behind us."

"Shh, I am. I do. What I realize now is that you were only sixteen-years old. What could you have done? What could either one of us have done. I just left."

"It was me who left you behind. It was me who never stuck around. And for that I'm sorry. Can you forgive me? Can you ever forgive me?"

Christine's eyes were now totally wet. Tears started to drip down her cheeks.

"Why are you saying this to me? Please stop talking. I want to go home. Please, don't talk about that day." She started to raise her voice. "Don't ever bring up that day again! I hate my mother and I hate you too! Why did you leave so fast? Why couldn't you wait around?" Why did you leave me there? Why did you leave me in Cyprus?" she asked as she started to cry hysterically. Andreas pulled her to him tight and held her as he whispered the words she always feared the most;

"I know about the baby. I'm sorry I left you but I didn't know," as he himself broke down in her arms.

"What? The baby? You know about the baby? Where were you? I needed you so much at that time. You disappeared. No one knew where you went. Your parents didn't even know. She made me go to the monastery. She made me give up my baby. I told Fr. Demitri but he didn't listen. I'm glad he's dead. I'm glad she's dead. She made me give up my baby. They pulled my baby out of my arms and took him away. He was a boy. A beautiful little boy and they took him from me. Where were you? I needed you. Why did you let them do that to me? I hate her. I hate all of you. I want my baby. How do you know about my baby? I want to find my baby. I want to hold my baby again." Christine was trying to breathe. She was hyperventilating. Andreas quickly brought her a glass of water. As he handed it to her she looked up at him and said, "I want to die."

Andreas grabbed her by the back of her head and faced her and asked; "Why would you want to die when I can take you to your son?"

"What? You know where he is? Where is he? They told me a family in Greece adopted him. How did you find out about him? Let's go. Let's get on a plane. How did you find him? Thank you. Andreas thank you for finding my son, our son."

"I didn't find him, he found me. He came to America looking for us."

"How? How did he find you?"

"Shh, listen, I'm going to give you the short story. Fr. Demitri, God bless his soul, lied to you and your mother. He never intended to let the baby go to Greece. None of us knew at the time, but my brother Costas and his wife Panayiota were having problems conceiving a child, so Fr. Demitri arranged to have them adopt the baby. My brother had him all this time. At first I hoped my brother didn't know that it was our child. But Fr. Demitri told Haji and Rebecca that he knew from the beginning. Why my brother never told me we'll never know. But it doesn't matter anymore. He's here. Our son is here. He's in a hotel room with Rebecca."

"Who's Rebecca, and they named him Haji?"

"His name is John Haji Ioannou. He likes to go by Haji. Rebecca is his school teacher. After the invasion they along with many other villagers escaped Vavla and went to the monastery for safety. They were safe for a short time. The monastery was then taken over and they were tortured before they were rescued. I get the impression that the women were repeatedly raped. After they were rescued, they were taken to the American Embassy. Let's go, now that you know part of the story, I want you to see our son."

"Where is he?"

"Let's go first. I'll tell you in the car." Andreas continued the story as he drove. "They flew in yesterday and checked into the International Hotel at Kennedy Airport. Rebecca went through the yellow pages and called the diners in Astoria until she found the right one."

"How did she know we had a diner?"

"Fr. Demitri told her. We were easy to find. We're listed in the phone books."

"Thank God for Fr. Demitri. I'm sorry what I said about being happy he's dead."

"I know you didn't mean it. That wasn't you talking. That was a very upset person who was forced to put her baby up for adoption."

"Thank you for understanding."

"Listen, at first I was upset that you never told me. But on my way out here I realized that you were afraid to tell me for fear of opening up old wounds. Believe me, I do understand and realize that I never should have left you, pregnant or not. But that's all behind us. We love each other and Haji will bring us even closer together," he said as he continued holding her hand.

Andreas continued explaining to Christine about Fr. Demitri telling Haji about the gold and some general taking half in exchange for passports for them.

"I told Rebecca that we would help her find an apartment and hopefully a teaching job at St. Demitrios where I would like to enroll Haji. We'll also need a two bedroom apartment for ourselves."

"What's Haji like?" What does he look like? I'm afraid to see him now. What will he think of me for giving him up? Will he resent me? I'm afraid. Andreas I'm so afraid."

"First of all, you *didn't* give him up. He was *taken* from you. So you have *nothing* to be afraid of. He's going to love you like the mother that you are. Second of all, you know what he looks like. You've been looking at him every day for the past nine years."

"What do you mean?"

"His photograph has been on our coffee table in the living room. He's been with us all this time and we didn't even know it."

"Oh my God Andreas. That's right."

"Besides, he's a very lucky young man."

"Why's that?" asked Christine.

"He has his mother's looks." Christine broke down again, this time with some joy. "He's tall. Tall like an Alexander. Thank God he doesn't have my height."

"I'm sure that he's handsome like his father. He's lucky that you are his father, as I'm lucky to have you as my husband. I love you so much. Another man would not have handled this the way you did."

"Thank you and I'm sorry that it was me who left *you*. There's the hotel. I'm going to call them from the lobby as to not surprise them at the door."

They got out of the car and Andreas held Christine by the hand. He knew she needed to be guided by the way her hand was trembling. They walked through the triple glass doors, went to the house phone, and without missing a beat Andreas dialed 407.

"Hello," answered Rebecca on the third ring.

"It's me, Andreas. I'm here. We're both here."

"Good, I'm coming down now. I'm going to the coffee shop while you three meet."

"No way, Christine wants to meet you too. You're family now. Just stay there, we're coming up."

"All right."

"Andreas, what was all that about?"

"Rebecca thought it would be best if the three of us met without her. She wanted to give us some privacy. I told her nothing doing."

"I'm glad. I can't wait to meet her too. But I'm also scared."

"There's nothing to be scared of," Andreas said as they walked into the elevator and pressed the number four. Andreas put his arm around Christine's shoulder and held her close to try to stop the shaking. When they stepped off the elevator they followed the sign to rooms 400-410 to the right.

"Let's go," he said as he led her by the hand to room 407 and knocked on the door.

Rebecca opened the door and pulled it back as she stayed behind it. Haji was standing next to the window looking as handsome as any twelve-year old can look. Christine took a step inside and started to cry.

"My baby," she cried. "I'm sorry. I'm so sorry. They *made* me do it. Can you ever forgive me?" as Andreas held her, while escorting her to Haji. Haji looked Christine in the eyes and said; "I think we look alike." Christine laughed with joy as she slowly caressed Haji's cheek.

"It's all right, he won't break," whispered Andreas. "You can hug your son."

Haji broke the ice first by hugging Christine. As she cried in his arms Andreas joined them. Within a few minutes the four of them were sitting and talking. Finally, Christine took her eyes off Haji and looked at Rebecca.

"Rebecca. My dear Rebecca. I understand that if it wasn't for you this would not be happening. I, I mean *we*, are indebted to you. I don't know how we can ever thank you. You are now part of our family."

"Thank you, Christine. Right now you three are the only people I know in America. I'm just as lost as anyone can be under these circumstances. I'm excited that Andreas can help me find an apartment and possibly a job. As you know, I'm a school teacher and would love to continue teaching. This hotel is expensive but for now it'll have to do."

"We have a small apartment but you can stay with us until you get your own place."

"Thank you but no. You three need all the alone time you can get. I'm fine for now. Tomorrow I'll take a taxi to Astoria and start looking for apartments. Andreas told me he knows real estate people."

"Yes, many realtors come into the diner. How about the four of us go looking together tomorrow? We're going to need a larger place anyway."

"That will be fine. Thank you."

CHAPTER

That evening Andreas took everyone out to dinner in Astoria. Christine insisted that Haji sit up front next to his father while she acquainted herself with Rebecca in the back while keeping her eyes on her son. They were excited to go to a restaurant together. They talked mostly about their future in America. When they finished dinner they strolled Ditmars Boulevard to familiarize Rebecca and Haji with the area since it was considered the Greekest part of Astoria.

When it was time to leave, Andreas drove by St. Demitrios Church to show Haji the school he would go to, and also show Rebecca where he would try to get her a job. Rebecca was impressed with all of Astoria, and seemed to love it. Haji, on the other hand was a little disappointed with the lack of space around. Astoria was in a big city. Haji was used to lots of land.

At nine o'clock Rebecca asked to be taken back to the hotel. Andreas waited in the car as Christine went with Rebecca and Haji to get his things. The two women chatted while Haji stuffed as much of his clothes into his overnight bag. The new clothes he bought today were still in four large shopping bags. Christine hugged Rebecca as did Haji when they left. Christine thanked Rebecca again for everything she did and told her that Andreas will definitely talk to Fr. Harry tomorrow about a job and also talk to a Cypriot lawyer friend about making sure all her paperwork was in order.

"Rebecca, we're going to keep the car all week, so Haji and I will pick you up at eleven tomorrow morning to go apartment hunting. Andreas will meet us sometime in the afternoon. He's going to open the diner and get things going there before he joins us."

"That'll be fine," Rebecca said as she watched them walk out of the hotel room feeling so alone.

During the car ride home Christine did most of the talking. Andreas didn't say much. He was doing a lot of thinking about the next few days. Haji's eyes lit up as Andreas passed Shea Stadium and told him that that's where the New York Mets played and sometime soon they were going to go there.

That evening when they were home it was already eleven o'clock. It was a little uncomfortable but they all made due. Christine made up the couch for Haji and promised him he would soon have his own bedroom. It would only be a matter of time.

Rebecca on the other hand enjoyed her long awaited hot bath thinking about her uncertainties.

Will she get a job?

Will she get an apartment?

Will she ever get Private Akman out of her mind?

CHAPTER

The next morning, Andreas was up at his usual time of 5:00 a.m. This time he left the house immediately to avoid waking Haji. At the diner, Yoyo put him through the mill with questions about where he was. Andreas didn't give her too much information. He did tell her that Christine was back and his brother and family were dead. She expressed her condolences and said that she's here to talk if he ever needs her.

At nine o'clock, Andreas left the diner and went to his lawyer friend and explained most of the last two days to him. The lawyer said that since the passports were official it shouldn't be an issue. The only problem they may have is that there were no birth certificates or Social Security cards. But that can be arranged through the Cypriot consulate and the Social Security office. Andreas thanked him and went home to Christine and Haji.

Christine and Haji prepared to get Rebecca. She told Andreas that she set up apartment appointments for one o'clock, but first she would take Haji and Rebecca to lunch. Andreas asked Haji if he wanted to go back to the diner with him but Christine thought it better to wait for something like that. They talked for about fifteen minutes before Andreas walked Christine and Haji to the car, and then walked back to the diner.

After the lunch crowd left and the diner started to slow down Andreas took a taxi to St. Demitrios to speak to Fr. Harry. They talked for over an hour. Because Fr. Harry was a priest, Andreas trusted him explicitly. Fr. Harry assured Andreas that his story was safe with him. As far as a job, there were two openings for the upcoming school year which started in two weeks. They were reviewing several applicants, but under the circumstances there shouldn't be any problem giving one to Rebecca. Fr. Harry made arrangements with Andreas to meet Rebecca tomorrow at noon. When their meeting was over Fr. Harry took Andreas into the church to pray. Andreas left St. Demitrios feeling light on his feet.

That evening they all met for dinner at *Koufous* restaurant on Ditmars Boulevard, where Andreas excitedly informed Rebecca that she had an interview with Fr. Harry tomorrow at noon.

"Thank you, Andreas. I hope it goes well. I don't know how I can ever thank you."

"Please Rebecca," Christine said as she held her hand. "Look what you've done for us," as she motioned towards Haji. "It's us who don't know how *we* can ever thank *you.*"

Before it became too emotional, Andreas asked how the apartment hunting went.

Christine explained that they found a nice size newly renovated one bedroom apartment for Rebecca on Ditmars Boulevard for $155 a month, a block from the elevated RR train. Christine also explained to Andreas how she took them both on the train to show Rebecca how to get to St. Demitrios in the hope that she would work there.

Rebecca was still beaming about tomorrow's interview.

"That sounds great, but what about us?" asked Andreas. "Did you find *us* an apartment?"

"No, we're not getting another apartment. I found us a house we can afford on 44th Street just two blocks from the diner. I think it's time we owned our own home with a backyard. It would not only be good for Haji but good for us too. You always wanted a vegetable garden, so now you can have one."

"Great idea. When can I see the house?"

"Well, Rebecca can move in September 1st which is in two days. We already went to *Sellenger Henshor* furniture store. She picked out some really nice furniture. They have everything in stock and will be delivered on the first. Our house is available to move in today. I figured if you like it we can move in immediately and pay the owners rent until we close."

"Sounds great. I'll see the house tomorrow. It looks like everything is going to be fine."

"Everything *is* fine," said Christine. "I can't wait to move into the house. It has three bedrooms, two bathrooms, a large kitchen, formal dining room, and a finished basement. It even has a garage. It's time we bought our own car too. You should see Haji's room. He's very excited, aren't you Haji?"

"Yes I am. It's a really nice house."

"Can I get a ride back to my hotel now?" asked Rebecca. "I have a busy day tomorrow."

"Sure," said Christine. "We can leave now."

Christine dropped Andreas off at the diner, and then drove Rebecca to her hotel. They agreed that an eleven o'clock pickup tomorrow morning will be perfect for her twelve o'clock meeting with Fr. Harry.

Once inside her hotel room Rebecca felt all alone. She missed Haji but knew that he was exactly where he belonged. She sat in the chair looking out of the window for an hour, nervous about her job interview tomorrow.

What if I don't get the job? I can't depend on Andreas and Christine the rest my life.

She needed a hot bath and filled the tub. She sat in the tub for an hour thinking about her past and present life. She could not get the rapes out of her head. The image of Private Akman kept going through her mind. At such a young age, he had become a monster. She wondered what kind of abuse he could be inflicting on some innocent soul at this moment.

Leaving the tub she stood naked in front of the mirror and noticed that all her bruises were gone. Not one black and blue was visible.

It was the invisible damage that scared her.

The emotional scars that she hoped would not be permanent.

CHAPTER

Three months had gone by since Haji found his biologic parents. He was now settled into his new home. He loved having his own room. He was enrolled at the St. Demitrios School and in his routine. Every morning Christine would make him breakfast. For the first two weeks Christine or Andreas walked him to school. But after those two weeks Haji insisted he walk alone. He was doing extremely well in his studies and making friends.

On Saturdays he worked at the diner washing dishes. Andreas felt that working will teach Haji responsibility and help build character. Yoyo was the only person who knew their story.

One Saturday, they were shorthanded on the second shift. So Andreas sent Haji home to spend time with Christine and do his homework. He needed him back at dinner time to stay until closing. Haji liked that. He liked the restaurant business and was excited about locking up the diner at night. He was starting to feel at home although he still missed his parents and little sister Mary.

That Saturday night a few minutes before closing, three teen-agers about sixteen-years old that looked like trouble came into the diner. Andreas knew these kids from the neighborhood. He didn't like them, especially the one named Melvin.

"Sorry, we're closed," said Andreas.

"Well, your doors were open," said Melvin.

"I know. I was just about to lock up."

"Bullshit. The door was open. You're serving us."

"Get out before I call the police."

"Call the police. See if I care."

Andreas started walking towards the phone when Melvin stepped in front of Andreas and put his hand on his chest to stop him.

"You're not calling anyone if you know what's good for you. Just go into the kitchen and make us three hamburgers and three French fries."

"I said get out. I'm calling the police."

"Melvin, fuck' um up," said one of his friends.

"Yeah, fuck' um up," the other chimed in.

As this was happening, Haji walked out of the kitchen and saw what was going on. By now Haji had grown another inch to 5'-8". He had seen too much abuse in his young age and still had a lot of anger in him.

"What the fuck are you looking at?" asked Melvin.

"If you don't get the out of here you're going to find out," said Haji.

"I'm shaking. Can't you see me shake?" Melvin motioned his hand shaking as he laughed.

Haji started thinking about Cyprus. All of a sudden he start-ed thinking about Private Akman.

"Haji, it's all right. Go back into the kitchen," said Andreas.

"Yeah, go back into the kitchen if you know what the fucks good for you," said Melvin.

"Why don't you come over here and show me what the fucks good for me," said Haji.

Melvin took a step towards Haji and Andreas instantly took a protective father's step in front of Melvin. Melvin put his hand on Andreas' chest and pushed him aside. Andreas lost his balance and fell to the floor.

"Don't ever put your hand on my father again!" Haji then walked up to Melvin and punched him in the nose and heard it break. The other two ran to Melvin's rescue but were met with nothing but flying punches. One went right down, the other put up his fists in a boxing position and waited for an opening to hit Haji. That opening never happened. Haji knocked him down with one punch. Then Haji got on top of Melvin and started beating him to a pulp. Andreas was shocked. The first thing he thought about was that he never heard Haji refer to him as his father. Let alone in a protective state.

Andreas instantly got up and pulled Haji off Melvin.

"I don't ever want to see you in this place again," Haji screamed at all of them.

"Haji, calm down, it's all right. Thank you. Where did you ever learn how to fight like that?"

"I don't know. I just got mad."

Andreas called the police but refused to press charges. The police informed Melvin and his friends that they are never to come back to the diner, or they would get arrested. They all agreed and wobbled out into the night not knowing what hit them. Andreas gave the police coffee and donuts to take with them but asked the police to stick around until he locked up. The police stuck around and even offered Andreas a ride home. Andreas thanked them but declined.

During the short walk home, Andreas expressed his feelings to Haji about the way he was non-stop beating up those guys. "I understand you wanting to protect me and I love you for it, but I think you went a little overboard."

"I'm sorry. I just couldn't help it."

"Forget it. Those guys are bad news. Be careful of them. I hope they don't try to get back at you."

"Don't worry. I'll stay away from them if I see them. But if they come after me, I'm not going to back down."

"Just be careful."

"I will."

⚊⚊

At home Christine was waiting up for them. The minute they walked in the house she knew something was wrong. Andreas didn't want to keep any secrets from her, especially about Haji. He told Christine what happened. She instantly started to cry as she hugged Haji.

"Be careful," she cried. "This isn't Vavla. There are some really bad people in New York. You must be careful. What if they had a knife?"

"I'm sorry. I won't do it again." But Haji knew. He knew what happened to his family in Vavla. He knew he wasn't going to let anything ever happen to his new family.

They sat talking a little while longer. Andreas expressed his feelings when he heard for the first time Haji referred to him as *my father.*

Haji lowered his head and realized it was time to refer to Andreas and Christine as his parents. They never pushed it. They knew it would take some time for Haji to totally except them.

"You know," Haji said. "In Cyprus I called my mother and father Mama and Baba. Here in America is it all right if I call you Mom, and Dad?"

Christine and Andreas instantly teared up.

"Of course you can," Christine said. "It would be music to my ears. It's something I thought I would never hear. Now, let's all wash up and go to bed. There's church tomorrow."

CHAPTER

Three weeks later it was a week before Christmas. Andreas and Haji walked to the Mike's hardware store where they sold Christmas trees while Christine waited home making hot chocolate. It was a happy time for everyone. Although Haji missed his parents, he was really trying to adjust. When they brought home the tree, Christine showed excitement. They were a family. They decorated the tree with love while they sipped hot chocolate.

That evening they drove to Macy's on Queens Boulevard to do some Christmas shopping. Andreas left Christine in the dress department while he took Haji to the jewelry department to get a few things for Christine from Haji. When they met Christine back at the dress department it was Christine's turn to take Haji to the men's department to buy Andreas some items. Then they went to the jewelry department to pick up something for Rebecca while Andreas waited in the car.

≒⊹ ⊹≒

That week Christine shopped for Haji. It seemed that she wanted to make up for lost time, because when Christmas morning arrived it was all about Haji and his gifts. Haji never saw so many presents under a tree before.

That afternoon Basil and Athena came over followed by Rebecca. The house was filled with love and presents. Christine was in her glory. She had a house full of people on Christmas day with the addition of her son. Haji was busy trying on his new Puma and Converse All Stars sneakers. He even got a brand new baseball glove along with so many various new clothes. Christine sat with the ladies in the living room as Athena and Rebecca were complimenting how great the house looked and how beautiful the table was set with her new Christmas china. Christine kept looking around as though she was dreaming. Here she was sitting in her living room with friends and family on Christmas day watching her son watch television, and seeing Andreas and Basil in the kitchen carving the prime rib together.

That was a sight she thought would never happen.

During dinner there was talk of all subjects. The one subject that was never talked about in front of Haji was Cyprus. They would never talk about it unless Haji brought it up, which was never.

"Rebecca, how do you like teaching at St. Demitrios?" asked Basil.

"I really love it. At first it was a bit of a challenge. I didn't know anyone, nor did I know their system. But after a few weeks it was great."

"What subject are you teaching?"

"Because I'm fluent in both Greek and English I'm teaching English as a second language. There are so many students from Greece that don't speak any English at all. I love the kids and I think they love me too."

"I'm sure they do. How do you like taking the train?"

"It's fun. In the beginning I actually walked home a couple of Fridays just to familiarize myself with Astoria. Besides I like the exercise. But I'm very busy with school work. I come home, I grab a bite to eat and I'm constantly making lesson plans and checking homework. I'm not complaining, but it's a lot of work."

"Have you made friends?" Athena chimed in.

"Not really. Everyone at the school is really nice and a couple of other women teachers and I have gone out to lunch and even dinner one time. I'm still new in this area. I'm not worried about making friends right now. I want to concentrate on being a good American school teacher."

But who was Rebecca kidding.

She wanted to make friends.

She was just afraid.

"Nonsense, all work and no play? That's not good. Have you gone to any of the Cypriot night clubs? There are quite a few. And there are countless Greek night clubs all over Ditmars Boulevard."

"Yes, I see them all the time. I've never gone inside. I can never go to places like those alone. That's just not me."

"I understand. How about next week? It's New Year's Eve. How about all of us go together? Basil knows the owners of several those night clubs."

"Count us out," Christine jumped in. "No night club for Haji. This year the three of us will stay home and watch the ball come down in Times Square together."

"You know your brother. He needs to go to a night club New Year's Eve."

"I have an idea," Athena said to Rebecca. "Why don't you come out with me and Basil on New Year's Eve?"

"I don't know. I'll have to think about it."

"Come on, a young attractive woman like you should not be home alone on New Year's Eve. You're coming out with us and that's final."

"I'll think about it. Thank you."

⊷ ⊶

Later that week, Christine took Rebecca shopping for a new out-fit for New Year's Eve. Rebecca was somewhat excited to go to a night club. She always wondered what it would be like but was not ready to venture inside alone.

"Now that's a beautiful dress," said Christine. "You're going to drive the men crazy."

"You don't think that it might be a little tight?" replied Rebecca as she admired herself in the mirror.

"Yes, it might be a little tight. But you have the figure for it."

"You know what, you're right. It does look good, doesn't it?"

"Yes it does, now let's go pick out a pair of shoes."

CHAPTER

New Year's Eve-1974

On New Year's Eve Basil and Athena parked their car in front of Rebecca's apartment at nine o'clock. Upstairs Basil's eyes lit up when Rebecca opened the door. She greeted them with the stunning blue dress that emphasized her gorgeous figure. Basil couldn't take his eyes off her. The dress was a little tight but it didn't cling. It was classy. It fit her perfectly, as she exposed the slightest bit of cleavage with her beautiful wavy dark brown shoulder length hair.

"You look stunning," said Athena. "And those shoes, they're beautiful. Look at her Basil. Isn't she gorgeous?"

"Yes she is," Basil smiled.

"Do you think so?" Rebecca smiled back. "I want to thank you both for inviting me out tonight. I know it's about time I ventured out but I could never find the courage to do it alone."

"And your apartment, it's gorgeous," said Athena.

"Thank you, let me show you around," Rebecca said as she proudly led them through her apartment. Athena kept complementing everything from her curtains, to her kitchen, and living room. When she showed them the bedroom it was all about the bedspread and the pillowcases.

"It's beautiful. You really have a nice place here."

"Thank you."

"Well ladies, it's time to go," said Basil. "Rebecca, I'm parked right downstairs but I think we should walk the three blocks; we'll never find another parking space on Ditmars."

"All right, let me get my coat."

When Rebecca went back into her bedroom to get her coat, Basil whispered to Athena, "It's not her shoes that I was looking at. She is gorgeous. I can't wait to introduce her around tonight."

When Rebecca returned with her coat, Basil, with a gentlemanly gesture helped her on with it.

"Thank you, now I'm ready. Let's go."

They walked the three blocks in the chilled air. Basil was in the middle with Rebecca on his left and Athena on his right. Athena was careful not to hold Basil's arm as she usually does for fear it might make Rebecca feel like the third wheel.

At the nightclub Basil checked the ladies coats, and they were then escorted to their table for three. Basil was careful not to overwhelm Rebecca with people. He knew she was shy so he wanted to keep it quaint. The waiter brought over a bottle of wine, compliments of one of Basil's many friends. This was all new to Rebecca being from a small village as she watched the waiter pour the wine and waited for Basil's approval before he left. No one ever waited for Rebecca's approval for anything.

"So, how do you like the place so far?" asked Athena.

"It's great. I love the music. I think I can get used to places like this," she said as she picked up a couple of hors d'oeuvres that the waiter just brought over.

By ten o'clock people were drinking and spending time on the dance floor.

"Come on Rebecca let's dance," said Athena. She motioned to the crowded dance floor where everyone held hands and went around in a circle; one of the many traditional Greek dances.

"Yes, let dance, it's been a long time. I'm out tonight. I need to have a little fun." A minute after they were dancing a successful thirty-year old banker friend of Basil's named Michael Stylianou came to the table and asked Basil who the pretty lady was that accompanied him and Athena. Basil explained that she was a friend of the family who recently came over from Cyprus.

"Why don't you go dance with them?"

Michael looked again towards the dance floor at Rebecca; he knew what he needed to do.

"I think I will. Wish me luck."

"Good luck."

Michael walked to the circle of dancers and suddenly had an idea. He decided not to cut between Athena and Rebecca. He decided to cut in on Athena's left as Athena held Rebecca's hand to her right. Athena has known Michael for quite some time and always liked him. He whispered to Athena that she looked tired as he glanced at Rebecca. Athena took the hint. As tradition goes with Greek dancing, when one leaves the dance line, she pulled the hands on each side of her and joined them together as she said she was pooped.

When Athena returned to her table, Basil laughed at what she did.

"Do you think it'll work?" Basil asked.

"I think it already has. Look at them. They keep leaning over to talk to each other. Michael's a really nice guy; I think they could be a nice couple."

"I don't know. I've been watching him; he hasn't looked at her shoes yet. But he is glancing at other parts of her," he laughed.

"Very funny. I like them together. They're a good match."

When the song finished the band switched to a slow dance. Michael quickly introduced himself and politely asked Rebecca for the next dance. When Rebecca accepted, Michael instantly held her. The dance took about five minutes. Michael let Rebecca do most of the talking as she told him that she recently came to America from Cyprus and was teaching at St. Demitrios School. Michael explained that he was also Cypriot and came to America when he was ten-years old and was an investment officer for Manufacturers Hanover Trust in Manhattan. When the dance was over Michael escorted Rebecca to her table and said hello to Basil.

"Michael, I see you've met Rebecca," Basil said as Michael again thanked Rebecca for the dance.

"Why don't you sit down with us for a while, we have this bottle of wine that we barely made a dent in," as he motioned for the waiter to bring a chair.

"Yes, please sit with us a little," added Athena as Michael looked at Rebecca as she nodded her head with approval.

"Sure, thank you." When the waiter brought the chair Michael ordered a bottle of champagne.

For the next thirty minutes they talked about Astoria and Cyprus. Surprisingly Rebecca was able to discuss some Cypriot politics, but Michael kept turning the subject over to Rebecca. She seemed interesting, and Michael wanted to get to know her better. Athena suggested to Michael to sit with them the rest of the evening since he came to the night club with several other single men.

"Yes, I also think it's a good idea that you stay," added Rebecca. "All right, I'm here for the night."

The rest of the evening went well for everyone. Rebecca and Michael danced and talked. Athena accompanied Rebecca to the ladies room a few times to talk about Michael. Finally when the band leader started the countdown 10, 9, 8, everyone started to chime in with him. When the band leader went 3, 2, 1, the place erupted. Everyone was yelling Happy New Year. Strangers were going around kissing each other. When Athena finished kissing Basil, she glanced over to Rebecca and Michael. She saw them kiss and heard Michael say that he was happy to finish off 1974 with her and to start off 1975 with her too.

"Yes," said Rebecca. "I'm also glad that we met. It's only been a few months but I'm starting to really feel like America is going to work for me."

The rest of the evening went quickly. The four sat and talked about many different subjects, but Rebecca wanted to dance, and Michael was only too happy to dance with her. It didn't matter what the dance was. It could have been Greek, American, fast, or slow. They were a match. For the first time since the invasion a little over five months ago, Rebecca wasn't thinking about that time.

Athena decided she needed to fake a headache. When she announced they were leaving, Michael immediately offered to escort Rebecca home. Once again Athena's plan worked.

By 3:00 a.m. the night club was closing. Michael took Rebecca's coat ticket and handed it to the coat check lady and left her a five dollar tip. When she handed him Rebecca's and his overcoat he wished her a happy and healthy New Year. The coat check lady thanked him and watched the tall handsome man with the expensive suit help Rebecca on with her coat. *What a lucky lady,* she thought.

Michael and Rebecca walked slowly down Ditmars Boulevard towards her building. When they reached her building, he escorted her upstairs to the safety of her door. She took out her key and saw the way Michael was looking at her.

"Rebecca, I had a wonderful New Year's Eve. I must admit, I really didn't want to come out tonight but my friends sort of twisted my arm," he smiled. "I'm so glad that I did. I had a wonderful time."

"Me too, I also didn't want to come out tonight but Athena and Basil talked me into it and I'm so happy that I did."

"I'm also happy you did." he said as he smiled at her and stared into her eyes. "Rebecca, I would like to see you again if I may. Can I have your phone number?"

"Yes you can, I would like that." Michael took out a pen and a small piece of paper he had in his overcoat and handed it to her. He wanted to play it safe without Rebecca having to invite him inside for a paper and pen if she didn't have one in her pocketbook. He didn't want to go inside her apartment. He wanted to be a gentleman. After she wrote it down, she looked into his eyes afraid if Michael would try anything with her. But Michael, being the gentleman that he was, accepted the paper, thanked her again, expressed the wonderful time he had, and gave her a small kiss on the cheek.

"I'll call you tomorrow."

"Yes, I would like that."

"Good night Rebecca."

"Good night Michael."

Rebecca entered her apartment, closed the door, and locked it. She leaned back against the door and smiled as tears rolled down her cheeks. After a minute she entered her bedroom and took off her coat. She looked at herself in the mirror and congratulated herself for holding it all together. She quickly undressed and put on her flannel nightgown and got into her bed. She laid there looking up at the ceiling thinking about her very first New Year's Eve in America.

Everything went perfectly. The food. The drinks. The company. Especially the company.

It was all perfect. Michael was a good man. He seemed to really like her, as she did him.

She looked forward to his phone call tomorrow.

Then she started to cry.

"Damn you, damn you," she cried. "Damn you Private Akman."

CHAPTER

The next morning, Rebecca woke up at eleven with puffy eyes. She didn't know if it was from crying herself to sleep or irritated from all the people smoking the night before. She took a long look at herself in the mirror and started to cry. She needed to get hold of herself. She desperately wanted to move on with her life but the only way that could happen is if she left the atrocities of her past behind.

She wanted to feel good.

She needed to feel good.

She put on her robe and went into the kitchen to make a cup of coffee. She loved her kitchen. Everything there was brand new.

Brand new.

Just like her life in America.

It's a new year.

A new country.

A new job.

A new life in a place that only Haji knew what she had been through. She filled her Pyrex coffee pot and put it on the stove to wait until it perked while she took out a plastic container of cottage cheese. She sat at the table thinking about what she was going to do with her spare time with the week off. She started looking over her lesson plans for the following week to pass a little time before her coffee was ready when the phone rang.

"Hello."

"Good morning Rebecca, I hope I didn't wake you."

"Good morning Athena, no, you didn't wake me. I've been up for a half hour or so."

"Good, did you sleep well?"

"Yes I slept like a baby." *She lied.*

"Good. We had a wonderful time last night. Wasn't it great?"

"Yes it was. I had a great time too. I wanted to call you later on today to thank you for inviting me, because if you didn't, I probably would have fallen asleep before the New Year."

"Now I'm even happier I invited you. So, what did you think of Michael? He's a great guy isn't he? He's handsome too. Did you know he's a very successful banker? He did walk you home, didn't he? What do you think of him? Do you think you'll see him again? Do you like him? I think he likes you. You two really looked good together."

"Athena, which question do you want me to answer first?" laughed Rebecca. "Everything was fine. Michael was a lot of fun and also a complete gentleman. He not only walked me home but he even walked me upstairs to my door. And in case you are wondering, I didn't invite him in, and he didn't ask to come in either. But he did ask me for my phone number and yes, I did give it to him. He said he would call me today."

"That's great. I'm happy for you. I'm happy for you both."

"Well, it's only a phone number. He didn't ask me to marry him or anything like that," Rebecca giggled.

"I know, I know. I just have a good feeling about all this."

"Athena, I really mean it when I said that I had a wonderful time. Thank you again for inviting me. I'll speak to you soon. Good-bye."

"Good-bye."

Rebecca hung up and felt a little better. She knew what Athena was trying to do and loved her for it. When her coffee was ready, she poured a large mug and sat at the table. Needing to feel secure, she continued looking over her students work. She loved her students and knew they loved her too. They made her feel important, as though she belonged.

She needed to be loved.

She needed to belong.

Halfway through her cottage cheese and coffee, Rebecca's phone rang again. This time it was Michael.

"Good morning Rebecca. Happy New Year to you again."

"Why thank you Michael. Happy New Year to you again too."

"Thanks. Did you sleep well?"

"Yes I did," she lied again. *Why is everyone all of a sudden interested in my sleep today?*

"Good, I'm glad to hear it. What are you doing now? It's almost lunch time. Can I come by and take you to lunch?"

Rebecca fell silence.

"Hello. Hello. Are you there? Did I say something wrong?"

"No no no. I'm sorry. I just took a sip of my coffee." She lied again. Everything was happening too fast. But deep down she wanted to go. "Michael, I know that it's almost noon, but right now I'm having my breakfast. I did go to bed after 3:00 a.m. Remember?"

"Yes I do. I was with you. Do you remember?" he laughed. "I'll tell you what. It is a little early. I do apologize for calling so early."

"Please don't apologize. I'm glad you called. I really am."

"All right then, how about we do this? Finish your breakfast and relax the rest of the afternoon. I'll pick you up at five and take you to dinner instead."

"You know what Michael? Yes, I would like that. Five o'clock sounds great. And Michael, please, nothing fancy. Okay? Please, something casual."

"Casual it'll be. See you at five."

Excited that Michael called, Rebecca sat and finished her breakfast. She was looking so forward to seeing him again. Since she did have a few hours before she needed to get ready, she decided to tidy up her apartment a little. Although it didn't need tiding up at all. She lived alone and worked a lot so her apartment was always clean. She washed her breakfast dish and coffee mug and went around dusting. Then she sat for an hour doing some school work. But between going to bed late, and all the school work she did, she decided that her still puffy eyes needed some rest. So she set her alarm clock for four o'clock and napped.

When the alarm woke her, she felt a lot better. She needed a shower from the night before. So she quickly got out of bed and brushed her teeth before she took off her dreadful flannel nightgown. She stayed under the hot water for thirty minutes washing away anything that needed to be removed. It didn't matter if it was sweat from the night before or anything that was on her mind. She needed to watch everything go down the drain. She spent twenty minutes blow drying her hair trying to put in a slight wave. Since she hadn't been out all day she didn't know what the weather was like so she turned on the news. She listened as she dressed. It turned out it was fifty degrees on that New Year's Day.

She wanted to look good for Michael but still needed to keep warm. So she decided on a pair of black jeans with boots up to her calves. Then she opened her lingerie drawer and chose one of her new Cross Your Heart bras. As she stood in front of the mirror looking at herself in her black jeans and white Cross Your Heart Bra that really lifted and separated her 36C sized breasts the doorbell rang. She ran to the door and looked into the peep hole and saw him.

"Just a minute Michael, just give me a minute." Before Michael had a chance to answer Rebecca ran into her bedroom and quickly put on her red turtleneck that emphasized her figure. She quickly looked in the mirror, fluffed up her hair, ran to the door, and opened it.

"Hi Michael," she greeted him with a small kiss on his cheek. "Please come in. I just need a minute to get my jacket."

"Take your time, you look beautiful today," he added.

"Thank you."

"You have a nice place here," he said as he watched her hurry into the bedroom to get her jacket. "It feels like a really warm home."

"Thank you," she said as she walked towards Michael trying to find a sleeve of her jacket.

"Here, let me help you with that," as he stepped behind her and helped her on with her jacket.

"Thank you."

"I really like your apartment. Are you sure you're a school teacher and not a home decorator?"

"Thanks for the compliment. But yes, I really am a school teacher that enjoys decorating."

"I can see that. I guess it takes a woman to add a woman's touch," he said as he admired the small little knickknacks on the shelves. "Are you ready to go?"

"As a matter of fact, I'm starving."

"Good, let's go."

Downstairs Rebecca felt the cold air and immediately zipped her jacket. She wasn't used to the cold. In Cyprus the weather was eighty degrees in the winter. So this cold weather was something totally new to her.

"Not used to the cold I see," Michael smiled.

"No I'm not."

"It's only fifty degrees with no wind. It's a heat wave," he laughed. "Wait until February and March. Sometimes it goes down to the single digits."

"I'm not looking forward to that. But I'm in America now. It's my home, so I'm getting prepared. By the way, where are we going for dinner?"

"There's a new restaurant that just opened a few blocks from here called The Parthenon. I understand that the Greek and Cypriot food there is terrific. You do like Greek and Cypriot foods don't you?" There was a slight hesitation; Michael quickly asked her if she would like to eat somewhere else.

"Well, since you asked, I'm going to tell you. I've been eating Greek and Cypriot food my entire life. And please don't get me wrong, I love our type of food. I'm especially proud of my heritage but one time a few of us teachers went out and we had Italian food that I really enjoyed."

"You like Italian food?" Michael asked surprised. "I love Italian food. There's an Italian restaurant a few blocks from here. The food there is out of this world. I just thought that since you're new to America you might be homesick for Cyprus."

There was silence.

Michael looked at her and saw her eyes water. "Rebecca, are you all right? Is it something I said?"

Silence again.

"Rebecca, what's wrong?"

Silence again.

"Michael, I'm sorry. I'm not feeling very well. I think I need to go home."

"Why? What did I say? You were fine a minute ago. Five minutes ago you were starving. What happened?"

"It has nothing to do with you. It's me. I'm just not feeling well. It just came on suddenly."

"Come on, the Italian food at Mamma Garuccio's is really out of this world. Come on; if you continue not feeling well I'll take you home. No questions asked. I promise."

"Well, I am still hungry."

"Good."

"Michael, can you do me a favor?"

"Sure, anything."

"I'm in America now. Please don't ask me about Cyprus anymore. Please."

Michael looked at Rebecca's sad eyes and wondered what was going on inside this beautiful person's head that was making her so sad.

He wanted to help her but didn't know how.

Those beautiful eyes looked so sad.

"You have my word. I won't bring it up again. Now, I don't know about you but I'm in the mood for Mamma Garuccio's lasagna."

"I never had lasagna before, the one time I ate Italian food I had chicken cutlet parmesan. But I'm willing to try the lasagna."

"I'll tell you what we'll do. We'll order one chicken cutlet parmesan and one lasagna and split it."

"Now that sounds great. I'm starving again."

"Good, let's go." They did an about face and walked in the opposite direction towards Mamma Garuccio's restaurant. This time Rebecca grabbed Michael's arm as they walked.

"Feeling better?" he asked.

"Much better thank you." They continued walking up Ditmars Boulevard towards 31st Street and turned right. They passed many restaurants that were full. Many had lines out the door. When they reached Mamma Garuccio's they noticed a line of about twenty people.

"Oh no, look at all those people. We'll never get in," said Rebecca.

"Don't worry; you want chicken cutlet parmesan, you're getting chicken cutlet parmesan. I'll show you how it's done." They continued walking past Mamma Garuccio's to the corner phone booth. Michael took out a business card from his wallet and dialed the restaurant.

"Mamma Garuccio's, how can I help you?"

"Dorothy?"

"Speaking."

"Hi Dart, this is Michael Stylianou."

"Michael, how are you? Happy New Year. What can I do for you?"

"I need a favor. I'm with a very dear friend of mine who is dying to taste a piece of your wonderful lasagna," he winked at Rebecca and she smiled back at him, "but the line is out the door."

"No problem. You know the ally in the back?"

"Yes I do."

"Good, go to the seventh door. I'll be waiting."

"Thanks Dart, I owe you one."

"Are you kidding, I still owe *you* a few."

As they started walking up the dark alley Rebecca went from holding Michael's arm to squeezing it.

"Do you know where you're going?" she asked.

Before Michael could answer, the door opened and there stood Dorothy Garuccio. Dorothy stood just 4'-9" tall and slightly overweight. But where she lacked in good looks, she made it up in personality.

"Michael, it's been too long. Come over here and give Mamma a Happy New Year hug." Rebecca let go of Michael's arm as Michael gave Mamma Garuccio a big hug.

"Mamma, it's great to see you. I'm glad business is good."

"Business is great, especially today. Everyone's hangover is subsiding and the whole world is hungry. Now, who is this beautiful young lady with you?"

"I'm sorry, this is my very dear friend Rebecca and she loves Italian food."

"Well you came to the right place with the right guy," she said as she gave Rebecca a hug. "Please, come in out of the cold. I have the perfect table for you." They followed Dorothy through the kitchen where all they heard was clanking of pots and pans and dishes along with only Italian speaking kitchen help. As they made their way through the kitchen Rebecca couldn't believe all the different types of Italian foods. The smells were to die for. They continued through the kitchen right out into the dining room to a small table for two ten feet from a beautiful fireplace that gave off just enough heat to feel the warmth without being too hot.

"The best table in the house, and I'm sending over Mario, my best waiter. Give me your coats. I'll have them checked." Michael helped Rebecca off with her jacket and then took off his and handed them to Dorothy.

When they sat Rebecca was impressed. She looked around at the place. There were bottles of wine on shelves along with pictures of Italy with photographs of different villages. She was especially impressed with all the vintage photographs of old Italian people.

"Michael, I love the restaurant. Dorothy seems very nice. How do you know her?"

"She's a client of mine. Remember, I'm an investment banker. I helped her make a lot of money."

"Good evening, my name is Mario. I'll be your waiter this evening. Dorothy asked that I bring you this bottle of wine." Michael's eyes lit up as he looked at the Bordeaux Merlot dated 1955. Rebecca watched as Mario opened the bottle and poured a small amount in a glass for Michael's approval. Michael swirled the wine, took a sip, and nodded his approval with delight. Mario then filled his glass halfway and filled Rebecca's the same.

"Michael, this is really a nice place. I did say casual, didn't I?"

"Yes you did."

"Well if this is casual I'm afraid to see what formal is," she smiled.

"To tell you the truth The Parthenon restaurant is a little on the casual side. But when you mentioned chicken cutlet parmesan I upped it a little. I hope you're not upset?" he smiled.

"Not at all," Rebecca said as she sipped her wine.

"Excuse me love birds." They looked up and saw Dorothy. "So Rebecca, you like lasagna?"

"Dorothy," Michel interrupted. "Rebecca is new to America. The only Italian meal she has had so far is chicken cutlet parmesan. I told her about your lasagna and she's dying to try it."

"I'm trying something new this year. I'm starting a tasting menu. It's something entirely new in the restaurant industry. There are so many different meals and everyone wants them all. So I now have a five course tasting menu. It starts off with a penne-alla-vodka, chicken cutlet parmesan, veal marsala, shrimp scampi, and lasagna. Plus a dessert. This way anyone who wants Italian food can taste a little variety. You can also substitute if you like."

"How does that sound to you Rebecca?" asked Michael.

"It sounds great, I can't wait to try everything."

The rest of the evening went great for Rebecca and Michael. They talked about her job and how she loved her students. Michael explained how he worked his way up from bank teller to one of the youngest senior vice presidents at Manufacturers Hanover Trust.

As an investment banker he advised Dorothy and her husband who died a year ago to invest in companies like IBM and a new TV computer game called Atari. They made a small fortune. Rebecca was extremely impressed with Michael. She couldn't remember ever having such a wonderful time. She kept emphasizing to Michael about how much she enjoyed all five courses.

At eight o'clock they left the restaurant. Rebecca gave Dorothy a big hug and thanked her for such a delicious dinner as Dorothy told Michael to be good to Rebecca, "She's a good catch, don't mess it up."

"I'll try not to," Michael said while hugging Dorothy.

Outside the weather was much chillier. This time when Rebecca held Michael's arm she nudged closer. They didn't talk much. Both were thinking about the wonderful evening. Finally Michael spoke.

"Well Rebecca, I know you have the rest of the week off but tomorrow I have to go back to work. I'll give you a call tomorrow night if that's all right with you?"

"That'll be fine. I'd like that."

"Great, what do you have planned this week that you're off? Anything exciting?"

"No, nothing too exciting. Tomorrow I'll spend part of the day at the laundromat and then I have some lesson planning for school. I need to do some food shopping. Stuff like that. Oh I almost forgot, I'm busy tomorrow night."

"Really," Michael said with a little concerned jealousy. "Can I ask what you're doing?"

"No need to ask. You know my plans. I'm going to be on the phone with you," she said as she looked him in the eyes and then put her head on his shoulder as he automatically kissed her on top of her head. They walked the last block with her head still on his shoulder with his arm around her.

When they reached her building, Rebecca insisted that since it was still early there was no need for Michael to walk her upstairs to her door. Michael didn't want to push the issue so he decided to leave it be. But before Rebecca went inside, she gave him a slight kiss on his lips and went upstairs, but not before thanking him for a wonderful evening and telling him that she was looking forward to speaking to him tomorrow night.

The next evening was Wednesday. Michael called Rebecca as promised. They talked for an hour. They both felt a connection. They wanted to continue to get to know each other further. Unfortunately, Michael had to go to Boston on business Friday morning and wasn't able to see Rebecca until the following weekend.

He promised to call her again from Boston which is exactly what he did almost every night.

CHAPTER

T he following Monday Rebecca was back at school. She decided to give her students a break before hitting the books again. They had an open class discussion on what they did during their Christmas–New Year's break. Most didn't do much. Only one student went to Florida to visit relatives. Before recess, Rebecca told her students that when they returned, they were going to hit the books.

Ten minutes after recess was over the principal came into Rebecca's classroom to inform her that she will sit in on her class temporally because Fr. Harry needed to see her immediately.

"What's wrong?" asked Rebecca.

"I'm not sure," *she lied.*

Rebecca grabbed her coat and walked down the three flights of stairs and exited the school to the church next door where Fr. Harry had his office.

"Miss Ioannou, Fr. Harry's expecting you," said Mrs. Noulis his secretary. "Just go right in."

"Thank you Mrs. Noulis and Happy New Year to you."

"Oh yes Miss Ioannou, thank you. Happy New Year to you too."

When Rebecca entered Fr. Harry's office she noticed Haji sitting on a chair in the corner. Haji looked sad, while Fr. Harry looked angry.

"Miss Ioannou, please come in and sit down." Usually Rebecca would do the respectful thing by kissing the priest's hand, but the way Fr. Harry motioned to Rebecca to sit, she knew Fr. Harry wanted to get down to business. "Miss Ioannou, thank you for coming on short notice. With Haji here I'm sure you figured there's a problem."

"Yes Father, what's going on?"

"Haji, would you like to explain to Miss Ioannou why you're here?" Haji didn't say a word. "Haji, I'm speaking to you," said Fr. Harry, this time a little louder. "You're in enough trouble as it is. I don't think you want to be in anymore trouble. Do you? If you don't start talking I'm going to suspend you."

Again Haji didn't say a word.

"Haji, what's going on?" asked Rebecca in a motherly tone. "Speak to me. Speak to me now."

Haji instantly answered Rebecca, as Fr. Harry watched the bond between Haji and Rebecca.

"I didn't do anything wrong!" he yelled. "I didn't do anything wrong! They started it! It was them! Not me!"

"What did they do?" asked Rebecca. "Who started it? And who is them?"

"It seems that Haji likes to fight," added Fr. Harry. "I'm beginning to think he's a bully. This is the fourth time since the beginning of the school year he's been to my office for fighting. His mother and father are on their way here now."

Rebecca knew about the fighting but never said anything. She didn't want to get involved. But now that Fr. Harry called her to his office she needed to step up. No one knew Haji the way Rebecca did. She knew all his inner secrets, as he knew hers.

She needed to protect him.

"Fr. Harry. May I have a little alone time with Haji please? I think I can get through to him."

"All right, you have my blessing. But this is it. I will not tolerate this sort of behavior in my school. You have about five minutes before his parents get here." Fr. Harry left his office thinking that he can never discipline Haji because of all the things he's been through. He was trying to imagine all the things Haji's been through that he didn't even know about from other heartbreaking stories from others who recently escaped from Cyprus.

"Haji, speak to me. I know about the fights. I know that there are more than four incidents. What's going on? You're the biggest kid in the school. I've never known you to fight. Haven't we've seen enough fighting in our lives. Fr. Harry thinks you're a bully. Haven't we've seen enough bullying? You and I have seen enough bullying for many lifetimes. Why are you doing this?"

"Miss Economou…"

"What did you say? Don't ever call me that again! Do you hear me? Miss Economou doesn't exist. Do you hear me? She doesn't exist," Rebecca scolded.

"I'm sorry, I forgot. No, I can't forget. I'm trying real hard to forget but I can't. I can't! I can't! I can't!" Haji cried. By now Haji was crying hysterically in Rebecca's arms. "I can't forget anything. You're the only person who knows what I've been through. There was so much I wanted to do to help the people in Cyprus but couldn't. I couldn't help anyone. I couldn't help you. I wanted to help you so bad but couldn't. I couldn't help my parents or my sister." he continued to cry. "I can't forget that. You remember.

You've been through more. How did you forget? I can't seem to forget anything. It's all still alive in my head. Why did they have to kill so many people? And the things they did to the girls. The things they did to you. How could you forget?"

"Forget? Me forget? I'll never forget. I've been trying to get those things out of my mind but to no avail. So let me give you some advice Haji. You will never ever forget, and neither will I." she cried. "You and I will have to learn to live with it. Do you hear me? We'll learn to live with it!"

At this time Christine, Andreas, and Fr. Harry entered the office and saw the two of them crying.

"Haji, what happened?" asked Christine. "What's going on? Are you all right? Fr. Harry told me you were in a fight. Are you hurt?"

"Not now!" Rebecca turned and yelled. "Not now! Get out! Get out of this room all of you! Do you hear me? Not now!"

"He's my son! Don't tell me to get out! He needs me! I'm his mother! Not you! I'm not leaving!"

"I know you're his mother! I know he needs you! But not now! Now he needs me! I need to talk to him alone! Get out! Get out now!" Rebecca repeated as she stood to face them. Fr. Harry quickly ushered Christine out of the office while Andreas stood there in a daze. "Please Andreas, I need you to leave too," Rebecca said in a low tone as she started to break down again. Andreas looked at Rebecca, then at Haji, and then at Rebecca again, and left to comfort Christine.

"Are you all right?" Rebecca asked as she turned to Haji.

"I don't know. I can't take it anymore. I didn't do anything wrong."

"You're fighting. Why are you fighting? I don't understand the fighting."

"I wasn't fighting. I was protecting."

"Protecting? Protecting who? Who were you protecting?"

"Kids. Kids that are being picked on every day, that's who I was protecting."

"Who's picking on whom?"

"Christos, do you know Christos, the fifth grader who walks around with his hand in his pocket?"

"Yes, I know the boy. What about him?"

"Do you know why he walks around with his hand in his pocket?"

"Yes I do. Most everyone knows why. He's missing two fingers and is embarrassed by it. So he keeps his hand in his pocket."

"I know too. We all know. The whole school knows. There was a bunch of kids in my class making fun of him. They were high fiving each other in front of him and asking Christos to high three them. Christos didn't want to but they continued to ask him. When Christos started to cry they took his hand out of his pocket and forced him to high three them. When I saw the way Christos was crying I couldn't take it anymore. It felt like I was back in Cyprus but this time there wasn't anyone with a gun to stop me. So I helped Christos. I beat the shit out of them."

"Haji, watch your language in Fr. Harrys office."

"I don't care," Haji cried. "I don't like Fr. Harry. I want Fr. Demitri. I wish Fr. Demitri was here. I miss Fr. Demitri. I want Fr. Demitri. The other day these kids from the public school were making fun of Louloutha because she was flat chested. They were pushing her around saying things like *let me see your itty bitty titties.* I was afraid they were going to do to her what was done to the girls in Cyprus. I was helping her. I wasn't hurting anyone. All I was trying to do was help people."

For several minutes Haji and Rebecca cried in each other's arms while wondering what the future will bring for them as peace of mind. Rebecca was especially concerned about Haji's violent behavior even though he was defending someone. She would try in the future to explain to him about taking the law into his own hands.

"Haji, are you ready to face your parents and Fr. Harry?"

"I guess so."

"Good, don't worry about anything. Remember, you're my little brother. I'll never let anything happen to you."

"And you're my big sister. I'll never let anything happen to you either."

Rebecca knew if she was going to protect Haji, she would have to take charge. She also knew she would have to sacrifice some of her own secrets to make them understand.

She opened the door and told them it was okay for them to enter. Fr. Harry wasn't happy about being given permission to enter his own office after being asked to leave but under the circumstances he went along with it. Christine gave Haji a big hug and kissed him while assuring him that she loved him and everything will be all right.

"Haji, go to class. I'll speak to your parents and Fr. Harry," said Rebecca taking charge.

"Wait a minute Miss Ioannou. Don't you think that we all need to speak to Haji together?" asked Fr. Harry.

"No! No I don't! Go ahead Haji! Go to class!"

As Haji started to leave Andreas put his hand on his shoulder and assured him that everything will be all right and that he loved him. Haji wrapped his arms around his father and then his mother and told them he was sorry and walked out the door.

"Please everyone, sit down," said Rebecca. "As you can see there's a problem. But before I start I want to apologize for my rudeness. But I had Haji's best interest in mind. I don't know what you know or don't know about Haji's and my past. I know that I briefed Andreas but I'm not sure if he got the full concept of what really happened to us in Cyprus. I'm going to tell you as much as I can without losing my mind.

"You need to know what happened in Cyprus so you can understand what's happening in Astoria.

"When Haji awoke in the middle of the night he found his sister with a rope around her neck standing on his father's shoulders, while his pregnant mother was repeatedly being raped. When a soldier noticed Haji, his father ran to protect him as his sisters neck snapped." Christine drew a breath of shock. "You haven't heard anything yet. The soldiers liked to bet on the sex of the unborn child that a pregnant woman carried. There was this one young soldier named Private Akman who was the last person to rape his mother that wanted to know what she was carrying, a boy or a girl. So he cut Haji's mother's belly open while she was still alive just to see if it was a boy or a girl." Christine started to cry as Andreas held her hand. "The next morning I was dragged into the house and stripped of all my clothing so they can watch twelve-year old Haji have sex with me."

"Oh my God. Those animals. I'm so sorry Rebecca," Christine said crying.

"Luckily it didn't happen because there was word that Cypriot soldiers were approaching the area. But as the days and weeks progressed, the rapes this poor young boy witnessed will be something that Haji will live with the rest of his life. And yes, I was one of the many rapes that he witnessed." At this point Rebecca totally broke down. Fr. Harry quickly got up and held her tight. Now Christine and Andreas were holding Rebecca as she cried uncontrollably.

"Hold it, hold it. Let me tell you about Haji."

"Are you sure you can continue?" asked Fr. Harry.

"I'm fine. I'm used to it. Now, Haji feels guilty that he wasn't able to help anyone in Cyprus. The thought of anyone hurting someone upsets him very much. Today some of the eighth graders were picking on Christos. Christos has two missing fingers and the bigger kids were teasing him. Instead of high fiving him they wanted to high three him. When Christos refused they started beating up this poor fifth grader and Haji helped him. Another time some kids were making fun of one of the girl's breasts and Haji was afraid they were going to do something that he witnessed many times in Cyprus. He's a good kid. He's just mixed up. He just can't bear to see anyone being hurt."

By now Rebecca was shaking while going through a dozen tissues. She wasn't able to continue. Christine was also crying, not only for Rebecca but for Haji. She started to feel the guilt of all the lost years she missed with him.

"Fr. Harry, please cover my class for the rest of the day. I'm not feeling well. I need to go home."

"Sure Miss Ioannou, you go home. Feel better. Take as much time as you need." They all took turns hugging Rebecca. Andreas offered to drive her home but Rebecca declined.

She needed to walk.

She needed fresh air.

She needed to be alone.

Reaching the door she turned and said, "Christine, Haji's a good kid. I know you're his mother. I'm not looking to take that job from you. Please don't get upset with me, but right now Haji's longing for the only mother he's ever known." She then looked at Fr. Harry and informed him that Haji really misses Fr. Demitri, and he shouldn't feel upset that he hasn't opened up to him the way he would have with Fr. Demitri. "I don't know if any of you know, but Haji and I refer to each other as brother and sister. I really look at him as my little brother, not like a son," as she glared at Christine. "I'll never let anything happen to him."

With daggers in her eyes she looked at each one of them and said, "I'll never let anyone hurt him."

Then she walked out the door.

CHAPTER

Rebecca started her walk home along 31st Street under the elevated subway line. Her mind wandered back and forth between Cyprus and America. She had to get her recent past out of her head. But how could she do it? She was living in Astoria where ninety percent of the population was Greek and Cypriot. Haji was also a constant reminder too.

That barbarian Private Akman was the worst thing she ever encountered.

Will she ever be totally free of him?

Rebecca passed many stores on her way to Ditmars Boulevard. To clear her mind, she window shopped and went into many stores along the way. She needed a pick-me-up. She bought some clothes and scarf from Eleni's boutique. When she crossed over Astoria Boulevard she went into the Neptune Diner and had a salad and a coke. She sat there for an hour thinking exclusively about how Haji would cope with the recent atrocities in the years ahead.

When she left the Neptune Diner she continued on 31ˢᵗ Street to Ditmars and went into Spiro's shoe store. She treated herself to two pairs of shoes with a nice sized heel with the thought of wearing them with Michael. She couldn't wait to get home to try on her new outfits.

That night Michael called Rebecca from Boston again.

"Hi Michael, I didn't expect you to call tonight."

"You're not upset, are you?"

"Of course not, it's just that you've been calling me every other day. Believe me when I tell you; I'm glad you called."

"Rebecca, what's wrong? You're not sounding your cheerful self. Is everything all right? Did anything happen to you?"

"No, nothing happened. I had one of those days." Rebecca started choking up. Michael heard the cracking in her voice. It was upsetting to hear her sad.

"Rebecca, what's going on? Is anyone bothering you? Are you hurt; are you in any kind of trouble?" He wanted to comfort her.

"No Michael, it's nothing like that. Can't a woman have a bad day?" Now Rebecca tried to disguise her crying voice.

"Yes, Rebecca, anyone can have a bad day. But when you're having a bad day I want to be around to comfort you. I can't comfort you from five hours away."

"Michael, listen to me. I had a really bad day. Then I did some shopping and it made me feel a little better. But when I got home I started feeling lousy again. But now that I'm talking to you and know that you care..." Rebecca started crying hysterically.

Michael felt helpless; he didn't know what to say. He thought he should let her cry it out for a minute or two before talking again.

"Rebecca! Rebecca! Do you hear me? Stop crying! What's wrong?"

"I'm sorry Michael. You're away on important banking business. You need to concentrate. I don't want to be a distraction to your job."

"Don't you worry about my job, and let me worry about you. I have a big presentation to do the next two days but if you need me I'll leave now."

"No. Do you hear me? No. Do not come home. It's nothing important. It can wait. You have no idea how much better I feel knowing that you care. Please, if you come home it'll only make me feel guilty. Please don't do that. Believe me when I tell you, if it was an emergency it would be a different story. I'm just having a bad day. You stay in Boston and do what you need to do. I'll be here when you get home. When do you plan on coming home, Thursday or Friday?"

"I finish up Wednesday night. Even if I left Wednesday night I wouldn't get to New York until at least eleven o'clock."

"Michael please. I'm fine. Wednesday night I want you to get a good night's sleep. Wake up Thursday morning and have a good breakfast and I'll see you Thursday night."

"All right then. Since you sound better, that's what I'll do. Good night Rebecca. Please take care of yourself until I get home. I'll speak to you tomorrow."

"Good night Michael, and thank you for caring." *I love you she said after she had already hung up the phone.*

CHAPTER

Surprisingly, Rebecca slept better than expected. The next morning she didn't feel like teaching. She was still embarrassed about opening up about her personal life in front of everyone in Fr. Harry's office.

She called Fr. Harry's office and left word with Mrs. Noulis that she was not feeling well and would not be in. Mrs. Noulis expressed her concern to feel better like she always did whenever someone called in sick.

After Rebecca had her coffee and cottage cheese breakfast while watching the morning news; she decided to go shopping again. The weather man said the temperature would reach forty degrees, so she decided to take the subway into Manhattan and spend the day. She needed to get out.

She took the RR train to 59ᵗʰ Street and Lexington Avenue. She spent an hour looking in several different stores. She didn't see anything she liked so she decided to take a taxi to Macy's on 34ᵗʰ Street. Now, this is a store she thought. She couldn't believe the size of it. She spent two hours looking around not wanting to buy anything before lunch.

She went outside where she remembered passing a pizza shop. She ordered a slice and a coke and sat at the counter while thinking about all the clothes she wanted to buy to feel better about her past and to look good for Michael. When she returned to Macy's, she ended up spending two hundred dollars. She didn't care. She had the money. Andreas and Christine insisted that she keep the money from the gold at the monastery. She did spend a little over two thousand dollars on clothes and furniture when she moved into her apartment but has been saving money since she started teaching.

On the subway coming home, she had difficulty carrying the bags but was still able to manage.

By the time she reached Ditmars Boulevard it was five o'clock and cold. Rebecca didn't wear any gloves and her fingers felt like they were going to snap off. When she finally reached her door she couldn't believe her eyes. In front of her door were the most beautiful dozen roses she had ever seen. She instantly put down her bags, lifted the flowers, and smelled them. She brought them into her apartment and then went back to get her bags. She quickly opened the card and started to cry as she read it; *when you hurt, I hurt, love Michael.*

Rebecca quickly put the flowers in water and placed them on the table. She sat there for several minutes rereading the card and holding it against her heart.

An hour later there was a knock on the door. She looked in the peep hole and opened the door for Christine. Christine really didn't know where to start so she just started to cry. Rebecca hugged Christine as she herself started to cry. When they separated Christine spoke first; "Rebecca, I'm so sorry. I had no idea it was that bad. I'm so sorry."

"It's all right Christine. I know you didn't know. What did you expect? Did you expect me to tell you? I just want to move on. And in time I hope I can."

"Rebecca, if there's anything I can do for you…"

"There's isn't anything anyone can do for me. I need to get through this alone."

"No Rebecca, you're not alone. You're an Ioannou now. You're part of our family now. You have *us*."

Rebecca started to cry again when she heard the word family as Christine held her tight as they both wept in each other's arms.

"Rebecca, they're beautiful," Christine said as she noticed the flowers. "Who sent them?"

"Aren't they? I met someone New Year's Eve. His name is Michael. He's really nice. He's away this week on business and he sent them to me."

"Athena did tell me that you met someone New Year's Eve but I hadn't heard anything since."

"Well, after he brought me home he asked for my phone number and he took me out to dinner the next night. He's been calling me regularly since then. Last night when he called he sensed that something was wrong. I told him I had a bad day but he sensed that there was something more.

"I don't know if you know but I called in sick today and went into Manhattan. Have you ever been to Macy's on 34th Street?" Rebecca didn't give Christine time to answer. She just kept talking. "I spent a lot of money but I needed to feel good. When I got home I saw the flowers. Aren't they beautiful?" Before Christine could answer Rebecca whispered, "Do you want to read the card?"

"Of course I do, let me see it." Rebecca ran into her bedroom to get it off her night table. She wanted it near her when she slept. Like a school girl Rebecca read it to Christine; *"When you hurt, I hurt, love Michael."*

Rebecca broke down again; "Christine, those Turkish soldiers were so mean to me. They did such terrible things to me. They made me do things to them that I cannot bare to think about. I feel so dirty. I cannot tell you how it feels to read this card and know that someone really cares for me. He wanted to come to me last night from Boston. Christine, Michael cares about me," Rebecca cried again as she hugged the card.

"Rebecca, stop doing this to yourself."

"Stop doing what? I can't help it!"

"No! Not about what happened! I'm not talking about those animals! I'm talking about how you feel about yourself! You have it all! Take a look in the mirror! How dare you call yourself dirty! You're beautiful! You're beautiful inside and out! Michael is lucky that he has someone like you interested in him!"

"I don't feel very beautiful lately. I feel ugly inside and out."

"Stop that! Do you hear me? Stop that now!"

Rebecca blew her nose so loud that they both laughed.

"Do you want to see the new clothes I bought?"

"I'm not leaving until I see them all. Come on, let's go see."

Each outfit that Rebecca tried on Christine complimented her more and more. Rebecca was getting the pick-me-up that she needed.

Afterwards Christine told Rebecca that Athena explained to her that Michael was very successful and on New Year's Day he called Basil excited that he was taking you out to dinner.

"Really? I'm happy to hear that, but believe me when I tell you; I don't care about successful. I'm just happy he cares."

"Christine, enough about me, tell me about Haji. What's going on with him? I'm very worried about him."

"Haji's having some problems. Fr. Harry thinks that he may need to spend some time with him."

"That might be a good idea but please don't push him. He's young; he'll be fine in due time."

"I hope so Rebecca. I've lost too many years without him. I just hope things get better so he can finally accept me as his mother."

"He will. It's going to take some time. I've been his teacher for some time now. He's a good kid. A really good kid. He'll come around."

Rebecca and Christine continued talking. Christine started opening up about her own life in Cyprus. She gave Rebecca more details about how life was living with her mother and her obsession with her coming to America and marrying someone rich.

"She should see me now. See should see how happy I am being married to Andreas and reconnecting with our son. The son that she made me give up so some rich guy can marry me. The son that Andreas and I would have never connected with if it wasn't for you." Now Christine broke down and cried in Rebecca's arms.

Suddenly the phone rang. Christine smiled hoping that is was Michael. Rebecca excused herself and went to answer the phone.

"Hello."

"Hi Rebecca, how are you tonight?" When Christine saw the way Rebecca's eyes lit up she whispered that she would see herself out and blew her a kiss. Rebecca smiled and lipped *thank you*.

"Hi Michael, I'm fine today."

"You sound much better. I can't tell you how happy I am to hear happiness in your voice. You had me worried last night."

"I'm fine today. Yesterday I just had a bad day. That's all it was, and thank-you so much for the flowers. They're beautiful."

"I'm glad you like them."

They talked for an hour. Rebecca was careful that the conversation wasn't only about herself. She asked Michael many questions about his presentation and the city of Boston. Michael explained that as far as work went all was going great, and was happy in his career. As far as the city of Boston, he didn't venture out much. It was all about work.

"So Rebecca, I'm leaving Thursday morning. I'll call you tomorrow night. How about we revisit Mamma Garuccio's Thursday night for a nice quiet dinner?"

"How about we don't? How about you come over to my house and I prepare you a home cooked meal? You've been eating out every night since we've met."

"Are you sure?"

"Yes, I'm sure."

"Then I accept. What are you going to cook?"

"How about I surprise you?"

"Great, I love surprises. I'm looking forward to speaking to you tomorrow night, and to your surprise dinner on Thursday. Good night Rebecca."

"Good night Michael." *I love you Michael, she said again after she had already hung up.*

CHAPTER

38

The next morning, Rebecca was up bright and early looking forward to an exciting day. She felt like all her batteries had recharged. She was prepared to go to school and be the teacher that she was. Yesterday's day off was a good decision.

She did her morning ritual of watching the news while eating cottage cheese and sipping her coffee.

She quickly showered and put on her new navy blue suit and white blouse. Looking in the mirror she thought, *I missed my students yesterday; I can't wait to see them.*

As she walked along Ditmars Boulevard, she noticed Mr. Stathis opening his butcher shop.

"Good morning Mr. Stathis, how are you today?"

Mr. Stathis turned to see the pretty young woman that said good morning to him and replied, "Good morning to you ma'am, I'm fine thank you. How are you?"

"I'm doing very well, thank you. I know you're not open yet but can you pick me out a couple of nice tender lamb shanks? I'll pick them up on my way home later."

"Of course ma'am, the only thing is, all my meat is tender," he said as he smiled at her.

At school Rebecca went directly to Fr. Harry's office to assure him that she was fine and he need not worry about her anymore and to concentrate on Haji. Fr. Harry was glad Rebecca was back after only taking one day off.

Since she had a few extra minutes she went into the second floor gym to check on Haji. Haji was playing basketball when he saw Rebecca come into the gym. He passed the ball to his friend and approached her.

"Haji, are you all right?"

"Yes thank you. How are you? Fr. Harry told me you were sick yesterday."

"Shh, I lied. I just needed a day off," she smiled.

Haji smiled back. "I'm glad you weren't really sick."

On Rebecca's way home, she stopped at the Mediterranean grocery store and bought rice and ingredients for a salad, and then picked up the lamb shanks from Stathis' butcher shop.

At home she marinated the meat and put it in the refrigerator to absorb overnight. Everything was in place for tomorrow evening. She made herself a salad and toast for dinner. She watched the news to see what was going on in the world while going over her students school work. At eight o'clock Michael called and they talked and talked. Before either one noticed, an hour had gone by.

"You know Rebecca, we haven't known each other very long but I feel we've known each other for years."

"Michael, I'm so glad you feel that way, I feel exactly the same way. I'm looking so forward to cooking you a home cooked meal."

"I'm glad, because I'm looking forward to eating it. But I'm looking more forward to seeing you again."

"Good night, Michael. Dinner will be ready at six o'clock to-morrow." *I love you Michael, she said after she hung up.*

"Good night Rebecca." *I think I'm falling in love with you, he said after he hung up.*

CHAPTER

The next day Rebecca followed her daily ritual, but had her mind on six o'clock. She couldn't wait to see Michael, but at the same time didn't breeze through her lessons. Her students' learning was important to her.

At recess, she went to see Fr. Harry to inquire how Haji was doing. Fr. Harry informed Rebecca that Haji hasn't opened up to him at all.

"When I ask him about Cyprus he uses one or two word sentences like, *very bad,* or just *yes,* or *no,* but you were right about one thing. There was a tremendous bond between him and Fr. Demitri.

"I believe eventually, Haji will be able to live with his recent experiences. You were correct when you said that he's a good kid. I can see that his parents have given him an excellent foundation along with your teaching skills and of course your recent guidance. But without taking anything away from his parents or yourself I can clearly see that the real foundation he has was from his spiritual Father Demitri.

"Miss Ioannou, I have very few regrets in my life. If I died today there isn't much I would regret not accomplishing. But if I had to regret something it would have to be not ever having the honor of meeting Haji's spiritual Father Demitri."

Rebecca left Fr. Harry's office all teary eyed. She started to recall the day she was tied up by Private Akman completely naked along with other women when the general told Fr. Demitri to choose one, and the way Fr. Demitri pulled out a gun and shot the general dead, and then the way the soldiers shot Fr. Demitri dead.

Fr. Demitri knew he was going to die.

He chose death before he would dishonor a woman.

Then Rebecca thought about her evening with Michael and put everyone else out of her mind. *Tonight I'm cooking for Michael and I'm not going to let anything distract me.*

At 2:25 pm, Rebecca quickly left school and started hurrying to the train when she saw a taxi and jumped in. She was home in ten minutes.

She boiled the water for rice and took out her lamb shanks. When the rice was halfway done she put it in the roasting pan, added her seasonings and her homemade broth with the lamb shanks on top and put it in the oven at 325 degrees. She then set the table. She didn't have any fancy dishes, but even if she did, she wouldn't have used them. She wanted to make it cozy and informal. She then made the Greek salad with all the toppings of tomato, red onion, and feta cheese. The only appetizer she had was *halloumi*; the traditional Cypriot cheese.

While the food cooked Rebecca gave the apartment a quick surface cleaning although it didn't need it. She always kept her place clean. She glanced around and noticed the way Michael's flowers were visible on her coffee table.

I want Michael to see them. She bent down and smelled them, savoring the scent.

Now she had to take care of herself.

Rebecca showered and spent thirty minutes blow-drying her hair. Still undecided what to wear she looked at her new clothes. She wanted to look casual but also needed to feel feminine. She decided to wear her Jordache Jeans along with her new pink crew neck top, with a pink bra, and pink panties.

The pastel color underwear gave her a sense of femininity.

When dressed, she examined herself in the mirror. Although she knew she looked good, all she thought about was how ugly and dirty she felt.

When Rebecca went into the kitchen it smelled the way a home should smell.

There's nothing better than a home cooked meal.

The doorbell rang five minutes to six. Rebecca took one last look in the mirror, checked the peep hole, and opened the door. Michael stood there holding a bottle of wine and flowers.

"Michael, come in. The flowers are beautiful. You shouldn't have. I still have the roses that you sent the other day," as she motioned towards the coffee table. "Please come in."

Michael stepped inside and put the wine and flowers on the table.

"Rebecca, let me look at you. You look beautiful." Michael said as she blushed like a school girl.

He held her hands, pulled her close to him, and kissed her on the lips. Rebecca made no attempt to pull away. They kissed for ten seconds before Michael unlocked their lips.

Rebecca looked Michael in the eyes and asked smiling, "I hope you're hungry. Let me hang up your jacket."

"I'm starved," he said as he took off his jacket. "It smells great in here. What are you cooking? Can I have a peek?"

"Sure, take a whiff while I put the flowers in water."

Michael opened the oven and saw the lamb shanks and loved the way they looked and smelled. When Rebecca returned to the kitchen, she gave Michael a corkscrew while she took the dinner out of the oven as he opened the wine.

"It smells great. I can't wait to bite into it," Michael said.

"Let's let it sit a few minutes," Rebecca said as she set it on the counter.

"Sounds great. Do you have any wine glasses?"

"Sorry Michael, I don't. Will any glasses do?"

"Sure, remind me to buy you some."

"That's not necessary."

"I know, it's just something I want to do for you."

Michael poured the wine into two highball glasses.

"Cheers," he said as they touched glasses.

"Cheers Michael, and welcome back. Tell me about your business trip."

"The trip was fine. I made a lot of new contacts; I think I might even be up for another promotion."

"That's great Michael. I'm sure you deserve it."

"Thanks Rebecca, that means a lot coming from you. Now, can we eat? The food smells great."

"Yes sir," she smiled. "I'm glad you're hungry," Rebecca said after another sip of wine.

Rebecca put the food in a platter and placed it on the table. Michael sipped his wine as he watched the woman he was falling in love with. *She's beautiful inside and out.*

Rebecca nervously watched Michael take his first bite. She smiled at his reaction.

"This is great, where'd you learn to cook like this?" Rebecca smiled and enjoyed the compliment. "I mean it, this is great."

"Thank you Michael. I like to cook. The only thing is I never have anyone to cook for."

"You do now."

"I'm glad you like it. Here, have some more."

After dinner they sat on the couch and watched the new TV show *Welcome Back Kotter*. They both laughed a lot. It turned out they loved the same type of shows. They talked for quite some time when Michael picked up the bottle of wine to pour Rebecca another glass.

"No Michael, I think I had enough."

"Me too," he said as he put the bottle back down.

At this point Rebecca and Michael were looking each other in the eyes. Rebecca sensed what was going to happen next.

"Rebecca, it's getting late. We both have work tomorrow. I think I need to get going. I cannot thank you enough for the delicious dinner. But even more important, I had a wonderful time. I'm so happy that our paths have crossed." Rebecca was sitting on his right. Michael put his right arm around her and with his left hand lifted her chin slightly and looked into her eyes.

"I really meant it when I said I'm happy our paths have crossed."

Then Michael leaned over and gave her a small kiss on the lips and then pulled away to see her reaction. When he looked at her she opened her eyes and smiled. He now knew he could continue. He pulled her closer as she put her right arm around him while he put his left hand on her waist. They sat there kissing for what seemed to be an eternity.

Michael felt her firm breasts against him. He wanted to touch them so badly but knew doing something like that would have to wait. He didn't want to rush things.

After all, Rebecca was a good Cypriot girl that he was sure was still a virgin.

CHAPTER

T he next evening Rebecca and Michael didn't see each other. Michael needed to work late to review his Boston trip on Monday. He needed to brief his New York office on the new banking regulations and other important banking matters. Rebecca stayed home and reviewed her week and planned next week's lessons. But Michael wanted to spend Saturday with her, so he picked her up Saturday morning at ten.

"So Michael, you told me to dress warm. Where are you taking me?"

"Have you ever heard of the eastern point of Long Island?"

"Sure, Montauk Point."

"No, not that point, the other point."

"You mean Orient Point?"

"Yes, and you say you're new around here," he smiled. "Don't get me wrong, Montauk's beautiful. But the north shore is very up and coming. There's a small town out there called Greenport. There's talk that it's going to be the next Astoria. The Greeks are going out there and buying up property and building summer homes. Some of my friends have already invested out there. I've been there a few times but now I want to take a better look."

"Are you thinking of investing?"

"Not so much for myself. My bank is being asked to lend a lot of money for investments out there. I figured it's worth a look. You never know. I might buy myself a piece of land. Even though it's cold, it's still a sunny day. Besides I want to spend the day with you. And I love the beach in the winter. It's so quiet and desolate. I can't wait to show you."

"I can't wait to see it."

Michael drove the Grand Central Parkway to I-495 east, which is also known as the Long Island Expressway, or the L.I.E. On a Saturday morning in January there's never traffic. But in the summer months it's nicknamed the world's largest parking lot because eastern Long Island has the nicest beaches in New York.

They took the L.I.E. to the last exit and drove Route 25 east. Michael took a detour by making a left on Northville Turnpike which was a country road to Sound Avenue that ran parallel to the Long Island Sound instead of staying on Route 25 with its traffic lights.

"Wow, this is a beautiful country road," said Rebecca. "Look at all the open land. What a difference from Astoria."

"Isn't it? I love it out here."

"I can see why. It's so peaceful."

"It is, but in the summer months there's a lot of traffic. People in New York for whatever reasons need to leave the city. When we get to Orient Point you'll see why."

"I can see why already."

They continued driving east along Sound Avenue. They passed through the towns of Mattituck, and Jamesport. As they approached the sign *Welcome to Greenport;* Michael pointed out *Town Beach;* the local beach that gets full of Greek speaking people.

"Even the life guards are Greek," he said.

They continued east towards Orient Point for another ten minutes. They passed the Blue Dolphin Motel where Michael had vacationed with his family every summer.

They passed Gardiners Bay Causeway and entered the town of Orient. Michael turned right into Orient State Park. He continued the two miles to the parking lot.

"Well Miss Ioannou, how do you like the view? Isn't it beautiful?"

"It's breathtaking."

"Come on, zip-up your jacket. Let's go for a walk."

They felt the chill when they exited of the car. Michael held Rebecca by the hand as they walked to the water. They stood there admiring the water view without saying a word for a minute.

"Come on," Michael said. "Let's walk a little."

After they walked a few minutes Michael let go of Rebecca's hand and put his arm around her. They were the only ones on the beach.

"Michael, do you know what this reminds me of?"

"No, tell me."

"In the movie, *The Planet of the Apes,* when they were walking along the beach, and they saw the Statue of Liberty."

"Yes, it does, but there's one difference."

"What's that?" she smiled

"In the movie, do you remember the beautiful woman walking on the beach with Charlton Heston?"

"Yes, she was beautiful." Michael then stopped and faced Rebecca.

"Well the difference between you and her is; she doesn't have enough beauty to tie your shoes." Michael then wrapped his arms around her and kissed her. This time he didn't look for her reaction. Once he started he didn't stop, and neither did Rebecca. They stood there kissing for several minutes, although they could have continued for much longer.

They continued to walk hand in hand, arm in arm, and stopping to kiss periodically. When they returned to the car Michael asked Rebecca if she was hungry for lunch.

"All that kissing has made me really hungry."

"Me too, there's a nice place right in the town of Greenport. You're going to love it."

"As long as I'm with you I'm sure I will."

Michael parked the car in front of Mitchel's waterfront restaurant. The hostess gave them a window seat overlooking the bay. They sat for an hour talking and holding hands while they ate. Rebecca was feeling the happiest she had ever felt.

After lunch Michael and Rebecca walked around the town of Greenport. Although most stores closed for the winter a few were open. They browsed in and out like tourists.

"Look Rebecca, here's a real estate office. Let's go inside."

"All right."

"Good afternoon, how can I help you?"

"Yes, I hope you can," said Michael. "I'm interested in commercial property."

"Sure, come sit down. I'm Carmine Costello."

"I'm sorry, I'm Michael Stylianou. This is Rebecca."

"Hello Rebecca, nice to meet you," Carmine said as he shook hands with both.

"I'm looking for a large piece of property. Preferably a corner lot on at least an acre."

'Sure, I can help you with that. I have several parcels that size. What type of business are you looking to open?"

Michael immediately glanced at Rebecca and winked. "I'm looking to open a restaurant. That's why I prefer a corner lot. I want something visible and accessible from two streets."

"Sure, I understand. My assistant isn't in today, so I can't show you around. But I can give you a list of properties I'm sure can meet your needs."

For the next ten minutes Carmine mapped everything out for Michael. They all shook hands again as Michael said he would get back to Carmine if anything was to his liking.

Outside, Rebecca asked Michael why he told Carmine he was looking to open a restaurant instead of opening a bank.

"Well Rebecca, if Carmine knew that Manufactures Hanover Trust was looking to buy property, the price would automatically double. So I'm starting out just looking for a place to open a restaurant. If and when I find something to my liking then Manufactures legal department will start negotiations."

For the next hour Michael drove around Greenport looking at prospective lots. He was impressed that Rebecca wasn't bored. She even had some interesting ideas.

"Rebecca, before we start heading back would you like to see my friend's house?"

"Sure, I'd love to."

"Good, it's ten minutes from here."

Michael headed West on Route 25. He turned right on Moores Lane and continued a quarter mile to Sound Drive and turned left.

"There it is. Isn't it beautiful?"

"Michael, it's gorgeous. I mean it. It's gorgeous."

"Isn't it. It belongs to my friend Foti. He had it built last summer. Come on, I want to show you the grounds."

"Do you think it's all right? Him not being home and all."

"Of course it is. I know him very well. He does a lot of business with my bank."

When they exited the car Michael led Rebecca to the back. Her breath was taken away. The house overlooked the Long Island Sound.

"Michael, this is the most beautiful house and grounds I've ever seen."

"Isn't it. Last summer when Foti had his house warming party I sat here mesmerized drinking a beer looking at the water. Foti told me last week that there's a lot for sale three houses away. Let's go take a look at it."

"I can't wait to see it."

"Good, lets walk," Michael said as he put his arm around her.

When they reached the vacant lot they instantly walked to the water.

"Oh, Michael. I can see myself living here. It's beautiful. Growing up in the mountains I always wished I lived near the water."

"Hey, you're still young. It can still happen."

Michael and Rebecca absorbed the scenery several minutes before they returned to the car.

During the ride home Rebecca fell asleep while Michael held her hand. When Michael exited at the Hoyt Avenue exit Rebecca opened her eyes.

"I'm sorry. I didn't realize I've slept for so long. You should have woken me to keep you company. I'm so embarrassed."

"There's nothing to be embarrassed about. Besides, you looked so innocent and beautiful sleeping. It made me feel good having you sleep while I drove."

"Why's that?"

"I felt like I was taking care of you. I like doing that."

"It feels good on my end too."

⟫⟪

Rebecca invited Michael up to her apartment. Once inside Rebecca poured two glasses of wine in the same highball glasses they used two days ago.

"Sorry Michael," she smiled. "Tomorrow I'm going to buy some real wine glasses."

Michael laughed and clanked glasses with Rebecca. They talked a while then Rebecca asked Michael if he wanted to take his spot on the couch.

"You bet I do."

They put their glasses on the coffee table and held each other in their arms. After a minute of kissing, Michael put his hand on Rebecca's breast. At first she felt a little uncomfortable but let him continue. She really loved that Michael was feeling her up not to disgrace her, but was doing it with passion. He started to ease his hand below her breast and under her shirt and started feeling her up over her bra. Rebecca continued letting him feel her up. She loved Michael's hand on her. It was only when Michael tried to pull her shirt off that she asked him to stop.

"Please Michael, no."

"Shh," Michael said as he stopped trying to remove her shirt but put his hand back on her breast. Rebecca was all right with that for the moment.

"Thank you for respecting me. It means a lot. It really does."

"I'll always respect you. I'll never do anything to hurt you."

They continued sitting on the couch holding each other while kissing. After a while Rebecca made a couple of sandwiches and a salad. They did a lot of talking and laughing. Then they watched *All in the Family*. They both laughed at Archie Bunker. They thought he was the funniest man alive.

"Well Rebecca, I don't want to overstay my welcome. I had a wonderful day. I know the minute I leave I'm going to start missing you. Let's get together tomorrow. Do you want to go to the movies or something?"

"Yes, I'd like that. We can do that in the afternoon. But what I'd really like to do before we see a movie is go to church together."

"Church? I haven't been to church since Easter. You like going to church?"

"I do. I go almost every Sunday."

Michael started thinking to himself that Rebecca must really be something special.

"I'm not much of a church goer but I would love to go with you."

"Great, can you pick me up tomorrow at nine?"

"Nine o'clock in the morning on a Sunday? Only for you Rebecca, only for you," he said as he wrapped his arms around her and hugged her tight.

"Good, I'll be waiting for you downstairs at nine," she said as she gave him a loving kiss. "Thanks again for a wonderful day and evening."

CHAPTER

 41

The next morning when Rebecca went downstairs Michael was already double parked waiting for her. As soon as she entered the car they both leaned towards each other and kissed. When Rebecca broke away Michael said to her; "Hey, I'm not finished yet," and then pulled her towards him and locked lips again." When he finally broke away Rebecca asked, "Finished now?"

"Yes I am, for now."

"Well now *I'm* not finished," and leaned over towards him and kissed him again. When she broke away, she told Michael that they both need to go to confession. Then they both laughed.

St. Demitrios' ten car parking lot was full when Michael pulled up to the church. They ended up parking two blocks away. As they walked to the church holding hands they discussed where they were going to eat breakfast and what movie they wanted to see. They agreed on the Neptune Diner and then to see the new blockbuster movie *Jaws*.

When they walked into the narthex (sort of a church lobby) Rebecca insisted on paying for both candles.

They both did the Sign of the Cross as is the tradition in the Orthodox Church. They found two seats together and stood while following the service. Many people couldn't help noticing the nice looking couple that just walked in. Michael took off his overcoat and stood handsomely with his navy blue suit, white shirt, and blue striped necktie. Rebecca unbuttoned her coat and left it on.

Halfway through the service, Rebecca noticed Christine and Andreas off to the side. Rebecca smiled at them while they smiled back at her. Rebecca sensed something was troubling Christine. At a second glance she noticed Haji. He was standing next to Andreas wearing a visible black eye. Rebecca automatically felt the older sister in her but knew she had to somehow keep her distance.

When church services end, most people visit the church hall for coffee hour. It's a time to socialize among fellow parishioners. Rebecca was introducing Michael to some people she knew, and was surprised that Michael also knew some of the parishioners, mostly through business.

While Michael was talking to a group of men about bank loans, Rebecca made her way over to Christine. Rebecca felt the only way to find out about Haji was to ask.

"Christine, how are you? I noticed Haji's eye. What happened to him? Is he all right?"

"Rebecca, I'm so worried about him. He got into a fight yesterday at the diner. Someone came in and started to make trouble and Haji threw him out. The guy came back with some friends and Andreas told them to leave. They actually listened to Andreas but

Haji decided to follow them outside and fought with three of them. I'm so worried. He needs to control his anger but he doesn't."

"Yes he does need to control his anger. I'll speak to him. Where is he?"

"He's in the hallway by the bathrooms with a few of his friends."

"I'll be right back."

"Rebecca no, please leave him alone. I'm afraid he might snap at you."

"Snap at me? I don't think so. I'll let you know what happens." Rebecca went into the hallway and saw Haji laughing with some of his friends. When Haji saw Rebecca he turned away. After all they've been through, to see Haji turn away, Rebecca felt like he stabbed her in the heart.

Not wanting to embarrass him she said, "Haji, can I see you a minute please?" Haji turned serious as he approached Rebecca.

"What?"

"What? Is that the way you're going to talk to me? What?" she repeated.

"What? What did I do?"

"If you're going to talk to me like that forget it."

Rebecca turned to walk away and almost bumped into Michael.

"What's going on?" Michael asked.

"Nothing Michael, are you ready to go?" Rebecca noticed that Michael sensed trouble so she decided to sugar coat it. "Michael, I want to introduce you to someone. Haji, this is Michael, a very dear friend of mine." Michael extended his hand and they shook. "Haji is Basil and Athena's nephew. Basil is Christine's older brother. That's Christine over there," Rebecca pointed. "That's her husband Andreas next to her."

"Oh hi Haji, I know your aunt and uncle. They're wonderful people. It's nice meeting you," Michael said as he shook Haji's hand again, this time giving an authoritative squeeze.

Rebecca walked away with Michael worrying how much Michael heard.

"Rebecca." Rebecca turned and saw Christine walking towards her. "Is this Michael?"

"Yes, come, let me introduce you. Michael, this is Christine, Basil's sister."

"Christine, it's nice to meet you. I want to thank you for having a brother."

"Why's that?"

"Because if it wasn't for him, I never would have met Rebecca," Michael said as he put his arm around Rebecca and pulled her towards him and kissed her on the head. Christine smiled at the two love birds at the same time watching Haji staring at Michael.

"Yes, I've heard. By the way, this is my husband Andreas."

"Hello Michael, nice to meet you."

"Nice to meet you too Andreas. I just met your son Haji. He's a big boy."

"Yeah, good thing he has his mother's height and looks," laughed Andreas.

"Oh stop it. He may look like me, but he's all you," added Christine.

The four sat and chatted together for a few minutes when Christine invited Rebecca and Michael to the diner for breakfast. Rebecca respectfully declined. She didn't want Michael knowing any of her connections to them, at least for now. Rebecca knew that if her relationship with Michael continued she would need to tell him about her past. But for now she still needed to be private.

When Rebecca and Michael were walking to the car Michael brought up Haji.

"Rebecca, is there a problem with you and that kid Haji?"

"No Michael, why do you ask?"

"I don't know. I just sensed that something's going on. And what's with the black eye?"

"Well to be honest with you, Christine is one of the first people I met when I came to America. Haji's big for his age. He seems to be getting into fights lately. He's also one of my students; so she asked me to talk to him, that's all."

"All right, I'm sorry; I thought maybe there was a problem. My mistake."

"No problem, no problem at all. Thank you for caring," she said as she gave him a kiss.

CHAPTER

As the months passed, life turned bitter sweet for Haji and Rebecca. Bitter for Haji, sweet for Rebecca. She was seeing Michael every weekend and at least twice during the week, and spoke on the phone nearly every night. Her life was moving along but Michael was getting impatient with her about having sex.

Haji on the other hand was having his problems. His anger went from protecting people, to starting fights. After his thirteenth birthday in June, he finished the school year at St. Demitrios and worked at the diner the entire summer. He actually liked the diner business and Andreas was happy to have him there. Andreas' only concern besides Haji's fighting were the friends he was keeping.

That following September, Haji attended Bryant High School a few blocks from the diner. Christine was a little concerned because it was a tough New York City school. Haji knew the school and had a few older friends who went there. Besides, he wasn't afraid. The word spread after he beat up Melvin, and two of his friends who had a reputation of being some of the toughest guys in the neighborhood. Haji already had the reputation of someone not to reckon with.

Halfway through the school year Haji became good friends with Tommy. Tommy was from the island of Rhodes. He was nicknamed Tommy-Two-Fingers because it was rumored that if anyone messed with him he'd just take out his gun and shoot them. As it turned out, Melvin and Tommy had exchanged words a few times after Melvin kept asking Tommy's girlfriend Kathy out, and many times he wouldn't take no for an answer.

One night Kathy and a few of her friends were studying at a friend's house for their PSAT's. By midnight they decided they had enough. Kathy and her friend Georgia started walking home together.

At the same time Haji and Tommy were hanging out in the Bryant High School schoolyard with a few of their friends smoking pot.

They also decided it was time to leave.

"Haji," said Tommy. "I have the marijuana munchies. Is your father's diner open?"

"Nah, he closes at eleven. He's already in bed."

"Shit, I could go for a cheeseburger."

"No problem. I got the keys. Let's go."

"Great."

Within minutes Haji was unlocking the diner.

"Tommy, let's keep the lights closed, otherwise people will think we're open."

"Good idea."

The minute they went into the kitchen they heard noise coming from the back alley. At first it sounded like cats. When they took a closer listen they realized it was crying. Haji quickly opened the door and ran outside into the night. Tommy followed behind already having his gun out. When they got to the crying Tommy couldn't believe his eyes. It was Melvin on top of Kathy and some other guy, neither Tommy nor Haji recognized was on top of Georgia. They were groping the girls as they were trying to remove their clothes. Tommy and Haji starting beating the shit out of them as the girls ran into the diner. After a few minutes Tommy brought Melvin and his friend into the diner at gun point. Meanwhile the girls were crying hysterically.

"You animals," yelled Georgia as she smacked Melvin.

"How dare you," said Kathy. "Who the hell do you think you are?"

"Listen girls," said Haji. "We're going to fix it so these two motherfuckers will never hurt you again. I don't want to call the police because they ask too many questions. Besides, if my father finds out I opened the diner he's going to get all pissed off."

"We can't call the police either. If my father found out I'll be in a lot of trouble. He'll think it's my fault because he thinks I dress like a slut," said Kathy

"Mine too," said Georgia, "we need to keep this between the four of us."

"Girls," said Haji. "You go home. Tommy and I are going to throw these two guys a beating and we'll see you tomorrow."

"Motherfuckers," yelled Georgia as she kicked Melvin's friend in the balls. "Come on Kathy, let's go." Kathy spit in Melvin's face as she walked past him.

Haji had never met Georgia before but instantly took a liking to her.

After the girls left, Tommy put the gun to Melvin's head and cocked it.

"Hold it Tommy," Haji said, "What do you think you're doing?"

"I'm going to blow their fuckin brains out, that's what I'm going to do."

"No way. Not now. Not here." Haji has seen so much torture in his young life. He knew that the threat was almost worse that the act. He knew what these two guys were going to do to the girls. They had to pay. But first they had to suffer. He went to the best school of humiliation. These two guys had no regard for human life. Haji knew what he had to do before he fixed it so they'll never hurt anyone ever again.

"Tommy, shoot them both in the knee caps."

"Are you shittin me?"

"Come on Two-Fingers. Shoot them both in their knee caps. I want them to be crippled."

Tommy fired four shots. They both went down. When they started to cry and moan Haji put two dish towels in their mouths.

"You like hurting people?" asked Haji. "Well, you're not going to hurt people anymore. Did you guys feel tough when you were about to rape two innocent girls," as he kicked them repeatedly.

Haji looked at them and saw Private Akman. He wanted them to suffer. He wanted them to bleed to death but he couldn't do it at the diner, it would have to wait. His father was going to open up in a few hours.

"We can't kill them here," said Haji. "Let's just let them go outside. If they bleed to death they bleed to death. If they don't, they don't."

Haji and Tommy threw them in the alley and told them if they told anyone they would kill them.

"Come on Tommy, we gotta clean up this blood. My father will be here in a few hours."

For the next hour they scrubbed the blood from the floor, made themselves something to eat and left. When they peeked in the alley, Melvin and his friend were gone.

"It's only a 22 caliber," Tommy said. "I knew it wouldn't kill them. They'll be fine. They're just going to limp for the rest of their lives."

"I really don't give a shit if they're fine or not. At the very least, I hope they have to walk with canes the rest of their lives. Give me the gun. I'm going to throw it down the sewer."

"Good idea, I'll buy another one next week, and Haji, I owe you one. If we didn't come here Kathy would have been raped."

"I just might take you up on it someday. In the meantime why don't you fix me up with Georgia?"

"Sure, I'll take care of that tomorrow."

CHAPTER

J uly, 1976
That following summer in July was the two year anniversary of
the invasion of Cyprus.

Rebecca and Michael had broken up.

Michael was as passionately in love with Rebecca as she was of
him. They enjoyed each other's company and were inseparable.
The problem was all Rebecca's fault and she knew it. The fur-
thest they had gone physically was feeling her up. She could not
bring herself to touch him on his manhood. A few times Rebecca
came close, but every time she tried she saw the face or penis of
Private Akman. She decided her love for Michael was so strong,
that she let the relationship slip away.

Michael deserved better, she thought.

So Rebecca buried herself in her work. She taught Monday through Friday, tutored on Saturdays, and taught Sunday school. Everyone loved her. Nobody could figure out how such a beautiful woman didn't have a boyfriend. Whenever somebody tried to introduce her to someone she always had an excuse.

One Friday night in October, Christine visited Rebecca unexpectedly. When Rebecca saw Christine, she immediately thought something happened to Haji.

"Christine, how are you? Is everything all right? Is Haji okay?"

"Everything's fine, and so is Haji. You really love him don't you?"

"Yes I do. Like a little brother." Rebecca said as she smiled.

"Rebecca, can I come in?"

"Oh yes, please, come in. I'm so sorry. What can I do for you?"

"Do for me? Why do you think I need something? Can't a friend stop by and visit a friend without needing something. I just wanted to see how you're doing."

"Christine, please. I think I know why you're here. Can't you please respect my privacy?"

"Come on, why are you talking to me like that? Do I really deserve it?"

"What do you want?" Rebecca snapped.

"All right Rebecca, why don't you cut the crap. What's going on with you? I can't figure you out. You're alienating yourself from the world. You're burying yourself in your work and you're not coming up for air. You have a man who's madly in love with you. You said it yourself; you loved the way that felt. You needed it! You got it! He gave it to you! I can't understand what's going on in that head of yours!"

"What's going on in my head?" screamed Rebecca. "What's going on in my head? How can you ask me a question like that? Do I need to give you a history lesson? Did you forget? Did you all of a sudden get amnesia?" Rebecca was crying hysterically now. "How many times do I have to tell you my story? Do you like hearing it? Is that what it is? You like hearing my misery? I can't! I can't! I can't! I just can't be with a man! Don't you think that I love Michael? Not a moment goes by that I don't think about him! I cannot begin to tell you how much I love him! I cannot continue rejecting him! It's not fair to him!"

"Then don't reject him! Tell him! Tell him your story! He'll understand when you tell him! He's in love with you! Don't you know that? He'll understand!"

"Get out! Get out of my house before I call the police! Get out," Rebecca cried while wrapping her arms around Christine and cried uncontrollably. "I'm sorry. I'm so sorry Christine. You're the only family I have here. The only family in the world. I didn't mean to yell at you. Can you ever forgive me? I just don't know what to do."

"Shh, Shh," Christine whispered. "I'm going to tell you what to do. You're going to tell Michael." Rebecca started shaking while trying to pull away. Christine held her tight. "Shh, shh," Christine continued whispering. "You're going to tell him, and he's going to understand."

Rebecca took a deep breath, pulled her head back, and looked at Christine. "I don't know if I can. What if he doesn't want me? I'm sure he thinks I'm a virgin. How's he going to want someone who had all the sex that I had. What if it still doesn't work? What if I still can't be with him?"

"Listen to me, and listen to me good! You didn't have sex! It was forced upon you! You were raped! Do you hear me? You were raped!" Rebecca started to sob again. "I promise you, he'll understand and have patience because he'll know why you've been rejecting him." Christine looked Rebecca in the eye, "Rebecca, he misses you. Believe me when I tell you. That man is so in love with you he can't take it.

"Rebecca, without details, do you want me to brief Michael or give him a hint so he can at least have the slightest idea? This way he'll know it isn't him that's being rejected. Then you can give him whatever details, if any that you might want to give him."

"What if he rejects me?"

"If he rejects you then he rejects you. It'll be his loss."

"Christine, I don't know what to do. I can't live like this."

"Then call him. Call him now. Ask him to come over."

"Now?"

"Now!"

"What if he doesn't?"

"Like I said before, it'll be his loss."

"Will you stay with me until he gets here?"

"I'll stay here as long as you need me to. Now go. Go call him."

Rebecca started walking towards the phone and turned to say something.

"Go! Call him! Call him now!" Christine ordered.

Rebecca dialed, and Michael answered on the third ring.

"Hello. Hello. Hello, is anyone there?" Rebecca froze. "Is anyone there?"

"Michael, hi, it's Rebecca."

"Hi Rebecca."

"Michael, how are you?"

"I'm fine, Rebecca, how are you?"

"I miss you."

"I miss you too." Michael said sadly. She felt the pain he was feeling and started to cry.

"Give me the phone!" Christine interrupted. Rebecca froze as Christine pulled the phone out of her hands.

"Michael, this is Christine."

"Christine?"

"Yes, Christine. Christine Ioannou. Basil Alexander's sister. Remember me? We met at St. Demitrios about a year ago. The day you met my son Haji, remember him? He was the one with the black eye."

"Yes. I do remember. Did you say Ioannou?"

"Yes I did."

"Are you related to Rebecca?"

"Yes I am. Well, kind of."

"I didn't know that."

"I know you didn't. There's a lot that you don't know."

"Evidently. What's going on?"

"There's a lot going on. It's just too much to tell on the phone. But there's one thing that I *can* tell you on the phone."

"Yeah, what's that?" Michael asked coldly.

"Rebecca loves you. She always has, and never stopped." Michael was silent. "Michael, I know you love her and right now you're confused about what's going on. Please Michael, please come over now, to Rebecca's, it's very important."

All of a sudden Michael showed he still loved Rebecca by getting protective and worried.

"What happened? Is Rebecca all right? Is she sick? Is she in any kind of trouble?"

"Nothing happened, yes she's all right, no she's not sick, and no she's not in trouble. She's in love. She's in love with you. If you come over now, you'll understand."

"Now? It's ten o'clock."

"I know it's ten o'clock. Please come over."

"Christine, I'll be there in an hour."

"Thank you Michael."

"No Christine, thank *you*. Christine, are you still there?"

"Yes Michael?"

"Even if it was midnight I'd come right over."

"I know, I know you would." Christine turned to Rebecca.

"He'll be here in an hour. Take that dreadful flannel nightgown off and shower. You look like a mess."

Rebecca laughed with excitement. "Didn't you once tell me that I was beautiful?"

"Yes I did, but not today. Now go before Michael sees you like this and you scare him away," laughed Christine.

Rebecca was out of the shower in fifteen minutes. Christine blow dried Rebecca's hair as she sat watching in the mirror. "I'm so nervous. I hope I can do this. I hope he doesn't reject me."

"Would you stop with the rejections? If he rejects you he's going to have a problem with me," laughed Christine. "Okay, your hair's dry. Let's get you dressed. Put on something that's going to make his eyes pop out."

"No Christine. I'm not playing that game. I'm putting on a pair of jeans and a top."

"That'll do it."

Rebecca and Christine talked for ten minutes before Michael rang the doorbell. When Rebecca heard the bell she almost jumped out of her seat.

"I can't do this. Send him away. I'm afraid."

"Listen, I'm parked downstairs. I'm opening the door and I'm going to brief him for thirty seconds then I'm going to go sit in my car. Is that all right? May I brief him? It'll break the ice."

"Go ahead. What do I have to lose?"

"What do you have to lose? You have nothing to lose. It's Michael who has everything to lose." Christine got up and leaned over Rebecca and hugged her. "He's a lucky man to have you."

Christine opened the door and slipped out into the hall as Michael was about to ring the bell again. She faced Michael for ten seconds as tears were dripping down her face.

"What's going on?" He asked with tears in his eyes. Christine just wrapped her arms tight around him and cried as she whispered in his ear.

"She loves you. She really loves you. She did not *just* come from Cyprus. She *escaped* from Cyprus. She was a virgin before she was taken prisoner during the invasion. She was abused in every way possible; she's been raped more times than she can count. The abuse was so bad, she's afraid she'll never be able to actually make love." Michael broke away and looked at Christine as she just nodded her head.

"It explains a lot," he said as he now wrapped *his* arms around Christine to express a thank you.

Christine quickly pulled away, "She's inside. Go to her. She needs you."

Michael almost ripped the door off the hinges as he flung it open and stepped inside. With tears in his eyes, he stood there looking at the most beautiful creature in the world that looked so lost. Rebecca picked up her head in embarrassment and folded her arms in shame and doubled over.

Michael pulled her from the chair and held her tight.

"Oh Michael, I'm so sorry I didn't tell you. You must have thought I didn't love you. I do love you. I'm just so afraid that it would be too painful. I so much wanted to be pure for you. I feel so dirty."

"Shh," Michael whispered as he continued to cry. "Pure? Dirty? You're as pure and clean as a new born baby. I'm so sorry for all you've been through. I'm here now. I now know some of what you've been through. You can tell me anything you want and it wouldn't change the love that I have for you. I'll never leave you again."

"Oh Michael my love, I'm so sorry. I tried to get my past out of my mind and I've hurt you in the meantime."

"Your past is your past. You can never get rid of your past. You must and will learn to deal with your past. Always remember, none of it was your fault my love. You did nothing wrong. Do you hear me? You did nothing wrong. I will help you deal with everything for the rest of my life if you allow me. Always remember; *when you hurt, I hurt.*"

"Thank you Michael. Thank you for loving me. Thank you for being you."

"No, it's me who should be thanking you for loving *me*. Rebecca, do you remember that night when we were coming back from Orient Point and you fell asleep?" Michael asked as he kissed her. "And when you said you were embarrassed? Do you remember what I said? I said that it felt like I was taking care of you. I like taking care of you. I want to take care of you. I promise I'll never let anyone hurt you ever again. Please let me protect you. Please let me take care of you...

"Rebecca my love, will you marry me?"

CHAPTER

44

That night Rebecca and Michael stayed up until one o'clock sitting on her couch. Michael didn't want to push Rebecca for information. He assured her that he felt her pain and would help her in any way he could; including getting professional help.

But most of the time they talked about their future. Michael wanted a big wedding while Rebecca wanted something small. But either way it didn't matter. They were getting married. They kissed and held each other without Michael trying to advance. Finally Rebecca looked Michael in the eyes.

"Michael my love, please hold me."

"I am holding you."

"No Michael, hold me like this," as she put his hand on her breast and held it there.

They sat there kissing for a few more minutes when Michael pulled away.

"Rebecca, I'm very worried about you; I'm not leaving you tonight. I'm sleeping on your couch."

"Oh no you're not. I will not allow you to sleep on my couch."

"But Rebecca, I don't want to leave you tonight."

Rebecca stood and took Michael by his hands and guided him up. She slowly pulled her shirt over her head and watched Michael stare at the way her voluptuous breasts filled her Cross Your Heart Bra. She then took both his hands and cupped her breasts with them. After a few seconds she removed his hands and turned around.

"Michael, please unhook my bra," she whispered.

Michael slowly unhooked the three snaps as she turned to face him. She slowly lowered the straps off her shoulders and tossed the bra on the couch as she passionately kept her eyes on his.

Michael lowered his eyes to the firmness of her breasts as the bra came off. Her breasts stood without sagging at all. Rebecca then took Michael's hands and cupped her bare breasts with his; this time massaging his hands on them.

"I'm sorry Michael; I cannot allow you to sleep on my couch. No fiancé of mine is going to sleep on my couch. You're going to sleep in my bed. Michael, please take me to bed."

Michael lifted her as Rebecca put her arms around his neck and kissed him.

After a few seconds Rebecca laid her head back and Michael carried her the rest of the way sucking on her breast.

CHAPTER

45

The next morning Rebecca rolled over and watched Michael sleep. He was totally naked as was she. Her love making did not yet include penetration but she did enjoy watching Michael's pleasure as she helped him release his manhood fluids. Her staring in his face woke him.

"Good morning beautiful, how are you this lovely morning?"

"I couldn't be better. I'm so happy you stayed the night. I think tonight will be even better," she said as she kissed him.

"I'm looking forward to going to bed, and waking up with you always. I can't wait to watch the sun rise, and set, on your beauty."

"Thank you Michael. Thank you for being you. How about some breakfast? I hope you're hungry."

"Sure I'm hungry; I'll get up and help you. We're a team, aren't we?"

"Yes we are, but this morning I'm making you breakfast while you sit and watch TV. Rebecca leaned over to kiss Michael and he grabbed her and pulled her towards him. She didn't resist at all when she felt his manhood against her. She closed her eyes and rolled over on her back as her eyes remained closed.

When Michael saw her closed eyes he whispered to her; "not now my love, how about we wait until tonight?" He wanted the moment to be right.

Rebecca sensed the disappointment in Michael and just said okay.

"I don't know about you but I could use a shower. Why don't you start breakfast and I'll be out in ten minutes," said Michael.

"Yes my love."

After Michael showered he had no choice but to put on his same clothes. When he entered the kitchen, he saw his future wife cooking breakfast and watched her.

Rebecca turned and saw him. She stopped what she was doing and gave him a long passionate kiss.

"What took you so long in there? I was afraid you snuck out the bathroom window," she joked. "I missed you."

"Sneak out the bathroom window? It's too late for that. You'll never get rid of me now. I'm here to stay. You're mine. You're mine forever."

Rebecca cried tears of joy in Michael's arms.

"Let's get married today," she said.

"Today? Nothing doing. We don't have time today. I have a busy day planned ahead for us."

"Oh yeah, tell me about the busy day you have planned for us that I know nothing about." Rebecca said as she kissed him.

"First of all, after breakfast I need to go home and change. Then I'm coming back to pick you up and we're going shopping."

"Shopping? Shopping for what?"

"Look at your hands?"

"What's wrong with my hands?" Rebecca asked as she looked at them.

"There's something missing."

"Missing? Did I lose a finger? Hold on," she laughed. "Nope, I still have ten fingers."

"Rebecca, do you remember what you said to me last night?"

"I said a lot of things to you last night. Mostly, *I love you*, why?"

"Let me remind you. You said; *"No fiancé of mine is going to sleep on my couch.* Well my love; *No fiancée of mine is going to walk around without a diamond engagement ring."*

Rebecca froze while she started to cry as she looked at her naked ring finger.

"Oh Michael, it's not necessary. I don't need a ring. I know you love me."

"For me it's necessary. For you, you deserve one and you're getting one. Case closed. Now, if you please, I like my eggs over easy."

"Oh Michael, I love you."

"And I love you too."

CHAPTER

A fter breakfast Michael and Rebecca talked briefly about the day's plans. Rebecca loved the way Michael took charge without actually bossing her around. They agreed on Michael picking her up at noon. They kissed goodbye and as soon as Michael left the phone rang.

"Hello."

"Hello Rebecca, it's Christine."

"Good morning Christine."

"Rebecca, you're making me crazy. I was afraid to call you. I sat in my car last night for over an hour and then fell asleep. How did it go? What time did Michael leave?"

"To answer your first question; everything went better than I could have ever expected. Michael is the perfect man. He asked no questions at all. He told me I can talk about it with him if

I want. If I don't want to talk about it he won't pressure me. Actually, he sounded a little like you, the way you've always said it wasn't my fault. He kept telling me that it didn't matter to him. What matters now is he wants to move forward in our relationship. Christine, Michael loves me. I mean he really does love me."

"Rebecca I'm so happy for you. Aren't you glad I talked you into calling him?"

"Yes I am. I can't thank you enough. We really *are* like family."

"Like family? We are family, and don't you forget it. So, it sounds like you two are back together since he wants the relationship to move forward."

"That's the other thing I wanted to tell you."

"What's that?"

"Do you want to know what move forward means?"

"Of course I do."

"He asked me to marry him," Rebecca said as she started to cry tears of joy.

"Oh my God Rebecca. I'm so happy for you. He really is a good man."

"Yes he is. Now, do you want me to answer your other question?"

"What other question?"

"Your first question was; *how did it go?* Your second question was; *what time did Michael leave?*"

"Well, what time *did* he leave?" Like a school girl Rebecca answered.

"About five minutes ago."

"What? He spent the night?"

"Yes, he spent the night."

"Oh Rebecca, I'm so happy for you. What happened? Did you do it?"

"I'm sorry Christine but that's private."

"I know, I'm sorry I asked."

"That's all right. Anyway, guess what else."

"What?"

"He went home to change and he's picking me up at noon. Guess where we're going. He's taking me to buy a diamond engagement ring."

"Ooooooh my God. You are a lucky girl."

"I thought you said that he was the lucky one to have me?" Rebecca laughed.

"I changed my mind. You're both lucky that you found each other."

CHAPTER

Michael waited for Rebecca downstairs for about five minutes since he showed up a few minutes early. The beauty Rebecca possessed almost stopped his heart as he watched her walk out of the building wearing black dress slacks, high heels, a tight orange pullover shirt, a short opened brown leather jacket, and a black shoulder bag.

She had a renewed confidence within herself this afternoon.

"Hello again my future husband," she said as she leaned over after she got into the car and kissed him.

"Hello again to you my future wife. You look stunning."

"Thank you."

"I love that necklace," Michael said as he slipped his hand under it while brushing the back of his hand on her breast. "I've never seen it before."

"Thank you. It was a Christmas gift from Christine and Andreas. I hardly wear it. Only on special occasions do I take it out of the box; and today my love is a special occasion."

"Yes it is special. Are you ready to go diamond shopping?"

"Like I said before, it's not necessary, but I'm very excited."

Michael put the car in drive and pulled out.

"By the direction you're driving we're not going to Steinway Street are we?"

"You're very observant this morning. I like that."

"Where are we going?"

"Manhattan."

Rebecca was thinking about Macy's on 34th Street. The one time that she's been there, she remembered the beautiful jewelry department. She couldn't believe it. She was going to Macy's for a diamond ring, or so she thought. When Michael crossed the 59th Street Bridge and turned left Rebecca expected him to continue driving south to 34th Street. But that didn't happen. Michael turned right on East 57th street. As he approached 5th Avenue he pulled into a parking space. Rebecca looked around a little disappointed that they weren't going into Macy's but nonetheless was still excited.

"Are you ready to dress up that finger of yours?"

"Excited, happy, and yes, ready."

"Good, come on. Let's go."

When they got out of the car Michael held Rebecca by the hand and they walked west a half block to 5th Avenue. They waited for the light to change and crossed 57th Street heading south.

"Well Rebecca, let's go diamond shopping."

Rebecca stopped in her tracks as she looked at the sign on the building.

"Michael, are you serious? Here? No. It's too expensive."

"Nothing is too expensive for you."

"For Christ's sake Michael, it's Tiffany's! Tiffany's!"

"Nothing but the best for you."

Once inside they went straight to the fourth floor where the highest priced jewelry was and were met by two armed security guards.

"Good afternoon, can I direct you to the right department?" asked one of the guards.

"Yes please," said Michael. "We'd like to see engagement rings please."

"Of course, congratulations." The guard pointed them to the counter at the middle of the floor.

"Thank you sir," said Michael as the guard gave a respectful smile to Rebecca as she smiled back at him proudly.

Michael led Rebecca to the counter. Several customers were being helped with two salesmen waiting to make their next sale. The salesman immediately approached them.

"Good afternoon, I'm Mr. Cohen. Is there anything in particular I can help you with?"

"Yes please, my name is Michael Stylianou and this is my fiancée Rebecca. We're looking for an engagement ring."

"Congratulations, you've come to the right place."

"Thank you," said Rebecca.

"Yes, thank you," added Michael.

"Is there any particular shaped stone you have in mind?" Mr. Cohen asked Rebecca.

"Can you show us what you have?" Michael asked taking charge.

After fifteen minutes of trying on several rings, Rebecca seemed to like the marquise shaped stone.

"I'm starting to read your mind sweetheart. I also think the marquise is beautiful. Besides, it fits your finger like a glove."

"Michael, can I speak to you in private for a minute."

"Sure, what's the matter?" he asked as they stepped away. "You're not changing your mind about marrying me are you?" he joked.

"Of course not. I saw the price tag. It's much too expensive."

"Let me worry about that."

"Michael, it's six thousand dollars."

Michael then took Rebecca by the hand after kissing her and telling her that he loved her, back to the counter, and said, "We'll take it."

"Good choice," said Mr. Cohen. "Just give me a couple minutes."

Mr. Cohen quickly brought over a ring cleaning machine, put on his eye piece, and examined the prongs to make sure they were tight. Then he put it in a beautiful blue velvet box and asked them to follow him to the cashier.

Mr. Cohen congratulated them again, shook Michael's hand, and smiled at Rebecca.

Michael paid using his credit card. When the cashier handed Michael the little bag with the ring, he instantly took the box out and opened it. He took the ring out, got on one knee in front of everyone in the store and asked; "Rebecca my love, will you marry me?" as he put the ring on her finger.

Everyone who saw clapped. Many of the men shook Michael's hand while the women hugged Rebecca as tears filled her eyes.

"Congratulations," one of the armed guards told them as they approached the elevator.

"What a nice couple," Rebecca heard the other guard say as the elevator doors closed as they went down.

Outside, Rebecca suggested they go for a walk. Michael held her hand and led her to central park where they sat on a bench and talked. Rebecca felt that now was the time to open up about her parents.

"I wish my parents were here to see me now. I know they'd love you."

Cautiously Michael asked, "Where are they?"

"They were killed in a car accident two years before the invasion. I don't have any brothers or sisters. I wish I had a sister to show my ring to. The closest thing to a sister I have is Christine. Let's go show her," Rebecca said excitingly.

"Yes of course, let's go now. But after that I need to take you to my parent's house."

"I'm sorry Michael. How selfish of me. Let's go to your parent's house first."

"No, that can't happen. Once we get there they'll never let us leave. We'll see them for dinner."

"That sounds better. The few times that I've met them I really liked them. I hope they feel the same about me."

"Believe me when I tell you; they do."

CHAPTER

As Michael was crossing the 59ᵗʰ Street Bridge to return to Astoria, he couldn't help noticing Rebecca.

"What are you staring at?" he smiled.

"My ring, as if you didn't know. I can't keep my eyes off it. I can't wait to show Christine. Michael, look at it. Isn't it beautiful?"

"On your finger it does look beautiful. In the box, it's only a ring."

"Michael, I want to tell you something."

"Let me guess. You love me?"

"Besides that."

"Go ahead."

"My last name wasn't always Ioannou. I was born Rebecca Economou. I had to pose as Haji's older sister to escape Cyprus. I bought myself a new identity."

"Sweetheart, now I'm beginning to understand the relationship. But I don't understand how you escaped with Haji. What was Haji doing in Cyprus when his parents were here?"

Rebecca started telling Michael her story as he listened in silence. She explained about Haji waking and finding his parents being tortured. She explained in detail about Haji's adoption and how she had to give up half the monastery's gold so General Franklyn would give them passports. At this time she left out all the atrocities.

"I'm starting to understand. I wish I was there to help you."

No you don't, Rebecca thought.

As Michael approached Christine's house he said, "This is great Rebecca, Christine has a driveway. I don't have to drive around looking for a parking space."

"Yes it is. They're very lucky. I can't wait to show her my ring."

As Michael turned into the driveway, Christine noticed them from the window. By the time Rebecca reached the front door Christine was already standing there with the door opened. Rebecca held up her finger.

"Oh Rebecca, it's beautiful. Congratulations. I'm so happy for you. I'm so happy for both of you," as she hugged Rebecca and motioned for Michael to form a group hug.

"Michael, come here. Let me give you a special hug. A welcome to the Ioannou family hug," as she wrapped her arms around him tight as Michael whispered in her ear, "Thank you for calling me last night."

Christine hugged them both again and cried.

CHAPTER

49

At this time Haji was keeping steady company with Georgia and double dating with Tommy-Two-Fingers and Kathy. Haji was still working at the diner with Andreas trying to keep his temper under control. It seemed whenever a customcr got out of control Haji always used violence.

Finally one Saturday morning, Andreas couldn't take it any-more. He didn't want to bother Rebecca because she was hap-pily engaged and planning her wedding. She didn't need to be reminded about her time in Cyprus with Haji. So he almost had to bodily put Haji into the car to bring him to Fr. Harry.

"Dad, I don't want to see Fr. Harry. Why do I have to go? I don't like him."

"Why don't you like him? He's a very good priest. You need to be spiritually connected to something. You have too much anger in you. Just talk to him. You must stop the fighting."

"Dad, I don't fight. I defend myself. There's a difference you know!"

"Don't try to convince me of the difference. I know the difference between defending yourself and constantly looking for a fight to show you're a tough guy, or to prove nobody's going to mess with you. Your mother and I are worried that one day you're going to really hurt someone and end up going to jail. You don't want to go to jail, believe me you don't."

Andreas pulled into the church parking lot and parked next to Fr. Harry's car.

"You see Fr. Harry's car Haji? It's a real piece of junk. Do you know why? It's because he makes very little money and any money he does have leftover he uses it to help people. He's a very good and caring man. Please, please give him a chance."

Andreas got out of the car while Haji sat in the passenger seat without moving. Andreas had to open the passenger door and pull Haji out.

"Let's go, you're coming inside with me now!"

Reluctantly Haji followed Andreas to Fr. Harry's office.

"Ahh, Haji, it's nice to see you," said Fr. Harry. "Please come in. How are you today?"

"I'm fine today, thank you."

"Good, good to hear it."

"Andreas, and you're also doing fine I hope?"

"Oh yes Father, I'm fine too. Thank you."

"Good, and Christine?"

"She's fine too, thank you."

"Great, everybody's doing fine. Andreas, can you give Haji and I a little time to be alone please?"

"Father, I thought maybe I should stay and talk too."

"Not today. Today I want to speak exclusively to Haji. Maybe it would be a good idea if you went home. It's warm out today. Haji can walk home. You're okay with that Haji, aren't you?"

"Yes Father," said Haji.

Disappointed, Andreas left and went home.

"So Haji, how are you today? I mean really? How are you *really* doing?"

"Like I told you before Father, I'm fine. You don't have to keep asking me."

"All right Haji, if that's the way you want to go, we can go that way."

"What way are you talking about?" Haji snapped back with an attitude.

"The way you're talking to me now," Fr. Harry raised his voice. "You need to change your attitude. You may be a tough guy out there, but in here you're going to respect me if you know what's good for you."

"Oh yeah, what's good for me? Huh? You tell me what's so good for me. I'm not afraid of you or anyone else."

"Oh really tough guy. Well let me tell you something tough guy! I'm not impressed! Your aggression should not be used the way you use it. Your aggression should be used for good. Not to hurt people. If you don't turn your anger into positive things I guarantee you you're going to get arrested. If you go to jail it's going to be all over for you. It'll give you a record that can never be erased.

"Do you have any idea what you going to jail will do to your parents? If you don't care what happens to yourself at least think of your parents! It took them twelve-years to connect with you! They don't want to lose you! Not only after two and a half years! I know you have anger in you! I know you want revenge! But these people you're fighting with here are not the ones that hurt you in Cyprus! These people didn't do anything to you! Wake up and smarten up!"

Haji fell silent. He didn't know how to answer because he didn't have an answer. Deep down Haji knew Fr. Harry was right.

When Fr. Harry saw the way Haji fell silent, he decided to change his tone.

"Look Haji," he started in his soft spoken pastoral voice. "I know you've been through a lot. I don't know all your details but I've heard many stories from others who escaped Cyprus with their lives. Like I've told you before, I'm here for you. Whenever you want to talk, I'm always available for you. Have you ever thought about your future?"

"I don't know what you mean."

"Your future. You're going to be fifteen-years old next month. You do want to go to college don't you?"

"I don't know. My parents want me to be a lawyer. I don't know. I'm beginning to think you're right. Maybe I do have too much anger in me. Right now I know I can never concentrate on college with my anger."

"So put your anger to good use. Keep your anger within the confines of the law."

"I don't know what you mean."

"Look, I would love nothing better than for you to satisfy your parent's dream of becoming a lawyer. Law school is a lot of money. I know your parents have the money. But unless you get that anger out of your system you'll never make it without getting into trouble. Control, you need control."

"Father please, tell me. How can I control my anger?"

"Like I said before. Keep it within the confines of the law. You're a big guy. You're also strong. Have you ever thought of playing football? That's a good sport to release anger. What about the YMCA? You can take up boxing. That's a sport that lets you punch people, and it's legal. What about this one? Join the army when you're eighteen. You can become Special Forces. These are only some of the ways to release some of your anger."

"I never thought of it that way. But to tell you the truth Father, there's a particular anger I have that I don't think I'll ever let go."

"Do you want to talk about it my son?"

"I don't know. I'm not sure. It's just…It's just there was this one person."

"What person my son? Who was it?"

"Well Father, I know you know what happened to my parents. My real parents and my sister. It was horrible. But after the Turks took over the monastery there was this one person that stood out among all the rest. Please don't get me wrong. They were all bad. Very bad. Very, very bad. But this one guy, his name was Private Akman. He was the worst. He seemed to get the most pleasure out of it. He was the one that cut my mother's belly open while she was still alive just to see what she was carrying, a boy or a girl. He needs to get killed. I would love to go back to Cyprus one day or wherever he is and kill him. He's the guy that's doing this to me. He was also bad to Rebecca."

"Let's keep Rebecca out of this. She's getting married in two weeks. This is a happy time for her. Let's concentrate on you. Haji, I'm sure that you're wondering how God can allow these things to happen. Let's not forget that the devil is the driving force in all evil. We make choices. Some of our choices aren't God loving choices. But nevertheless, the choices are ours.

"Do you see what's happening here? This Private Akman is taking over your mind. You escaped him. Or at least you think you escaped him. He's beating you up every day in your mind and you don't realize it. Please, please try to count your blessings. Your ultimate goal is to forgive him, because if you don't forgive him then he still continues to have complete power over you."

"Now you're starting to sound like Fr. Demitri with all your forgiveness stuff."

Haji's eyes were starting to swell up. Deep down Haji knew Fr. Harry was right. But he could never bring himself to forgive Private Akman.

"Listen to me Haji. I don't believe in coincidences. Why do you think you're here?"

"Where?"

"Here at St. Demitrios Greek Orthodox Church. Your spiritual Fr. Demitri is just another way to pronounce St. Demitrios. Isn't that something? I believe somehow Fr. Demitri sent you to St. Demitrios."

After an hour of talking, Fr. Harry asked Haji do a little soul searching after he went home, but not before taking him into the church to pray. He assured Haji that he had his entire life ahead of him and it was up to him to decide which direction it will go.

"Thank you Fr. Harry. You opened my eyes today. I'll try my best to change my ways."

"That's all I ask of you. You're a good kid who's turning into a man. I'll see you in church tomorrow. All right?"

"All right Father."

CHAPTER

The Wedding, June 1977

Christine and Andreas insisted on Rebecca sleeping at their house the night before the wedding. They were her family. They wanted everyone to know. Besides, no woman should wake up alone on the morning of her wedding.

Andreas sat with Michael when the wedding was being planned and explained; "The least Christine and I can do is to pay for the wedding since if not for her we would have never connected with Haji." By now Michael knew just about everything there was to know about how Rebecca came to America with Haji to find his biological parents. Michael agreed to let Andreas pay.

The wedding was beautiful. Christine was the matron of honor. Andreas wanted to walk Rebecca up the aisle, but Rebecca wanted Haji to give her away. Andreas was happy to step aside for his son. Michael decided to have Christine's brother Basil as his best man; the perfect choice since it was Basil and Athena who introduced him to the love of his life.

Rebecca was the most beautiful bride the one hundred and fifty guests had ever seen. When the limousine driver opened the door, Rebecca stepped out looking like a goddess. Against Christine's advice, Rebecca wore her hair like she always wore it. Her hair fell down naturally straight with a slight wave.

Under no circumstances was Rebecca going to make herself up with a phony up-dee-do.

Rebecca wanted to look like Rebecca.

Haji looked as handsome as ever in his tuxedo as he slowly walked Rebecca up the aisle as her prince charming stood there waiting for his future wife.

Fr. Harry did a splendid job preforming the wedding service. The entire church clapped as he said; *"Michael, you may kiss the bride."*

The wedding reception was at none other than the Chrystal Palace, the place where Andreas and Christine reconnected after ten years. When the maître d' announced, "For the first time as Mr. and Mrs. Michael Stylianou," Christine broke down in Haji's arms.

Haji was happy his parents allowed him to bring his girl-friend Georgia. They were keeping steady company even though Georgia's parents weren't happy with him because they heard through the grapevine that Haji's been getting into trouble in school. Besides, he was Cypriot and her family was from the island of Nisyros.

When the time came for Michael to dance with his mother, she cried tears of joy in his arms. She worried that her son would never settle down. The minute she met Rebecca, she knew she was the one for her only child. For the few months that Michael and Rebecca had broken up, it actually devastated her.

Since Rebecca didn't have a father, she danced with Haji even though he was slightly embarrassed. By now Haji was fifteen-years old with broad shoulders, already six feet tall and handsome. All of the guests watched Rebecca as she danced with who many thought was her younger brother.

The next morning Michael and Rebecca were on the plane headed to the beautiful island of Mykonos for their honeymoon. Rebecca dozed off staring out the window. When she awakened, she thought about the time a few short years ago when she was on the bus going from the American Embassy to the airport. She saw Private Akman smiling at her while he held his crotch. Then she thought;

I'm on my honeymoon you jerk. I'm not going to let you ruin my honeymoon. Because of you I can never have peace. Because of you, as long as I'm alive I'll always look over my shoulder for fear that I'll see you. But not now. Not today. Not this week. I'm on my honeymoon.

CHAPTER

51

"Haji, look at the time. Where were you?"

"Dad, I was out with Georgia."

"Georgia? It's one o'clock in the morning. Georgia's parents let her stay out this late?"

"Well not really. We went to the movies and then I took her home."

"Why did you lie to me?"

"I didn't lie. I *was* with Georgia. I dropped her off then I went to hang out with my friends."

"Friends? You call those pot smoking bums friends? I don't want you hanging out with them. They're trouble."

"They're not trouble. They're good guys."

"Haji, please listen to you father," cried Christine.

"Come on Mom. I'm not doing anything wrong. I'm just hanging out with my friends."

"Till one o'clock in the morning?" yelled Andreas.

"Dad, today was the last day of school. I wanted to celebrate with my friends."

"I understand, but you told me you wanted to open the diner tomorrow morning. It's one o'clock in the morning. How are you going to open? What kind of shape will you be in?"

"Dad, you go to bed at one o'clock in the morning and wake up at five."

"Listen to me son," Andreas whispered; thinking it's better to change his tone. "Yes I do get to bed late and wake up early. And I am happy you want to help out with opening the diner, but I want you to get enough sleep. I need to know that you can handle it. Your mother and I are afraid that you're going to get arrested for smoking marijuana. You need to work this summer and save your money."

"Yes Haji," chimed in Christine. "You also need to change your friends. We really like Georgia. She's such a wonderful girl. I'm afraid she's not going to want to be your girlfriend anymore if you continue to smoke marijuana. Continue to go out with Georgia, but come home after you drop her off. Please stop hanging around those guys in the school yard. Remember, you're going to college. You're going to be a lawyer."

"I'm tired. I want to go to bed. Can we talk about this tomorrow?"

"All right son, go to bed," said Andreas. "I'll be relieving you tomorrow after lunch. Please be careful opening."

"Thanks Mom, thanks Dad. I know that you care. I'll try to make you proud of me."

"Stop hoping," replied Andreas. "We're already proud of you."

CHAPTER

The next morning Haji was awake on time. As he approached the diner, Tommy-Two-Fingers was waiting by the door.

"Tommy, what are you doing here so early? Your parents throw you out?"

"No, everyone's been breaking my balls to get a job. So my father got me a job working for an exterminating company. You believe this shit? Me becoming an exterminator, just so I can remove rats from traps?"

"You gotta be kidding. Is that what you're going to do all summer? Clean rat traps?"

"Yep, that's me. Even Kathy wanted me to get a job. So hurry up and open the doors. I need to eat something before I go to work."

"Sure thing, how about some rats and eggs?"

"Don't be a fuckin wise guy."

CHAPTER

53

The rest of the month everything went well for everyone and continued to do so. Michael and Rebecca came back from their honeymoon and moved into a beautiful high rise apartment building on Park Avenue. Michael thought it would be better for him to live close to his job since he worked late almost every night. Especially since many of his high profile clients also lived in Manhattan.

Michael and Rebecca became the perfect host and hostess. The word spread that they hosted the most beautiful cocktail parties. As always, whenever they hosted a party, Rebecca was, without a doubt, the glamour of the party; *Admired by men, and envied by women.*

Through Michael's wealthy clients he was able to get Rebecca a teaching job at a prestigious private school in Manhattan making five times the salary she made at St. Demitrios.

As happy as Rebecca was at her new job she missed her students at St. Demitrios because the kids at the private school were a little on the spoiled side. But all in all teaching was always her passion.

Every night no matter how late, Rebecca always waited for Michael to eat dinner together. Rebecca loved being married to Michael. She had never seen an angry side of him. The patience he had for her was second to none. But in the end it paid off for him. Their love making was as part of their lives as was eating and sleeping. As far as Michael was concerned, Rebecca's past atrocities were a thing of the past.

But Rebecca's love for Michael made her the world's best actress. Michael had no idea that whenever they made love, Rebecca only saw Private Akman. Her biggest fear still, was that one day Private Akman would somehow find her and rape her again.

Haji was working six days a week at the diner. In the three plus years he's been in America, he learned the diner business as well as anyone. He opened in the morning, and worked through lunch. At night he had dinner either at home or at Georgia's house. Georgia's parents were beginning to accept Haji because they knew their daughter loved him. They were beginning to face the fact that at fifteen-years old their daughter might end up with a Cypriot.

CHAPTER

"Tommy, hey Tommy, where you going?" yelled Haji one Saturday afternoon when he left the diner.

"I gotta go into Manhattan."

"Manhattan? What for?"

"There's this filthy piece of shit restaurant that has more rats than cockroaches. I have to go there every morning as the owner opens and remove all the dead rats caught in the traps during the night."

"Holy shit. That must really suck."

"You have no idea. Sometimes I have to scrape them off because my boss, the cheap fuck that he is, makes me reuse the traps with blood all over them."

"It's the middle of the afternoon, you're late."

"I know. My boss got a new account at some catering hall on Long Island. He needed me to set traps. I'm getting tired of all these fuckin rats."

"I would tell you to tell them to get a cat, but I don't want you to lose your job to a cat. Then you'll have no money to take Kathy out."

"First of all at this place they don't need a cat, they need a lion. That's how big and many the rats are. Second of all, Kathy will never leave me; I'm too much of a stud."

"Oh yeah? That's not what she tells me," laughed Haji.

"Very funny wise guy. By the way, what are you doing now?"

"Right now, nothing, why?"

"Why don't you come with me to The Bowery and see what a real man's job is like?"

"I can't. I told Georgia I was going to take her out for pizza."

"Pussy whipped."

Haji thought for a few seconds. "You know what? Fuck it. Give me a minute, let me call her and tell her I'm going with you to work. I also need to tell my father I'm going with you too; otherwise he'll think I got killed on the way home.

Haji ran back into the diner and called Georgia. Georgia was fine with it. She told Haji that she would be home watching TV. Andreas on the other hand was not as accepting. He knew Tommy was one of Haji's' friends that smoked marijuana. But after a second thought, he didn't give Haji too much of a hard time because Haji was accompanying Tommy to work. Andreas knew what type of work Tommy was doing this summer, and felt it would be good for Haji to see what other jobs were like.

"Haji, be careful, don't get bit. Most rats carry rabies. If one of those rats bites you you're going to need twenty needles in your stomach."

"Yeah Dad I know. One of the guys Tommy works with got bit and that's exactly what happened to him."

"I'm sorry someone got bit, but I'm glad you're aware."

"Thanks Dad, I won't be late."

⊱✦⊰

"Haji, what took you so long," asked Tommy.

"You know my father always gives me the be careful speech."

"Yeah, what is it with fathers? How come they're always lecturing us on being careful?"

"The fuck do I know."

CHAPTER

Leaving the subway at Delancey Street and The Bowery they walked along The Bowery for two blocks.

"There it is Haji, the Takeout Grill. The dirtiest piece of shit place around."

"Sure looks like it. So what do we do now? Just go in there and clean off the rat traps?"

"Yeah, that's exactly what we're going to do. The only thing is Tahar works from three until closing at midnight."

"So what?"

"Tahar's the owner's cousin. It's five o'clock, and he's in there now."

"So what, what's the big deal?"

"He's a real fuckin scumbag. Just watch the way he acts. He acts like he owns me. Fuckin guy is always yelling at me, calling me rat trap and shit. He's always telling me I'm not doing my job because he still has rats. But I figured out his problem."

"Yeah, what's his problem?"

"He's afraid of rats. Last week there was a rat under the counter. You should have seen him jump. Then he started yelling at me, like it was my fault. If I didn't need this job I'd shove a rat up his ass."

"You're cruel to even think of doing something like that."

"Yeah I know. Anyway, let's get this over with, besides, you know that I'm a crazy motherfucker, but I can never really shove a rat up someone's ass. But I'll tell you this; I would love to beat the living shit out of him."

Haji was a couple of steps behind Tommy as they walked towards the Takeout Grill. Tommy opened the door and held it for Haji to go in first.

"Look at that," said Tommy. Over there in the corner. See the rat? They're all over the fuckin place. Look at the size of it"

When Haji looked inside his heart stopped. He froze in his tracks. He kept staring into the restaurant as Tommy continued holding the door.

"Haji, what the fuck? You coming or not?"

Haji just stood there. It was as though he was in cement shoes. Finally he spoke.

"Give me a minute," Haji said calmly. "I need to call Georgia and let her know I'm not taking her for pizza."

"I thought you did that already."

"I tried. Her phone was busy. I need to try again."

"Go ahead pussy whipped. Go get your girlfriend's permission," laughed Tommy.

"Hey rat trap. You're fuckin late," Tahar said. "You were supposed to be here this morning. I don't need to get to work and see all those dead rats like I did today."

Tommy wanted to put down his bag of rat bait and start pounding on Tahar but knew better. He wasn't going to get fired over this little piece of shit. He knew at the end of the summer he would have some of his friends get pleasure out of beating the shit out of him. So for now, he bit his tongue.

"I'm sorry Tahar. My boss sent me somewhere else this morning and this is the first chance I had to get here all day."

"Just go downstairs and do your thing rat trap! And don't give me any of your shit!"

Tommy took a deep breath to control his temper.

"Yes sir, I'll only be a few minutes."

"Hurry the fuck up and do what you gotta do, and don't steal anything. I know what's down there."

That remark was almost the straw that broke the camel's back. Tommy stopped in his tracks, turned around, walked up to Tahar, looked him in the eyes, and said; "Look motherfucker. I'm not a crook. Do you hear me? I'm not a crook. If you don't believe me why don't you follow me and watch?"

"Just go do your fuckin job rat trap, and don't tell me what to do."

"I know why you don't follow me downstairs."

"Oh yeah, why?"

"It's because you're afraid of rats. That's why."

"Me? Afraid of rats? Very funny. I'm not afraid of anything or anybody."

Tommy waited a second or two and then quickly looked down towards Tahar's feet and yelled; "Look out, there's a rat!"

Tahar almost hit the ceiling as he screamed.

"Yeah, you're not afraid of rats. You're not afraid of anything," laughed Tommy as he turned around and went into the basement.

When Tommy entered the basement all ten rat traps were full. It was exactly what he expected. For the last month, Tommy had been there six days a week and always all ten traps were full. If there were a hundred traps they would be full. The subway ran directly under the street and the New York City subway system has always been a haven for rats. Tommy and his boss knew it was a losing battle but as long as they kept killing rats no one could really accuse them of not doing their jobs.

When finished, Tommy went back upstairs and opened the back door into the alley and put the bag of dead rats into the dumpster and came back inside.

"Tahar, all done. Ten killed and ten traps reset. Someone will be here tomorrow afternoon."

"Tomorrow afternoon? Bullshit! I want someone here tomorrow morning!"

"Well, all I can say is call the office."

Outside, Tommy looked around for Haji. He was nowhere to be found. *Chicken shit,* he thought.

He's probably just as afraid of rats as Tahar.

CHAPTER

56

Haji sat in the back of the pizza shop the entire time Tommy was in the Takeout Grill. When he first got inside he knew that he needed to see Tommy leave. So he positioned himself in the back. He wanted to make sure Tommy wouldn't see him.

The moment Haji saw Tommy pass the pizza shop he went directly to the nearest phone booth. After the third ring she answered.

"Hello."

"Hi Rebecca, it's Haji, how you doing?"

"Haji, it's nice to hear your voice. I'm doing well thank you. What about you? You're doing fine I hope?"

"Rebecca, you know me. I'm always doing fine."

"All right little brother, what's wrong?"

"Nothing's wrong. Can't I call my big sister just to see how she's doing?"

"Yes you can, I'm sorry. Where are you?"

"I'm in Manhattan. When you and Michael were over for dinner on Sunday, Michael said he was going away this week on business. Is he still away?"

"Yes he is. He's flying home from Boston on the red eye tonight. He should be home by one o'clock in the morning. Why do you ask, and what are you doing in Manhattan?"

"Well, you know my friend Tommy?"

"Yes, he's one of your marijuana buddies, why?"

"Well, he's an exterminator this summer and I came with him to clean out some rat traps in some restaurant downtown…"

"Haji, that's disgusting," Rebecca interrupted.

"I know. When I got to the restaurant, I saw a rat and chickened out; so I left. I figure since I'm off tomorrow, and I'm already in Manhattan and Michael's away we can have dinner together."

"That's so sweet of you Haji. Of course I'll have dinner with you. What do you want me to make for dinner?"

"No no no, we're going out. I'm taking my sister out."

"You know what Haji, let's do it. I've been home alone every night. Yeah, let's go out."

"I'll tell you what, I'll take the subway up to your apartment and we'll go out somewhere near where you live.

"That sounds great."

"Can you do me a favor? Can you call my parents and let them know my plans? I don't have any more change."

"Of course, I'll call them as soon as I hang up with you. I'll also tell the doorman to expect you."

"Great, see you in about half an hour."

CHAPTER

57

A t Rebecca's apartment building the doorman greeted Haji and asked if he could help him. Haji introduced himself and the doorman rang Rebecca to announce him. When Haji walked into the apartment Rebecca greeted him with open arms. Haji loved the way Rebecca decorated the apartment. It was not too overwhelming. It was just right. Nothing fancy about the place. Neat and clean with a warm home feeling.

"Haji, what a surprise, it's so nice to see you."

"It's nice to see you too."

"Here, sit down. Visit with me a little before dinner."

Haji sat and they talked for a while. Rebecca asked how Georgia's doing, and if Haji was looking forward to the upcoming school year. Haji knew he needed to tell Rebecca what she needed to hear so he just yessed her.

"Haji, what's wrong? There's something wrong. I can see it in your eyes."

"Nothing Rebecca, I guess I'm just hungry, that's all, and I did get a little queasy when I saw the rat."

"All right then, let's go. I'm hungry too, and do me a favor. I don't want to hear another word about rats."

"I promise."

Downstairs Haji asked the doorman to call them a taxi.

"Why do we need a taxi?" Rebecca asked as the doorman stepped away.

"When I was downtown I saw an Italian restaurant. Let's go try it."

"Great, you know I like Italian food. Now I'm really hungry."

Haji gave the intersection of The Bowery to the cab driver. Rebecca couldn't understand why Haji wanted to go to a restaurant on The Bowery but didn't question him. When the driver stopped, Haji paid him and got out with Rebecca.

"Haji, where's the restaurant? I don't like this neighborhood."

"Sorry Rebecca, I made a mistake. I feel so stupid."

"Stop that, you just made a mistake. You're not stupid."

"I know, thanks. Anyway, we're only a few blocks away. Come on."

As Haji passed the pizza place he had eaten in, he led Rebecca to the Takeout Grill, peeked inside, and saw it was empty.

"Come on, let's go."

"Where?"

"In there."

"I'm not eating in there."

"Oh yes you are," Haji said as he took her by the hand, opened the door, and guided Rebecca directly in front of him.

"Haji, what's going on? What are you doing? This place is filthy," she whispered.

Tahar had his back to the door. When he heard them come in he turned around and faced them.

"Can I help you?" asked Tahar.

Rebecca was standing an inch away from Haji directly in front of him. If Haji wasn't behind her, Rebecca would have fallen onto the floor.

"Excuse me, I asked if I can help you. If you're not ordering anything I'm busy," Tahar said with arrogance.

Rebecca started to shake. Haji guided her to a small chair to sit as she started to cry.

Haji turned around, locked the door, and turned the sign from open to closed.

Then he walked behind the counter.

"Hey, what the fuck are you doing back here?" said Tahar.

Haji looked around and saw the staircase that led to the basement.

"As a matter of fact you *can* help me Private Akman."

CHAPTER

58

Rebecca stared at Private Akman as she sat reliving those hellish days.

How many times did he beat her?

How many times did he humiliate her?

How many times did he rape her?

She didn't even know, as she sat there in shock. She couldn't believe he was standing right there. Right there in front of her. *Why did Haji bring me here?*

"I haven't been called Private Akman since I got out of the Turkish Army. By the way, I got promoted to Sergeant Akman before I was honorably discharged. Do I know you?"

Honorably discharged? Rebecca thought trembling. They honored him?

When Rebecca heard him ask if Haji knew him she started to shake uncontrollably.

"Don't you recognize me?" asked Haji.

"No"

"What about her?" Haji asked as he pointed to Rebecca. "Do you recognize her?"

"No. What's her problem?"

"I'll show you her problem."

Haji towered over the 5'-4" 145 pound Private Akman, as he grabbed him by the hair and flung him across the room like a ragdoll toward the stairs, as Private Akman screamed in pain and confusion. Haji then slowly walked to Private Akman, lifted him by his hair, and threw him down the stairs as Private Akman screamed in agony as bones were heard breaking.

"Come on Rebecca, let's go. Come on I said. Let's go. Let's go downstairs."

Rebecca froze. She was glued to the seat. She couldn't move. Haji walked over to her, pulled her by the hand, and forcibly took her into the basement.

Private Akman was lying on the floor trying to move.

He couldn't move.

Downstairs Haji noticed the rat traps all full. He picked one up and put it on top of Private Akman's chest. Private Akman started to scream.

"Get it off of me, get it off of me! Please get it off of me!"

"Haji, what are you doing? Why did you bring me here? What's the matter with you?" cried Rebecca.

"Closure, that's why I brought you here. Closure. You see this piece of shit. He doesn't even remember us."

"Who are you people? Help me. I need help. I can't move my leg or shoulder. I think they're broken."

Private Akman's apron was lifted up to his waist. He was wearing shorts on this warm summer night. Rebecca clearly saw his leg broken at his shin, although the bone was not exposed, as he laid there on his back unable to move.

"Shut the fuck up," yelled Haji as he picked up another trap with a dead rat in it. He took it to the butcher block table, picked up a cleaver, chopped the rat in half, and shoved it into Private Akman's mouth.

Private Akman immediately started to choke so Haji pulled out the rat and shoved it down Private Akman's pants.

As Private Akman regained his composure, he started to whimper when he spoke.

"What's going on? Why are you doing this to me? Who are you? How do you know who I am?" as he tried to wiggle away like the little worm that he was.

Haji looked over at Rebecca to see her reaction of Private Akman's questions. He suddenly noticed the take charge part of her that she possessed when they first came to America to find Andreas and Christine. She walked up to Private Akman, looked down at him, and started to answer his questions.

"Who are we? Who are we you ask? You savage! You're going to find out who we are! Don't you recognize me? Huh? Don't I look familiar to you, you piece of garbage? Take another look! Think! Think real hard!"

"Who are you people? What the fuck are you talking about?" Private Akman cried.

"How dare you not remember," Rebecca screamed as she stepped on Private Akman's balls.

"Ouch! What the fuck? You crazy bitch!"

"Crazy bitch? I'll show you crazy bitch," Rebecca yelled as she stepped on Private Akman balls again. "So, you don't remember us Mr. Private Akman who has done such a great job and got promoted to Sergeant Akman! Well Sergeant, you don't mind me calling you Sergeant do you?"

Private Akman stared up at Rebecca in total confusion.

"Well Sergeant, I'm going to remind you who we are."

"Cyprus! 1974. The Monastery. Remember the monastery? Huh? You little worm," she said as she kicked him repeatedly in the balls as he screamed. "Here, how about this? All the women you raped up there in the monastery. You forgot? How about when you burnt down The Holy Cross and you grabbed twelve-year old Anna? She was twelve-years old and you made her get on her knees in front all those people to satisfy your sick mind. Then you told her mother that she was next so she had something to think about all day until the evening. Is your memory coming back now?" Rebecca continued to cry as she kicked him in the balls again.

"What about all those times you held back food from the children, just so you can have their mothers beg you for sex, just to satisfy that sick mind of yours? Remember that?

"Remember Fr. Demitri? He was the holiest man alive. Remember that morning? No? I'll remind you, you savage." She said as she kicked him in the balls again. "Remember when Fr. Demitri and Haji here," as she pointed to Haji as he sat on the steps staring at what was going on with tears dripping down his cheeks as *he* remembered.

"Remember when they came out of the chapel after being locked in all night? You had ten of us on our knees completely naked with our hands tied behind our backs and you told our dear Fr. Demitri to choose one of us? Remember? Then you grabbed me by the hair and pulled my head back and told him to pick me because you already warmed me up? Then you kicked me in the back of the head and sent me face first onto the stone ground and started laughing. Remember? You don't remember warming me up you demented barbarian? You don't remember laughing when I landed face first?" As she this time stepped on his broken leg, as Private Akman screamed in excruciating pain. "Then Fr. Demitri pulled out a gun and shot your piece of garbage uncle, the general? I was so sorry that Fr. Demitri didn't shoot you too. But not anymore. I'm glad he missed. I'm glad you're here now. I'm glad *I'm* here with you."

Haji stood from the steps and slowly walked over to Private Akman and looked down at him.

"What about my mother?" he whispered, "Huh? My dear pregnant mother. You remember her, don't you? You were the last one to rape her before you took out your knife and cut her belly open to see if she was carrying a boy or a girl. Do you remember that? You held my dead baby brother by his leg and yelled; it's a boy. Then you just left the baby on top of my mother as she bled to death. Is any of this bringing back any memories?"

Haji walked away and picked up the cleaver and held it over Private Akman's head.

"Don't worry; I'm not going to chop off your head. You need to suffer, and suffer you will. Chopping your head off would be much too easy of a death."

Then Haji went back to sit on the steps to watch Rebecca do her thing.

Private Akman stared up at Rebecca as he continued crying.

"Remembering now, aren't you?" Rebecca whispered.

"That was you?" Akman said. "It was part of the war. The war is over. Get on with your life. I'm getting on with mine."

"Get on with my life? You despicable excuse of a human being! Get on with my life? How dare you tell me to get on with my life! There hasn't been a second since that time that I haven't thought of you, and the things you made me do, and you don't remember me? How dare you not remember me!" she yelled as she stepped on his balls three more times."

All of a sudden Private Akman started to shake as he looked towards the wall.

Rebecca looked over to the wall to see what it was. It was a rat walking around.

"Hey Rebecca," chimed in Haji. "Our Honorably Discharged Sergeant is afraid of rats. Look at him. He's shitting in his pants. Rebecca, come here a minute. I want to show you something."

Rebecca didn't know what Haji wanted to show her but she kicked Private Akman in the balls again and went to the middle of the staircase to see what Haji wanted.

"Watch this," Haji stood and closed the basement lights. Holding Rebecca's hand, he told her to be quiet for a minute. After a few seconds Haji turned the lights back on and they both couldn't believe their eyes. There were about thirty rats that came out from under all the shelves where there must have been holes leading to the subway system. The minute the lights were turned on, the rats scattered back to where they came from with Private Akman screaming.

"See that shit? I told you, he's afraid of rats."

"Please, please, I'm sorry," cried Private Akman. "I remember now. I'm sorry. Please, please, I'm begging you. I can't move my leg. I can't move my shoulder. I need to go to the hospital. Please! Please! I'm begging you! Please!"

"Haji, I have an idea. Listen to me and listen to me good. Don't ask me any questions. Take the rat out of our Sergeant's pants."

"Why?"

"Just listen to me and don't ask me any questions I said!"

Haji jumped at the way Rebecca snapped at him.

"Take the two halves of the rat with the trap and put it in one of those bags over there. Clean off the cleaver and the butcher block table that you chopped it in half on. We can't leave any sign that anyone was here. Take the dead rat off him and put it back where it was. Wait a minute. Take the trap out of the bag and remove the other half of the rat. Throw the empty rat trap where you found it. I want the empty trap to look like a rat got away."

Haji put the trap with half the rat back on the butcher block table and scrapped it off with the cleaver. Then he cleaned off the butcher block and the cleaver again and threw the empty rat trap on the floor where he found it.

Rebecca looked around and liked what she saw. Everything looked perfect. She then walked up to Private Akman and asked him where exactly his leg hurt.

Private Akman slowly pointed to the spot that hurt on his leg.

"Here?" asked Rebecca as she kneeled down and gently stroked the spot where the leg was clearly broken.

"Yes, that's the exact spot."

Rebecca then noticed the wet spot between Private Akman's legs as she smelled urine.

"I see you peed your pants. I like that. It shows me you're scared," Rebecca smiled. "You've scared many people. You've made many people pee themselves. That's good. I'm glad you're scared." Rebecca continued as she slowly breathed in the smell of Private Akman's urine. "Ordinarily, the smell of urine would gross me out. But not now. Not *your* urine. Your urine smells like fear. And I love the smell of *your* fear."

Rebecca then squeezed the spot as Private Akman started to scream. Then Rebecca grabbed his leg with her other hand and started to bend it until she felt the bone completely separate, as the bone was now completely exposed through the skin.

She watched the blood ooze out as he screamed in agony.

Rebecca then stood, looking down at Private Akman and smiled as she stepped on his shoulder that was clearly dislocated, as Private Akman continued screaming.

"Now Honorable Sergeant, I'm sure you can't move at all."

"Please help me. I'm sorry. Please have mercy on me. Please, I'm begging you."

"You're begging me? I've begged you. Many people have begged you. All that begging did was make you happier. Now you want mercy? Mercy? You merciless barbarian!"

Rebecca then took the cleaver and made several small cuts on Private Akman's body as he screamed and continue begging for mercy. Then, while smiling down at him she slowly cleaned off the cleaver with his shirt.

"Haji, take the cleaver. Wash it off good and dry it thoroughly. I don't want to leave fingerprints. She then went to the staircase where Haji was enjoying the show and turned off the lights. After a minute or two Rebecca turned the lights back on and saw rats all over Private Akman's open bloody wounds as he was screaming and begging for mercy.

Rebecca looked down at Private Akman as he was shaking with fear as one of the rats continued to nibble on one of the several small cuts that she made.

"Sergeant, I need to leave now. Just in case you're not sure what's going to happen next, I'll tell you. I'm going to give you something to think about like you gave Anna's mother. I'm going to turn off the lights and go home while all those rats are eating you up alive. Did you hear me? I said; eat you up alive. Sergeant! Look at me. I want the last thing you see to be the smile on my face as you are being eaten alive. Good night Sergeant. Sweet dreams."

Rebecca quickly turned off the lights and followed Haji up the stairs while they heard Private Akman screaming and begging for Rebecca to come back.

"This way Rebecca. Let's go out the back door through the alley."

Rebecca followed Haji out the back door and watched Haji open the top of the dumpster to throw away the bag with the two halves of the rat.

"Haji stop!" Commanded Rebecca.

"What's the matter Rebecca?"

"Don't throw the bag into the dumpster. We're going to walk a few blocks and throw the bag down a sewer. I want to leave nothing to chance."

"Good idea big sister."

They walked the first block in silence. Immediately after Haji threw the bag down the sewer Rebecca asked; "Haji, are you all right?"

"Never felt better. I hope *you're* all right."

"Me? I'm perfect. Thank you for bringing me here. I now really have closure."

"So do I."

Rebecca knew that when Private Akman was found the next morning, it would look like he locked the front door to go to the basement for something, fell down the stairs, broke his leg, fell unconscious, and got eaten by the rats.

Just in case, they walked ten blocks as evidence that they weren't there before they hailed a taxi, and took it to Macy's on 34th Street. When they exited the taxi Rebecca hailed another taxi and told Haji to go home. Before Haji entered the taxi he hugged Rebecca and told her that he really loved her like an older sister and they both promised they would never speak about this evening ever to anyone. Not even to each other.

"Rebecca, what are you going to do now?"

"Macy's closes in thirty minutes. I need a new outfit."

"A new outfit? Now?"

"Yes little brother. Now."

Rebecca watched the taxi drive away as she walked into Macy's and went straight to the lingerie department. She looked around for a few minutes, decided on what she wanted, and paid for it.

When Rebecca exited Macy's she felt like the large weight that she had been carrying on her heart for the last three years had finally been lifted. It's a beautiful evening she thought. So she decided to walk home.

CHAPTER

When Haji arrived home his parents were watching TV. When he saw them, he walked up to his mother and bent down and hugged her. Then he went to his father and hugged him.

"Mom, Dad, I love you very much."

"Well son, we love you very much too," said Christine.

"Yes, son, we love you. How was dinner with Rebecca?" asked Andreas.

"Oh, it was pretty good. We did a lot of talking. I also did a lot of soul searching. I want to tell you both that I'm really sorry about the way I've been acting. I think I've figured it all out. Please give me a chance to show you. I want to go to college. I'm not too sure about being a lawyer, but I'm definitely going to college."

"I'm happy to hear that son," said Andreas.

"You can be anything you want," said Christine. "You have our support."

"Mom, Dad, can I tell you something?"

"Sure son," Christine answered.

"People always say to look at the bright side of things. Well, there is no bright side of what I went through in Cyprus, but I'm happy that I found you both. Am I making sense?"

The three of them just held each other and cried.

CHAPTER

Rebecca was starving by the time she reached home, so she decided to make a salad. She cleaned up and watched a little TV. At midnight she showered and thought about the heavy heart that no longer existed. She stood in the mirror and looked at her naked body.

She now knew it could never happen again.

She was finally free.

She slowly watched herself in the mirror as she put on her new shear black bra and panties. Michael loved to see her walking around in a black bra and panties although she always felt more feminine in pure white.

But tonight it is was all about Michael.

She watched herself as she put on her new shear white cover-up that only emphasized the black bra and panties.

Rebecca asked the doorman to buzz her when Michael was in the elevator on his way up. When Michael entered the apartment Rebecca was standing in front of him.

"Lock the door!" She commanded.

That evening they made love like they have never made love before.

The entire time, Rebecca did not close her eyes.

She kept staring into Michael's, and only Michael's eyes.

The End

EPILOGUE

After graduating college with a business degree, Haji decided to stay in the family business. Besides the Broadway Diner, he owns three others.

Since his Uncle Basil and Aunt Athena were unable to have children of their own, they willed everything to Haji.

As successful as Basil was, Haji built an enterprise. He expanded Basil's buildings into hotels, shopping centers, and malls.

Haji, together with his wife Georgia, are living on Long Island. Their four children, Mary, Andreas, Demitri, and Emanuel, along with their twelve grandchildren, often visit them either at their home, or their beautiful summer house in Southampton.

Rebecca and Michael are retired living in Manhattan, while spending their weekends and summers in their beautiful house in Orient Point, overlooking the Long Island Sound. Their frequent visits from their three children, Michael, Demitri, and Anna, along with their seven grandchildren fulfill their time.

Rebecca never returned to Cyprus, although she and Michael have vacationed the world.

Haji and Rebecca never forgot the promise they made to each other about returning the gold to the monastery. Over the years they have financed several million dollars to build another monastery in Cyprus.

True to their words, Rebecca and Haji have never mentioned the evening they left Private Akman to be eaten alive by the rats.

Nor have they ever given it a second thought.

AUTHOR'S NOTES

It has been over 40-years since the illegal invasion of Cyprus; although there have been multiple talks by many governments. Including the United Nations.

Nothing has happened to reclaim access to those homes that were lost.

Too many lives have been lost.

What happened to the 1,587 missing?

How many were murdered?

How many were enslaved?

How many women were dishonored?

I cannot, and will not complete this book without listing the names of those that are still unaccounted for. I owe them at least that. They are:

Last Name	First Name	Place of Origin
Achilleos	Argyros	Pano Dheftera
Achilleos	Panayiotis	Pano Zodhia
Adamides	Argyris	Strovolos
Adamou	Adamos	Sotira, Famagusta
Adamou	Adamos	Xylotymvou
Adamou	Loukas	Nicosia
Adamou	Panayiotis	Tymbou
Adamou	Vrionis	Famagusta
Adhamou	Pieris	Dherynia
Afxenti	Constantinos	Acheritou
Afxentiou	Andreas	Eptakomi
Agapiou	Nikos	Trachoni Kythreas
Agathokleous	Andreas	Pentayia
Agathokleous	Christakis	Yermasoyia
Agathokleous	Heraklis	Ayios Tychonas
Aglantziotis	Panayiotis	Kythrea
Agrotis	Kyriakos	Nicosia
Akathiotis	Petros	Trypimeni
Akrita	Sofia	Kato Zodhia
Akritas	Georghios	Kato Zodhia
Aladiastos	Andreas	Ayios Epiktitos
Alexandrou	Andreas	Stylli
Alexandrou	Christakis	Nicosia
Alexandrou	Eleni	Sysklipos
Alexandrou	Nicos	Ormidhia
Allayiotis	Georghios	Potami, Morphou
Americanou	Christos	Ayios Epiktitos
Analytis	Georghios	Greece
Anamisi	Demetrios	Trikomo

Last Name	First Name	Place of Origin
Anastasiadou	Flourentza	Famagusta
Anastasiou	Christofis	Sotira, Famagusta
Anastasiou	Michalakis	Famagusta
Anastasiou	Zenon	Limassol
Andrea	Antonakis	Kambi Farmaka
Andrea	Petros	Xylophagou
Andreou	Andreas	Stylli
Andreou	Angeliki	Trachoni Kythreas
Andreou	Angelos	Nicosia
Andreou	Aristofanis	Kontemenos
Andreou	Charalambos	Oikos Marathasa
Andreou	Christakis	Famagusta
Andreou	Costas	Orounda
Andreou	Evgenios	Sysklipos
Andreou	Georghios	Alona
Andreou	Irini	Neo Chorio Kythreas
Andreou	Koulla	Famagusta
Andreou	Maria	Sysklipos
Andreou	Maro	Trachoni Kythreas
Andreou	Sotera	Famagusta
Andreou	Soulla	Trachoni Kythreas
Andreou	Stelios	Anayia
Andreou	Tassos	Famagusta
Andreou	Themistoulla	Trachoni Kythreas
Andreou	Yiakoumis	Palekythro
Andritsopoulos	Eleftherios	Greece
Anemas	Demetrios	Greece
Angeli	Agathangelos	Latsia
Anthis	Eleftherios	Greece

Last Name	First Name	Place of Origin
Antona	Christakis	Larnaca
Antoni	Antonis	Vitsada
Antoni	Panayiota	Neo Chorio Kythreas
Antoni	Theophanis	Neo Chorio Kythreas
Antoniades	Andreas	Tremetousia
Antoniades	Andreas	Kythrea
Antoniades	Georghios	Arminou
Antoniades	Savvas	Yiolou
Antoniou	Andreas	Pallouriotissa
Antoniou	Antonakis	Strongylos
Antoniou	Antonios	Pelendri
Antoniou	Antonios	Petra
Antoniou	Antonios	Angastina
Antoniou	Apostolos	Tymbou
Antoniou	Charalambos	Kambos
Antoniou	Christodoulos	Vouno
Antoniou	Chrysi	Lefkonico
Antoniou	Efterpi	Famagusta
Antoniou	Kypros	Potamos tou Kambou
Antoniou	Kyriakos	Ayia Marina Skyllouras
Antoniou	Panayiota	Lefkonico
Antoniou	Stelios	Kyperounda
Antoniou	Varnavas	Trachoni Kythreas
Antzouli	Andreas	Palekythro
Apostolides	Andreas	Neo Chorio Kythreas
Apostolides	Michael	Kythrea
Apostolides	Savvas	Neo Chorio Kythreas
Apostolou	Andreas	Larnaca
Apostolou	Andreas	Lythrodontas

Last Name	First Name	Place of Origin
Apostolou	Antonios	Livadhia
Apostolou	Chrystallou	Exo Metochi
Apostolou	Paraskevas	Livadhia
Aresti	Panayiotis	Famagusta
Argyrou	Andreas	Polystipos
Argyrou	Andreas	Neo Chorio Kythreas
Argyrou	Georghios	Ayios Serghios
Aristidou	Georghios	Kellaki
Aristodemou	Ioannis	Ayios Georghios, Kyrenia
Aristodemou	Ioannis	Drymou
Aristodemou	Kyriakos	Strovolos
Aristotelous	Andreas	Limassol
Aristotelous	Andreas	Kambos
Artemi	Charalambos	Ayios Georghios Spatharikou
Artemiou	Andreas	Strovolos
Artimatas	Costas	Paralimni
Ashikallis	Constantinos	Kaimakli
Aspris	Antonis	Latsia
Aspris	Panayiotis	Aphania
Asprou	Anastasia	Eptakomi
Assiotis	Costas	Ashia
Athanasi	Georghios	Karmi
Athanasiou	Athanasios	Limassol
Athanasiou	Costas	Menico
Athanasiou	Georghios	Sotira, Famagusta
Athanasopoulos	Demetrios	Greece
Attas	Charalambos	Lyssi

Last Name	First Name	Place of Origin
Attas	Costis	Lyssi
Atteslis	Marios	Nicosia
Avaratziis	Michael	Argaki
Avlonitis	Spyridon	Greece
Avraam	Arestis	Potamos tou Kambou
Avraam	Areti	Mia Milia
Avraam	Lefteris	Livadhia
Avraam	Loizos	Koma tou Yialou
Bitsakis	Stavros	Greece
Challouma	Michael	Tremetousia
Challouma	Procopis	Tremetousia
Chambou	Charalambos	Nicosia
Charalambides	Michalakis	Kyrenia
Charalambides	Theodoros	Greece
Charalamboudi	Yiannis	Yialousa
Charalambous	Andreas	Piyenia
Charalambous	Andreas	Pedhoulas
Charalambous	Andreas	Nicosia
Charalambous	Andreas	Kyrenia
Charalambous	Angelis	Vasilia
Charalambous	Antonios	Ergates
Charalambous	Antonios	Ashia
Charalambous	Antonis	Ayia Varvara
Charalambous	Christakis	Pera Orinis
Charalambous	Christofis	Petra
Charalambous	Costas	Tseri
Charalambous	Costas	Vasilia
Charalambous	Costas	Nicosia
Charalambous	Demetrios	Eptakomi

Last Name	First Name	Place of Origin
Charalambous	Georghios	Pera Orinis
Charalambous	Koumis	Lympia
Charalambous	Kyprianos	Ashia
Charalambous	Kyriacos	Xylophagou
Charalambous	Michael	Kythrea
Charalambous	Michael	Argaki
Charalambous	Michalakis	Nicosia
Charalambous	Nicodemos	Klirou
Charalambous	Nicos	Famagusta
Charalambous	Panikkos	Synchari
Charalambous	Paraskevou	Troulli
Charalambous	Takis	Kyrenia
Charalambous	Theodoros	Sysklipos
Charalambous	Theophanis	Kyrenia
Chari	Antonios	Neo Chorio Kythreas
Chari	Costantis	Exo Metochi
Chari	Kyriacou	Exo Metochi
Charilaou	Ioannis	Kyra
Cheretakis	Michael	Greece
Chimonas	Vassos	Athienou
Chiratou	Neophytos	Pelendri
Chrisostomidou	Archontou	Morphou
Christaki	Andreas	Dherynia
Christaki	Leontis	Ashia
Christides	Christos	Kythrea
Christodoulides	Efstathios	Prastio Morphou
Christodoulou	Adamos	Yeri
Christodoulou	Antonis	Arnadhi
Christodoulou	Christakis	Dhali

Last Name	First Name	Place of Origin
Christodoulou	Christakis	Ayios Amvrosios
Christodoulou	Christodoulos	Famagusta
Christodoulou	Demetrios	Kythrea
Christodoulou	Demetris	Peristeronopyghi
Christodoulou	Eleni	Petra
Christodoulou	Elias	Kambi Farmaka
Christodoulou	Georghios	Mandres
Christodoulou	Marios	Nicosia
Christodoulou	Michael	Pentayia
Christodoulou	Nicos	Nicosia
Christodoulou	Nicos	Mia Milia
Christodoulou	Othonas	Limassol
Christodoulou	Savvas	Karmi
Christodoulou	Takis	Yiolou
Christofi	Andreas	Kythrea
Christofi	Christakis	Askas
Christofi	Christofis	Ypsonas
Christofi	Evangelos	Lapithos
Christofi	Georghios	Limassol
Christofi	Katerina	Famagusta
Christofi	Leontios	Eptakomi
Christofi	Marikkou	Peristeronopyghi
Christofi	Melpomeni	Lapithos
Christofi	Nicolaos	Kythrea
Christofi	Papachrysostomos	Dhavlos
Christofi	Paris	Limassol
Christofi	Phivos	Nicosia
Christofi	Polykarpos	Lapithos
Christofi	Stelios	Kalo Chorio, Lefka

Last Name	First Name	Place of Origin
Christofides	Andreas	Nicosia
Christoforou	Adonis	Achna
Christoforou	Andreas	Kambos
Christoforou	Elias	Fterycha
Christoforou	Andreas	Ayios Georghios Spatharikou
Christoforou	Christoforos	Potami, Morphou
Christoforou	Christoforos	Potamos tou Kambou
Christoforou	Costakis	Kato Dhikomo
Christoforou	Ioannis	Amargeti
Christoforou	Panayiotis	Kiti
Christoforou	Renos	Polystipos
Christoforou	Savvas	Nicosia
Christoforou	Stavros	Dherynia
Christoforou	Stelios	Nicosia
Christoforou	Xenophon	Astromeritis
Christou	Andreas	Nicosia
Christou	Andreas	Malounda
Christou	Andreas	Angastina
Christou	Christos	Ayia Napa
Christou	Costakis	Neo Chorio Kythreas
Christou	Costas	Paliometocho
Christou	Ionas	Dhali
Christou	Kyriacos	Kato Dherynia
Christou	Paraschos	Nisou
Christou	Stelios	Aradhippou
Christoudia	Christos	Neo Chorio Kythreas
Christoudias	Michael	Ashia
Christoukkou	Andreas	Ashia

Last Name	First Name	Place of Origin
Chrysanthou	Adamos	Vitsada
Chrysanthou	Chrysanthos	Lythrodontas
Chrysanthou	Savvas	Mesa Yitonia, Limassol
Chrysiliou	Tassos	Nicosia
Chrysostomides	Yiannakos	Morphou
Chrysostomou	Christos	Nicosia
Chrysostomou	Neophytos	Limassol
Chrysostomou	Pantelis	Famagusta
Chrysotomou	Athina	Famagusta
Constantinides	Georghios	Nicosia
Constantinou	Andreas	Analyondas
Constantinou	Andreas	Tseri
Constantinou	Andreas	Kyrenia
Constantinou	Andreas	Eptakomi
Constantinou	Antonios	Syrianochori
Constantinou	Charalambos	Kyrenia
Constantinou	Christos	Pallouriotissa
Constantinou	Constantinos	Ayios Serghios
Constantinou	Constantinos	Kyra
Constantinou	Constantinos	Ormidhia
Constantinou	Costas	Ormidhia
Constantinou	Costas	Kaimakli
Constantinou	Costas	Livadhia
Constantinou	Demetrios	Kyperounda
Constantinou	Demosthenis	Mandria
Constantinou	Eleftherios	Nicosia
Constantinou	Evangelos	Greece
Constantinou	Leontios	Lythrodontas
Constantinou	Michalakis	Larnaca

Last Name	First Name	Place of Origin
Constantinou	Neophytos	Famagusta
Constantinou	Nicos	Kalopanayiotis
Constantinou	Pantelis	Ashia
Cosma	Christakis	Yialousa
Cosma	Nicos	Ormidhia
Costa	Costas	Avgorou
Costa	Ioannis	Nicosia
Costa	Kakoullou	Aphania
Costantakopoulos	Ioannis	Greece
Costanti	Costas	Asgata
Costanti	Philippos	Nicosia
Costanti	Stylianos	Argaka
Costantinides	Costas	Kythrea
Costantinides	Loizos	Nicosia
Costi	Christos	Pera Chorio Nisou
Costi	Theodoros	Exo Metochi
Costi	Vassos	Ashia
Costrikkis	Costis	Ashia
Damaskinos	Christakis	Morphou
Damaskinou	Neophytos	Elia, Kyrenia
Danezi	Panicos	Nicosia
Daniel	Panayiotis	Anoyira
Dedevesis	Demetrios	Galatsio, Attika, Greece
Demetis	Kyriacos	Lapithos
Demetriades	Demetrios	Petra
Demetriades	Demetris	Nicosia
Demetriades	Themis	Kato Dherynia
Demetriadou	Maritsa	Petra
Demetriou	Andreas	Famagusta

Last Name	First Name	Place of Origin
Demetriou	Charalambos	Ayios Epiktitos
Demetriou	Christakis	Dromolaxia
Demetriou	Christina	Troulli
Demetriou	Demetrios	Stylli
Demetriou	Demetrios	Dhali
Demetriou	Georghios	Strongylos
Demetriou	Georghios	Xylotymvou
Demetriou	Kyriacos	Nicosia
Demetriou	Lambros	Voni
Demetriou	Leontis	Trikomo
Demetriou	Loukas	Lympia
Demetriou	Michalakis	Dhali
Demetroudi	Maritsa	Kato Dhikomo
Demosthenous	Demos	Famagusta
Demosthenous	Leonidas	Chloraca
Demosthenous	Neophytos	Limassol
Deritziotis	Nicolaos	Greece
Diakou	Andreas	Vasilia
Diakou	Costantis	Exo Metochi
Diakou	Savvas	Vasilia
Diarkou	Andreas	Ashia
Diarkou	Antonas	Ashia
Dracos	Gregorios	Nicosia
Dracos	Themistoklis	Kambos
Drousiotis	Photis	Limassol
Drousiotis	Soterios	Larnacas Lapithou
Economides	Georghios	Voni
Economides	Porphyris	Fterycha
Economidou	Pagona	Kyrenia

Last Name	First Name	Place of Origin
Economidou	Xenia	Kyrenia
Economou	Elias	Elati, Trikkalla, Greece
Efseviou	Christakis	Trachonas
Efstathiou	Costas	Ayios Georghios, Kyrenia
Efthymiou	Antonios	Dhali
Efthymiou	Chrystalla	Karavas
Efthymiou	Costas	Syrianochori
Efthymiou	Costas	Neo Chorio Kythreas
Efthymiou	Efthymios	Ayios Amvrosios
Efthymiou	Nicos	Lapithos
Eleftheriades	Andreas	Palechori
Eleftheriou	Christakis	Vasilia
Eleftheriou	Eleftherios	Vasilia
Eleftheriou	Eleftherios	Famagusta
Eleftheriou	Elpiniki	Vasilia
Elia	Andreas	Trachoni Kythreas
Elia	Krinos	Pentayia
Elia	Neophytos	Strovolos
Elia	Odysseas	Yialousa
Eliopoulos	Panayiotis	Greece
Ellinas	Kyriacos	Kyrenia
Ellinas	Miltiades	Kythrea
Englezou	Antonakis	Ashia
Englezou	Christakis	Ashia
Englezou	Georghios	Ashia
Englezou	Nicos	Ashia
Englezou	Yiannakis	Ashia
Englezou	Yiorgakis	Ashia

Last Name	First Name	Place of Origin
Epaminonda	Evangelos	Nicosia
Ermogenous	Christos	Aradhippou
Erotokritou	Costas	Lapithos
Erotokritou	Linos	Famagusta
Evangelou	Evangelos	Nicosia
Evangelou	Gregoris	Lapithos
Evdokiou	Emilios	Aphania
Evgeniou	Elli	Sysklipos
Evgeniou	Stelios	Larnaca
Evripidhou	Andreas	Larnaca
Evripidhou	Evangelos	Ayios Dhometios
Evripidou	Chrysanthos	Limassol
Fantaros	Charalambos	Kambos
Farfaras	Andreas	Famagusta
Ferekides	Loucas	Nicosia
Findiklis	Kleanthis	Nicosia
Flamoudhiotis	Michael	Ashia
Fori	Georghios	Ashia
Foullis	Sophoklis	Limassol
Frangeskidou	Aphroditi	Kythrea
Frangopoullos	Artemis	Ashia
Frangopoullos	David	Ashia
Frangou	Kyriacou	Famagusta
Frangoulides	Ioannis	Pano Zodhia
Frantzis	Kyriacos	Pelendri
Frixou	Kyriacos	Nicosia
Frydas	Antonios	Morphou
Fteroudis	Charalambos	Vasilia
Galactiou	Demetrios	Kyrenia

Last Name	First Name	Place of Origin
Galinis	Erotokritos	Klirou
Gatana	Christodoulos	Lapithos
Gavriel	Costas	Troulli
Gavriel	Gavriel	Livadhia
Gavriel	Yiannis	Aphania
Georghiades	Nicolaos	Nicosia
Georghiades	Vasilios	Kaimakli
Georghiou	Andreas	Mosphiloti
Georghiou	Andreas	Latsia
Georghiou	Andreas	Famagusta
Georghiou	Andreas	Kyrenia
Georghiou	Antonios	Mammari
Georghiou	Charalambos	Ayios Vasilios
Georghiou	Christakis	Karmi
Georghiou	Christodoulos	Avgorou
Georghiou	Christos	Dromolaxia
Georghiou	Costakis	Strovolos
Georghiou	Costas	Troulli
Georghiou	Eleftherios	Aradhippou
Georghiou	Eleni	Petra
Georghiou	Georghios	Nicosia
Georghiou	Georghios	Aphania
Georghiou	Georghios	Kathikas
Georghiou	Georghios	Larnaca
Georghiou	Georghios	Pera Chorio Nisou
Georghiou	Georghios	Ayios Amvrosios
Georghiou	Georghios	Koma tou Yialou
Georghiou	Kyriacos	Mia Milia
Georghiou	Michael	Alambra

Last Name	First Name	Place of Origin
Georghiou	Michalakis	Famagusta
Georghiou	Pavlos	Marathovounos
Georghiou	Petros	Palekythro
Georghiou	Prodromos	Kythrea
Georghiou	Savvas	Kato Dhikomo
Georghiou	Savvas	Aradhippou
Georghiou	Soterios	Kalopsida
Georghiou	Sotiris	Trachonas
Georghiou	Yerolemos	Angastina
Georghiou	Yiakoumis	Nicosia
Georghiou	Yiannis	Famagusta
Germanos	Alexandros	Kyrenia
Germanos	Andreas	Kyrenia
Giorgallas	Georghios	Paralimni
Giorgalli	Georghios	Synchari
Giorgatzi	Costas	Sysklipos
Giorgatzi	Hadjivassilou	Sysklipos
Glarentzos	Charalambos	Greece
Glikenou	Symeon	Paralimni
Gourounias	Georghios	Paralimni
Gregoriou	Costas	Lapithos
Gregoriou	Elpida	Trypimeni
Gregoriou	Michael	Pano Dhikomo
Griva	Christos	Greece
Groutas	Michael	Dhali
Hadjiangeli	Nicolaos	Syrianochori
Hadjiantoni	Antonis	Ashia
Hadjiantoni	Costas	Vatyli
Hadjiantonis	Demetrios	Trikomo

Last Name	First Name	Place of Origin
Hadjiavgoustides	Anastasios	Greece
Hadjicharalambous	Demetrios	Pano Lefkara
Hadjichristodoulou	Andreas	Alambra
Hadjichristodoulou	Andreas	Lapithos
Hadjichristodoulou	Christodoulos	Kato Zodhia
Hadjichristodoulou	Georghios	Angastina
Hadjichristodoulou	Neophytos	Episkopi
Hadjichristoforou	Pantelis	Kontemenos
Hadjichristou	Soteris	Kythrea
Hadjichristoudhia	Christakis	Ashia
Hadjiconstanti	Antonakis	Kato Dhikomo
Hadjiconstanti	Chrystallou	Kato Dhikomo
Hadjiconstanti	Diomedes	Ashia
Hadjiconstanti	Petris	Kato Dhikomo
Hadjicosta	Christos	Karmi
Hadjidaniel	Michael	Ashia
Hadjidemetris	Pavlos	Yialousa
Hadjieftychiou	Costakis	Lapithos
Hadjigavriel	Andreas	Angastina
Hadjigavriel	Elias	Ashia
Hadjigeorghiou	Panayiotis	Nicosia
Hadjigeorghiou	Panayiotis	Korakou
Hadjihambi	Liasis	Akanthou
Hadjikallis	Panayiotis	Ayios Epiktitos
Hadjikoumi	Andreas	Famagusta
Hadjikoutsou	Georghios	Ashia
Hadjikyprianou	Constantinos	Xeros
Hadjikypris	Ioannis	Pano Dheftera
Hadjikyriacos	Hadjiyiannis	Kythrea

Last Name	First Name	Place of Origin
Hadjikyriacou	Georghios	Neapolis
Hadjikyriacou	Nicolaos	Famagusta
Hadjikyriacou	Philippos	Famagusta
Hadjikyriacou	Stephanos	Famagusta
Hadjikyrou	Georghios	Ayios Amvrosios
Hadjilois	Soteris	Vasilia
Hadjiloizou	Andreas	Famagusta
Hadjiloizou	Marcos	Tymbou
Hadjilouca	Andreas	Kato Dhikomo
Hadjilouca	Hadjieleni	Massari
Hadjilouca	Panayiotis	Karavas
Hadjimamas	Kyriacos	Peristerona, Morphou
Hadjimichael	Petros	Kato Zodhia
Hadjineophytou	Costas	Morphou
Hadjinicola	Athanasis	Voni
Hadjinicola	Georghios	Katokopia
Hadjinicola	Georghios	Lapithos
Hadjinicola	Hedjieraklis	Sysklipos
Hadjinicola	Kyriacos	Yerani
Hadjinicolaou	Christos	Yialousa
Hadjinicolaou	Stavros	Ayia Varvara
Hadjioannou	Maria	Famagusta
Hadjiona	Andriana	Exo Metochi
Hadjipanayi	Soteris	Mandres
Hadjipanteli	Panayiotis	Lefkonico
Hadjipantelis	Savvas	Yialousa
Hadjipaschalis	Iacovos	Trikomo
Hadjipavlou	Costakis	Famagusta
Hadjipavlou	Michalakis	Famagusta

Last Name	First Name	Place of Origin
Hadjipavlou	Pavlos	Argaki
Hadjipetrou	Charalambos	Kato Dhikomo
Hadjiprokopiou	Loizos	Ayii Trimithias
Hadjisavva	Anastasis	Lapithos
Hadjisavva	Marios	Nicosia
Hadjisavva	Savvas	Massari
Hadjisolomou	Evanthia	Filia
Hadjisoteri	Andreas	Famagusta
Hadjisoteri	Antonis	Komi Kebir
Hadjisoteri	Kyriacos	Komi Kebir
Hadjistavris	Nicolaos	Athens, Greece
Hadjistavrou	Nicolaos	Nicosia
Hadjitheodoulou	Costas	Chandria
Hadjittofi	Georghios	Ashia
Hadjittofi	Ttofis	Ashia
Hadjitzirkallou	Kyriacos	Ashia
Hadjiyiakoumi	Andreas	Kythrea
Hadjiyiakoumi	Soteris	Kythrea
Hadjiyianni	Hadhichristodoulos	Katokopia
Hadjiyianni	Spyros	Morphou
Hadjiyianni	Yiannis	Famagusta
Hamouriotakis	Georghios	Greece
Hanna	Antonios	Famagusta
Haritou	Haritos	Politiko
Hdjiyianni	Georghios	Neo Chorio Kythreas
Hdjiyianni	Hadjivassilis	Famagusta
Hdjiyianni	Michael	Pano Dhikomo
Heperi	Maritsa	Ashia
Herakli	Despina	Exo Metochi

Last Name	First Name	Place of Origin
Herapetti	Eleni	Neo Chorio Kythreas
Herapettis	Elias	Neo Chorio Kythreas
Hilimintri	Demetrios	Peristeronopyghi
Hountalas	Prokopios	Greece
Iakovides	Costakis	Lapithos
Iakovides	Pavlos	Larnaca
Ignatiades	Ioannis	Greece
Ignatiou	Sophoclis	Lapithos
Ioannides	Anastasios	Larnaca
Ioannides	Eleftherios	Nicosia
Ioannides	Evdoras	Kato Dhikomo
Ioannides	Evelthon	Neo Livadhi, Morphou
Ioannou	Andreas	Menico
Ioannou	Andreas	Limassol
Ioannou	Andreas	Neo Chorio Kythreas
Ioannou	Chariton	Galini
Ioannou	Christakis	Pareklishia
Ioannou	Costas	Kato Dhikomo
Ioannou	Costas	Kyrenia
Ioannou	Demos	Voni
Ioannou	Eleftherios	Menico
Ioannou	Gavriel	Aphania
Ioannou	Ioannis	Kalogrea
Ioannou	Ioannis	Nicosia
Ioannou	Kypros	Nicosia
Ioannou	Kyriakos	Kythrea
Ioannou	Marios	Kakopetria
Ioannou	Minas	Kokkinotrimithia
Ioannou	Papaepiphanios	Angastina

Last Name	First Name	Place of Origin
Ioannou	Photios	Pano Zodhia
Ioannou	Soteris	Ayios Dhometios
Ioannou	Theodoros	Nicosia
Ioannou	Theodoros	Voni
Iona	Angeliki	Lefkonico
Iona	Savvas	Famagusta
Iordanou	Kyriacos	Mathiatis
Iosif	Chrystallou	Sysklipos
Isidorou	Costakis	Ayia Varvara
Isidorou	Isidoros	Ormidhia
Kafetzi	Antonakis	Paralimni
Kailas	Nicolaos	Kokkinotrimithia
Kaimakamis	Christoforos	Kyrenia
Kaizer	Christos	Kyrenia
Kakouri	Iacovos	Ayios Epiktitos
Kakouris	Savvas	Kato Dhikomo
Kakoutsas	Georghios	Komi Kebir
Kalaitzis	Chrysanthos	Potamos tou Kambou
Kalaphatis	Demetrios	Engomi, Famagusta
Kalapodas	Christakis	Ashia
Kalapodas	Vassos	Kato Dhikomo
Kalari	Marios	Pallouriotissa
Kalatha	Kyriacos	Avgorou
Kalatzis	Yiannis	Galini
Kalbroutzis	Stylianos	Thessaloniki, Greece
Kalli	Stavros	Famagusta
Kalli	Theodora	Ayios Ermolaos
Kalli	Yiannis	Ashia
Kallikas	Kyriacos	Aradhippou

Last Name	First Name	Place of Origin
Kallistratou	Costas	Agridaki
Kamenos	Christodoulos	Sysklipos
Kamenou	Anastasia	Sysklipos
Kamilari	Kyriacos	Trikomo
Kamilari	Nicos	Lythrodontas
Kaminarides	Ioannis	Nicosia
Kampouri	Charalambos	Kakopetria
Kampouri	Demetris	Ashia
Kanarini	Charita	Sysklipos
Kangaris	Frantzeskos	Lyssi
Kanni	Christos	Neo Chorio Kythreas
Kanni	Rodhou	Neo Chorio Kythreas
Kantonis	Georghios	Peristeronopyghi
Kaouras	Andreas	Kato Zodhia
Kaoutzanis	Christodoulos	Ayia Trias
Kapnetis	Kyriacos	Pano Dhikomo
Kappides	Kyriacos	Komi Kebir
Kapros	Costas	Trachoni Kythreas
Kapsokartis	Costantis	Tseri
Kapsos	Panayiotis	Mia Milia
Kapsouri	Socrates	Karavas
Karafilli	Loizos	Koma tou Yialou
Karamani	Andreas	Marathovounos
Karamani	Michalakis	Vasilia
Karamanou	Despina	Mia Milia
Karangounis	Charalambos	Greece
Karantokis	Kyriakos	Aphania
Karantonas	Panayiotis	Ayios Amvrosios
Karaoli	Panicos	Lythrodontas

Last Name	First Name	Place of Origin
Karatzas	Anastasis	Xylophagou
Karayiannis	Ioannis	Mandres
Karayiannis	Phivos	Mandres
Karayiannis	Prodromos	Kythrea
Karayiorgis	Panayiotis	Potamia
Karayiorgos	Athanasios	Greece
Karefyllides	Christos	Kyrenia
Karefyllides	Christos	Kyrenia
Karmios	Loizos	Voni
Karoulla	Achillou	Gaidouras
Karoulla	Andreas	Stylli
Kasia	Andreas	Koutsoventis
Kasiouri	Georghios	Eptakomi
Kassapis	Andreas	Ashia
Katalanou	Costas	Ayios Epiphanios
Kateifis	Andreas	Mia Milia
Kateifis	Georghios	Mia Milia
Katountas	Nicolaos	Greece
Katrakakis	Theocharis	Greece
Katsarou	Michalakis	Trikomo
Katselli	Nicolaos	Limassol
Katsiambris	Andreas	Lemythou
Katsidiaris	Panayiotis	Katokopia
Katsouris	Michael	Neo Chorio Kythreas
Katsouris	Savvas	Stylli
Kattou	Panayiotis	Kyrenia
Katzi	Andreas	Xylophagou
Katzi	Nicos	Xylophagou
Kavalierou	Yiasoumis	Komi Kebir

Last Name	First Name	Place of Origin
Kazamia	Chrysostomos	Ashia
Kefalonitis	Christodoulos	Paphos
Kelepeshi	Charalambos	Ayia Irini, Kyrenia
Kelle	Panayis	Kontea
Kelloura	Spyros	Petra
Kemekis	Panicos	Yialousa
Kentonis	Costakis	Morphou
Kentras	Constantinos	Greece
Kermanou	Savvas	Liopetri
Kermentis	Nicos	Ormidhia
Kimis	Theocharis	Tsakkistra
Kinanis	Michalakis	Strovolos
Kiotti	Panayiotis	Famagusta
Kiratzis	Christos	Ayios Amvrosios
Kitas	Costas	Politiko
Kittou	Nicolaos	Paralimni
Kkafa	Antonis	Ashia
Kkimis	Kyriacos	Ashia
Kkolias	Vassilios	Marathovounos
Kkolos	Kyriacos	Achna
Kkolou	Andreas	Liopetri
Kkolou	Georghios	Yerolakkos
Kleanthous	Andreas	Ayios Ermolaos
Kleanthous	Georghios	Kathikas
Kleovoulou	Nicos	Mandria
Klitou	Klitos	Lefkonico
Klokaris	Pantelis	Marathovounos
Kofou	Spyros	Exo Metochi
Kogkoni	Andreas	Voni

Last Name	First Name	Place of Origin
Kokkini	HadjiKyriacos	Ashia
Kokkinos	Ioannis	Achna
Kokkinos	Loucas	Famagusta
Kokkinovoukkos	Kostantis	Kontea
Kokkinovoukos	Michael	Kontea
Kokotas	Costas	Paleosofos
Kokotsis	Michael	Syrianochori
Kolaniou	Georghios	Dherynia
Kolanis	Demetrios	Lyssi
Koliantris	Alexandros	Pentayia
Kolios	Kypros	Kythrea
Kolokasis	Nicos	Mia Milia
Kolokotronis	Nicos	Akaki
Kolovos	Soteris	Chartzia
Komiati	Polycratis	Famagusta
Komodromos	Michael	Peristeronopyghi
Komodromou	Sotera	Peristeronopyghi
Konis	Antonis	Eptakomi
Konnaris	Michalakis	Trimiklini
Kontonicolas	Demetrios	Aradhippou
Kontos	Andreas	Neo Chorio Kythreas
Kontos	Yiannakis	Akaki
Kontou	Andreas	Achna
Korellis	Antonakis	Kythrea
Korkou	Nicos	Rizokarpaso
Kostriki	Demetrios	Ashia
Kotsios	Costas	Neon Ambeliko
Koufterou	Efrosyni	Dhikomo
Koukkoularis	Christos	Greece

Last Name	First Name	Place of Origin
Koukkoulis	Loizos	Ayios Dhometios
Koukos	Costas	Mia Milia
Koukou	Chrystallou	Mia Milia
Koukou	Costas	Dhikomo
Koukoumas	Andreas	Yeri
Koullis	Kyriakos	Neo Chorio Kythreas
Koullouros	Savvas	Kyra
Kouloumas	Nicos	Kythrea
Koumbarides	Charalambos	Nicosia
Koumbarou	Panayis	Famagusta
Koumettou	Rogiros	Kormakitis
Koumi	Michalakis	Famagusta
Koumi	Theodoros	Paralimni
Kountouri	Michalakis	Moutoullas
Kountouri	Yiannis	Strongylos
Kountouros	Adamos	Achna
Koupanos	Ioannis	Klepini
Koureas	Thomas	Paliometocho
Kouris	Christodoulos	Mia Milia
Kouroufexis	Andreas	Palechori
Kourouna	Andreas	Potamia
Kouroupis	Pavlos	Greece
Kourras	Michael	Lefkonico
Kourris	Avgoustis	Peristeronopyghi
Kouspi	Chrysostomos	Lapithos
Kouspou	Soteris	Ayios Amvrosios
Koutalistra	Christos	Morphou
Kouti	Kyriakos	Ashia
Koutis	Yiakoumis	Ashia

Last Name	First Name	Place of Origin
Koutroullis	Stephanos	Greece
Koutsias	Gregoris	Exo Metochi
Koutsoftas	Ioannis	Mandres
Koutsou	Soteris	Peristeronopyghi
Koutsoullou	Kyriacos	Spathariko
Kouvaros	George	Mia Milia
Kozakos	Costas	Karavas
Kozakos	Yiannakis	Karavas
Kozakou	Despina	Karavas
Kratimenos	Anastasios	Greece
Kritikos	Nicolaos	Greece
Kymissi	Andreas	Kythrea
Kypri	Alexandros	Sysklipos
Kypri	Kyriacos	Stroumbi
Kyprianou	Andreas	Nicosia
Kyprianou	Anthimos	Pedhoulas
Kyprianou	Chrysostomos	Marathovounos
Kyprianou	Georghios	Nicosia
Kyprianou	Michael	Yeroskipou
Kyprianou	Michael	Limassol
Kyprianou	Phivos	Elia, Kyrenia
Kyriacou	Andreas	Trachoni Kythreas
Kyriacou	Costas	Pretori
Kyriacou	Despina	Pano Dhikomo
Kyriacou	Loucas	Eptakomi
Kyriacou	Petros	Ashia
Kyriacou	Stephanos	Peyia
Kyriakides	Georghios	Neo Chorio Kythreas
Kyriakides	Ioannis	Larnaca

Last Name	First Name	Place of Origin
Kyriakides	Theophylactos	Nicosia
Kyriakidou	Rodou	Neo Chorio Kythreas
Kyriakou	Andreas	Limassol
Kyriakou	Andreas	Makrasyka
Kyriakou	Andreas	Mitsero
Kyriakou	Andriani	Famagusta
Kyriakou	Christos	Larnacas Lapithou
Kyriakou	Costas	Peristerona, Morphou
Kyriakou	Costas	Mitsero
Kyriakou	Costas	Ormidhia
Kyriakou	Epiphanios	Lefkonico
Kyriakou	Georghios	Trachonas
Kyriakou	Kika	Kato Dherynia
Kyriakou	Kyriakos	Oroklini
Kyriakou	Kyriakos	Pyroi
Kyriakou	Kyriakos	Lapathos
Kyriakou	Mamas	Peristerona, Morphou
Kyriakou	Maria	Kato Dherynia
Kyriakou	Neophytos	Myrtou
Kyriakou	Nicolaos	Strovolos
Kyriakou	Nicos	Trikomo
Kyriakou	Nicos	Aradhippou
Kyriakou	Panais	Ayios Georghios, Kyrenia
Kyriakou	Savvas	Akaki
Kyriakou	Stylianos	Alambra
Kyrris	Costas	Ayios Georghios, Kyrenia
Lambi	Elias	Chartzia

Last Name	First Name	Place of Origin
Lambi	Michael	Chartzia
Lambi	Michalakis	Chartzia
Lambrides	Andreas	Nicosia
Lambrides	Costas	Nicosia
Lambrou	Ioannis	Eptakomi
Lambrou	Panayiotis	Lythrodontas
Lambrou	Vassos	Kaimakli
Laphazanis	Andreas	Ayios Epiktitos
Larcou	Andreas	Lyssi
Lavithis	Georghios	Ayios Vasilios
Lazarou	Agathangelos	Alambra
Leandrou	Savvas	Neo Chorio Kythreas
Lefteri	Andreas	Kontemenos
Leondi	Kyriacos	Ashia
Leondiou	Leondios	Ashia
Leoni	Christodoulos	Trachonas
Leonida	Charalambos	Mia Milia
Leonida	Polyxeni	Paleosofos
Leonidou	Andreas	Kythrea
Leonidou	Leonidas	Ashia
Lephas	Kyriacos	Ayios Serghios
Liasi	Panayiotou	Limnia, Famagusta
Liasi	Yiannakis	Yialousa
Libertos	Christos	Voni
Liggis	Nicolaos	Achna
Livadhiotis	Georghios	Akaki
Loizides	Andreas	Kythrea
Loizides	Andreas	Tymbou
Loizides	Vassos	Nicosia

Last Name	First Name	Place of Origin
Loizou	Andreas	Komi Kebir
Loizou	Christakis	Palekythro
Loizou	Christodoulos	Ayia Varvara
Loizou	Christofis	Arnadhi
Loizou	Costas	Pentayia
Loizou	Georghios	Palekythro
Loizou	Georghios	Milia
Loizou	Georghios	Famagusta
Loizou	Loizos	Gouphes
Loizou	Loizos	Ayios Epiktitos
Loizou	Maria	Skylloura
Loizou	Michael	Gouphes
Loizou	Panayiotis	Ashia
Loizou	Vassos	Gypsou
Loizou	Zenon	Galini
Lontou	Nicolaos	Galini
Louca	Christodoulos	Mammari
Louca	Ereneos	Ayios Serghios
Louca	Myrophora	Skylloura
Louca	Panayiotis	Marathovounos
Louca	Yiangos	Melini
Louloudis	Antonis	Limassol
Loumbas	Nicos	Klepini
Lourmbas	Demetrios	Greece
Lygkos	Thomas	Greece
Lyssis	Costas	Sotira, Famagusta
Lytras	Evangelos	Athienou
Madellas	Pantelis	Nicosia
Makaritis	Andreas	Lyssi

Last Name	First Name	Place of Origin
Makrides	Andreas	Lefkonico
Makrides	Stylianos	Anayia
Makrides	Theodoros	Anayia
Malakides	Demetrios	Aradhippou
Malekides	Savvas	Ayios Ioannis Agrou
Malli	Michael	Lyssi
Malliappi	Christakis	Ashia
Malliappi	Costis	Ashia
Mama	Yiangos	Kalo Chorio, Lefka
Manoli	Tassos	Limassol
Manti	Elenitsa	Kythrea
Mantilas	Iason	Marathovounos
Mantis	Sotirios	Ayios Georghios, Kyrenia
Mantoles	Andreas	Karavas
Mantralis	Constantinos	Lapithos
Maouris	Georghios	Famagusta
Maouzis	Christodoulos	Voukolida
Mappis	Savvas	Exo Metochi
Maratheftis	Charalambos	Vasilia
Maratheftis	Soterios	Letymbou
Markatzis	Demetrios	Ashia
Markou	Christos	Klirou
Markou	Tasos	Paralimni
Markou	Yiasoumis	Phrenaros
Maronitis	Michael	Neo Chorio Kythreas
Maronitou	Maria	Neo Chorio Kythreas
Masias	Demetrakis	Liopetri
Masouras	Andreas	Kato Zodhia

Last Name	First Name	Place of Origin
Mastichis	Panayiotis	Kokkinotrimithia
Mastrappas	Andreas	Lapithos
Matsangos	Andreas	Koma tou Yialou
Mavrommatis	Georghios	Kalo Chorio, Lefka
Mavrommatis	Koumis	Yialousa
Mavrou	Andreas	Tymbou
Mavroudi	Michael	Dhikomo
Mayias	Panayiotis	Kythrea
Mazarakis	Christodoulos	Philousa
Mazoula	Aphrodite	Famagusta
Mazoulas	Gregorios	Famagusta
Melachrinou	Costas	Strovolos
Melas	Yiannakos	Neo Chorio Kythreas
Melifronidis	Georghios	Orounda
Melissos	Costas	Karavas
Melleha	Anastasia	Troulli
Mellehas	Georghios	Troulli
Menelaou	Menelaos	Drymou
Menelaou	Vassos	Ayios Demetrios
Menikos	Savvas	Lapithos
Menikou	Costas	Famagusta
Menikou	Kyriakos	Neo Chorio Kythreas
Merakli	Costas	Kapouti
Merakliyiannis	Georghios	Argaki
Meranou	Phivos	Famagusta
Mesaritis	Andreas	Ayios Epiktitos
Mesaritis	Sotirios	Ayios Epiktitos
Mettis	Andreas	Filia
Mias	Christos	Ashia

Last Name	First Name	Place of Origin
Michael	Andreas	Troulli
Michael	Andreas	Exo Metochi
Michael	Athanasis	Malounda
Michael	Charalambos	Eptakomi
Michael	Christakis	Tersephanou
Michael	Drosos	Pyrga, Famagusta
Michael	Georghios	Morphou
Michael	Georghios	Trachonas
Michael	Georghios	Larnaca
Michael	Loucas	Angastina
Michael	Matheos	Ashia
Michael	Michael	Strovolos
Michael	Michael	Kyrenia
Michael	Michael	Xylotymvou
Michael	Michael	Nicosia
Michael	Nicolaos	Aphania
Michael	Nicolaos	Komi Kebir
Michael	Nicos	Lythrangomi
Michael	Panayiotis	Lefkonico
Michael	Samson	Neta
Michael	Simos	Famagusta
Michael	Soterios	Lefkonico
Michael	Vassilis	Koma tou Yialou
Michael	Vassos	Pyroi
Michael	Yiannis	Stylli
Michaelides	Andreas	Nicosia
Michaelides	Cleanthis	Kyrenia
Michaelides	Xanthos	Kythrea
Michalos	Nicolaos	Neo Chorio Kythreas

Last Name	First Name	Place of Origin
Mikeou	Charilaos	Kaimakli
Milikouris	Georghios	Dhali
Milikouris	Vassilis	Palekythro
Milioti	Eleftherios	Pyrga, Famagusta
Miltiadous	Emilios	Kyrenia
Miltiadous	Georghios	Strovolos
Miltiadous	Polyxeni	Sysklipos
Miltiadous	Stavros	Lefkara
Mina	Charalambos	Pera Orinis
Mina	Elias	Mia Milia
Mita	Gregorios	Trachonas
Mixias	Michael	Vitsada
Monachos	Vassilios	Kastri, Ighoumenitsa, Greece
Moniatis	Vrionis	Souni - Zanatjia
Morphaki	Elpiniki	Ayios Georghios, Kyrenia
Mosphili	Pashalis	Mandres
Mouis	Costakis	Lapithos
Moullotou	Evangelos	Limassol
Mourikis	Athanasios	Greece
Mouskos	Takis	Lyssi
Mousoullos	Stavros	Xylophagou
Moustaka	Costas	Ashia
Moustakas	Georghios	Kyrenia
Moustakas	Kakoullis	Lympia
Mouzouras	Angelos	Ashia
Mpakka	Yiannis	Peristeronopyghi
Mparris	Nicolaos	Ayios Georghios, Kyrenia

Last Name	First Name	Place of Origin
Mpourekas	Asimakis	Greece
Mprodymas	Constantinos	Greece
Mythillos	Georghios	Mia Milia
Nearchou	Kyriacos	Ayios Demetrianos
Neochoritis	Stavros	Famagusta
Neocleous	Andreas	Ayii Vavatsinias
Neocleous	Christakis	Agros
Neocleous	Pavlos	Kalavasos
Neophytou	Andreas	Emba
Neophytou	Constantinos	Ashia
Neophytou	Demetrios	Salamiou
Neophytou	Neophytos	Gypsou
Nestoros	Panayiotis	Nicosia
Nicodemou	Christakis	Ayios Georghios, Kyrenia
Nicola	Christodoulos	Angastina
Nicola	Chrysostomos	Komi Kebir
Nicola	Epiphanios	Vitsada
Nicola	Georghios	Kyrenia
Nicola	Irini	Sysklipos
Nicola	Loukia	Famagusta
Nicolaides	Michael	Angastina
Nicolaou	Antonios	Nicosia
Nicolaou	Christakis	Ayios Georghios Spatharikou
Nicolaou	Costas	Politiko
Nicolaou	Eleftherios	Lympia
Nicolaou	Georghios	Kyrenia
Nicolaou	Gregoris	Vatyli
Nicolaou	Iacovos	Famagusta

Last Name	First Name	Place of Origin
Nicolaou	Ioannis	Kythrea
Nicolaou	Kypros	Lythrodontas
Nicolaou	Marios	Omorphita
Nicolaou	Nicolaos	Psimolophou
Nicolaou	Nicolaos	Gastria
Nicolaou	Nicos	Marathovounos
Nicolaou	Nicos	Alambra
Nicolaou	Nicos	Kyrenia
Nicolaou	Nicos	Famagusta
Nicolaou	Panayiotis	Exo Metochi
Nicolaou	Panayiotis	Larnaca
Nicolaou	Pantelis	Pera Orinis
Nicolaou	Soterios	Kyrenia
Nicolatzi	Theodoros	Elia, Kyrenia
Nicolettis	Panayiotis	Lyssi
Nikiphorou	Pantelis	Alambra
Nikita	Costas	Karavas
Nikitopoulos	Lambros	Ayios Sostis, Messinia, Greece
Nistikou	Andreas	Voni
Ntouri	Philippos	Aradhippou
Odyssea	Kyriacos	Ayios Epiktitos
Olymbiou	Alexandros	Nicosia
Ombashi	Tomis	Gypsou
Orphanides	Andreas	Lythrodontas
Orphanides	Stylianos	Neo Chorio Kythreas
Orphanou	Andreas	Aphania
Orphanou	Georghios	Tymbou
Orphanou	Theodokis	Potamos tou Kambou

Last Name	First Name	Place of Origin
Orphanou	Theophanis	Tymbou
Orthodoxou	Andreas	Trikomo
Pachoullaras	Georghios	Lythrodontas
Pafiolis	Constantinos	Greece
Pagonis	Michael	Aradhippou
Pais	Christakis	Pano Zodhia
Pakkalian	Rosa	Trachoni Kythreas
Paleologou	Dionysios	Morphou
Palmas	Andreas	Mosphiloti
Palmas	Charalambos	Peristerona, Morphou
Pamboulos	Soteris	Aphania
Pamis	Costakis	Kyra
Panayi	Andreas	Mitsero
Panayi	Andreas	Kyra
Panayi	Antonis	Pallouriotissa
Panayi	Avraam	Milia
Panayi	Christofis	Pano Dhikomo
Panayi	Costas	Larnaca
Panayi	Demetrios	Alaminos
Panayi	Panayiotis	Marathovounos
Panayi	Panicos	Mesoyi
Panayi	Soterios	Lapathos
Panayi	Yiakoumis	Aphania
Panayides	Marios	Limassol
Panayides	Michalakis	Prodromos
Panayiotou	Andreas	Famagusta
Panayiotou	Andreas	Latsia
Panayiotou	Aristides	Amargeti
Panayiotou	Artemisia	Exo Metochi

Last Name	First Name	Place of Origin
Panayiotou	Demetrios	Famagusta
Panayiotou	Nicos	Lythrodontas
Panayiotou	Panayiotis	Alona
Panayiotou	Panayiotis	Omorphita
Pantazis	Philippos	Famagusta
Panteli	Antonios	Sotira, Famagusta
Panteli	Christakis	Kontemenos
Panteli	Elpiniki	Prastio, Famagusta
Panteli	Kleovoulos	Trachonas
Panteli	Nicos	Ayios Amvrosios
Panteli	Nicos	Dhali
Panteli	Varnavas	Nicosia
Pantioras	Theodoros	Greece
Pantouri	Costas	Lapithos
Pantouris	Georghios	Trimithi
Paourtas	Panais	Exo Metochi
Papachristodoulou	Nicos	Kontemenos
Papachristoforos	Alexandros	Nicosia
Papachristou	Georghios	Latsia
Papadopoulos	Costas	Kaimakli
Papadopoulos	Ioannis	Greece
Papaelisseou	Elisseos	Limassol
Papageorghiou	Antonis	Avgorou
Papageorghiou	Georghios	Voni
Papageorghiou	Hadjicostas	Sysklipos
Papageorghiou	Iosif	Sysklipos
Papaioannou	Antonios	Nicosia
Papaioannou	Christakis	Kambia
Papalambrides	Georghios	Ioannina, Greece

Last Name	First Name	Place of Origin
Papalambrou	Vasilios	Greece
Papalli	Christofis	Acheritou
Papamirmingi	Iacovos	Kythrea
Papanastasiou	Artemisia	Athienou
Papantoniou	Iacovos	Trachonas
Papapanayis	Elias	Nicosia
Papapavlou	Constantinos	Athienou
Papapavlou	Elias	Vavylas
Papapolydorou	Costas	Mesoyi
Papathoma	Andreas	Akaki
Papathoma	Michalakis	Akaki
Papatryfonos	Andreas	Peristerona, Morphou
Papatsanis	Athanasios	Greece
Papavasiliou	Minas	Nicosia
Papayianni	Andreas	Marathovounos
Papayianni	Nicos	Kato Dhikomo
Papayiannis	Ioannis	Neo Chorio Kythreas
Paphitis	Andreas	Trachonas
Paphitis	Apostolos	Ashia
Paphitis	Costas	Ashia
Paphitis	Georghios	Ashia
Papoutsis	Costas	Ayia Varvara
Paraschou	Michael	Yialousa
Paraskeva	Androniki	Famagusta
Paraskeva	Georghios	Neo Chorio Paphou
Paraskevopoullos	Vasilios	Lefkonico
Paroutis	Michael	Pano Zodhia
Parpa	Constantinos	Strovolos
Parpa	Maria	Troulli

Last Name	First Name	Place of Origin
Parpa	Maritsa	Kato Dhikomo
Parpa	Nicolas	Kato Dhikomo
Parpas	Nicolas	Troulli
Paschalis	Ioannis	Trikomo
Paschalis	Panayis	Sotira, Famagusta
Pasiarti	Sofia	Kato Dhikomo
Paskas	Panayis	Ashia
Passias	Stelios	Orounda
Patera	Georghios	Ashia
Patinios	Alexis	Kyrenia
Patounas	Panicos	Sykopetra
Patsalides	Marios	Lapithos
Patsalou	Christodoulos	Pyroi
Patsanas	Constantinos	Greece
Patsi	Georghios	Dhavlos
Patsia	Kyriacou	Lefkonico
Pattishis	Sotiris	Exo Metochi
Pavlides	Antonis	Kato Dhikomo
Pavlides	Phivos	Evrychou
Pavlou	Charalambos	Klirou
Pavlou	Christos	Liopetri
Pavlou	Costas	Karakoumi
Pavlou	Georghios	Marathovounos
Pavlou	Panayiotis	Polystipos
Pavlou	Pavlos	Xylotymvou
Pavlou	Pavlos	Xylotymvou
Pavloudes	Pavlos	Greece
Pediou	Kyriakou	Lefkonico
Pediou	Lysandros	Lefkonico

Last Name	First Name	Place of Origin
Pekri	Michalakis	Vatyli
Peletie	Victoria	Kythrea
Pelia	Georghios	Lyssi
Pelopida	Polyvios	Varisia
Pepekkos	Andreas	Ayios Epiktitos
Pepes	Nicos	Neo Chorio Kythreas
Peppou	Anthousa	Pano Dhikomo
Perdios	Anastasios	Ormidhia
Pericleous	Nicos	Dhali
Perikkou	Takis	Syrianochori
Perikleous	Stelios	Limassol
Petrasides	Andreas	Palekythro
Petrasites	Andreas	Famagusta
Petri	Christos	Kythrea
Petrides	Nicos	Episkopio
Petrides	Yiannis	Neo Chorio Kythreas
Petrou	Andreas	Mitsero
Petrou	Andreas	Pyla
Petrou	Andreas	Exo Metochi
Petrou	Andreas	Famagusta
Petrou	Antonakis	Stylli
Petrou	Christakis	Xylotymvou
Petrou	Costas	Evrychou
Petrou	Efstathios	Sotira, Famagusta
Petrou	Kyriacos	Pano Dhikomo
Petrou	Modestos	Komi Kebir
Petrou	Petros	Nicosia
Petrou	Petros	Mitsero
Petrou	Petros	Ora

Last Name	First Name	Place of Origin
Petrou	Petros	Nicosia
Petrou	Stelios	Dherynia
Petrou	Yiakoumis	Pano Dhikomo
Petsa	Stavros	Vouno
Peyiotis	Yiannakis	Stroumbi
Phaedonos	Phaedon	Limassol
Pharmakalidou	Rozalia	Famagusta
Phili	Demetrakis	Aradhippou
Philippides	Andreas	Kato Lakatamia
Philippou	Andreas	Pyroi
Philippou	Georghios	Trikomo
Photi	David	Ashia
Photi	Kyriacos	Palekythro
Photi	Nicolaos	Neo Chorio Kythreas
Photiou	Costas	Peristeronopyghi
Photiou	Panayiotis	Vasili, Famagusta
Physentzides	Marios	Nicosia
Pienis	Gregoris	Kambia
Pieri	Lambros	Ashia
Pieridi	Priamos	Limassol
Pierou	Kyriacos	Eptakomi
Pikis	Georghios	Athienou
Pilatou	Georghios	Avgorou
Pilatou	Sotiris	Famagusta
Pilavas	Andreas	Nicosia
Pillatsis	Lefkos	Nicosia
Pirintzis	Costas	Voni
Pisis	Andreas	Kapouti
Pitsiataris	Georghios	Prastio Morphou

Last Name	First Name	Place of Origin
Pitsillos	Efstathios	Lapithos
Pitsillou	Soteris	Voni
Pitta	Anastasis	Ayios Ioannis Agrou
Pitta	Iakovos	Angastina
Pittas	Georghios	Ashia
Pitti	Marcos	Dhali
Plarkos	Andreas	Livadhia
Poirazis	Andreas	Strongylos
Poirazis	Georghios	Strongylos
Poirazis	Loizos	Strongylos
Poirazis	Savvas	Strongylos
Poirazis	Stavros	Strongylos
Polos	Christakis	Trachonas
Polos	Pavlos	Trachonas
Polydhorou	Antonis	Xylotymvou
Polydhorou	Polydhoros	Mesa Yitonia, Limassol
Porca	Hadjigeorghios	Trypimeni
Porti	Evangelos	Mia Milia
Porti	Savvas	Mia Milia
Potamitis	Charalambos	Morphou
Poullaides	Andreas	Vatyli
Pourgourides	Antonis	Komi Kebir
Pourgourides	Panayiotis	Nicosia
Poyiatzis	Andreas	Vatyli
Poyiatzis	Georghios	Larnaca
Poyiatzis	Vasos	Paralimni
Ppalazi	Nicolaos	Menico
Ppasias	Ttofis	Xylophagou
Pratsi	Andreas	Ashia

Last Name	First Name	Place of Origin
Pratsi	Stylianos	Ashia
Pratsis	Polykarpos	Morphou
Prodromou	Charalambos	Ayios Amvrosios
Proestos	Michalakis	Kyrenia
Proestos	Panayiotis	Lapithos
Prokopiou	Soterios	Kyperounda
Prokopiou	Thalia	Kyrenia
Psaltis	Yiannakis	Aradhippou
Psara	Kyriacos	Koma tou Yialou
Psaras	Costas	Belapais
Psaras	Nicos	Paralimni
Psatha	Panayiotis	Arnadhi
Psillis	Costas	Lapithos
Psillos	Kyriacos	Paralimni
Psillou	Pantelis	Lythrodontas
Psoma	Milia	Fterycha
Pyrgou	Nicos	Larnaca
Pyrkas	Demetrios	Mammari
Rahovitsas	Gregorios	Greece
Rayias	Fanos	Morphou
Rimis	Michael	Mia Milia
Rossides	Costas	Akaki
Rossos	Andreas	Nicosia
Roti	Lefkios	Nata
Rousos	Georghios	Pera Chorio Nisou
Rousou	Xenis	Lyssi
Rousounides	Stavros	Nicosia
Roussis	Seraphim	Greece
Roussou	Christodoulos	Kato Dhikomo

Last Name	First Name	Place of Origin
Roussou	Efrosini	Kato Dhikomo
Sakkas	Yiannis	Marathovounos
Sakki	Yiannis	Marathovounos
Salaforis	Andreas	Koutsoventis
Salaforis	Stylianos	Kythrea
Sarris	Yiannakis	Limassol
Savva	Andreas	Kontemenos
Savva	Andreas	Alambra
Savva	Andreas	Sysklipos
Savva	Andreas	Dora
Savva	Christos	Neo Chorio Kythreas
Savva	Chrystallou	Trachoni Kythreas
Savva	Costakis	Limassol
Savva	Georghios	Limassol
Savva	Herodotos	Tsada
Savva	Kleanthis	Ashia
Savva	Kyriacou	Neo Chorio Kythreas
Savva	Michalis	Lympia
Savva	Petros	Ayios Amvrosios
Savva	Prodromos	Kythrea
Savva	Savvakis	Karavas
Savva	Savvakis	Larnaca
Savva	Savvas	Lympia
Savva	Savvas	Kalogrea
Savva	Theodoros	Lympia
Savvides	Demetris	Famagusta
Savvides	Ioannis	Nicosia
Savvides	Pavlos	Trachoni Kythreas
Savvides	Savvas	Dhali

Last Name	First Name	Place of Origin
Savvides	Soteris	Trachoni Kythreas
Savvides	Stelios	Yialousa
Savvopoulos	Andreas	Famagusta
Sazos	Georghios	Limnatis
Schizas	Nicolaos	Kapouti
Scoutari	Christodoulos	Angastina
Serghi	Loucas	Ayios Georghios, Kyrenia
Serghides	Joseph	Nicosia
Serghides	Michael	Nicosia
Serghiou	Adamos	Eptakomi
Serghiou	Andreas	Koma tou Yialou
Serghiou	Charalambos	Acheritou
Serghiou	Demetrios	Ayios Georghios, Kyrenia
Siakallis	Demetrios	Mia Milia
Siakallis	Michael	Morphou
Sialouna	Michalis	Eptakomi
Siamishis	Andreas	Sysklipos
Siamptanis	Antonis	Ashia
Sideras	Michalakis	Famagusta
Sideras	Stavros	Karavas
Siekkeris	Andreas	Livera
Sigas	Theophanis	Paliometocho
Sini	Argyrios	Greece
Siokkos	Chrysostomos	Lefkonico
Sioumma	Savvas	Ashia
Siourlas	Constantinos	Greece
Skalias	Christakis	Kyrenia
Skalistis	Ioannis	Nicosia

Last Name	First Name	Place of Origin
Skitsa	Antonios	Ormidhia
Skordis	Christoforos	Dhali
Skoulias	Georghios	Lympia
Skourides	Alexandros	Nicosia
Skourlis	Demetrios	Greece
Skouros	Andreas	Ashia
Skouros	Menelaos	Lapithos
Skouros	Neophytos	Lapithos
Smirlis	Vassilios	Navplio, Argolida, Greece
Socratous	Georghios	Akaki
Socratous	Ioannis	Galini
Socratous	Loizos	Polystipos
Socratous	Socratis	Agros
Socratous	Socratis	Kolossi
Sofroniou	Christakis	Peristeronopyghi
Sofroniou	Sofronios	Yermasoyia
Sofroniou	Sofronios	Odhou
Solomi	Pavlos	Komi Kebir
Solomi	Solon	Komi Kebir
Solomou	Soteris	Lapithos
Solomou	Theodoulos	Aphania
Sophocleous	Adamos	Lapithos
Sophocleous	Adamos	Engomi, Famagusta
Sophocleous	Andreas	Sysklipos
Sophocleous	Andreas	Yourri
Sophocleous	Christodoulos	Larnaca
Sophocleous	Jack(Kyriacos)	Kythrea
Sophocleous	Vathoulla	Kythrea
Sophocli	Angelis	Chartzia

Last Name	First Name	Place of Origin
Sophocli	Pantelou	Sysklipos
Soteriou	Marios	Larnaca
Sotiraki	Christos	Psimolophou
Sotiraki	Evgenios	Psimolophou
Sotiriou	Andreas	Angastina
Sotiriou	Sotirakis	Acheritou
Spanos	Andreas	Ayia Varvara
Spanou	Georghios	Kyra
Spaou	Constantinos	Paralimni
Spyrou	Antonios	Ashia
Spyrou	Demetrios	Eptakomi
Spyrou	Georghios	Tymbou
Spyrou	Panayiotis	Arsos
Spyrou	Panayis	Lyssi
Spyrou	Soteris	Kyrenia
Stamati	Marikkou	Exo Metochi
Stamatopoulos	Constantinos	Greece
Stathopoulos	Andreas	Greece
Stavraki	Andreas	Voni
Stavraki	Christodoulos	Kythrea
Stavraki	Stavros	Voni
Stavraki	Theocharis	Voni
Stavrak	Yiangos	Voni
Stavri	Chrysostomi	Ayios Georghios Spatharikou
Stavrinou	Andreas	Marathovounos
Stavrinou	Georghios	Tseri
Stavrinou	Ioannis	Kapouti
Stavrinou	Stavros	Lemythou

Last Name	First Name	Place of Origin
Stavrou	Andreas	Trachoni Kythreas
Stavrou	Demetrios	Nicosia
Stavrou	Demetrios	Latsia
Stavrou	Soterios	Greece
Stavrou	Stavros	Lythrodontas
Stavrou	Stavros	Xylophagou
Stavrou	Theotokis	Galini
Stephanides	Charalambos	Arsos
Stephanou	Stephanos	Lythrodontas
Stergenakis	Georghios	Paliometocho
Stivaktas	Nicolaos	Greece
Stivaros	Andreas	Arsos
Stratis	Kyriacos	Dhikomo
Stratoura	Costantis	Ashia
Stratouras	Georghios	Kyra
Strongylos	Georghios	Kyrenia
Strouthou	Demetris	Lyssi
Stylianopoulos	Errikos	Limassol
Stylianou	Andreas	Ktima
Stylianou	Andreas	Kakopetria
Stylianou	Andreas	Paralimni
Stylianou	Christakis	Myrtou
Stylianou	Chrysanthos	Ayios Georghios, Kyrenia
Stylianou	Diomides	Vouni
Stylianou	Iacovos	Fterycha
Stylianou	Ioannis	Fterycha
Stylianou	Kyriacos	Pachna
Stylianou	Panayiotis	Pano Dheftera

Last Name	First Name	Place of Origin
Stylianou	Savvas	Nicosia
Stylianou	Stelios	Kokkinotrimithia
Stylianou	Stelios	Makrasyka
Symeou	Charalambos	Engomi, Nicosia
Symeou	Costakis	Aradhippou
Symeou	Savvas	Nicosia
Symeou	Symeon	Lapathos
Syzinos	Demetrios	Gypsou
Taliadoros	Andreas	Dhali
Taliadorou	Stavros	Nicosia
Tambi	Michael	Ashia
Tanteles	Georghios	Neo Chorio Kythreas
Tappas	Eleftherios	Prastio, Famagusta
Tarapoulouzis	Christakis	Morphou
Tasiakis	Costas	Lapithos
Televantos	Angelos	Kyrenia
Telli	Theognosia	Peristeronopyghi
Tellis	Eleftherios	Peristeronopyghi
Tenekedzis	Georghios	Syrianochori
Tengeris	Nicolaos	Sysklipos
Thalassinos	Sotiris	Ayios Epiktitos
Thanopoulos	Demetrios	Greece
Themistokleous	Eleni	Trachoni Kythreas
Theocharides	Demetrios	Nicosia
Theocharides	Evgenios	Nicosia
Theocharis	Sofoklis	Lapithos
Theocharous	Charalambos	Dhali
Theocharous	Theocharis	Angastina
Theodorou	Andreas	Famagusta

Last Name	First Name	Place of Origin
Theodorou	Andreas	Ayia Anna
Theodorou	Andreas	Malounda
Theodorou	Ioannis	Katokopia
Theodorou	Maroulla	Elia, Kyrenia
Theodorou	Phivos	Syrianochori
Theodorou	Savvas	Anayia
Theodosiou	Christakis	Prastio Kellakiou
Theodosiou	Demetrios	Nicosia
Theodosiou	Panayiotis	Strovolos
Theodosiou	Theodosios	Kato Deftera
Theodoulou	Andreas	Karakoumi
Theodoulou	Antonios	Tymbou
Theodoulou	Michalakis	Famagusta
Theodoulou	Theodoulos	Livadhia
Theodoulou	Theodoulos	Palekythro
Theodoulou	Theodoulos	Neo Chorio Kythreas
Theoharous	Christos	Kalo Chorio, Lefka
Theologou	Charalambos	Filia
Theophanous	Kyriacos	Kythrea
Theophanous	Theophanis	Xylophagou
Theophanous	Vassos	Ashia
Therapi	Demetrakis	Larnaca
Therapontos	Kyriacos	Neo Chorio Kythreas
Thoma	Christos	Voni
Thoma	Demetrios	Latsia
Thoma	Eleftherios	Lapithos
Thomaides	Thomas	Larnaca
Thrasivoulou	Lazaros	Myrtou
Tikis	Andreas	Trypimeni

Last Name	First Name	Place of Origin
Tikkos	Christos	Ayios Georghios Spatharikou
Tombolis	Georghios	Shia
Tooula	Costis	Kato Dhikomo
Toumazou	Charalambos	Lefkonico
Tourapi	Michael	Tseri
Tourourou	Georghios	Palekythro
Tourourou	Panayiotis	Palekythro
Tourtouris	Loucas	Marathovounos
Toutas	Costas	Ashia
Triantaphyllides	Manousos	Potamies, Heraklion, Greece
Trianti	Vassilios	Greece
Trifylli	Panayiota	Peristeronopyghi
Trigki	Georghios	Belapais
Trigki	Savvas	Belapais
Tringis	Georghios	Kyrenia
Tryfonos	Marios	Tembria
Tsangari	Andreas	Filia
Tsangari	Christoforos	Larnacas Lapithou
Tsangari	Ioannis	Dhymes
Tsangarides	Andreas	Ayios Georghios, Kyrenia
Tsangarides	Constantinos	Kyrenia
Tsangarides	Loizos	Kyrenia
Tsangarides	Nicolaos	Neo Chorio Kythreas
Tsangaridou	Efrosyni	Ayios Georghios, Kyrenia
Tsaousis	Demetrios	Aphania

Last Name	First Name	Place of Origin
Tsiakka	Varvara	Morphou
Tsiakkas	Andreas	Peristeronopyghi
Tsiakkas	Constantinos	Greece
Tsiakkas	Panayiotis	Karavas
Tsiakkas	Savvas	Karavas
Tsiaklides	Michael	Mia Milia
Tsianakkas	Evangelos	Trachoni Kythreas
Tsiapouta	Pantelis	Prastio, Famagusta
Tsiattalos	Stavros	Kato Dhikomo
Tsiattalou	Annousou	Kato Dhikomo
Tsidirides	Constantinos	Greece
Tsielepis	Nicos	Dhali
Tsigo	Michael	Ayios Serghios
Tsikouris	Christos	Ashia
Tsimbides	Michalis	Morphou
Tsippouri	Irini	Pano Dhikomo
Tsirkakas	Demetrios	Ayia Varvara
Tsitsou	Panayis	Ashia
Tsolakis	Loucas	Phrenaros
Tsomallouris	Theodoros	Phrenaros
Tsonis	Elias	Greece
Tsouknidas	Demetrios	Greece
Ttantiri	Loucas	Tymbou
Ttantiri	Nicolaos	Tymbou
Ttofa	Apostolos	Ashia
Ttofas	Christos	Ashia
Ttofi	Nicos	Phrenaros
Ttooula	Christodoulos	Trachoni Kythreas
Tylliros	Christodoulos	Ayia Irini, Kyrenia

Last Name	First Name	Place of Origin
Tylliros	Christodoulos	Nicosia
Tylliros	Stylianos	Nicosia
Tyllirou	Maria	Ayia Irini, Kyrenia
Tyrimou	Evagoras	Avgorou
Tyrimou	Michalakis	Nicosia
Tyrranou	Costas	Myrtou
Tzakouras	Kyriacos	Nicosia
Tziamas	Christos	Kythrea
Tziampos	Andreas	Neo Chorio Kythreas
Tziortzi	Christos	Neo Chorio Kythreas
Tzirkas	Kyriacos	Exo Metochi
Tzirkas	Nicolaos	Exo Metochi
Vais	Iacovos	Greece
Vakis	Yiannakis	Nicosia
Valanides	Costas	Agridhia
Vanezi	Christofis	Kythrea
Vardakis	Lambros	Achna
Varnava	Andreas	Lympia
Varnava	Panayiotis	Mia Milia
Varnava	Themistoklis	Trachoni Kythreas
Varnava	Varnavas	Trikomo
Vasilaras	Evdoros	Strovolos
Vasilediou	Anastasia	Morphou
Vasiliou	Synesis	Rizokarpaso
Vassiliou	Charalambos	Limassol
Vassiliou	Serghios	Avgorou
Vassilopoulos	Minas	Tochni
Velonas	Demetrios	Greece
Velousi	Petros	Lefkonico

Last Name	First Name	Place of Origin
Vereis	Pieris	Dherynia
Violari	Chrystalla	Sysklipos
Violaris	Nicos	Kalo Chorio, Klirou
Violetti	Eleni	Kato Dhikomo
Vlachou	Nicos	Ayios Amvrosios
Vlachou	Yiannos	Komi Kebir
Vlamis	Costas	Voni
Vlamis	Themis	Voni
Voniatis	Georghios	Famagusta
Vorka	Eleni	Pano Dhikomo
Voskou	Andriani	Kato Varosi
Voskou	Antonakis	Ashia
Voskou	Costantis	Ashia
Vourka	Alexandros	Fterycha
Vourkou	Costas	Ayios Georghios, Kyrenia
Vourti	Elengou	Neo Chorio Kythreas
Vyras	Andreas	Kythrea
Vyras	Vassos	Kythrea
Xanthos	Panayiotis	Trachoni Kythreas
Xeni	Christofis	Lyssi
Xeni	Xenis	Famagusta
Xenophontos	Demetrakis	Trikomo
Xenophontos	Georghios	Ayios
Xenophontos,	Nearchos	Anayia
Xenos	Theodoros	Greece
Xinari	Maria	Pano Zodhia
Xydhias	Ioannis	Greece
Yatana	Savvas	Lapithos

Last Name	First Name	Place of Origin
Yerolemou	Costakis	Limassol
Yerolemou	Ioannis	Eptakomi
Yerolemou,	Neophytos	Komi Kebir
Yerondis	Spyridon	Krinas Korinthias, Greece
Yeropapas	Antonios	Lyssi
Yeropapas	Ioannis	Lyssi
Yiaoumi	Andreas	Paralimni
Yiahoutis	Loucas	Akanthou
Yiakouma	Marios	Trachoni Kythreas
Yiakouma	Nikolaos	Trachoni Kythreas
Yiakouma,	Pantelitsa	Trachoni Kythreas
Yiakoumettis	Iakovos	Peristeronopyghi
Yiakoumi	Christos	Ashia
Yialiali	Savvas	Lapithos
Yiallourides	Andreas	Strovolos
Yiallourides,	Sotirios	Morphou
Yiallouros	Neophytos	Kokkinotrimithia
Yiangou	Costas	Ayios Dhometios
Yiangou	Costas	Voni
Yiangou,	Ioannis	Tseri
Yiannadji	Ktoris	Lefkonico
Yiannakas,	Vasilis	Eptakomi
Yiannaki	Theodosis	Achna
Yiannakis	Minas	Greece
Yiannakopoulos	Nicolaos	Greece
Yianni,	Christofis	Aphania
Yianni,	Giorghis	Makrasyka
Yianni,	Loucas	Kato Dhikomo

Last Name	First Name	Place of Origin
Yianni,	Petros	Mosphiloti
Yianni,	Yiannis	Famagusta
Yianni,	Yiannis	Paralimni
Yianni,	Yiannis	Lythrangomi
Yiannikou	Ioannis	Nicosia
Yianno	Savvas	Kythrea
Yiannou,	Kyriacos	Lyssi
Yiannou,	Yiannos	Ashia
Yiasemides	Costas	Mia Milia
Yiatrou,	Christoforos	Ayios Ioannis Agrou
Yiatrou,	Soteris	Exo Metochi
Yiettimis	Kyriacos	Nicosia
Yiorgalli	Georghios	Neo Chorio
Yiorgalli,	Kyriacos	Famagusta
Yiorgalli,	Savvas	Aphania
Yiorkakouthiou	Petros	Pano Dhikomo
Yiorkouni	Charalambos	Ashia
Ypermachou	Ypermachos	Tersephanou
Zachareas	Evangelos	Greece
Zacharia	Georghios	Kythrea
Zacharia,	Panayiotis	Ayios Andronicos
Zacharia	Zacharias	Ayios
Zachariades	Andreas	Kythrea
Zachariades,	Costas	Kythrea
Zakou,	Christofis	Kokkinotrimithia
Zambas	Michalakis	Limassol
Zambas,	Pavlos	Kythrea
Zampakkide	Theocharis	Kythrea
Zannettou	Christos	Ashia

Last Name	First Name	Place of Origin
Zaou	Nicolaos	Tseri
Zavou,	Loizos	Dhali
Zeniou,	Klitos	Peristeronopyghi
Zenonos	Therapon	Lythrodontas
Zenonos,	Zenon	Nicosia
Zervomanolis	Georghios	Greece
Zervos	Sofoklis	Neo Chorio Kythreas
Zevlaris	Andreas	Kythrea
Zissimos	Andreas	Famagusta
Zographou	Panayiotis	Trikomo
Zorpi	Andreas	Famagusta
Zotti	Eleni	Kato Dhikomo
Zotti,	Myrofora	Kato Dhikomo
Zotti,	Pantelis	Kato Dhikomo
Zouvannis	Yiannis	Vrysoulles